TRINITY

∽◯

LAUREN D. FRASER

For Anna Elizabeth

CONTENTS

ACKNOWLEDGEMENTS

Thank you to the following people who helped me bring my imagination to light:

My dear husband, Andrew, for his never-ending encouragement;

Nicole Olinger, Lois Dillon, Kim Scalise, Tracy Ware-Justice, Robin Lanager, Julie Beltrani, Janine Cerra, Kristin Kline, and my sister Tiffany Heineman. Thank you for your thoughtful discussion and especially your time. I am forever grateful for your wisdom and support;

Jeremy Sumpman, who motivated me and inspired me to tell my story, and who reminded me that a cavalry attack on a castle is a strategically bad idea;

My mom, Meredith Chapman, for her critical eyes;

My dad, Robert Heineman, for always reminding me to "get to the point;"

My sister, Heather Donnelly, for providing me with a lifetime of character inspiration;

And my dear friend Patricia Krahnke, for teaching me that it is never too late to pursue your passion.

1

RESOLVE

I was breathing so hard I could barely hear my own thoughts, let alone anyone else's. The twisted pretzel corridors seemed so much longer this time and the stairways appeared darker and steeper as I made my way to her chambers. If only I had been able to avoid the confusion present on the battlefield, I would already be with her, ready to defend her and protect her as I promised I would.

I started to wheeze.

"No!" I whined aloud, "Not now for God's sake!" Asthma was never convenient, especially at this particular moment in my life. I stopped in the middle of the hall to try to cough and catch my breath. My throat was so dry, as if I had taken a drink of sand. I had no choice but to dig into the leather pouch hanging at my right hip. My bloodied hand was shaking as I pulled out my inhaler, took two puffs, stuffed it back into the pouch and started running once more. A drink could wait. I was so close.

I reached for the shiny glass knob on the chamber door and leaned all of my body weight into the massive wooden barrier between her and me. I stumbled forward. The door was already open, just as I feared.

All I could actually see was a trail of blood leading from where some had pooled by the window. I was too late. I had to find her, to see her one last time. Perhaps she was all right. Maybe I was wrong and she managed to escape her attackers. I walked toward the window where just minutes ago she had probably been watching the battle ensue below, half frozen in anticipation and even hope. I stood for a moment, almost sensing her presence when I glimpsed a hand reaching toward my right side from behind me. Before it could take me by my neck, I grabbed the wrist and twisted. I turned around to see a familiar face.

"Your Grace, we must get you out of here. They're still in the palace. It is not safe here." The man to whom the hand belonged was like me, soiled with blood and dirt from the battle-field. Dark red blood dripped from his left hand and even his violet eyes were reddened probably with the fatigue of battle.

"But she…" I began to say to him.

"Is gone. We must go." He pushed me through the doorway into the corridor. Again, I was running down hallways and stairways, oblivious to where I was going and clueless about what I was to do next. I felt tightness in my chest - the sensation of my heart fighting with my head over the pain of my perceived loss. I had to remain strong and I had no time for tears, but I could not stop the tears from falling. If she was gone, we were fighting for nothing.

"Not 'nothing,' Avery. Fight for them! Fight for the Trinity. I love you," a familiar voice spoke to me in my thoughts. The warm feeling of resolve came over me. I reached into my sheath and pulled out my blade. I knew I had to get back to my people in the field.

"Let's go," I said as we ran through the great hall toward the front gate.

"I am Avery de Hazaro. This is <u>my</u> house!" I announced.

We pushed our way through the crowd of loyalists doing their best to keep the enemy from destroying Pilton Palace, until we reached the imposing front steps. The last time I saw these steps, she was still alive - optimistic that we would fulfill all the hopes and dreams of the Kingdom. With that memory, I felt more determined to lead my people to victory over these oppressors and I felt an increased obligation to keep the rest of my family safe.

I began to race down to the base of the stairs and realized the man was no longer with me. I turned back and he was gone, somewhere in the crowd of metal on metal. I called out for him and hearing no response, I continued toward the ridge. I listened closely for my sisters voices and ran west, along the perimeter walls until I could finally see them. They had reached the high ground and were completely out of harm's way, for now.

2

A SHARED DREAM

I shot out of my sleep with a jolt, gasping for air. It was the same dream; always the same dream, nightmare really. I could always hear the voices, frantic and confused, but I could never see any faces nor could I understand what was happening. It was foggy and the air smelled the way Timber's fish tank smelled when it had not been cleaned thoroughly. Then suddenly, darkness. All I could hear was the faint whisper of a man's voice that I recognized: "Sleep well my petal. Look after the others." And that is when I would awaken.

"Ugh!" The time on my digital clock read 5:46 am. Of course. Since I had to wake up in twenty minutes anyway, I switched on my bedside lamp. At least I could get some more studying in before my Pre-Calculus test first period. The people at my school who thought that advanced math first thing in the morning was a good idea deserved to be punched in the face, repeatedly. I blindly reached for my textbook, which was on the floor, still open to the practice test questions on page 124, and found the cat stretched across the pages.

"Come on Tulip, move it," I whispered harshly at the twelve pound ball of white and gray fur. She opened her eyes, yawned and ignored my request. For whatever reason, the cat never took me seriously.

"Aww, come on Tulip, please?" I begged of the cat, a little louder than my first plea. Again, no cooperation from Tulip.

"Seriously? What's wrong with you?" I had awakened the "Beast." Marena was sitting up on the darker side of our shared bedroom. "Why are you up and why did you think it was a good idea to wake me up?" All good questions.

"I'm sorry. I had the dream again and - sorry, sorry." I whispered.

Marena huffed and flopped herself back onto her pillow. I decided to give up on Pre-Calc. I had studied for four hours last night before bed and I knew I was ready for this test. Math had never been my favorite subject, or my best, but I carried a B average so, for once, I decided to cut myself some slack and try to remember the elements of the dream I kept having. I turned the lamp off and closed my eyes again to force the visions to come back to me, but all I could see was darkness. Just then, our bedroom door flew open.

"Did you?" It was Timber, very animated and louder than necessary for before 6 am. I could see in the shadows that her arms were flapping, her signature "I'm really, really excited about something" gesture.

"Shhh," I warned, "the 'princess' is still asleep."

"No I'm not, jerks!" Marena muttered. She threw a star shaped pillow at her twin sister in the doorway. The pillow toss fell short and instead disturbed Tulip, who then decided to relocate herself under the bed. I took the opportunity to reclaim my Pre-Calc book.

"I had the dream again, the one about the boat and the fog!" Timber exclaimed.

Now she had my absolute attention. "I had a dream too," I replied, "but it's still the same. I can't really see anything."

"Me either."

The lamp on the other side of the room suddenly illuminated Marena. Even half asleep, she was absurdly pretty; blonde hair, blue eyes and the fullest lips, which were now molded into a pout.

"You two really have to give up on this dream business. Dreams are dreams. Nothing," she whined and headed over to her closet to begin the morning ritual of pulling out every possible combination of outfit appropriate for one of the most desirable girls in school.

Although Timber and Marena were twins, and only fifteen months younger than I was, we were all very different girls. They had just turned sixteen years old on March 2nd, while I had turned seventeen and got my drivers' license in December.

Marena was elegant, graceful and popular while Timber was somewhat self-conscious and more interested in sports than boys and clothes. Both of them were gorgeous, but Timber was not as interested in showing off her beauty as Marena. Timber had a more subtle beauty that in some ways was more attractive than Marena's "in your face" kind of good looks.

Marena and Timber were not identical twins, but they looked remarkably similar. Marena had blue eyes and Timber had hazel eyes. Timber was slightly shorter than Marena with a more boyish figure. Both of them had the loveliest blonde waves. Marena typically wore her hair down like a glamorous movie star. Timber preferred her hair pulled off her face, usually in a ponytail. She was the true athlete among us while Marena was the artist and musician. We all played tennis very well; that was our one shared athletic pursuit.

Then there was me: shorter with reddish brown hair and brown eyes. There was a resemblance between us, of course, but you had to look for it. I was popular among my friends, but our high school was big and it was easy to find friends. Even the loners were not loners there.

With the exception of my spot on the tennis team, my involvement in school was limited to academics although I was on the student council and was National Honor Society President, a title that came to me by default. No one wanted to be president of the nerds, and I only took the job to add something impressive to my resume for college.

Timber was becoming even more animated in response to her twin's somewhat apathetic reaction to a very perplexing situation.

"Come on Rena, you have to admit that it's interesting Avery and I have such a similar dream and that we usually have it at the same time, right?" Timber asked, knowing that Rena rarely found anything interesting.

"I guess it's weird, but Avery always had this dream. You just started having it so it's probably just because you've been hearing Avery drone on and on about it for the last year and a half," Marena sniped.

Though personally, I thought Marena was simply jealous she had been excluded from our strange dream circle, she might have had a valid point. A few years ago, I realized that many of my early memories of our house in Scotland were from photographs and people talking about the pictures, not necessarily from having actual memories of the events. Still, I never prompted Timber to tell me about her dreams, she always spoke freely about the details, and they were eerily similar to the visions that I often had.

Timber wisely decided to ignore Marena, and turned back to me, "Avery, I heard something new this time. It was a woman and she said 'je suis prest…'"

"'I am ready' - I heard it too," added Marena almost in a trance. She slowly turned to face Timber and me, dropping the skirt she had been holding onto the floor. Her face became pale.

"Wait, what?" Timber stammered. I was just as surprised as my younger sisters were. Marena slowly lowered herself and sat upon her unmade bed.

"It's dark and cold and the air smells like seaweed or something," she began, her voice even-toned and oddly expressionless. "People are running, but I cannot see them. A heavy blanket or some kind of material covers me, over my face. It smells like spices, like potpourri at the spa - cloves - I don't know, and suddenly the voices seem more excited and nervous. Someone has their arms around my shoulders and is saying 'Shh, sweetness, shh. Rest now.' Then I hear the woman say 'je sui prest, I am ready!

"This was the dream I was having right before Avery woke me up. I never had it before, but it was so vivid. This is <u>the</u> dream?" Marena asked, still stunned.

"Yes," I told her, "But I don't think it's just a dream."

3

THE QUEEN'S CHAMBERS

Riva awoke when the sun began to peek through the wooden shutters. She was not ready to rise, but knew she had to face this day at some point. She placed her feet on the cold wood floor and forced her slender body to stand. Riva shuffled toward the wardrobe passing the full-length mirror and paused to glimpse at her profile. She smoothed the auburn waves that cascaded down her back. At least she would look as beautiful as possible today. She owed them that. Riva would leave them all with the memory of her as the beautiful, young woman she had become. Perhaps the next time they would see one another, Riva would still be that young woman, she hoped.

Heat and tears began to overtake Riva and she let out an audible gasp as she collapsed to the floor in front of the wardrobe. She melted into the floor with a piercing cry that alerted Tartine to hurry into the room without invitation or hesitation. Tartine had been ready for this day; she had been preparing for months.

"Majesty?" She knelt down to stroke Riva's back. "There, there."

Riva turned her face into the aging woman's shoulder to muffle her sobs.

"I can't. I just can't let them go," she cried, lifting her head just enough for Tartine to see the pain in her hazel eyes.

"This is the only way," Tartine reminded her Queen, "You want them to be safe. This is the only way to ensure the future of the realm. This is the way it must be done, Riva. You must find your strength. This day will be difficult for us all." Tartine walked to the windows and opened the shutters as she did each morning.

Riva swept the back of her left arm across her wet face, lifted her head and slowly rose to her feet. "I know. I must bear this," she said to Tartine who remained on her knees on the floor.

"But…" Riva was interrupted by the figure of her husband at the door to her bedchamber. She lowered her head as she curtsied to her King.

Tartine rose from the floor only to bow into a deep curtsy to the young man. His commanding presence was due more to his handsomeness than his position alone. After all, his wife was the true ruler of the Kingdom. His sand colored hair glistened from the sunshine that now streamed into the room. His brilliant blue eyes, which ordinarily sparkled when he came into a room containing his strikingly exquisite wife, were dull this day.

"Good morning, my love, madam," Philson's voice cracked with what seemed to Riva to be the stress of the seriousness of this day. She lifted her eyes and met his gaze. She saw that his eyes were red and his skin pale. Riva and her young King held each other's stare for what seemed like a lifetime. He knew by the look in her eyes that she bore the burden for his broken heart and he could not bear to witness her pain. Philson broke first and looked to his wife's most trusted lady in waiting, Tartine. Riva looked back at the floor.

"Please, have her ready, Tartine. We only have two hours before the mist clears. My sister has been summoned. She will be led to the nursery first and we will begin the process from there," Philson turned to look at his sullen wife, "Riva, I - I will see you to break our fast," Philson turned away from the women and strode out the door closing it behind himself. Riva crumpled to the floor once again.

After a moment of silence, with her eyes still fixed to the floor, she directed Tartine, "My cream and burgundy gown."

"Yes, Majesty."

"And the formal jewels as well. I want them to remember me at my best," Riva remained on the floor. "I need a moment, Tartine. I will be ready. I do not want to disappoint the King or the Council with any unnecessary emotional displays. You know, I considered putting up a fight. I considered running with them myself, but I understand that this is the only way. I trust the seers just as my husband does. But…" sobs began to choke her words, "my heart bleeds - I…"

Tartine crossed the room and knelt down to take Riva by both of her hands. She looked directly into her eyes, "The kingdom's heart bleeds today, Majesty, but it will heal as will you. Your mother…"

"Yes!" Riva interrupted raising her voice, "My mother committed the same horrid act and where are they? Where is my family now?" Abruptly, Riva stood and backed a few steps away from Tartine. She did not want to consider that she was following the path her mother had chosen so many years ago.

"My decision, the decision Philson and I have made is not the same resolution my mother came to when she sent me away. She made that decision based on a false prophecy and fear, and paid for that choice every single day of her life. If I am doomed to repeat her mistake, then I tell you now that my life is over," she declared dramatically, stamping her bare foot on the floor.

"I did not mean to upset you, Majesty," Tartine apologized, bowing her head in respect to the young Queen, who was clearly feeling the burden of her responsibility. Tartine laid the beautifully embroidered coronation gown on the bed.

"Out!" Riva ordered the older woman. "And send in the other ladies to dress me. I cannot keep the King waiting. I want you to know that today is the last day of my life,"

"Your majesty…"

"After today, I will be a ghost." She turned her back to Tartine and steadied herself on the mattress by placing her hands flat against it. "If I must do my duty, know I do it for my heart. Send them in. I need to dress."

Tartine withdrew from the Queen's bed-chamber without turning her back to the now sobbing young woman and with a nod, directed the five young ladies-in-waiting to serve their Queen. Without hesitation, the women scurried into the chambers to do their duty. They too had prepared for this day.

I continued to peer into my rearview mirror where I saw the young Queen and this dramatic scene unfolding.

"Avery! Red light! Red light!" Marena screeched. I slammed on my brakes.

"I know!" I shouted back.

"Well then wake up and please try not to kill us before first period!"

4

TGIF!

We got to school right on time, despite Timber forgetting her History book and forcing us to turn around and go back to the house, and Marena insisting on stopping for coffee at the Dunkin Donuts. I parked my well used Honda Accord in my new reserved spot in the junior lot, and we walked into the front entrance of Woodport High School together, as we always did. Despite being the oldest of my sisters, every morning I was aware of my shorter stature walking with Marena and Timber, both of them slender and blonde. They were like bookends flanking me as we entered the building. Marena smoothed her hair in the reflection of the glass doors.

The bell rang, alerting us to get to our first classes and we broke off from each other, silently. Timber headed to the opposite side of the enormous school building, waving down her friends whose smiles sparkled from all the metal in their mouths.

I turned toward the math and science wing, equations running through my mind. I was walking behind Marena and her friends, who met her in the common every morning - two of the most annoying creatures on the planet, Misty Walters and Alexis Thoms. They were busy complimenting my stunning sister on her choice of wardrobe today; dark skinny jeans with a pale blue v-neck sweater that, "Like, totally matches Bradley Jacobs eyes!"

I choked back a snicker as I headed into Mr. Monahan's classroom and took my seat. I really could not understand why Marena spent time with such dolts.

"Book bags, under your desks. Take out your graphing calculators and a pencil and let's go," the middle-aged man at the front of the classroom instructed as he began to hand out what looked like the thickest packet of graphs yet this year. I could feel the pre-test jitters beginning in my belly, tickling my insides. I tried to inhale and exhale slowly to relax. I reached into my book bag with my left hand, fishing for a good pencil with a reasonably useful eraser.

I tried to accomplish this task one handed, and without having to look directly at the bag to find the pencil, but as with most things I tried to do to look cool or smooth, I failed.

"I'll get that for you, Avery," my friend Paul cheerfully told me as he handed my purple mechanical pencil to me. Paul was a nice kid and always so eager to be helpful.

"Thanks. Good luck, Paul."

"You too," he replied, smiling his best sixteen year old smile at me. Every time I would look over at him in math class, I would notice he had a kind, sweet face.

I was done with the test with about four minutes left in the period so I checked over some of my less confident answers, but I did not really have time to do any of the problems over, even if I found a mistake.

"Oh well," I thought to myself, "I did the best I could." I sighed and put my head down on my arms, waiting for the bell. I could tell this would be a long day.

I was exhausted by the time lunch period arrived and I was probably not very good company for my friends. My mind wandered and my imagination took off in a bizarre direction. I was trying to mentally compile all of the dreams and daydreams I had had over the past year. They were growing in frequency and clarity. Maybe I was imagining a past life, but that did not explain why my sisters were having the same dreams now. None of my possible ideas made any sense. Who were these people in my dreams and why were they so sad? They were definitely strangers, but at the same time, so familiar.

Just as I thought my brain was going to explode, I turned my attention to the lunch table. My friends were all going on and on about the prom. I did not have the energy to talk about something that was still two and a half months away.

"Do you think Adam will ask you?" Kerri was looking right at me and it took me a few beats to recognize she was expecting an answer from me.

"Umm - I don't know," I replied.

"Really, because - well, haven't you been spending a lot of time together lately, you know movies and stuff?" I could tell she was just fishing for information since she had a serious crush on Adam Martin since the seventh grade. He was a year ahead of me in school, but our paths often crossed through school activities and sports. While he played football in the fall, he was the first singles player on the boys' tennis team in the spring season. Our coach encouraged the better players on the boys and girls teams to work out together and hit together on the weekends and between seasons.

Kerri Jeffers was not someone I considered a friend, but we were both friends with Karen Rossi and forced to tolerate one another ever since Karen bought us both best friend charms in the fourth grade. Kerri had some good qualities; she was very smart and musically talented. Nevertheless, her annoying traits out-shined her positive ones. She was bossy, nosy, gossipy and judgmental, the last trait being the one negative characteristic I truly could not tolerate, and I always wondered how Karen could be friends with such a mean girl.

"Actually, I heard Avery and Adam were doing more than just watching a movie last weekend at Jim Shipley's house," reported Brian Manning, the male version of Kerri.

"What? Aww, come on…" I could feel that I was turning the same color as the sauce covering Brian's mysterious and allegedly Italian lunch. It was hard to protest, since Adam and I did have a rare opportunity to get somewhat familiar on the Shipley's basement couch - all very PG, but all a bit too much for Kerri to handle. I was not the least bit surprised that Adam had shared this information with Brian; I just wished Brian had the wherewithal to keep it to himself. Suddenly, Kerri's eyes became glassy and red and she had to go to the bathroom.

"Ok Brian, enough. Now Kerri is all upset. You know she likes Adam, so cool it, ok? For the record nothing is going on because Adam and I are just good friends," I explained.

The truth was that I was madly in love with Adam Martin, and would do anything to have him reciprocate the feelings, but he was way out of my league. I was not interested in giving myself to a guy who probably wouldn't talk to me the next day, but who would most certainly report his conquest to every guy on the football team. That fact did not stop the way my heart palpitated out of my chest every time he walked near me in the halls, however.

Aside from Kerri storming away from the lunch table in near tears, the rest of the day was free of drama. I got an A on my essay on Federalism in US History, which was a pleasant surprise since I was not confident I actually understood all of the concepts I wrote about in my essay.

I was quite eager to get home to start my weekend. I had no plans. I almost never had weekend plans but I was eager to talk to my sisters about our dream, maybe even talk to Uncle Bob and Aunt Bea about it all. As the final bell rang, I collected my books from my locker and headed toward the junior lot.

Timber was already at the car, leaning on the hood, talking to a boy. Even though she was only sixteen, she had the look of a much more mature girl. She had recently had her braces removed and was starting to look less and less like a child. The boy she was speaking to was clearly still a boy, with his pudgy cheeks and high-pitched voice.

"See ya Monday, Timber," the boy said to my little sister as he watched my approach, "I'll call you tomorrow. Maybe you can go bowling with me and Sam?" he asked.

I always thought it was funny when people called my sister by her nickname. In fact, I doubted anyone at school knew her real name. Aside from the fact that "Timber" was a shortened version of her full name, Timberose, we always called her Timber because she has such bad balance. From the time she was little, Timber would trip over nothing and everything and each time she would fall, we'd always yell "Timber!" and she would giggle and get up to try again. Rose probably would have been a more normal or acceptable nickname, but Timber fit my sister so well.

Her closest friends picked up on the inner meaning of her nickname, especially when she began playing sports. While she was incredibly agile and athletic, chances were that Timber would fall or get knocked down at least once in every soccer or basketball game she played and her friends would call out "Timber!" She loved it.

"Sure, I'll ask my aunt," she replied, "bye Tyler."

"Tyler? He's new, right?" I asked.

"Yup, and he told Heather Miller that I'm the coolest girl in our homeroom so I let him walk me to the car, but I'm not going to bother asking Aunt Bea about bowling. I know she'll say no anyway."

"You'll have plenty of time to hang out with boys when you get to college and even then, you won't want to. They're boring and weird," I told her. Our Aunt Bea was very strict and did not allow us to formally date boys just yet. We assumed she was strict because she had some weird, unfounded fear about teenage pregnancy or something. Of course, we could hang out with boys as friends as long as other girls were around. Marena learned the loophole in this rule and typically invited Timber and me to join her on "non-dates." But Timber always followed the rules to the tee.

Just then, our other sister came prancing up to the car with her entourage of dimwits. They said their adieus complete with air kisses and Timber, Marena and I got into the car.

Marena spoke first, "So what should we do? I mean, this has been driving me crazy all day."

"I know," I said as I turned into the Plaza, "maybe we should ask Aunt Bea?"

Timber sighed, "You think that'll get us anywhere? Aunt Bea never tells us anything." Timber had a point. Aunt Bea was never particularly forthcoming about the events that led to her gaining custody of her brother's daughters and she would likely be just as unhelpful in helping us dissect and analyze our dreams.

As we pulled onto Indian Trail, after much debate, we decided to see what information we could get from Aunt Bea at dinner. It was Friday, after all, and we remembered that Friday night dinner meant a bottle of wine for Bea and Bob.

Ordinarily, we would go off and do our own things on Friday nights so that our Aunt and Uncle could also have time to themselves. Marena would most likely meet up with a scatterbrained member of her dominion and Timber would spend her time before bed comparing notes with her friends about the week's gossip. I would typically bide my time reading whatever my English teacher thought was appropriate torture for a seventeen year old. If it were not for our new plan that night, I would have been holed up with Moll Flanders.

Friday night dinner was the closest thing we had to a weekly family tradition. Aunt Bea called it our weekly "family meeting" where we would recap our week in school for them and talk about upcoming events or projects.

Bea and Bob got married when they were very young, supposedly so they could take care of the three of us. We used to live in Scotland, but they brought us to the United States when we were still very little. It was never clear why we moved here, but Bob was immediately able to get a good job with Port Authority driving the ferryboats. Aunt Bea had been able to go to college at night after caring for us all day, and was now studying for her doctorate in Celtic anthropology and folklore, which seemed like a weird thing to study. She told us the subjects she was studying made her feel closer to home.

Bea had to go back to Scotland once a year to attend a four week research conference, which she always looked forward to very much. She was currently working on a book about Scottish legends that she said could be confirmed through anecdotal evidence. Timber had been hoping Bea would prove the existence of the Loch Ness Monster, but I did not think that was the sort of legend Aunt Bea was researching.

They never had children of their own, and even though we always knew they were not our real parents, they were the only parents we had. Considering the fact that they were still so young, they did a good job raising us. I was sure our parents would be quite pleased with them if they knew how we had turned out so far. That is, if our real parents even cared one way or the other.

Bea and Bob worked hard to give us a nice life, and so we did whatever we could to make life easier on them. Like most of my friends with sisters, Marena, Timber and I did not always agree or get along. Marena tended to be the toughest one for me to deal with at times, but we worked out any sisterly problems amongst ourselves. Bob and Bea just about never heard or saw our fights, which could last for days like the time last summer when Timber "borrowed" Marena's new sundress and accidentally ruined it with bike grease when she fell off her bike down at the boardwalk. Marena had saved up for that particular dress for two months and I thought she was going to kill Timber, but the three of us worked it out on our own and Bob and Bea were kept out of it. Marena got a new dress and Timber's life was spared.

"We need to orchestrate this plan perfectly tonight," I instructed as we dropped our book bags onto the kitchen table and headed for the fridge. Bea had just been to Costco, which meant we had an enormous supply of chocolate Jell-O pudding packs, perhaps the most perfect after school snack ever invented.

"My suggestion is to be blunt and just tell Bea that we have this dream and we know she can tell us what it means," Marena stated.

"Well, we don't know that Bea knows what it means, first of all. And secondly, being blunt makes people act defensively, Rena. I think we should be more subtle and try to feel out whether Bea knows anything before we make her feel uncomfortable and ruin her evening," suggested Marena's more sensitive twin.

"We have a few hours to think about it and I have to run over to baby sit Bailey Reynolds until his mom gets home," Marena replied, referring to our neighbor, "So let's talk about it when I get back, before dinner."

I knew what she was up to, but let it go. Marena wanted to do things her way, as usual. She had no patience. Ever since she overheard Bob and Bea speaking in hushed tones about what she believed was our parents about a week before her sixteenth birthday, she has been suspicious that they were hiding something from us.

Obviously, they did not intend for her to hear their exchange, and it likely had nothing to do with us, but Marena was very insistent that we find out the details of their conversation. She believed she heard them mention our mother, and something about how now that Marena and Timber were sixteen, they would not be safe. Believing this nebulous conversation was just a comment about our mother's drug use, Timber and I voted to wait and not immediately attack our aunt and uncle about this perceived secret until we had more facts. Marena disagreed with our chosen tactics and had nagged us about launching a "full investigation" for weeks.

It was our understanding that both our mother and father were involved with drugs and that was why Aunt Bea and Uncle Bob obtained custody of us. That explanation never really made very much sense to any of us and it sounded more like something you would see on a Lifetime Original Movie, especially since Bea was about fifteen when we were taken from our mother.

Bea explained that the courts "do things differently" in Scotland since we had no other living blood relatives, but we never bought the explanation for our past. Any time we would challenge Bea's story or ask questions, she would cry and make us feel horrible. We knew there had to be more to the story, though it never seemed very important.

Obviously, our parents did not love us or else they would have worked out their alleged drug problem, found us and raised us. Obviously, Bea and Bob did really love us as their own children, so where we came from never mattered to us.

That is, until we all started having the same dream.

5

OPERATION "SPILL THE BEANS"

"More wine, Uncle Bob?" Marena asked. She did not wait for an answer before pouring the red wine into his glass.

Marena's role in our diabolical plan that we were calling "Operation Spill the Beans," was to get Aunt Bea and Uncle Bob to relax and be comfortable. She was already acting overly solicitous. Marena was not completely self-centered - only the majority of the world revolved around her - so, the fact that she was incredibly interested in Bea's day lecturing to undergrads at The College of Saint Elizabeth was a dead giveaway that she wanted something.

"My goodness, Rena," Bea remarked in her Scottish brogue, "When did you develop such an interest in Scottish folklore?"

All I could think was "Abort mission, abort mission! Our cover has been compromised!" Marena could not help herself.

"I've always been interested in ancient history!" She squealed. Her expression was priceless. She looked dejected, as if offended, that our dear Aunt Bea was unaware of her interests. Marena was a wonderful actress.

"Well, you are more than welcome to come to one of my classes and sit in one day, as long as you don't have a test or anything important going on in school. You can take the train back from Convent Station and your sister can pick you up at the Dover Station." Bea's invitation to Marena was extremely appealing to me.

"Um, sure Aunt Bea. Love to come - sounds so educational," Marena was looking to Timber and me for help. Timber and I made eye contact with each other and just laughed. Uncle Bob understood the joke and snickered right along with us. Marena pouted. Perhaps her performance was not as believable as she had hoped.

"All right girls, what's going on? Special dinner, you're pouring our bottle of wine…?" Bea did not miss a trick. She was younger than any of us when she stepped in as our mother, but her sense of teenage trickery was stronger than it should have been for someone forced to grow up so quickly.

In response to Bea's query, Marena batted her eyelashes and gave her most innocent expression - the "I have no idea what you are talking about" look that she usually gave in response to "did you take my new CD?" or "did you eat the last pudding pack?" Timber cracked up yet again.

"Come on lassies," Bob coaxed, "what is it?" As the oldest, I knew the twins were looking to me to start this conversation. For all of her bluster, Marena generally chickened out of difficult exchanges. I took a breath.

"We've been having this dream," I started, "and we were hoping maybe you could shed some light on it for us."

Bea gave Bob the kind of look that meant something. It was a somewhat guilty look. Bob nodded at Bea as if to say, "Go ahead and tell them." I have always been very good at reading body language and expressions so at this point I understood that Bea knew about our dream.

"Well," Bea began nervously, "I don't know much about dreams or psychology, but why don't you tell me about your dream and maybe we can figure it out together," Bea offered. I wanted to tell Bea to cut the act, that I knew she knew more than she would admit, but I had to tell myself to be patient. We would get to the bottom of all of this at some point. We just needed some clues.

"You see, the three of us have had a similar dream. It's the dream I told you about last year with the fog and the voices. Marena and Timber just started having pretty much the same dream," I reported.

Timber interjected, "Except, in my dream I hear a lady say 'jest sui prest…'"

"I am ready," answered Bob under his breath, but loud enough for us to hear.

"It's French, right Uncle Bob?" Timber asked. I could tell she was as curious as I was. How did he know the translation? As far as we knew Bob was familiar with the English language only, and sometimes we doubted his relationship with even that, given his habit of using the urban slang he would pick up from the guys who worked on his ferries.

Bob nodded and I caught him glancing at Bea again. This time the look he gave her was a bit sheepish, as if he knew he had spoken out of turn. I wondered if my sisters were witnessing all of the weird looks, too.

"And you've all been having the same dream?" Bea inquired.

"Pretty much," Marena told her as she topped off Bea's wine glass with a little more of the Pinot Noir Bob had brought home from his last trip to Merke's Fine Liquors.

Bob was partial to Merke's since he was invited to play on the store-sponsored men's softball team a few years ago. Bob had never played baseball as a kid, or even softball, but he was so honored to have been asked that he spent hours in the batting cages at Skylands Park getting ready for his first debut. He actually became a very good player and he turned his experience into a lesson for us, "You can do anything you set your mind to girls if you practice," he had said in a proud, fatherly moment.

"Any idea what that's all about, Aunt Bea?" Marena prodded with a hint of sarcasm in her voice. Marena was feeling the same way I was. Of course, they knew. They just were not sharing the answer with us.

"Perhaps you are remembering a place where you had been together, like the time we visited our friends on Staten Island and took you to see where the ferries go. It was foggy that day, so maybe you are remembering that," Bea suggested.

She seemed pleased with herself and clearly accepted her reasoning and analysis. It sounded as if she was inventing that explanation on the spot. While I was impressed with her improvisational skills, her explanation left a lot to be desired. Perhaps if we were much younger, we would have accepted her answer as the end of the conversation.

Timber and I were on the same wavelength.

"Well, Aunt Bea - um - I don't want to sound rude or anything, but that doesn't come close to explaining why we would each have the same dream, or why we would have it at the same time. Avery, Marena and I all dreamed the same dream last night. We each had variations of it, but for the most part, the same exact dream. I think that goes beyond mere coincidental reminiscing," Timber challenged.

Bea looked nervous. She glanced at Bob who shrugged back at her as if to say, "I don't know, what do you think?" Bea and Bob had that sort of relationship where they could speak without words. I admired that, even envied it. I hoped that when I found my true soul mate - and I did believe in soul mates - we would have a similar understanding.

Marena was getting impatient. "Aunt Bea?"

Bea clearly had no competent response to Timber's question. It was a good one.

"I don't know Marena. What do you want me to say? That you are all remembering the day you left your home? That..." Bob finally spoke up and interrupted our poor, struggling aunt.

"Beata," he rarely called her that, "let us not give them ideas that have no real meaning!"

Suddenly I recalled a line I loved from Shakespeare – "the lady doth protesteth too much," or something close to that. As usual, Timber was thinking along with me.

"You mean Scotland? That we are all remembering Scotland?" Timber asked anxiously.

"Maybe. I don't know. There's plenty of clouds and fog there." Bea rose from her seat at the dining room table.

In an attempt to act casually, she turned to the wall behind her and inspected her reflection in the long Pottery Barn mirror. Despite their limited incomes, both Bea and Bob had expensive taste. They preferred furniture and decorative accessories that were well made and regal looking. Apparently, Pottery Barn and other retail stores like Restoration Hardware satiated their preference for fine things at what they considered reasonable prices. Of course, I never thought spending nearly a thousand dollars for a mirror was reasonable, but what did I know?

Bea was combing through her brown waves with her fingers in front of the mirror. While she seemed to be looking at herself in the mirror, I could tell she was also looking for the expressions on both Timber and Marena's faces.

"I have an idea," Bea stated as she turned back from her reflection, "the next time any one of you has a dream that you believe to be questionable in meaning, write it down and I will contact my friend Dee in the Psych Department at school. She is writing a paper and researching the meaning behind certain dreams and repressed memories in adopted children. I am sure she will have some insight into what you girls are experiencing. Now, anyone for dessert? I picked up some ice cream sandwiches when I was at Costco," Bea announced.

That was classic Bea, avoid answering a difficult question and then distract us with dessert. Aside from pudding packs, she knew that ice cream sandwiches were our kryptonite, and, not unlike almost every other time she employed this tactic, she was successful here. Timber was the first to crack.

"Yes!" She exclaimed. "Come on Marena, it's our turn to clear the table." They both got up from their seats and began collecting dishes. I glanced at Uncle Bob who winked and smirked at his wife, clearly proud of her cleverness.

I was not budging. "Ok, but Aunt Bea, we haven't really resolved the issue about the dream we already had. Can your friend tell us about that without even meeting us? How can she determine the meaning of our dreams when she doesn't know us?"

I was making a good point. I could tell by the look Bea delivered to Bob, as if to say, "This kid just doesn't quit!" Marena and Timber returned from the kitchen to the dining room to hear Bea's response.

"I'll talk to Dee and maybe she will want to meet with the three of you and we can get to the bottom of this issue. All right?" Bea did not wait for my response. "Good. Let's enjoy dessert, Avery. You and Marena should turn in early tonight. You have a match with the Jacobs girls tomorrow morning at the Racket Center."

"Ugh," groaned Marena, "I totally forgot about that." Actually, so had I. The Jacobs girls were home on spring break from their respective colleges and had run into Bea at the Stop and Shop last week. They were a few years older than we were, so we never associated with them socially. We were in the same tennis clinics at the Woodport Racket Center and competed in the same local tournaments since we could hold a racket.

Both Karla and Kristen Jacobs played college tennis and I suppose they were eager to practice against us. Tennis was the one sport that Bea and Bob wanted us to know how to play. Bea called it the "sport of princes," which made sense to me as a six year old, since I did use a "Prince" brand tennis racket.

We did love tennis, and all three of us were quite good at it. Woodport had an exceptionally competitive team at the high school, and the three of us soared quickly through the ranks. Really, Marena and Timber were better players than I was, but our coach was interested in

OPERATION "SPILL THE BEANS"

winning and he did not feel a close camaraderie with the league rules that required that the best players fill out the top spots on a team.

Marena and Timber were undefeated for two years as the First Doubles team, and despite the fact that they both defeated me in our team-seeding matches, they remained at First Doubles this year while I jumped to the First Singles position. While I had a very respectable 12-2 record, with my losses coming at the NJ State Singles Tournament and our Northern Regional match against Old Tappan High School, Marena and Timber were again undefeated. When they played together, they moved in fluid, synchronized motion. They rarely ever spoke when they played, but they covered the court with such grace of movement, you would think they had to be communicating somehow. Their adversaries had no chance, when you really thought about it. Twins!

Reluctantly, my sisters and I obeyed Aunt Bea and retired to our rooms after dinner to engage in our typical Friday night activities - Marena almost immediately upon turning on the light to our room jumped onto the computer and logged onto Facebook; Timber was on the phone; I was struggling through <u>Moll Flanders</u>. We kept to ourselves and went to sleep as usual.

I was disappointed that Aunt Bea refused to provide us any credible insight into our dream. I was replaying some of the information she gave us in my head. Specifically, I was thinking about "maybe you are remembering the day you left your home." It was getting late, so I figured I would think more about it the next day.

6

THE LETTERS

"Help them. Please, protect them," the young woman pleaded on her knees. Her face was wet with tears and partially covered by a veil that cascaded to her shoulders from a headpiece that kept her long, auburn waves away from her cheeks.

"I love you, my sweet petals." The young woman rose from her feet and lifted her veil, revealing a most beautiful porcelain complexion. She wore an embroidered gown, right out of a Holbein painting from the 16th Century. Her sparkling eyes pierced mine as she looked directly at me.

"I love you. Come home. It is time. We need you. We need the Trinity," she told me.

I shot out of my sleep with my heart racing as if I had just sprinted around a track. Marena could not turn on the lamp by her bed fast enough and knocked it to the floor, startling Tulip who had chosen Marena's bed for her evening nap. I turned on my lamp.

"Did you - did she…?" Marena could not formulate a thought let alone a sentence.

"Yes, yes!" I practically screamed at her. I could not calm myself. Who was this woman? She was the same woman in my other dreams as well. The bedroom door flew open and Timber slid inside.

"Did you guys…?"

Marena finished her thought, "Yes, I think so. I did. Avery?"

"A young woman with my hair and your eyes. Old fashioned - and she said, 'Come home?'"

"We need 'the Trinity'" Timber clarified.

"Yes," I said.

"Yes," Marena agreed.

"Should we tell Bea and Bob?" Marena asked looking to me for guidance. Both of my sisters commonly looked to me to have all of the answers.

"No. What is the point? She is just going to deny knowing anything about it. No. Let's do this. We should set up a journal on the computer, with a folder for each of us to input our impression of our dreams. From that, we can do our own research and analyze it ourselves. Then, if we can come up with a viable theory, we can approach Bea with that," I suggested. Marena jumped onto our shared Mac computer, opened a Word document and started typing.

"Don't mind me. I just don't want to forget a single detail," she told us.

"Good point. Make sure you put in everything you remember including what the lady looked like, what the room looked like and all the little details," I told them both. Timber ran out of the room and returned with her laptop, tripping over my slippers on the way back into our room. As the only one without a tool to record my dream, I reached for my math notebook and purple mechanical pencil and started writing. I did not want to forget the sound of her voice, or the tears streaking down her face, or the beautiful purple and gold gown she was wearing.

⌒◯

Our friendly tennis match with the Jacobs sisters became unfriendly when Kristen made a snide comment about Marena's outfit. Accusing my sister of shopping off the clearance racks at Dick's Sporting Goods, while probably accurate, was akin to accusing her of kicking a puppy. Marena was incensed to say the least, but Kristen just laughed at Marena's reaction and told her she was "just kidding."

Kristen and Karla were your typical Woodport girls, self-absorbed and completely convinced that they were better than everyone else. In many ways, these particular Woodport girls were better than everybody was, but unfortunately, they did not know how to be humble. It was incredibly unattractive to us, but they got on well with their fellow Woodport girlfriends when they were in high school. My sisters and I were certainly not underprivileged, but Woodport was full of those who have and those who have slightly less, and those who have were not shy about letting the rest of us know about it.

"Can you believe that Kristen?" Marena asked me as soon as we got into the car. I did not want to tell her "yes."

"I wouldn't worry about Kristen Jacobs, Rena." I tried to get her to relax while we drove home. We turned into our driveway and noticed that neither Bob nor Bea was home. I looked at Rena and Rena looked at me. We must have had the same thought, and apparently, so did Timber because as soon as we opened the front door, we could hear Timber rummaging all the way down in the basement.

"Timber? Is that you down there?" Rena called.

"You guys have got to come down here and see what I found!" She screamed back to us. Marena and I dropped our racket bags behind the couch, specifically where Aunt Bea asked us not to leave our things. Anxious to unravel the mystery of our dreams, neither Marena nor I were particularly concerned with the safety of others at the moment. In fact, I was not confident we even closed the front door.

Amid a sea of boxes, Timber was turning the pages of what looked to be a photo album.

"Check this out, guys," she said waiving us over to her position. She was making a mess, obviously digging through the archives of our family's past.

"Holy moley, Tim! You better clean this up before Bea and Bob come home," Marena ordered her twin. "By the way, where did they go?"

"Bob's work holiday party in Weehawken. Remember, it got postponed because of the snowstorm in December and then postponed again because of the blizzard in February?" Timber reminded us.

"Oh yeah." That February snowstorm was awesome. It dumped about two feet of snow, which closed school for two days. Timber, Marena and I, and some of the neighborhood kids built forts and had a two-day snowball war. We also had sledding races right down the middle of our street before the plows arrived. It was so much fun and it was the first time in a long time that all the kids on our street interacted with one another. Then, once we were back to the regular routine of school that forced our neighborhood into cliques and castes, our two days of unified fun were soon forgotten, and we ignored each other in the hallowed halls of Woodport High School.

"Let me see that," Marena ordered her twin, grabbing the album from her.

"Hey, this is from our house in Scotland. I haven't seen these pictures in years," Marena cooed as she flipped the pages.

"Rena, that's not what I wanted to show you," Timber said yanking the album back from her, "It's this letter," she told us raising handwritten pages. Timber handed it to me in a move akin to an acknowledgment of my seniority. I read the short letter aloud:

"My Dear Sister,

Thank you for the images you sent to us. What a brilliant and magical machine that makes such lifelike paintings of my baby girls. The twins are growing so quickly. I feel like it was just yesterday that I was nursing them and holding little Avery in my arms. I cannot repay you enough for your protection of them, Beata. When you are all able to return to the Kingdom, you and Bobril will be rewarded handsomely for your loyalty and bravery.

I must tell you that this may be my last letter for some time. Anyon has taken the Kingdom and reunited us with Mordith. He has named our cousin, Ginter, as Regent. While I remain Queen in name, Ginter is charged with the task of leading the Council under the direction of Anyon. Your brother, and my dearest love, has been taken as a prisoner, locked in the Tower. I have received no word as to his condition and I fear the worst. Ginter comforts me, but only as much as a distant relative can. I miss your brother dearly. My heart aches for him as much as it aches for my children. Ginter acknowledges my losses, and patronizes me, but I am still not assured of his loyalty.

The Order of the Heather has suggested that I refrain from writing to you until they are sure of your safety and mine. Please tell my girls I love them and I will be with them soon.

With all my heart, Your sister and your Queen,
Riva de Hazaro."

We were silent with our astonishment.

"Did you find any other letters?" I asked Timber. She reached into a box labeled "Fort Augustus" and pulled out a pile of handwritten papers. She handed them to me and I divvied them up among the three of us. I looked at Marena, who was speaking as she wandered over to the patio chairs in storage for the winter beside the basement stairs. I thought I heard her ask me, "Is this our mother writing to Aunt Bea?"

"It looks that way," I answered her.

"What? Who are you talking to?" Marena asked me.

"You. You just asked me 'is this our mother writing to Aunt Bea?' and I just said 'looks that way.'"

"Marena didn't say anything, Avery. No one said anything," Timber told me as we all sat down on the patio furniture, which was arranged like a living room in the basement.

Bea preferred that we not use the furniture when it was stored in the basement, and would remind us of her preference each time she knew we were spending time down there. Our basement had become a bit of a hang out spot for our friends and us. Uncle Bob set up an old television and DVD player as well as a mini fridge, old couch and microwave oven creating a living room area for us. We even had a ping-pong table and dartboard.

Apparently, Bea had read an article in Parenting Magazine about allowing teenagers to have their own space and privacy and felt that setting aside a corner in the basement for us was a reasonable attempt at being "modern parents." In reality, we enjoyed spending time with Bea and Bob. More often, my sisters and I needed privacy and space from each other, not our parental figures.

"I could have sworn I heard you say that, Rena." I was confused. I knew what I had heard, and then I heard her say, "You're obviously hearing things!"

"I'm not hearing things. I know what you said," I retorted somewhat offended. I could tell they didn't believe me.

Lately, I would imagine things happening that clearly had not happened yet, and when they would occur I would say, "See I told you that would happen." Marena and Timber would crack themselves up mocking me and calling me Nostradamus.

"Wait, Avery what did you hear me say?"

"'You're obviously hearing things' is what I heard," I replied.

"I didn't say that out loud. I literally just thought it! How did you know I was thinking that exact phrase?" Marena seemed amazed. "Here, try again. What am I thinking now?" She challenged.

I laughed aloud, "That Tulip didn't eat Timber's turkey rollups on Wednesday…" I started giggling as soon as Timber's expression changed. She was obviously waiting for me to complete Marena's thought. "I swiped them off the plate when she went to the bathroom and ate them."

"I knew it! You're such a jerk," Timber laughed. "Gosh, I am too gullible!" Aside from pudding packs, Timber's favorite after school snack was what she called a "rollup," some deli meat and a slice of American cheese rolled up and essentially shoved into her mouth. As our resident athlete, Timber could certainly eat a great deal of food. Bea did not keep many unhealthy foods in the house, so we all grew very accustomed to creating our own delicious snacks out of whatever we had in the refrigerator or pantry.

Marena was hysterical, laughing and slapping her legs, "You are easy to fool, Tim - but how in the world are you able to read my mind like that, Avery?"

"I don't know. I have never tried to do that before, and I was not trying now. I just could. If I concentrate, I can actually hear your thoughts sometimes. To be honest, I noticed that I could do this a few weeks ago, after your birthday party," I told them.

"Why didn't you tell us?" Marena asked. I shrugged.

"I just thought it was in my head. I guess it is in my head," I giggled.

"This is clearly something. I do not know what. But something. Between the dreams and this - well, there's something weird going on here," Timber warned.

"Don't get excited, Tim," Marena tried to calm her sister, "and don't be over dramatic."

"No, she's right. This is all a little too weird," I added. We were all studying the letters Timber had divvied up among us, and silence filled the basement.

We read in silence for about an hour, scouring the pages for clues about our mother and our life in Scotland. I attempted to concentrate exclusively on the written pages, but Timber and Marena's thoughts were cluttering my own. They were both sad and confused, as was I.

This was not the drug-addicted mother we believed had left us to the care of our aunt and uncle. From the letters I read, this was a young woman tormented by a choice she was forced to make. Our mother was a young Queen of some sort, concerned about the welfare of her children who were far from her and concerned about the welfare of her kingdom. It was difficult to understand what I was reading. A Queen? Queen of what – of where?

Timber broke the silence, "Fort Augustus! We have to go to Fort Augustus." We did not answer her, but Marena and I both agreed with our younger sister.

7

SICK DAY

Monday, Marena feigned a sore throat and convinced Aunt Bea she needed to stay home from school. The three of us had already worked out our plan - "Operation History Lesson" - to have Marena stay home to continue our research. Bea did not have to work on Mondays and typically used the day to accomplish housework and grocery shopping. It had rained all weekend, washing away the last evidence of winter. It was still raining when Timber and I left Marena and headed to school. Since our school now had a new attendance policy that required a doctor's note if you were sick and wanted your absence excused, Bea made an early appointment for Marena to be examined by Dr. Lane.

According to a text message from Rena at 10:04, Dr. Lane passed off Marena's "sore throat" as a consequence of an earlier than normal allergy season and prescribed Nasonex and antibiotics "just in case." I laughed aloud in AP History when I saw that. Marena should get an Oscar for her performance.

School ended at 2:18 and by 2:20, Timber and I were at the car, ready to head home. We did not want to get our hopes up that Marena had found anything helpful, especially since Marena could be so easily distracted when left on her own. She had promised us she would do her best and frankly, she was the only candidate for the job. I had a <u>Moll Flanders</u> quiz in English as well as a National Honor Society meeting at lunch and Timber had a big Geometry test she was afraid to miss.

"Hey Avery, Rena sent me a text an hour ago. Looks like she found something," Timber announced while were stopped at the traffic light by the post office. "She also asked for a medium French Vanilla, light and sweet from Dunkin Donuts."

"Ugh. I don't have any money left, do you?" I had used up the last of my lunch money at the Snapple machine after gym eighth period. We played floor hockey and the gym was especially hot and dry today. I normally did not waste my money on the vending machines, but I was so thirsty and water fountain water was not satisfying my thirst. Aunt Bea only leaves each of us $5.00 per day for lunch and I had already spent my gas money filling up my car on the way to school.

"Yeah, I have birthday money left, but I want to get paid back," Timber demanded.

"When don't I pay you back?"

"I know you're good for it, but Rena is the worst. She never repays me. It's almost embarrassing to ask her for money sometimes because all I get is the "we're family and family helps each other" speech."

"So basically, she humiliates you into forgiving her debt?" I laughed as I waited to make a left into the parking lot by Dunkin Donuts.

"Exactly," she laughed in reply, "never underestimate Marena. She's that good!"

Timber jumped out of the car to get Marena's coffee. I realized after she went into the shop that I could also use a coffee, but I was too lazy to leave the driver's seat. I turned up the music on my stereo. I wondered what a medium hazelnut coffee with cream and sugar would taste like. Ordinarily and in fact regularly, I would order a French Vanilla, light and sweet just like Marena. But if I were to have a coffee right now, I would try something new for a change. Of course, I was not particularly motivated at that point to bother getting out of the car, so the new flavor would have to wait for another day.

The after school line at Dunkin Donuts was longer than usual. I could see Timber chatting up one of Marena's friends while waiting in line. I looked around the parking lot for familiar cars. Adam Martin's blue Nissan Altima, a hand-me-down from his older sister, Laura, was parked a few yards away by the CVS Pharmacy. Next to him was a jeep I recognized as belonging to Morgan Jeffers, Kerri's older sister. As much as I disliked Kerri, I disliked her sister even more. Morgan was just mean and she would pick on me when Kerri, Karen and I would play at Kerri's house. Morgan was exceptionally popular with all the boys.

She was not tall, but had the figure of a woman, with large breasts that were generally on display through a low cut top. Morgan had perpetually bronzed, almost orange skin from the fake glow that she received free twice a week when she worked at Suntastic, the local tanning salon. Her hair was long and brown with streaks of gold in it and her eyes were a sort of purple from the color-contacts she wore. Rumor had it that Morgan was caught in a rather unladylike position in the boys' locker room with the freshman boys' soccer coach last year. She denied it, but he no longer worked at the high school after that, and she was finishing her senior year at Saint John's.

Just then, I saw Adam walking through the sliding doors at CVS. I did not have time to think, so I got out of the car and prepared to walk toward him. We had not spoken in over a week, not since the Shipley basement couch encounter. I felt almost guilty that I had refused his persuasive advances. What was I waiting for anyway? I was afraid that he was completely losing interest in me and prom bids were already on sale.

"Hi Adam!" I exclaimed as I came upon his car. He seemed sheepish when he saw me.

"Oh, hi Avery. What's up?"

"Nothing really, I just wanted to say hello. I thought maybe you were avoiding me or something. I didn't see you at the NHS meeting at lunch today. We gave out blood drive assignments."

"That was today? I totally spaced. Sorry," Adam seemed nervous. The heavy rain had subsided earlier in the afternoon, but it was still drizzling. He was not wearing a jacket, just a light gray football hooded sweatshirt. The rain was creating dark spots on his shoulders.

"That's ok," I replied cheerfully even though I meant to appear nonchalant and suave. "I just signed you up to do registration with me. It's the easiest job. Are you good with that?"

"Sure," he replied. Something was distracting his attention. I turned to look toward CVS. Kerri was practically skipping over to us.

"Here, you jerk," she said as she thrust a small white bag into Adam's chest, "that was so embarrassing. Next time you can buy your own stupid - oh, hi Avery." Kerri was unnecessarily loud and peppy. He quickly shoved the bag into his sweatshirt pocket and looked away.

Kerri acted as if she was surprised to see me, but I could tell she had seen me standing there the whole time. I started to feel hot. I knew exactly what was happening. I looked to Adam who was staring at his keys in his hand. Now I understood his awkwardness when I first approached him.

"Come on sweetie," Kerri addressed Adam, "let's go work on our homework." The word "homework" was surrounded by air quotes and I felt nauseous. A week ago, Adam was telling me what an "awesome chick" he thought I was and everyone was congratulating me on my handsome potential prom date. I blew it! I told him to stop, that I did not want to go any further with him and that was all it took. My head was reeling and I felt this terrible tightness in my chest.

I turned briskly and walked back to my car.

"See ya, Avery," Kerri called after me. I could still hear her giggling as I closed my car door. I sank into the driver's seat and allowed the tears to flow freely. Timber came out of Dunkin Donuts with three coffees and gingerly opened the car door.

"What happened?" She asked as she handed me a medium sized coffee.

"What's this?" I asked ignoring her question.

"Medium hazelnut, cream and sugar. It's what you wanted, right?"

"Yeah, but how did…?"

Timber smiled. "You're not the only one who can perform tricks!"

◦

On the ride home, I ranted and raved about Kerri and Adam, and how humiliated and pathetic I felt. Timber consoled me the best that she could. I was heartbroken and I was angry with myself.

"I love Adam Martin and I let him get away by being prissy," I complained as we walked into the house. Bea's car was not in the garage, which was a good thing. This sort of conversation was not one I would publicly broadcast throughout our home.

"She's a total slut, Avery, and you are so much better than her," said a voice from the couch. Marena was lying there with her comforter, Timber's laptop and Tulip.

"Hey, you can read our minds now too?" Timber asked.

"What? No, Karen Rossi called for Avery. She said your phone is off or something and wanted to know if you are all right. She just spoke to Kerri Jeffers or something. Naturally, I asked the appropriate follow up questions and found out that Adam is taking Kerri to the prom, they are going out… and she puts out. Avery, Kerri is so gross and Adam is even grosser."

"All right, all right! I don't want to talk about it anymore." I rummaged through my book bag for my cell phone. Sure enough, it had turned completely off since I had forgotten to charge the battery last night.

"I have to go charge my phone," I announced as I walked through the dining room into the kitchen. I could feel myself tearing up once again and I tried desperately to control myself. I plugged my phone into the charger on the counter. Timber was hot on my trail.

"Get me one!" Marena yelled from the living room. Timber opened the refrigerator and took out three pudding snacks. She handed one to me as I stood silently crying. I did not have the strength to turn around and take it from her. All of my energy was presently devoted to sucking back my sobs. Timber put her arms around me from behind.

"Avery, please don't cry. There will be other boys. I mean, you always say that to me. I hope you weren't lying to make me feel better." Timber could be so adorable sometimes. I tried to laugh, but instead choked on my tears and started coughing, which actually made me laugh even more.

"Try not to drown in there!" She said silently as she left me to my own thoughts in the kitchen. I took a few deep breaths, but Marena was becoming impatient.

"Get in here Avery," she yelled from the couch, "I want to show you what I found!"

8

THE LEGEND OF KIRANA

"Girls, dinner is ready," Uncle Bob sang as he slowly opened my bedroom door and looked in on us. "Working on a school project, are you?" For the last four hours, my sisters and I had been printing and reading our online research. Papers were spread out all over Marena's bed and the floor.

"Uh huh," Marena replied without looking up from Timber's laptop. She had relocated from the couch to her bed when Aunt Bea came home.

"We'll be down in a minute," I reported to our uncle, "just helping these two with some research." Uncle Bob nodded and walked out of my room slowly. I could tell he was suspicious. We rarely worked on school projects together.

"Check this out," Marena remarked. "This article written by Dr. Douglas Smith from the College of St. Elizabeth's Anthropology department says that the legend of Kirana dates back centuries and that it is believed to be located somewhere northeast of Scotland."

"Northeast of Scotland is - I don't know, Norway or something, right? Or maybe Iceland?" Timber commented looking up at an apparently invisible map of the world on the ceiling. "What does the article mean, 'believed to be located'? They don't even know where it is?"

"Hang on - here, it says Scottish historians and explorers in the early 20th century attempted to recover treasure thought to have been on board the British ship, HMS Gray, which sunk in a storm in 1499 off the coast of John O'Groats in Scotland. The ship had been carrying gold to be delivered to the government in Spain, blah, blah, blah - oh, here - approximately 10 years later, in 1510, three men came ashore in Scotland alleging to be survivors of the boat wreck. They told tales of a beautiful, mystical island where they lived for a little over a year until they were able to return to Scotland. One of the men who survived with them, a young physician named Hazaro remained in this land. They called the land, 'Kirana.' James IV, King of the Scots had the men executed as heretics, but not before they had printed maps and described their land to a Catholic Bishop in Edinburgh who apparently shared this information with members of a Catholic abbey on Loch Ness…" Marena stopped reading for a moment and looked up from the laptop.

"That's got to be our abbey, in Fort Augustus!" She exclaimed. Timber and I exchanged a smile. "Our" abbey in Fort Augustus was our home in Scotland before we came to live in Woodport. We lived in a little cottage on the abbey grounds. The abbey was right on the southern bank of the famed Loch Ness. Marena was clearly on to something important.

"Well, what else does it say? Keep going!" Timber encouraged.

"Um, ok - yes - it says that Kirana was described in a series of letters written between the priest and the abbey, as existing off of Scotland's coast, somewhere between the Orkney and Shetland Islands. These letters were discovered in 1822, hidden in a wall in Edinburgh Castle. The various brothers of the abbey who wrote to the Bishop were intimately familiar with Kirana and had ongoing relationships with some of its natives who frequented the shores of Loch Ness, blah, blah - the letters are preserved in the Abbey at Fort Augustus, Scotland and copies of the translated letters are kept in an archive at The College of St. Elizabeth in New Jersey."

"Girls, your dinner is going to be cold, let's go. Bob called you ten minutes ago!" Aunt Bea shouted from the bottom of the stairs.

"We'd better go," I instructed, "bookmark that page, Rena so we can finish it after dinner." I was very encouraged by our research and the fact that suddenly Aunt Bea's affinity for the Scottish culture and legends, as well as her long - standing relationship with the College of St. Elizabeth all began to make a lot of sense.

Dinner consisted of chicken breasts, brown rice, and steamed asparagus. I generally avoid asparagus, but I had been in such a hurry to return to our research, I did not even notice that I had practically swallowed it whole. Bea noticed and seemed pleased by my new taste for a healthy vegetable.

Timber, Marena and I practically knocked each other down the stairs trying to be the first to continue reading the article Marena had found about Kirana. Naturally, Timber was first to the stairs, up the stairs, and to the article. The information Marena had found on her "fact finding mission" did lead us to this article, but Timber and I agreed that if she had actually been doing the research during her "sick day" instead of watching Gilmore Girls re-runs, she we would have found this information hours earlier and we would be on to the next bit of research.

Upstairs, Timber continued to read the article to Marena and me from the end of Marena's bed. The conclusion it made was that people had tried to find Kirana, but couldn't and the story of those washed up sailors was probably based upon hallucinations they experienced due to Post Traumatic Stress.

"I bet there's more to it than that!" Marena announced when Timber finished paraphrasing the last few paragraphs of the article.

"Me too," I agreed. "There must be a connection to the abbey in Fort Augustus. I don't think it's a coincidence that we lived there, do you?" My sisters shook their heads.

"So we should go there with Aunt Bea when she goes to Inverness," Marena suggested.

"And miss softball tryouts? No thanks!" Timber said. Timber was competing for the Varsity catcher spot and had been working out with Uncle Bob to improve her throw down to second base.

"We could meet her there toward the end of her trip. Then she doesn't have to take time out of whatever project she's working on to deal with us and you don't miss tryouts. That is our Easter break anyway," I recommended.

❦

"Absolutely not!" Bea was not as enthusiastic or as remotely interested in our brilliant plan as we had hoped.

"But why?" whined Marena.

"You'll miss a week of school, for one thing…"

"Not if we go the third week, that's our Easter break and we have the whole week off," Marena retorted.

"Look girls, your Aunt is going to be very busy. Maybe we'll plan a trip to Scotland for all of us next summer after Avery graduates," Uncle Bob proposed. That idea sounded great, actually. Of course, it did not fit our fact-finding mission scheme, "Operation History Lesson," which had now evolved into "Operation Go with Bea." Admittedly, it was not our most original name for a scheme.

"Next summer is too late, Uncle Bob," Timber added. I wished she had not said that and I could tell she immediately regretted what she said. Consequently, we next heard from Aunt Bea:

"Why is next summer too late? What is so important that you must be in Scotland this spring, huh?" None of us answered her. "That's what I thought. So that's good, we should all plan a trip for next year, yes?" With that, I caught Aunt Bea as she raised her eyebrows at Bob as if to suggest that they just dodged some bullet.

It was subtle, but I have seen that look in the past, like when Marena asked Aunt Bea and Uncle Bob why she could not head to the New Jersey shore for the weekend with her friends on her own last summer. There was not a good reason why not, especially since one of her goofy friend's mothers was going to be there with them, but Aunt Bea knew they would not be supervised the entire time and told Marena "no." She and Bob had exchanged this same look when Marena finally accepted their verdict, a look that meant, "That took a great deal of effort, glad we got through it."

"Fine," I said. Silently, I told my sisters we should retreat to my room to further discuss the issue. Timber heard me and motioned to Marena. In an almost choreographed move, we spun around on our heels, headed back toward the stairs, and ascended them with Timber in front and me in the back.

❧

"Now what?" Timber asked me as we all took our places back in my room. I was always expected to have all of the answers.

"Well, what if we exhaust all of our resources here?"

"You mean go to St. Elizabeth's?" Marena asked.

"Precisely. Bea said we could join her there whenever we wanted. What do you guys have on Thursday? Any quizzes or anything due?"

"Not me," Marena reported.

"Me either," said Timber.

"So in the morning, let's ask her if we can take the train to Convent Station ourselves and hang out to use the library. You guys have those big English papers due for Honors, right?" I had to prepare that paper last year and I remembered spending a lot of time in our school library working on the thing. It was an in-depth paper on the significant historical and cultural events occurring during the time our chosen book was authored. I chose Kurt Vonnegut's <u>Player Piano</u> and wrote about post war America and capitalism.

"True, we have to have rough drafts with all of the research in by next Friday, and I'm only partly finished," Marena responded. "We can sit through one of Bea's lectures and then spend the rest of the day working on our research. Although, I think I really should do some work on my paper."

"You know, I'm going to mention it to Bea now," I got up from the desk chair and headed downstairs. I could hear the television. Our aunt and uncle were enjoying a recorded episode of Chef Gordon Ramsay's "Kitchen Nightmares." Bea and Bob were captivated by our DVR, which was just the same old cable box we always had but with recording capabilities. I always thought it was cute how interested they were in modern electronics, especially the DVD player and computers. Along with the TV, I could hear the sound of Bob's voice.

"Bea, you must relax. They'll hear you," he said. I stopped on the stairs and crouched down to listen to what seemed to be a conversation of importance.

"You're right of course, but I thought we had more time," Bea replied.

"Oh Bea, you know these girls are too clever to keep secrets from them. Why not take them to Scotland?" I liked Bob's question.

"Bobril that simply cannot work!" Bea did not like Bob's question. "Once they set foot in Fort Augustus - no, as soon as they land in Scotland they will be in danger. I cannot allow that without first securing their safety with the Order of the Heather." I was taking mental notes as my right foot started to fall asleep. I hated that feeling of pins and needles, and I attempted to move my foot in a way that might alleviate the weird and mildly painful feeling without alerting Bob and Bea to my covert position on the staircase. I felt rather accomplished that I had neither been detected nor fallen down the stairs when Marena popped her head out of the bedroom.

"Hey," she whispered, "what are you doing?" Apparently, it was not obvious to my sister that I could not answer her aloud so I glared at her, pointed downstairs, and put my finger to my lips to shush her. I hoped at some point she would be able to hear my thoughts, like Timber could. Marena mouthed to me that I should hurry up and that I did not need to be rude. Luckily, she had only distracted me for a moment.

"Look Beata, all I am saying is that these girls deserve to know who they are and who they are about to become in this world." Yes Bob, tell her!

"But we are not dealing with this world. I hate to deprive them of all they have accomplished here in America. Kirana is so different from here, in fact I wonder if we will be able to re-assimilate. I have lived in this world longer than my own, Bob."

"I know my dear, but we always knew the day would come when our return to Kirana would be expected and required. They will be called back. Consider these dreams the girls keep talking about. Seems that Riva is already calling them back." I remained silently on the steps. I knew I had to report to my sisters all that I had heard, but I still was not sure what I was hearing. I waited a few moments when it seemed that Bob and Bea's conversation had concluded and headed down the stairs into the living room.

"Aunt Bea? We were wondering if we could come to college with you on Thursday?" She had no reason to say yes, but probably no reason to say no either.

"Sure, Avery. You may, but you will have to park at the Dover Station and take the train to Convent Station, like you did for the Open House in the fall, all right?" Transportation was the least of our concerns.

"We can do that! Thanks Aunt Bea. I will tell the others. They have to work on their English papers and I have some research to do myself for - history," I ran up the stairs to report back to my sisters.

9

THE MAN IN THE CLOAK

The rest of the week dragged on, as expected. Anytime we had something exciting planned, the days leading up to that event seemed longer than necessary. I had decided to spend my lunch period in the National Honor Society office in order to avoid Kerri Jeffers' stories about how "amazing" her weekend with Adam was since her parents were out of town. The reality was that I no longer cared about Adam, or anyone else, for that matter. My new obsession was with Kirana and deciphering the clues we had found. I was attempting to discover the truth about the lives of my sisters and me, and with each day came a new revelation.

On Tuesday night, I had another bizarre dream. In it, Aunt Bea was getting into an old-fashioned looking sailboat with a man in a cloak. She did not seem to be in any distress, but when I awoke, I felt extremely anxious as if what I had been dreaming was not supposed to be occurring. I did not share this dream with my sisters yet, because it was so vague.

Physics was my least favorite class. Now that Woodport High was on a block-scheduling program, I only had Physics three times a week, but for an hour and ten minutes. The idea of physics always fascinated me, but once I realized how much math, specifically Trigonometry, was involved in the course, my interest faded somewhat. I was doing fairly well on the tests and labs in the class, despite my disinterest. Today, we were finishing a lab on velocity. My lab partners and I were working out some of the final calculations when I suddenly had a vision.

I saw Aunt Bea speaking to the man in the cloak on the shore of a lake. She was significantly smaller than he was and she seemed distraught. Her hands were covering her face at one point. Fog was billowing around them as they walked together onto the dock. The man removed the hood of his cloak revealing a very handsome face. He appeared to be in his early to mid-thirties, perhaps – maybe a little younger than Uncle Bob was. He had almost violet eyes that sparkled when he smiled at Bea as he faced her. The man placed his right hand on her shoulder, as if to comfort her. Then he got into a small rowboat at the end of the dock. He reached out his hand out for Aunt Bea and she stepped into the small boat. After untying the lines, the rowboat disappeared into the mist.

"Avery? Avery? Hello!" One of my lab partners was attempting to get my attention. I refocused my attention to her direction and indicated that I was listening.

"What do you have for the velocity on 2C?" Taylor asked me. I must have been daydreaming for a quite a while. Of course, my answer on 2C was an integral part of the rest of the problem we had to solve for this particular lab.

"I'm sorry, I didn't get it yet," I replied, "I'll do it right now."

⌒⌒∂

"He was wearing a cape? Who wears a cape?" Marena asked. I laughed.

"I know, right? But I am less concerned with the goofy costume and more disturbed by the fact that I watched Aunt Bea leave in a boat with this guy through this crazy haze. I wonder why our dreams have fog in them…"

I pulled into Dunkin Donuts. It was an unusually warm day for mid-March so we decided on Iced Coffees, as did half of the junior and senior classes. The other half of them were on line at Rita's Ices on the other end of the parking lot. Timber went into the shop to buy our drinks and Marena and I waited for her in the car. We lowered the windows and turned up the music to hear a Taylor Swift song about teardrops on her guitar.

"This song is so lame," Marena commented.

"No it's not. I like it." The truth was, I more than liked that song. I had downloaded it onto my iPod a few weeks ago and it became my go-to crying song when I thought about Adam Martin. I really did not want to have another emotional episode at this point, so I turned the radio off to satisfy Marena who preferred upbeat dance music anyway.

"There, happy?"

"Ugh! Why did I wear a sweater today? It's so hot!" Marena complained. She opened the car door, swung her legs out and stood up in the parking lot. Then, as if she was in a movie, she removed her light green Gap sweater over her head to reveal a white lace tank top. She shook her blonde waves out and sat back in the car. I noticed that about six junior boys were standing outside of the Dunkin Donuts, staring at my sister. She noticed too and waved at them, which prompted the boys to pretend they were in a deep, philosophical conversation.

"How do you do that, Rena?" I laughed. She shrugged her shoulders and changed the subject.

"Adam Martin is breaking up with Kerri," she reported.

"Really? Too bad I don't care anymore," I replied turning my gaze out the driver side window. If only that statement were true.

"Don't you want to know why?" She coaxed.

"I'm sure you are going to tell me."

"Apparently, he told Josh Camon who told Dave Walsh in my English class that Kerri hooked up with this senior from Saint John's so he's going to dump her for being such a slut. But this is the best part - oh wait you don't care…"

"What is it, Rena? You have my attention."

"He wants to ask you to the prom! Isn't that awesome?" Suddenly, I realized that it was not "awesome" at all.

"Ehh," I grunted. "I'll see if he actually asks me, but I am sort of over Adam. This is the second time he's jerked me around like this and if I allow it, it won't be the last time."

"Good for you! Who needs Adam Martin? So anyway, Aunt Bea said that we can meet her for her 9:10 class in her office tomorrow by 8:45, so we have to take the 8:10 train from Dover." Marena was happy to change the subject to discuss our plans for our St. Elizabeth's College visit.

"Ok, so we should leave the house by 7:30 then. What are you wearing?" I figured Marena had already planned her wardrobe and would have a good idea of appropriate dress for a college campus. Apparently, she hadn't thought about her clothing yet, which was very unlike her, but her justification was that the students in the undergraduate day classes at St. Elizabeth's were all female, so she didn't really care. I suppose she had a point, but I still wanted to look the part of college student.

"Ok, see you Friday!" Timber was exiting the Dunkin Donuts and yelling back at someone still inside. As if in slow motion, Timber caught her foot on the door, tripped and spilled the forward most iced coffee in the carrying tray, on the sidewalk. The boys who had been lost in fantasy eyeing up Marena, were now lost in hysterics laughing at her twin.

"Oh shut up!" She hissed at them. Marena and I got out of the car to help her with the other coffees. "I'll get another one," she moaned and headed back into the store.

⌒೦

Aunt Bea's lecture to her "Social and Cultural Changes of Scotland, 1600 - 1900" class was more interesting than I had thought and Aunt Bea was a very lively presenter. She discussed the importance of the poet, Robert Burns to the average Scotsman during the 1700's. She recited the Burns' poem, "Ode to a Haggis," which we heard every year at the local Scottish Society's annual supper. Robert Burns' memory and contribution to Scottish society was honored each year at the supper we attended and at similar events all over the world. Bea's lecture gave me a very good idea for my A.P. European History project due at the end of the marking period.

Class was over at 10:30 and Aunt Bea had a department meeting at 11 am for which she had to prepare. She walked us over to the library and told us to wait for her there and she would take us to lunch at the faculty-dining hall after her meeting.

"We probably only have about an hour and a half, maybe two hours before Bea gets back," I whispered, "so let's find the letters first."

The archive librarian, an older woman named Nancy, showed us where the library kept the translated letters Dr. Smith spoke about in his article. Apparently, we needed special permission to sign them out to look at them, but luckily, as Professor MacLeod's girls, we were already very special. The translated letters were bound in an oversized leather book entitled "The Legend of Kirana – Bishop Grayson's letters 1510 - 1512."

"When you are through with the book, you can bring it back to me at the Archive Desk. Photocopies are not permitted due to the age of this book, and it cannot be removed from the library, unfortunately," Nancy informed us. We thanked her and headed over to a table in the back of the archive section where we could dive into the book of letters.

By 12:40, we had not heard from Aunt Bea and we were actually quite hungry, so Timber sent her a text message, which resulted in the reply "on my way." We returned the book of letters to Nancy and told her we would be back in about an hour to continue our research. The letters had proven to exceed our expectations in terms of providing information about Kirana and its people. It sounded like a fairy tale land, but what we still had not found were any clues as to our connection to Kirana.

Lunch with Bea was abbreviated. She apologized, but she had to eat and run back to teach her Celtic Folklore and Fantasy course at 1:15, which of course was fine with us. She also told us to just finish our work and get home for dinner. Although she would be working late preparing her Graduate Teaching Assistant to cover her courses for the next four weeks while she was conducting her research in Inverness as she did every year, Bob would be home and said he would take us to dinner at Hoppes' Restaurant in the Plaza. That was Bob's favorite local restaurant because it was a micro-brewery. He said that their ales and lagers were close to what he enjoyed in Scotland.

We finished our lunch and even had a little cheesecake for dessert before racing back to our new friend Nancy at the library. We agreed that Marena should work on her English paper while Timber and I continued to look at the letters. Marena headed over to the bank of computers to search the library for the texts she needed for her paper. Timber and I wandered back to our table in the archive section and went back to taking notes on the book of letters.

By 4 pm, we were ready to head home. Having found some interesting descriptions of mythical creatures and beautiful landscapes, we determined that we were just not going to find what we desired. Without saying a word aloud, as we left the library and headed across campus to the train station, my sisters and I shared our disappointment.

I had a restless sleep Thursday night and awoke in a sweat at about 3:15 am. Having experienced the dream with Aunt Bea leaving on a boat into the fog with a stranger in a cloak once again, I began to wonder whether defying Aunt Bea's wishes and traveling to Scotland was our only way to uncover the mystery of these weird abilities I seemed to be developing, and of our true past. Bea left for the airport right after dinner and was on her way to Scotland.

"Rena, are you awake?" I whispered.

"Yeah, you woke me up with your bad dream or whatever that was. You kept saying 'no Aunt Bea, don't go.'"

"I did? Oh, sorry about that. I had the dream with the cloaked man again. This time I could feel the tension between Bea and this man. She obviously knew him and she seemed torn about going with him. This time, in this dream, she did not seem like she had a choice." I suddenly felt the hair stand up on the back of my neck as I remembered more details from the dream.

"Oh my God! He took her from the Abbey!"

"Are you sure? It's just a dream, Avery," Marena was attempting to downplay the importance of my vision, but I could tell by her tone that she was not convinced that the dream had no measure of importance.

"I saw the boathouse and the dock and the clock tower. Rena, this is going to happen when she goes to Scotland, I just know it!" I could feel my heart beating through my chest.

"Shh, calm down. You're going to wake up Timber, Bob, and probably half the neighborhood," Marena warned and as if on cue, our bedroom door creaked open and Timber slid through with Tulip under her arm.

"Sorry, I didn't mean to get so loud Timber," I apologized.

"Duh, Avery. I can hear your thoughts - both of you. I was just too lazy to come in here until now. I agree with you, Avery, we need to get to Scotland sooner rather than later. Remember what we read in those letters today? About how the sailors came back from Kirana like ten years after the boat sunk and how they thought it had only been a year? What if that's true? What if the guy in the cape is taking Bea to Kirana? We won't see her for years!" Timber seemed panicked.

"First of all, it was a cloak, and secondly I don't know where he's taking her," I replied, trying to organize my problem solving skills.

"Avery, if a guy in a cloak is taking Bea anywhere, it's got to be Kirana. Normal people do not wear cloaks. Remember that dream we had about the lady in the medieval dress?" Marena added.

"That's true. So then, we should follow her, right? I mean if she is in danger, we can be there to help her. If this guy is taking her to Kirana, we can follow her there and maybe figure out these dreams and our mind reading trick," that was the best plan I could come up with at 3:30 in the morning. Marena jumped onto the computer.

"Bea flew out - today!" Marena just realized that it was Friday already. "She left from JFK - hmm…" Timber and I gathered around the computer screen. Marena had pulled up the United Airlines website and was searching for available flights out of Newark Liberty Airport.

"There are three seats on a flight leaving Newark at 7:30 pm on Saturday night. It lands in Glasgow on Sunday morning. What do I do? Should I click to book them?"

"Holy moley, Avery! A one way ticket is $1200.00? We're going to be so busted!" Timber warned.

"Yeah, but what choice do we have?" Marena asked.

"Well, we can tell Bob what we think we know and at the very least, he can warn her," I suggested.

"All well and good except that does not help us figure out these dreams. Do you really think Uncle Bob or Aunt Bea are going to listen to us about a dude in a cape? It doesn't make sense," Marena said.

"Cloak," Timber corrected.

"Whatever! Point is, if we want to get to the bottom of these dreams, Avery's visions, the letters, and every other weird thing, we need to get to Scotland. Period."

Marena was right. Yet, every fiber in my body was telling me that we should not disobey Bea and Bob, except one - my heart. My heart was telling me we needed get to Scotland as soon as possible. I walked over to where I had tossed my backpack, reached inside for my wallet, and removed my "in case of emergency" Visa Check Card, which was connected to one of Bob and Bea's bank accounts. Once I started driving, I had been given explicit instructions that this card was to be used only in cases of extreme emergency. I felt strongly that this was such an emergency.

10

HOMECOMING SCOTLAND!

O ur flight was not as horrible as I feared, although Timber would disagree. Almost six hours of relative inactivity was driving her insane. I could hear her complaining that she was cramped in the seat; that Marena was too close to her; that she was too anxious to sleep. Timber complained in her thoughts while Marena slept for the majority of the flight. Marena was always able to fall asleep no matter where we were or how nervous or excited she was. If I suddenly had this mind reading gift, Marena's gift was sleep. Of course, most teenagers probably had the ability to sleep hours on end, but I doubt any were as peaceful or beautiful while they were sleeping than Marena.

We arrived at Glasgow airport at seven in the morning. While it was an overnight flight having departed Newark Airport at 7:30 pm, it was only about six hours. Despite the restful sleep, Marena was still tired. Timber was cranky and I was sleepy myself, but it was up to me to lead my sisters to the Highlands and the abbey in Fort Augustus. I needed my wits about me and my map.

"Maybe we should just get a cheap hotel room and take a nap?" Timber suggested as her mouth was gaping open in a yawn.

"Eww! Brush your teeth much?" Marena scowled as she shoved her twin aside so that she could walk between us through the busy airport as we headed to customs with the crowd from our flight. Timber made a face and rummaged through her backpack for gum, offering it both to Marena and me before taking one herself.

"There is no time to rest, guys. Bea has already been there for a full two days and who knows if she has left with that guy already or not," Marena reasoned referring to the dreams and visions I had been having right before we left New Jersey.

My visions were coming to me more vividly than they had previously. In fact, they were no longer weird dreams but more like premonitions. Some of the things I would see, like Timber scoring the winning three-pointer at her last basketball game against High Point Regional to win the game, were visions of events that would happen almost immediately after I saw them. Other visions were more vague, like this one with Bea leaving on a boat with a strangely dressed, but very handsome man, through the fog. The mental pictures I would have were much stronger and less hazy when the subject matter was my sisters. They were coming to me more often now and with the knowledge my sisters and I had gained through our trip to the College of St. Elizabeth library, these images were beginning to make more sense - at least I was trying to tell myself that.

"Ugh! I feel like I'm going to throw up, I'm so tired," Timber whined.

"Pull it together, Timber. Rena is probably right. You can sleep on the train to Inverness, although you'll miss all the Harry Potter scenery," I cajoled. Timber had become very excited about our prospective train ride through the Highlands up to the city of Inverness once she learned that parts of the Harry Potter movies had been filmed in the area and the train would take us right through it.

"I'm so tired I want to die!" Now she was just being cranky and over dramatic. Marena and I ignored her last comment as we plodded through customs, a much less painful experience than expected, and we headed to baggage claim.

As we waited for the carousel to deliver our shared rolling duffel bag, Rena pointed out a young man holding up a sign with our name on it, "MacLeod."

"Do you think that hottie is waiting for us?" She asked me, knowing how silly the question sounded. I just gave her a "seriously?" look and she laughed.

"Too bad," she said, "At least in Scotland no one will mispronounce our last name," she joked. That was a pet peeve of Marena's - people constantly pronouncing our name phonetically, "Ma clee odd," rather than "Ma cloud." It annoyed me as well, but not to the same degree as my sister.

"True. I'm sure there are a million MacLeods here."

"Oh, thank God!" Timber exclaimed triumphantly as she pulled the Columbia blue "Woodport Girls Basketball" duffel bag off the conveyor belt. "Now let's get to the train station before I pass out," she ordered us.

Just then, the handsome young man with the "MacLeod" sign came up to us. Marena gasped.

"Good morning ladies. I will help you with your bags. I have a car waiting for us," he smiled the most brilliant smile I have ever seen. The three of us were too astonished to respond. He looked so familiar to me. I felt as though I knew him, even though I was fully aware that was impossible.

The young man, had light brown hair, dazzling blue eyes and was what my freshman year English teacher, Ms. Stelton would call "a tall drink of water." He was ruggedly handsome and wore cargo pants and a traditional cream-colored Scottish wool sweater. He also wore what appeared to be Doc Marten boots in black.

"You are Beata and Bobril's girls, right?" The man asked us.

"Uh huh," was all that Marena or any of us could utter in response.

"Oh, thank goodness. I was starting to worry that I approached the wrong trio of beautiful young girls," he told us. Marena laughed her nervous laugh, which sounded a lot like a birdcall. Timber and I laughed a little as well, at Marena of course.

"How did you...?" I began to ask, but I answered my own question. Bob! We underestimated Bob. Bob had to work the weekend, which was a bit of luck for us. He would be home late on Friday and have to leave very early in the morning on Saturday to get to the Port Authority. We left him a nebulous note on Friday night that we were spending the weekend with friends working on school projects. This was Marena's idea, but it was not overly credible that all three of us would be working on school projects at the same time, together at the same place. Nevertheless, Bob called me around 9 pm on Friday night to confirm that we were all at Jenna Ryan's house on Sunset Lakes Road. We were there. He did not ask how long we would be there, he just wanted to make sure we had gotten there safely. We had, and he also told us to be good house guests this weekend.

The real problem with our plan was that we had not come up with a way to explain the rather large debit from my emergency check card use in the wee hours of Friday morning. At some point, Bob would have received a notice from the bank that a debit had been made, and checked on it, perhaps thinking that Bea had changed her flight plans, only to find that his sneaky nieces purchased three one-way tickets to Scotland. Stupid online banking technology!

I imagined that Bob would be both panicked at our absence and angry that we disobeyed him. I decided to turn my cell phone back on and sure enough, I had five missed calls. Two calls were from Aunt Bea and three from Uncle Bob with one voice mail message from 8:36 pm, Saturday evening. I listened:

"Avery, this is your Uncle Bob. Your Aunt and I are very disappointed in you and your sisters. Bea is sending one of her students to meet you and take you to her. Stay with him at all times. We will deal with your punishment when you come home." I breathed a heavy sigh.

"Totally busted," I said silently to my sisters.

"So, can I take your bags?" The man asked. None of us moved as I communicated silently with my sisters, briefly describing the gaping hole in our escape plan.

"I'm sorry, but we don't talk to strangers," Marena told the young man in her most sultry and adult voice, "you know who we are, but we don't have the slightest idea who you are."

"You are right and I apologize if I am rude. My name is Adelio. I am one of your aunt's research assistants while she is working in Scotland this season. I am a student at Inverness College," he told us somewhat nervously. It sounded as though he had rehearsed this introduction. "Your aunt asked that I meet you at the airport and bring you to Fort Augustus. Your uncle will be joining us as well as soon as he can get a flight from your home."

I made eye contact with my sisters, "We are complete boneheads!" I told them silently.

"And completely grounded!" Timber added.

"Shall we?" Adelio asked.

"Shotgun no trades!" Marena shouted at us.

"Pardon?"

"Yes, we are ready," I reported on behalf of my sisters and myself.

11

THINKING OUT LOUD

"Adelio, is that Italian? Doesn't sound very Scottish," Marena probed our new guide and apparent babysitter from the front seat. She had not stopped talking since getting into the Volvo station wagon outside the airport. Her "shotgun" claiming skills had hit an all-time high when she invented the "no trades" rule. Often, she would have to hand over the front seat to Timber or me when we would remind her that we had previously done her a favor, usually one that required us to cover for her nefarious activities like sneaking an extra cookie or when she was older, sneaking out to see a boy. Then she instituted the "no trades" rule by saying "I don't care, tell if you want" to us, destroying our leveraging power. Timber and I were yet to come up with a solution to her strategy, and typically found ourselves in the back seat, grumbling about Marena's cleverness.

"Umm - I'm not sure. I think it's a family name," he replied as he turned expertly into another roundabout. We had only left the airport about an hour ago and Timber was already fast asleep.

"How quaint," she flirted, "so, what are you studying with my aunt?"

"Well, we are working on a project about - uh - well, it's complicated. I don't think you would be interested," he replied nervously.

"Oh no, I would! I am so intrigued by everything Bea studies and especially everyone she works with. You know, I'm thinking of studying Celtic History when I get to college," Marena offered.

"What a liar! Until last year, you thought Celtic History involved a professional basketball team from Boston!" I thought. Unfortunately, Marena heard me.

"Shut up, Avery!" She hissed.

"I didn't **SAY** anything," I replied practically through my teeth. One of the last conversations Timber, Marena, and I had as our airplane taxied to the runway at Newark Airport was to be sure that we did not needlessly reveal our mind reading abilities to anyone. That meant being careful not to verbally reply to each other's thoughts. Marena's ability to hear my thoughts and Timber's thoughts was still in its infancy so on the plane for the first hour, we played a game kind of like Simon Says to practice only replying to verbal comments. Marena was finally getting the hang of it when Timber fell asleep and the in-flight movie, "How Do You Know," starring my favorite actor, Paul Rudd started. Clearly, Marena needed some more practice.

"I did not hear Avery say anything," Adelio added.

"Oh," she laughed, "Well, anyway…as I was saying…"

Just then, Adelio pulled off the main road. It was an abrupt turn onto a dirt road. The sign before this new road said, "Luss" with an arrow to the right. I checked my map. We were not anywhere near Fort Augustus.

"Where are we going?" I asked, "This is definitely not the way to Fort Augustus."

"Breakfast," Adelio replied, although he could have just as easily had said, "Anything to quiet your sister."

Luss was a quaint village on the banks of Loch Lomond. It looked very much like the typical small town you would imagine existing in a far off land in a storybook. I had remembered to bring my camera and wasted no time snapping shots of the homes, the beautiful rose gardens and the view of the famous loch, which Marena kept referring to as a lake. Timber corrected her about four times:

"It's a loch Marena. We have lakes. The Scottish have lochs."

We had something called an "all day breakfast" at the only restaurant in town. Adelio recommended that we order it to fuel up for the rest of our trip. Timber did not hesitate to order what turned out to be an enormous meal of eggs, toast, fried bread, beans, some interesting piece of pork and "blood pudding." Blood pudding was nothing like our favorite snack and after one small bite, we all decided to skip that part of our breakfast. Adelio noticed our faces after trying the blood pudding.

"Everything all right with your breakfast?" He asked in his strong Scottish brogue. His voice was beginning to sound like a melody.

"Yes, but what is blood pudding made out of?" Timber asked him. Adelio looked at all three of us in a way that answered the question.

"Hey, what's a vampire's favorite after school snack?" Marena thought and then answered her own silly riddle, "Jell-O blood pudding packs!" Timber and I cracked up over her corny joke and rewarded her quickness in our thoughts. Adelio looked as if he was missing a private joke between sisters.

"Have you always been able to do that?" He asked.

"Do what?"

"Read each other's minds," he replied. Timber dropped her fork and it clanged onto the plate. Marena nervously reached for her water glass and it nearly toppled over into her dish. No one, not even Bob and Bea knew we could hear each other's thoughts. We obviously were not hiding our secret gift very well. So much for our practice session on the plane. We needed to be more careful, we all agreed. After all, we certainly did not want Adelio, let alone anyone else believing we were some circus sideshow act.

⌒〇

After our "all day" breakfasts, Adelio suggested we take a stroll around the town. Marena was disappointed that her cell phone was not working and approximately ten minutes into our walk, told us she would meet us at the car. Timber asked to borrow my camera so she could take some pictures down by the loch. Adelio and I were left to wander Luss together. I could feel myself blushing with this handsome man walking to my right. I had never known a more attractive boy. Adam Martin had nothing on Adelio. If you could call a boy beautiful, that is what you would call Adelio. I could tell that he was kind too. His eyes and his gentle smile informed me of that fact.

There was something so comfortable and familiar about Adelio. Perhaps we were related? Maybe he was really our uncle or brother and he was waiting for an appropriate time to introduce himself properly? I did not believe that he was Aunt Bea's research assistant at Inverness because I never heard her mention him before and in the weeks leading up to her trip, she spoke of Caroline, Lorraine and Andrew. I would have remembered "Adelio."

We walked in silence through an old churchyard dotted with hundreds of headstones dating back far into the 1500s and 1600s. I was thinking how amazingly ancient that seemed considering America was still an unconquered wilderness at that point in history.

"That's nothing," Adelio stated, "wait until we get into the Highlands and Loch Ness. There is even deeper history there."

"What?" My palms began to sweat. Was mind reading a Scottish gift? Now my entire body was beginning to sweat, clearly from nervousness since it was only about 35 degrees Fahrenheit currently. "Did you just - how did you…?" I managed to stutter. Now I was sweating out of embarrassment for sounding like an idiot.

Adelio let out a chuckle, clearly amused by my sudden anxiety, "We have a lot of things in common, Avery," he announced as Timber came running up to join us.

"You are not going to believe what I just did!" She exclaimed. "Excuse us for a minute, Adelio. I need to show my sister something."

"Why don't we just meet back at the car in ten minutes? We should probably get going soon. Looks like rain. Of course, it always looks like that in Scotland," Adelio added.

"Ok," Timber replied over her shoulder as she yanked me up the dirt road.

"By the way, I think you are beautiful too, Avery," I thought I heard Adelio say. I gasped, but when I turned to look back at him, he had already turned around the corner out of sight.

12

THE GINGER CAT OF LUSS

"Timber that is a cat. We have one at home," I said slowly as if I was speaking to a five year old. My little sister rolled her eyes at me as we walked up to the front stoop of a little stone house where a rather well fed orange cat was sunning herself in the morning's light.

"Avery, I can understand her. She meowed at me and I heard her say 'welcome to my home, mystical one. I am called Ginger and it is an honor to be in your presence.' Then she bowed her head." We were now right upon the cat that, unlike Tulip who would typically turn and scamper off when strangers approached, stood at attention and looked me dead in the eye. She was a sweet, older looking cat. She 'meowed' at me, began to purr and rubbed up against my leg affectionately. As much as I like cats, I did not want to pet this one since she looked as though she might have recently taken a roll in the dirt.

"Ginger says she is honored to meet you and she is at your service," Timber translated.

"Ok, Tim. Perhaps another nap will do you some good when we get back to the car. Say goodbye to the nice kitty." I grabbed her shoulder to turn her away when Ginger meowed again.

"Wait, Avery. She needs to tell us something about Fort Augustus." Timber then stared at Ginger who stared right back, apparently engaging my sister in some silent conversation. I was beginning to get aggravated. She had pulled me away from Adelio at a most inopportune moment, to play Dr. Doolittle. Timber gasped.

"Avery, Ginger knows about us!" She exclaimed. "Ginger says that one of her kittens lives at the Abbey in Fort Augustus and reported to Ginger that Bea was there, but left with a man called Ginter to return to Kirana. Kirana is where our mother lives. Our mother is Queen Riva de Hazaro of Kirana!" Timber was getting more excited, and I was becoming even more agitated. We already knew this information, with the exception of one detail: the name Ginter.

"Ok, Dr. Doolittle ask Ginger who this Ginter guy is," I instructed. As I made the request aloud, the possibility that Ginter was the man I saw in my vision of Bea leaving with a man dawned upon me. She and the cat resumed their staring match.

"Ginger doesn't know," Timber translated with a bit of disappointment in her voice. "Thank you, Ginger." Timber knelt down and rubbed the cat behind her ear. Ginger purred and rubbed her head on Timber's left pant leg.

"Come on Tim, let's go find Rena and Adelio," I coaxed. There was a sudden sadness in Timber and at the same time, a bit of anxiety that I rarely ever saw in her. Marena was more likely to act anxiously or at times, as if she were depressed. Mostly, that was just to get attention. Marena tended to be somewhat dramatic, while Timber was more often even-keeled and laid back. Whatever conversation she thought she had with this cat, has led her into a rather blue mood.

"Are you all right?" I asked.

"Sure," she replied.

"Then what is it?"

"I don't know. I mean, I feel like we're too late or something."

"Too late for what?" I felt like I was adopting some of Timber's anxious emotions.

"To save Aunt Bea."

❧

Timber and I walked up the main street in Luss in silence until we came upon the Volvo and our sister with her right arm in Adelio's left. Before we saw them, we could hear Marena's laughter. Timber and I looked at each other and thought the same, exact thought: "Marena's in love." We both cracked up at the fact that we had the same simultaneous thought, but then, my heart sank. As we came upon Adelio and Marena sitting together, with linked arms, laughing and enjoying an ice cream cone with a piece of chocolate in it, I could feel my entire body become warm.

"Anyone but him," I hoped I thought to myself. Timber grabbed my hand. She heard me, but Marena kept giggling and playfully poking Adelio in his left side.

"Hey guys! You have to get one of these. Vanilla ice cream with a Flake in it. You remember Flakes, right?" Marena was overly excited. Flakes were delicious British chocolate bars. Every so often, Aunt Bea would remember to bring Scottish chocolates like Flakes, Malteasers and Buttons back home from her trips to Scotland.

Marena's voice was high pitched and louder than necessary. I hated when she was "excited Rena." She often took on this persona when she was with her girlfriends in school. When she acted this way, it was difficult to avoid paying her attention.

Timber suddenly perked up, "I love Flakes," she replied to her twin, "Want one, Avery?" Timber asked while heading over to the ice cream shop that was only a few yards from where we were parked. I was surprised she had any money on her. Timber rarely ever carried any cash let alone British pounds. We had all taken some money out of Bea's stash before we left for the airport. I left Bea an IOU, for whatever it was worth.

"I'll just have a lick of yours," I told her as I stared at Marena and Adelio. My stomach was starting to hurt.

"If you don't mind, let's get a move on," Adelio suggested, "At this point, we're going to have to stop off soon anyway." Timber trotted over to the ice cream shop, which was really more like the ice cream trucks that would come through Station Park in the summers when we had soccer games, or when we went to watch Uncle Bob in his softball games.

"No!" I yelled in an unnecessarily loud voice, "We need to get to Fort Augustus."

"Avery, Adelio and I have talked about it and we think it's best that we stop off in a few hours at a place Adelio knows, called the Drover's Inn," Marena informed me.

I could feel my blood pressure begin to rise. "We talked about it? We think?" In twelve minutes, Marena was suddenly picking out china patterns with Adelio. This was just like my sister. As soon as Adam Martin began to show even the slightest bit of interest in me, Marena began sitting with him in their shared lunch period. As much as I wanted to believe Marena was trying to ingratiate herself with Adam to help me out in his eyes, in my heart I knew she was running interference. Marena could attract any guy at our school that she wanted, but more likely than not, she would set her sights on the boys that Timber or I liked. In all honestly, I don't think she meant to act that way. I think she can't help it.

Timber was already back with her ice cream cone.

"Drover's Inn?" She asked enthusiastically, "That sounds cool!" Timber would be excited about it. She loved staying at hotels. She had a weird habit of taking the little soaps and shampoos hotels would provide. The linen closet in our shared bathroom at home had a stash of them. She would not let us use them. Timber just collected them. We all found it to be a very strange habit.

"It does sound cool, Tim, but I really think we should try to push on to Fort Augustus today," I told them, "I - that is, we don't want to miss anything, right?" The rest of that thought was completed and shared with my sisters silently. They knew what I meant and they sensed my anxiety concerning this cloaked character and Bea.

"I know you are anxious to see your Aunt, girls, but there's no point to rushing up there. You are all obviously exhausted and this time will give us a chance to have a nice dinner and…"

"Talk? Get to know each other better? I couldn't agree more, Adelio," Marena had cut him off mid-sentence. He glanced over at me, but I turned away to watch a tourist bus almost hit a Volkswagen in the parking lot. I needed to do my very best to restrain my thoughts. There was no use starting a fight with my sister.

"Sure," replied Adelio. I was clearly going to lose this battle and honestly, I was incredibly tired.

"Fine, Drover's Inn it is," I acquiesced. We did have a long way to go.

13

THE DROVER'S

We left Luss and Loch Lomond and headed north toward the Highlands. Within fifteen minutes, Timber had to use the bathroom. She undoubtedly had the smallest bladder of anyone we knew. When Timber was little, Aunt Bea and Uncle Bob would ask her if she had to "use the potty" ten times before we would leave the house and it was never until we were as far from a restroom as possible that she would suddenly have to go. Luckily, there was a gas station not too far from Luss. Adelio stopped there and Timber jumped out of the car. He also got out of the car to use the pay phone to contact Bea, no doubt, although I was surprised he didn't have a cell phone.

"So, guess what Timber can do?" I teased Marena.

"Is this a bathroom joke?" Marena asked with a sigh. I was notorious for my inappropriate bathroom humor.

"No," I laughed, "this is serious. Timber can hear animals and communicate with them."

Marena gave me her best "seriously?" look just as Adelio returned to the car. I completed the story of Timber and Ginger in my head and Marena did not seem overly surprised or nearly as impressed as I was. Nevertheless, we agreed to keep that bit of information from our handsome guide.

Timber fell asleep again and Marena continued to talk with Adelio about what seemed to be anything and everything. They really seemed to hit it off, and in listening to their easygoing conversation, I wondered why I could not be as natural as Marena. I watched her gently stroke Adelio's hand when she wanted to make a point and effortlessly twirl her hair through her long fingers. I sighed and looked out the window at the amazing scenery.

Before long, we were pulling into the lot of the Drover's Inn. Adelio had told us that it had been voted pub of the year, 1705. It looked as if it had not been updated since the year 1705. We entered the building to check in and the lobby was decorated with a multitude of stuffed, wild dead animals from deer to bear.

"Uncle Bob would love this place," Marena thought and the three of us laughed aloud. Adelio caught my eye and laughed too. I suppose he wanted to feel a part of our inside jokes. Marena rubbed his right arm as she giggled at the thought of Uncle Bob feeling right at home at the Drover's. Bob loved to hunt and fish. Deer season in New Jersey was his favorite American holiday. He would prepare for weeks, cleaning his shotgun, buying new camouflage outfits, and organizing hikes into the woods searching for deer droppings. Timber was the only one who liked to go with Bob during hunting season. She told us she would go only so she could "warn" the deer that Bob and his friends were coming to do them harm. Bob had not bagged a buck in the last five years she had been "hunting" with him.

"Well hello, love," the woman behind the big reception desk said to Adelio, "Long time no see," she shrieked. The woman was older and probably attractive in her day, but today she looked as if she had smoked one too many cigarettes and drank one too many pints in the pub.

"Looks like she's been here since 1705," Marena snidely commented in her thoughts. Timber cracked up and had to walk away from us to contain herself.

"Aye Mary, have you got us a couple rooms for the night?" Adelio asked in his thickest brogue yet. He sounded as if he was putting on a stronger accent suddenly.

"Wish I did. Hell for Leather is playing the pub tonight and all the rooms are taken already. You should have called ahead, Adelio," she told him. Marena unglued herself from Adelio's side and excused herself to go to the ladies' room. Timber went with her, which was a wise move for Timber since it seemed as though we would be on the road again shortly.

"Oh, wait - we do have a room, suite actually. Two beds and en suite. Do you want that?" Mary asked him.

Adelio reluctantly replied, "Thanks Mary. That'll be just fine." He handed her a credit card.

"Wait," I interrupted. "We have money, let us pay."

Adelio laughed, "No, I owe your Aunt Bea at least this. Please, allow me. I'll let you girls treat me to fish and chips in Fort Augustus tomorrow."

"Ok," I replied. I did not like the way he called us "girls." How old was he anyway? He could not be much more than a year or so older than I was.

"Twenty-two," Adelio declared.

"What?"

"I'm twenty two. Wait here for your sisters and I will meet you all at the car to collect your things. We should rest a little before dinner," Adelio instructed.

"Uh huh," was all I could say.

Our suite was not exactly what I expected. Actually, the Drover's Inn was not like any motel or hotel in which we had ever stayed. As we ascended the creaky stairs to room number eleven (of twelve), we all thought the same thing, "well, this is creepy." Timber giggled at our common feeling. Enormous portraits of very serious looking people lined the stairway. Their eyes followed us as we climbed from the lobby to the third floor. The place smelled like the Assisted Living facility I volunteered at with the National Honor Society last year, musty and damp.

It was no wonder the air felt moist. As soon as we got to the car to collect our bags, it started pouring. We were soggy and so was the Inn. The creaking stairs were beginning to bother me as we continued to our room.

"No need to be nervous, girls. I've stayed here a dozen or more times and I've never seen a ghost," Adelio informed us with a smirk.

"A what? A ghost? You mean this place is haunted?" Marena asked.

"Not really, but there have been reports of weird happenings here since the 1800s," Adelio responded.

"Oooh," Marena cooed, "Promise to stay close and protect me?"

"Of course," Adelio dutifully replied. I wanted to vomit, but I knew I could neither voice my disapproval nor ruminate about it in my thoughts without the other two knowing how I felt. Instead, I stepped in front of Adelio and opened up room number eleven for my sisters.

"Uh oh," Timber said as we all walked in, "I thought there were supposed to be two beds."

"There are two - one double and one single next to it," Adelio pointed out to us.

"Well where is everyone supposed to sleep?" Timber asked.

"You and Avery can sleep in the big bed and I'll take the little one and Adelio can share…" Marena was going too far.

"No," I interrupted, "Adelio can have the little bed and we can all share this big one. It's just for the night."

"That's fine. Thank you Avery." Adelio threw his backpack onto the twin sized bed. Marena grimaced.

"Why don't we change our clothes and head down to the dining room for dinner," Adelio suggested, "then we can get to bed early and head out to Fort Augustus first thing in the morning."

"Great idea," I replied. It was only about four thirty in the afternoon, and none of us were hungry after our hearty breakfasts, but it seemed like the only logical thing to do.

"What's 'en suite,' Avery?" Timber whispered to me as we set our bags down on the big bed.

"Bathroom in the room," I replied back in a whisper.

"Oh, right. I hope they have little soaps and stuff."

⁓᎒

By five twenty, we were all dressed and ready for dinner. Marena insisted on taking a shower, which of course slowed us down a bit and caused a logistical problem. The bathroom, although it was in our room and not a shared bathroom like some of the other rooms in the Inn, was quite small. In fact, it was so small Marena could not get dressed in it without stepping in the puddles she had created with her shower. Adelio agreed to forgo changing his shirt and head down to the pub to wait for us so that Marena could dress. It was so unnecessary, but I was glad to see that Adelio was a gentleman at least.

We sat down in the dining room for dinner. Adelio recommended we try the haggis with neeps or turnips and tatties, potatoes, a dish we were all too accustomed to eating on special occasions. Unfortunately, the haggis we usually ate left much to be desired considering the FDA had banned its production in the United States for a while. That ban required that haggis be imported into America. Most of the haggis I had tried was from a can. Uncle Bob loved haggis so we had no choice but suffer through this "delicacy" a few times a year. Adelio promised that we would not taste better haggis than at the Drover's Inn. I ordered it, as did Timber, but Marena ordered chicken. She was not very adventurous when it came to food, but I could tell that she regretted her meal choice when she saw Timber and my reactions to our first bites of the haggis. It was delicious!

"They key is the sauce. Scottish whiskey sauce – the best around!" Adelio told us.

"Bob would love this!" Timber exclaimed. At that moment, I had a pang of homesickness, not because I missed home but because I was worried about Uncle Bob. Now that he was on his way to Scotland, I was worried about what he would do to us when he caught up with us in Fort Augustus. I suppose, that was a selfish worry. Worse, I worried we would remain without answers to all of our questions about our mother and who we really were. It troubled me that Aunt Bea and Bob would not share any details with us. What was the big secret?

Timber put her hand on my shoulder, "It'll be all right," she whispered.

"I guess, but Bob's going to be so angry and disappointed in us for sneaking out, despite our reasoning for doing so," I whispered back. Timber nodded in agreement as our dessert was served. Adelio recommended the sticky toffee pudding. I began to realize that pudding in Scotland was a completely different creature than the pudding to which we were accustomed in America. It was nothing like the delectable delicacy that came in plastic cups at home. Here, pudding was more like a spongy cake or in the case of our breakfast of blood pudding, a dry, gritty patty of questionable constitution. I ordered my pudding with cream on the side and Timber ordered hers with vanilla ice cream. Marena asked to share with us since she could not possibly eat any more food. I rolled my eyes with that request, considering I had often witnessed both Marena and Timber ingest entire pizzas by themselves, but slid my plate halfway between us across the table so she could share with me.

After our dessert, despite the sugar rush that I was feeling, my eyes started to get very heavy. I was ready to crash into our bed upstairs. Before I could excuse myself and suggest that we all get to sleep, the sound of bagpipes filled the dining area.

"Hey, that band is starting. Can we go to the pub?" Timber asked. Suddenly, she seemed to have caught a new wind of energy, which was funny given the incessant whining earlier this morning.

"Sure, why not?" Adelio replied.

I could think of a number of reasons "why not," but I could tell my vote would be irrelevant as my sisters jumped out of their chairs and headed toward the pub. As I stood up at the table, Adelio came to my side to move my chair out for me. No boy had ever done that before for me.

"Oh, thanks," I said.

"Don't worry, we won't stay long," he assured me, "I'll keep an eye on those two if you want to head up to the room and get some sleep."

"I'm not tired," I lied. Adelio laughed.

"Ok." He put his left arm around my shoulder, "Come on then. I'll get you a pint."

"Oh, I can't - I mean, I'm not old - well, that is, I don't usually drink beer," I was stammering and tripping over my words. I knew I sounded like an idiot; a young, immature idiot, no less.

"That's all right. No one is checking your birth certificate here. Where I come from, everyone enjoys a bit of ale." I did not really hear what Adelio was saying as we walked into the pub. My temporary deafness was a result of a combination of the fact that Adelio was touching me, and that was making me breathe heavily, and the fact that the band was so incredibly loud in an already overcrowded pub. Marena and Timber had found a small table to the right side of the bar.

"I'll get us a few pints, all right?" Adelio had removed his arm from my shoulder and was directing me to sit with my sisters. I nodded and followed his instruction.

Once I sat down, Timber elbowed me in the side, "He likes you. I can tell," she told me silently. I shrugged as the tempo of the music quickened and the bagpiper started playing a song I recognized, "Bonnie Dundee." Marena squirmed in her chair. She seemed have heard Timber's thought to me. I reminded myself I had to be careful with what I said in my thoughts to my sisters. We still hadn't figured out how the whole mind reading thing worked. I seemed to be able to hear both of them, but they only heard my thoughts or each other's at certain times. Marena then leapt up out of her chair to take two pints of beer from Adelio. He joined us with two more pints, one for me and one for himself.

"Cheers," he said lifting his glass.

"To Fort Augustus!" Timber exclaimed.

"To Fort Augustus!" We replied.

14

FALLING HARD

I walked through the room toward him. The only sound I could recognize was that of my own heart beating far too quickly. I wished I could just calm down, and ordinarily, I could take a deep breath and relax just a little when I was nervous. Not this time. This time was different. This walk through the archway was the walk that was about to change my life for the better. The air smelled sweet like honeysuckles or cherry blossoms. I tried to breathe it in.

I was so nervous, but also excited because I knew what was about to happen: this was the moment for which I had been waiting. Now I was close to him. I reached out my left hand and he took it in his. He kissed it, ever so lightly. The moonlight streamed into the room, which was lit only by candles. I began to cry, not for sadness but for total and complete joy. He began to speak, his voice unsteady. I gazed up at his face. His eyes were glassy but glimmering from the candles and the same emotion that had washed over me as soon as the doors opened to permit my entry into this chamber.

"Avery, you are the woman I was born to love. Be my wife?" he asked, and although it was a question, it was as absolute as any declaration I had ever heard.

"My life begins today," I replied through my tears, "Adelio, you are the man I was born to love." With one motion during one heartbeat, he took me in his arms and kissed me on the lips. No man ever had or ever would kiss me this way. It was an embrace that made me realize I was home.

Then I felt a punch to the arm.

"Avery, wake up." I opened my right eye and then the left. Timber was leaning over me whispering, clearly without having brushed her teeth yet.

"What time is it?" I asked. "And why are you breathing on me?" I sat up in bed to avoid Timber's hot breath only to find it impossible to avoid seeing my other sister snuggled up next to Adelio on the impossibly small second bed.

"Are you kidding me?" I threw my bare feet onto the tartan carpet between our two beds. I stood over Marena and Adelio with my fists clenched as tight as my teeth. I could feel my ears burning.

"Avery…" Timber whispered in a way meant to caution me. "Avery, what are you doing?" Nothing. I was not going to do anything. I never did anything when Marena flirted unapologetically with Adam Martin, even before Kerri Jeffers got to him. I never did anything when she asked Brian Fleming to the Sadie Hawkins Dance after I said I was going to ask him. What was I going to do now? I watched them sleep, breathing in tandem.

Beyond the fact that sleeping in the same bed with a person we knew for all of one day was completely inappropriate, I could not contemplate how this scene could have transpired. The last thing I remembered was my head hitting the pillow last night. Timber had come up to bed with me. Then I remembered; Marena had stayed down in the pub with Adelio for one last song. Obviously, it had turned into more than "one last song." As I continued to stare at Marena and Adelio, I could feel the heat spreading from my ears to my face.

"Avery? Don't cry," Timber whispered as she slid over toward me on the bed.

"I'm not," I protested. The tears were trickling down both my cheeks. "I'm taking a shower," I announced. I walked over to the foot of my bed where I had stationed my bag and grabbed my necessities, including clean underwear, and locked myself in the bathroom.

⌒◯

"You're unbelievable, Rena! She's really upset so you'd better explain yourself!" I could hear Timber lecturing her twin as I combed my wet hair in front of the mirror.

"Get over it, Tim. And Avery can get over it too! Adelio and I had a great night last night when you babies went to bed. If she was so interested in him, she wouldn't have practically passed out at the table in the pub!" Marena hissed. "I'm sorry he likes me, ok. What am I supposed to do about it?" As angry as I had been when I saw Marena practically attached to Adelio's back in the twin bed, I realized she was right. If Adelio liked Marena, what could she do about that? More importantly, what could I do about it?

Timber knocked on the bathroom door, "Are you almost done, Avery? I really have to get in there." I unlocked the door and let her inside.

"Let me just grab my clothes, and it's all yours," I told her as I collected my belongings.

"Are you all right?" She asked me silently. "I know Marena can be a total jerk sometimes."

"I'm fine - really. And I'm not mad or anything. I was just surprised, is all," I reported as sincerely as possible.

"Oh, thank goodness!" Marena sighed as she poked her head into the bathroom. I pushed past her to put my things back in my backpack.

"Where's Adelio? We should really get moving if we want to get to Fort Augustus," I said as cheerfully as possible.

"Getting us tea and toast," Marena replied in her best Scottish brogue. She had already changed her clothes and packed her bag. "See you downstairs?"

"Yeah, I'll be right down when Tim gets out of the bathroom." Marena practically skipped out the door, obviously delighted by the notion that she was going to reunite with her precious Adelio. I sat on the bed and waited for Timber to get ready.

⌒⊙

By the time we got downstairs and into the parking lot, Marena had already claimed the front seat of the Volvo and was gesticulating wildly, her arms flailing about as she spoke in her "excited Marena" voice to Adelio. I must have groaned or made some sort of noise of discontent. Timber grabbed my left elbow and pulled me along to the car.

"Forget Marena. She can't help being Marena," she told me. I put my left arm around my little sister's shoulder and squeezed her to me.

"How did you end up the sweet one?" I asked her as I tickled her belly with my other hand. She giggled, took my backpack and slung it into the trunk. Adelio met us at the back of the car with tea in Styrofoam cups. I could not look at him, and I knew I would never be able to look at him the same way today. I really felt as though we had made a personal connection in Luss, but whatever moment I thought we had was completely eradicated by the vision of Marena snuggled up with him in that small bed.

Timber climbed into the left side of the car, behind Marena. As I turned to walk to the other side, Adelio caught my left hand with his right hand. I stopped and turned toward him. I think my heart skipped a beat.

"Yes?" I asked aloofly.

"Are you, I mean are we all right, Avery?" He did not give me an opportunity to answer him. "I know you saw Marena in the bed with me and - well - I want you to know I would never act dishonorably or inappropriately - and, well - nothing happened - your sister is very nice, but I do not..." This time I did not let him finish.

"I get it. It's fine. You like her. Everyone likes Marena."

"Well, yes of course I like her, but I did not know she crawled..."

"I already know. She told me. It was all very innocent," I interrupted. Why did he feel he needed to explain himself to me? Were my feelings so obvious? I knew I needed to get us both past this awkwardness.

"Oh, good then," he replied with a hint of suspiciousness in his voice. "You girls really do share everything." I smiled and turned to get into the car. He followed behind me and soon enough, we were back on the road north to Fort Augustus.

Marena had purchased a copy of Hell for Leather's CD and it played loudly through the Volvo's stereo system. She sang along, pretending to know the lyrics, which would have been incredibly annoying if it was not so funny. I realized, as did Timber, that Marena was trying very hard to capture Adelio's attention.

Within a few miles, Timber fell asleep again and I watched the scenery out the window. I could not get the memory of that dream of Adelio and me out of my head, even knowing that he seemed to have chosen my sister upon whom to bestow his attentions. Still, the dream was palpable. I closed my eyes to try to recapture the visions in my dream. I could smell the sweet cherry blossoms wafting in the air and I could feel Adelio's lips, soft and moist on mine. I could smell his breath and I moaned as he squeezed my waist. Then I realized I had moaned aloud. I opened my eyes and caught Adelio's gaze in the rearview mirror. I quickly looked out the window. We were climbing higher and higher into the Highlands.

15

A GOOD PLAQUE

We stopped at a "scenic" overlook in a place called Glencoe. All four of us got out of the car to stretch. Timber grabbed our camera and went off with Marena to take some photos. The weather was typical Scottish weather, rainy with a chance of dreary. I did not mind it at all, although my hair was beginning to disagree with the climate. I reached back to smooth my hair into a ponytail while I read the plaque commemorating the Massacre at Glencoe in 1692. I was a sucker for a good plaque at an interesting site.

"You like history?" Adelio asked me. He had been about three steps behind me from the moment we opened the car doors.

"I do," I replied, "You?"

"I do." I felt the tension of our idle chitchat. Our conversation was so much more natural only a day ago.

"Avery?"

I looked at Adelio. He was now standing at my left, still in front of the Glencoe plaque. I was hoping he was not going to say something more about the whole "Marena in bed with him episode."

"No, not that. I wanted to ask you something." I was so confused. I had not said anything out loud. Adelio leaned closer to me and began to speak softly. I leaned into Adelio because I could barely hear what he was saying:

"Your dreams - have you dreamt of me?" I felt warmth from my toes all the way to my eyebrows.

"What? Why would you ask such a weird question? No," I lied. I tried to sound mildly offended, but I think my attitude was more offensive to Adelio based on his reply.

"Well, I apologize, Your Highness. I did not realize the thought of me was quite so repulsive," he sulked.

I attempted to alter my outward attitude, to sound much less defensive, "I mean - well, why do you ask that?" I focused my gaze on the plaque as if I had missed some important information. Adelio's shoulders relaxed with my question, but I could tell he was not convinced of my sincerity. Of course, the truth was that I had dreamt a rather vivid fantasy of Adelio just last night. But the sight of my sister so close to him this morning erased the memory of the details of that dream.

Adelio put his hands on my shoulders and turned me toward his direction, forcing me to make eye contact. He was so much taller than I was. With his broad chest and shoulders, he had the build of a man, not like the boys to whom I was accustomed. He also possessed the most mesmerizing blue eyes I had ever seen. I began to feel incredibly anxious and uncomfortable. This moment had become unnecessarily melodramatic. Before I could protest, Adelio spoke to me:

"Avery, I need to explain something to you," he did not move his lips as he spoke to me, "Don't be alarmed." I was. If he could speak to me as my sisters and I had been communicating, then he could certainly understand my thoughts as well. A layer of embarrassment cloaked me. I pulled away from him. I was more mortified than frightened.

"Please Avery, I can't hear everything that goes on in that overactive mind of yours, just the things directed to me." That was a relief! I was still not ready to speak, silently or otherwise.

Adelio stepped toward me and continued, "And, I can only hear you." That last statement intrigued me.

"Why only me?" I asked silently.

Adelio smiled, "Your heart speaks to me," he said and smiled again. Was he being facetious or sarcastic? I had so many more questions, but as usual, my sisters' timing was impeccable. Timber and Marena came trotting up to us.

"Can we get moving? Someone has to use the bathroom." Marena announced.

"Shut up! I don't this time." Timber clarified to Adelio as she pointed to Marena. We all walked back to the car and took our same positions until Adelio made a special, silent request.

"Sit by me," he said, "we need to continue this conversation before we get to Fort Augustus."

16

BROKEN SILENCE

Marena reluctantly agreed to take my seat in the back of the Volvo, only because Adelio asked her to switch positions with me. If I had asked, she likely would have denied my request. She and Timber tuned us out with their iPods. Marena listened to music while Timber watched episodes of her favorite TV shows, which she had downloaded onto the device before we left. Bob and Bea had bought us all iPod Touch devices for Christmas this past year. We were probably the last teenagers in Woodport to have one.

We were well on our way to Fort Augustus before Adelio attempted to speak with me again. One breathtaking vista after another had passed by my car window. I turned around to my sisters in the backseat to grab the camera and was able to capture some brilliant shots of the landscape. We had only lived in Scotland for a few years before moving to America and Woodport with Bob and Bea, and I hardly remembered living here at all. I certainly did not recall how unique and beautiful the land was, and even if I had, I am sure I would not have appreciated it.

Woodport was also quite beautiful with a number of lakes, mountains and it even had its own glen. In many ways, Woodport and Sussex County reminded me of some of the scenery I was witnessing out the passenger window. Adelio finally broke the silence, but did not move his lips.

"There are things I need to tell you," he began. "And some of this might be alarming and may be unbelievable to you, but I need you to trust me." I nodded.

"First, you need to know that I'm not your aunt's graduate assistant. I doubt she remembers who I am at all, to be perfectly honest. I am not even from Scotland, exactly. I'm from the Kingdom of Kirana…" I interrupted him.

"Kirana? That's where our mother is from!" In my excitement, I made that statement aloud, which I immediately regretted once again forgetting our in-flight training on how to properly respond to silent communication.

"What about our mother?" Timber asked, taking her earphones out of her ears.

"What?" Followed Marena. So much for Adelio confiding in me.

He gave me a look, sighed and silently said, "I'll have to tell you most of this another time."

"Sorry," I mouthed. Adelio seemed disappointed and I wondered what part of his story he did not want to share with my sisters. The practical truth was, they would find out eventually anyway. We had no secrets at this point.

"I was telling Avery that I am from the same kingdom as your mother," he announced.

"I thought you were Aunt Bea's research assistant from Inverness or something," Timber said.

"Well, I want to explain that. I was sent from Kirana to protect your Aunt Bea, but I failed," Adelio told us.

"Failed? What do you mean 'failed?' What were you protecting her from anyway?" Timber was raising her voice.

"Shh," I cautioned, "this isn't a train station. Let him explain, Timber. Go on, Adelio."

He sighed again, "Well, the short version is that I was sent from Kirana to prevent exactly what has transpired over the past three days. Your Aunt Bea was taken to Kirana and it appears that it was not of her own accord. That is to say, it seems that she agreed to leave Fort Augustus for Kirana, but she was subsequently taken once the boat upon which she was traveling cleared the Kiranian border.

"By the time I realized what was happening, it had already happened. I was too late to stop the men who took her. Your Uncle contacted Bea to tell her you girls were on your way so these men know you are in Scotland. I believe the men who took Bea are coming back for you. You are who they really want."

"Well what are you doing wasting your time with us then? Why didn't you follow them and get Bea back? Some protection you are!" Timber was becoming more and more upset.

"It's not quite that easy, Timber…" Adelio protested.

"Wait, why would these men want us? Who are 'they'?" I asked him.

"You are the rightful heirs to the throne of Kirana and they take orders from Anyon, the King of Mordith. Anyon currently has control of the Kingdom." Suddenly, all of the questions we had had over the past few months and all of the information we had gathered through our research began to make some sense, in sort of a Disney fictional way. The missing piece to the puzzle of who we were was suddenly uncovered. Adelio was correct. What he was telling us seemed strange and impossible.

Suddenly Marena was very interested, "We're princesses?"

"Yes and you are the only hope the people of Kirana have right now."

"Only hope for what?" Marena questioned.

"Freedom and peace."

"If I had a dollar for every time someone told me that…" Marena joked. Timber cracked up, which lightened the mood in the car. We were just passing through the Ben Nevis mountain recreation area. According to a sign on the side of the road, "Ben Nevis, with its elevation of over 4000 feet is the highest mountain in all of Great Britain." It certainly dwarfed our highest point back home, the aptly named High Point at 1803 feet above sea level. The scenery and the sights of the first busy town we had come across since we left Glasgow, Fort William, temporarily distracted us all. Timber broke the silence.

"So what's the plan? How do we get Bea?"

"We obviously have to go to Kirana, right Adelio?" Marena chimed in.

"I'm taking you to the abbey on Loch Ness in Fort Augustus before we do anything. You will be safe there, but not for long. Once they can see where you are in Scotland, they'll come for you next."

"Ok, but who exactly are 'they'?" I asked.

"They are Anyon's men from the Kingdom of Mordith, the territory to the North of Kirana. Mordith is our only enemy. Anyon conquered Kirana and has controlled the kingdom for the last sixteen years. Well actually, it has been two Kiranian years. Your mother, the Queen, is essentially a prisoner, although Anyon allows her to live in the royal palace while her cousin, Ginter has served as acting Regent of Kirana. Although, it is unclear if Ginter has any power whatsoever under Anyon's rule. We do know that he often acts on Anyon's behalf."

"Ginter? Did he take Aunt Bea back to Kirana - on a boat through some fog?" I asked. Adelio had already lost me at "Kingdom of Mordith." There was obviously a lot of information we needed to understand, and not enough time to explain all of it.

"Yes, but how do you know that?"

"I saw it in a dream," I replied, now trying to remember every detail.

"Avery, Ginger told us about Ginter in Luss yesterday, remember?"

"Of course I do, dummy. It was yesterday," I snapped at her. She was interrupting my attempt to recall the exact details of my dream about Aunt Bea. Clearly, this vision had been a view into the future, not unlike many of the dreams I had been having of late.

"You don't have to yell at me," Timber pouted.

"Sorry, I didn't mean it. Just give me a minute," I requested silently. We had followed Aunt Bea to Scotland based on that dream and the information we had obtained at the College of Saint Elizabeth. It had not been clear to me that Bea was taken as a prisoner from Fort Augustus. In my dream, she did not seem to be in any danger. In fact, it appeared that she was simply leaving on a trip on Loch Ness. I wondered how my impression had been so off the mark.

"It wasn't, Avery," Adelio assured me silently, "you had no reason to know what Ginter wanted with Bea. Ginter may not even know what he wants with Bea - Anyon may not have informed him. Anyon wants you, ultimately. Anyon assumed that you would follow Bea to Kirana or at the very least follow her to Fort Augustus."

"How would he know what we would do? This is so freaky!" I replied aloud. I was now monumentally confused. This Anyon fellow was relying on my having a vision about Aunt Bea and then bravely undertaking a rescue mission? I never bravely did anything so how could this guy know any of this?

"I'll explain later, but for now just understand that there are mystical powers at play here that will be difficult for you to grasp at first," Adelio assured me silently. I nodded, still attempting to problem solve this puzzle.

"So why don't we just go with those men if they come for us too?" Marena asked. "They will obviously lead us to Bea."

"They don't want to take you on a trip to Kirana. In fact, they don't intend for you to leave Fort Augustus." Adelio replied. He looked to me. I knew what he meant. He did not need to say another word about it. There were no more questions from my sisters either.

We drove silently for what seemed to be an eternity and came into Fort Augustus at about 3 pm. Adelio pulled onto a long driveway that led to a beautiful old abbey. Timber commented to Marena and me in her thoughts that the place looked a bit like Hogwarts from her Harry Potter books.

"Hey, they have tennis courts! Too bad we didn't bring our rackets," Marena said.

"Rena, this is not exactly a vacation," I reminded her somewhat sarcastically.

"I know, Avery. I was just making an observation," she replied with equal sarcasm. We parked around the back, got out of the car and Adelio wandered over to an intercom.

"Brother, we've made it," he told the voice on the other end of the intercom.

"Praise Heaven," the voice declared through a thick brogue. Then the large iron door opened. Adelio led us through.

"This way," he instructed.

17

FORT AUGUSTUS

Adelio lead us down a long unlit hallway to a set of double doors. We passed through those doors into another hallway, this one lit by the sunlight. I looked around and noticed there were regular, electric lights spaced throughout the corridor. This disappointed me in a way, because the artificial lighting took away from the antiquity of the building. I felt a nervous anxiety in my stomach, like pre-exam butterflies in Physics or History in school. I took a deep breath and exhaled slowly to try to relax.

It was still not clear to me from Adelio's explanations what exactly was happening. Was Aunt Bea in danger? It did not seem that way, but apparently, we were in some danger. I was still hung up on the fact that Adelio could read some of my thoughts. It was terribly disturbing to me.

We walked through the long corridor until we came to another set of doors, these leading through a courtyard. I remembered this place; we had been here before. I remembered playing in the grass of this very same courtyard as a little girl with my sisters and other children

Marena remembered it too, "Hey, we used to play here!" Marena practically shouted to us in her thoughts, "Remember those big picnics in July? All the kids would run around on the grass!" For the few years that we lived in Fort Augustus, the abbey would throw a picnic for the "Friends of the Abbey," who I suppose were benefactors. I never knew exactly who it was that came for that party, just that it was the one time of year that Aunt Bea and Uncle Bob would truly be at ease. They knew everyone who came to the abbey for that weekend and we loved playing with the other children, which was a change since it was usually just us at our cottage the rest of the year.

"I wonder where all those kids are now and if they'd remember us," Timber added.

"I was not even six years old when we left Scotland, and most of those kids were around that age, so I doubt it," I told them. I smiled at Adelio, who was walking to our left. We had been silent for quite some time, and I felt a little badly that he was left out of our conversation.

"Does this courtyard look familiar to you?" He asked aloud.

"Yes, we were just thinking about it," I replied. Marena shoved her left elbow into my side.

"Hey, oww!" I complained. "What'd you do that for? Adelio knows we can read each other's minds already, Rena."

"He does?" Timber asked.

"I do. In fact I know a lot more about you girls than you probably do at this point," he teased. "But come along. I believe the brothers here will help you understand." Marena seemed pleased and came around to Adelio's left side. She grabbed his arm.

"Adelio, I'm scared. Will you promise to protect us?" Her sugary sweet voice was such a put on and just an attempt to rekindle the flirtation she had begun in Luss.

"Of course I will," he replied. "Don't worry Marena, I'm here for you girls." I was again mildly nauseated by the theatrical hero and victim game Marena was trying to play with Adelio. This was classic Marena - pretend to be a needy girl requiring the protection of the strong boy to keep his attention. They all fell for that act. Who could resist her? She was adorable.

"Don't worry Avery, I am here especially for you," Adelio assured me without a sound. Despite the death grip Marena had on his left arm, he put his right arm around my neck and pulled me to him playfully.

"Hey," I giggled. "Get in here, Timber." Timber linked her arm with my right. Marena began to sing, "We're off to see the wizard, the wonderful wizard of oz…" Timber and I chimed in, "We hear he is a wiz of a wiz if ever a wiz there was…"

⌒๏

We crossed through the grass into yet another hallway on the other side of the courtyard. Here, a jolly looking man of probably sixty or so years old met us. He seemed very happy to see us.

"My goodness how you've grown into women! Come into the light and let me look at you," the man instructed. His accent was not Scottish, perhaps Irish, but his voice was incredibly familiar to me.

"Girls, this is…"

"Brother Thomas!" I recognized the man and the instant familiarity caused me to throw myself into his arms for an embrace.

"Yes, yes," he replied and hugged back, "so wonderful to see you. It has been many years, although your Aunt Beata has sent us so many photos of you and tells us of your lives in America, so we feel like no time has passed at all!"

Marena and Timber had both stepped back from this mini family reunion. I could tell they did not remember Thomas as I had. It was Thomas who provided me with my earliest appreciation for books and stories. He would often come by our home at night to meet with Bea and Bob and before he left, I would ask for a bedtime story. Together, we would invent stories about faraway lands, of princesses and fairies. And he would always say, "good night, Your Highness," to me, and then bow as he left the room. Looking back, and knowing what we know now, apparently that was appropriate.

"Don't be frightened," I told my sisters without words. "He's a dear, dear friend. Like an uncle or grandpa." They did not seem convinced, but both of my sisters dropped their shoulders and seemed to accept that at the very least, Thomas was not a creepy stranger.

"Thomas, your real brother is Father McGee in Woodport, at our church there, right?" If I was remembering correctly, it was Brother Thomas who essentially sent us to New Jersey. His brother was the priest at Our Lady of Constant Sorrow church in Woodport and when we moved there Father McGee, who we called Father Dan, helped us to find a house and settle in. In fact, we lived in the rectory with him until our house on Indian Trail was ready for us.

He was a wonderful man, just like Thomas. Although we were not Catholic, we attended Sunday Mass at church when we were younger. More recently, only Bea and Bob attended since they had given us the choice as to whether we wanted to go to church when I was about thirteen years old. For some reason, Bob and Bea did not believe that religion in general was a particularly good idea, and we were not Catholic. They did like the idea of the community coming together one day a week and both of them volunteered time and money to various charities. They attended Mass for what they considered fellowship. My sisters and I preferred to sleep in and work on homework while they were gone. We had our own sisterly fellowship, much to the chagrin of Father Dan, who still regularly visited our home a few times a month. Father Dan would tease us since in addition to the church, he was also headmaster at Saint John's High School, Woodport's cross-town parochial rivals. We would make friendly wagers on which team, Woodport or Saint John's, would win the annual football game. My sisters and I raked many leaves at the rectory. Saint John's was a really good team.

"Of course," suddenly Marena recognized Brother Thomas. "We love Father Dan! It's nice to see you too," she gave Thomas a hug.

"And little Timberose, do you remember me?" He asked Timber. I could see her physically shudder at hearing her full name.

"I think so," she replied, "and it's Timber. Everyone just calls me Timber." I had not heard her full name used in years. Once a year, she had to endure new teachers struggling to pronounce it and then asking what type of name it was. Timber had the same answer for that ill-conceived question from the time she was twelve, "my parents were obviously on drugs." Timber gave Brother Thomas a somewhat half-hearted hug.

"Come, let's go into the drawing room, have some tea and biscuits and talk." Thomas opened a door with beautiful stained glass panes and led us into a large room full of more stained glass windows and very antique looking furniture. We sat on the soft red velvet couches as some younger looking monks served us delicious smelling black tea and shortbread.

"Girls," Brother Thomas began, "I have some unpleasant news to share."

18

WHO AM I ANYWAY?

We brought our bags up to our room, a beautiful suite with three bedrooms, two full bathrooms, a kitchen and cable TV. We even had a wireless internet connection, which caused Timber to squeal since she had brought her laptop computer and had regretted carrying it in her backpack, despite its purported lightweight. She was excited that she could use her computer here. The brothers at the abbey may have taken a vow of poverty, but you wouldn't know it looking at the fine accommodations we were provided.

Given the news that Thomas had recently delivered to us over tea, Adelio insisted on taking the front bedroom, which incidentally was the nicest one complete with its own bathroom. Timber and Marena raced up the stairs to claim the loft and I was left with the small room down the hall from the bathroom and Adelio's room.

"Should we unpack?" Timber yelled to me from the loft. Their bedroom overlooked the living room where I had plopped myself on one of the leather couches.

"You might as well," I replied.

"I would not get too comfortable girls, we may need to leave in a hurry at some point," Adelio advised as he entered the living room.

"Fine," Timber yelled back to him.

"Should we at least take some clothes out? I mean, we are going to be all wrinkly," Marena complained, very loudly from the loft. I was already tired of all of the shouting.

"Whatever. Do what you want, but please stop yelling. You guys are giving me a headache!" I moaned.

"Wah, wah, wah…" Marena mocked silently. I did not have the energy to respond.

"I'm taking a shower, or a bath or whatever they have here and Timber wants to take a nap. Ok?" Marena asked through my thoughts.

"Yes, fine, fine."

Adelio sat on the couch directly across from me. He had a map and what looked like a notebook or journal that he was studying intently. Before I could ask aloud, Adelio answered my question.

"I'm trying to figure out our best route into the kingdom," he told me silently, "I think we are going to need to go sooner than later, given what Thomas said." Brother Thomas had delivered us some sobering news earlier.

"Maybe," I whispered back, "but Brother Thomas said we would be safe here. This place is fortified. I mean you saw those men outside when we walked over here. Those are Highlanders! No one is getting through those guys, at least without us knowing about it."

"Avery, you don't quite understand the people we are dealing with here. They have powers. Brute force only gets us so far against Anyon and his minions." Adelio was right. I could not fully comprehend the powers he and Thomas had described.

"Well, we have powers too," I protested. I hated the anxiety I was feeling. I was so scared of these unknown and perhaps unfathomable forces that were planning to hunt down my sisters and me and end our lives. More than the fear of the unknown, I hated the fear of not knowing what to do about it or how to protect us.

How do I protect my sisters and myself from an enemy I have never met or seen who has been planning my demise since my birth? We intended for our trip to Scotland to be a fact-finding, reconnaissance mission to meet our mother and understand our background.

I never dreamed we would learn that our mother was the Queen of a mystical kingdom filled with unicorns and fairies called Kirana. I never imagined we would discover that we were heirs to this magical kingdom and that the survival of our people was essentially contingent upon our ability to stay alive. Moreover, I never contemplated, in my wildest dreams, that my sisters and I were this enchanted "Trinity" destined to rule a kingdom, or that we would have to win back control of our kingdom from a malevolent invader. Prior to tea and biscuits with Brother Thomas, I thought I was just Avery MacLeod, age seventeen of Woodport, New Jersey, formerly of Fort Augustus, Scotland, good student and nice person.

I could not understand how Marena and Timber could remain so calm. Perhaps they assumed that like everything else in their lives, I would have the answer to the problem. I could hear them saying to each other, "Don't worry, Avery will know what to do." Not this time.

My head was spinning and without realizing it, I was crying. Adelio noticed and rushed over to the couch to sit next to me. Then I just felt like an idiot.

"I'm sorry," I apologized through my tears, "I just don't know what we are going to do and I don't understand…" I mumbled into my hands. I had to pull myself together. I was embarrassing myself. Freaking out was clearly not a viable solution to our very ominous problem.

"There, there lass. It is all going to be all right. Nothing will happen to you or your sisters while I am with you," Adelio consoled me as he smoothed my hair from away from my face, which was probably all puffy and blotchy. "We've been preparing for your return to Kirana since you left. We have considered the possibilities and the challenges, as well as the dangers. I am sorry Brother Thomas scared you, Avery, but you don't have to be scared if I'm here, all right?" Adelio's voice was so soothing, I already felt much better about our predicament and our ability to solve the problem. I trusted him and at that moment, I believed that it was all going to be all right. Without thinking, I leaned into his body sitting next to me on the couch and threw my arms around his neck, giving him a strong squeeze.

"Thank you!" Adelio put his arms around my back and hugged me in return. We remained in that position for a few moments, not long enough in my opinion. I breathed in his scent. It was sweet like the honeysuckle and cherry blossoms in my dream. I started to get dizzy, my heart began to race and a warm feeling overcame my entire body. I felt tingly as if an electric current was running through me, head to toe as Adelio held me. I was hoping Adelio was not hearing my thoughts at that moment. That realization forced me to pull out of our somewhat platonic embrace. Adelio jumped up abruptly from his spot on the couch and relocated to his original position in front of his map.

"You like history, right? Well, have I got a lesson for you, your Highness." Adelio was remarkably cheerful.

"Yeah, ok," I replied trying to match his cheer, "but you don't have to call me that."

"Actually, I do."

19

AN EDUCATION

Marena apparently finished her bath and then collapsed on the bed next to Timber in the loft. Adelio and I were left alone to discuss our very important matters. I made us some tea and Adelio gave me my history lesson:

"You, Princess Avery, are descended from a long line of strong leaders. The rest of us lowly peasants refer to you as 'the Hazaro line' or 'de Hazaro.' Come closer and look on this map. You see, this is where Jonwell, one of the leaders of the Order of the Heather, discovered Hazaro many, many years ago. Right about here, on the south western shore," he said pointing to the map, "I'm a descendant of Jonwell, but I'll get to that later…" Adelio was very animated and seemed excited to tell me the story of Kirana as he pointed to a spot on the map on the southwest corner of what looked like an island. I was already completely entranced and decided I would not interrupt, but rather save my questions for the end of his impromptu presentation.

"Hazaro was a young physician's apprentice who came to the Kingdom of Kirana quite accidentally when he was twenty years old. He came from England, but he was likely originally from Spain. The ship on which he was traveling sunk in an amazing storm in the North Atlantic. He drifted ashore with three other sailors and was discovered by a member of the Royal Order of the Heather, a fairy named Jonwell, who nursed him back to health.

"Hazaro had no recollection of who he was or where he had been. While he lived among the fairies, Hazaro came to learn that Kirana was embroiled in a time of great unrest. King Milas of Kirana had been murdered by his brother, Frondin. As a result, the Kingdom was experiencing significant turmoil.

"Frondin was an unstable personality, to say the least, who had hated his brother, Milas, since birth. Milas had inherited the throne from his father King Donveld, who not unlike

Frondin, was unpredictable and paranoid. King Donveld was incredibly fearful of the people and creatures of the forest after encountering a coven of fairies he believed were trying to bewitch him. In fact, when his wife died in childbirth soon after this encounter, he believed it was the fairies that had cursed him and ordered a mission into the forests to seek them out and destroy them. While that mission proved unsuccessful, his luck got worse with the illness and death of his oldest son and heir. Donveld vowed revenge against all of the mystical people.

"Until this time, the fairies of the world lived for the most part among themselves and did not mix with the mortal humans. Their legends were well known and although they possessed magical powers including the ability to see the future, they were considered harmless.

"Nevertheless, Donveld raised his army and attempted to conquer the lands of the fairies and mystics and was killed in the process. His next eldest son, Milas assumed the throne and brokered a peace with the fairies, but within a year of rebuilding the peace in Kirana, his brother Frondin conspired against Milas, murdered him and resumed his father's ill-conceived mission to exterminate the fairies.

"In response to the war, the usurped Council to Milas formed the Order of the Heather. The Council believed, as Milas had, that at least some of the mystical people were peaceful and useful, and at the very least, harmless.

"The Order of the Heather included leaders of all the tribes and clans of Kirana including the fairy leaders. They were searching for a young, charismatic and brave leader to overtake the forces of Frondin. They had "seen" a young man rising to help them in their visions. That is when Hazaro arrived upon the shores of Kirana.

"Hazaro, having no sense of who he was or why he was in Kirana, became fond of the people who had given him a new life. He was inspired by their kindness as well as their mystical powers. He wanted to help them in their quest for peace and agreed to fight with them. Hazaro fell in love with Jonwell's beautiful daughter, Amara.

"Jonwell had had a vision of a young stranger leading them to victory and became convinced it was Hazaro. The Order trained Hazaro to be a skilled soldier. In the great and final battle of the Nolan Glen against Frondin's army, when he saw that the Order's military leader had fallen and their army had been pushed back, Hazaro bravely assumed the leadership and defeated Frondin. It had appeared to Frondin's army that Hazaro had employed some magic to win the battle and they all knelt and hailed Hazaro as the new King of Kirana."

I had closed my eyes and as Adelio described the great battles, I could see the event unfolding in my mind. I imagined something right out of a Lord of the Rings movie or perhaps Narnia; an epic scene where man and creature fought together, side by side for their freedom and survival.

"Hazaro married Amara and their marriage as well as his reign was blessed by the mystical people," Adelio went on. "Together Hazaro and Amara had three beautiful daughters, within five years of assuming the throne. Kirana entered a long period of peace and prosperity." This seemed like a good spot to interrupt Adelio.

"Ok, so I assume at some point this peace and prosperity ended. What happened?" I asked as I refilled both of our teacups.

"Thank you, yes indeed. Well, I do not want to bore you with all of the details, but more contemporary Kirana has experienced a disrupted peace. You see, the line of Hazaro succession runs through a ruler's daughters in Kirana, not the sons. This reality does not sit well with many potential male heirs, but part of the reason for this succession involves the blessing upon Hazaro's line. He had three daughters and therefore since that time, all of the full mystical powers have been bestowed upon the daughters born to the crown.

"It is the women of this line who are required to rule in order to maintain the peace in the land between all of the kingdoms. It is three, or a trinity, of daughters that continue this mystical line. The crown passes to the eldest daughter once she has turned eighteen years old provided the two younger sisters have each reached the age of sixteen. It was found that the full powers of the Trinity develop once all three girls are sixteen years old." Adelio explained. These details were getting complicated, and I had so many questions, but I figured that an overview of the facts were really all I needed at this point. Still I had to ask:

"So, if my sisters and I are the new trinity, what about my mother? Does she have two other sisters? Why can't they just rule Kirana?" Adelio turned a page in his journal to what appeared to be a flow chart or family tree.

"Yes, Queen Riva did have two sisters. Riva's grandmother, Huldi, had passed the throne to Riva's mother, Galina once her two other daughters had turned sixteen. Soon after taking the throne at age nineteen, Galina had three daughters, Riva, Fawna and Zeilda. Galina and her two sisters ruled Kirana together for only five years when their younger brother, Tindol became suddenly unhappy with his station in life, serving his three sisters.

"Despite Huldi's plea to her son to obey and accept his fated place in life, Tindol conspired to take the throne. The royal seers uncovered his plot and he was banished from Kirana. Galina saw that Tindol, despite his banishment was intent on taking power from her. He sought the assistance of the Kingdom of Mordith in the north and began to raise an army.

"The seers envisioned great danger for Galina's daughters and it was thought best to protect them by sending them to the fairies in the forest, while Galina and her sisters stood their ground in Kirana. Tindol's army invaded Kirana and defeated Galina and her sisters."

As Adelio explained this history, again I could envision the scene: my grandmother in full armor, like Joan of Arc or Queen Elizabeth, riding out to rouse her rag-tag army of peasants and noblemen upon a white horse. I could see the great battle, the violence and all of the lives lost to this cause. Adelio continued,

"The people of Kirana, unaware that Galina's heir was still alive, lost hope and accepted the leadership of Tindol. In order to repay the debt to the King of Mordith, Tindol allowed the kingdoms to unite, or so he thought. The King of Mordith, Sosna, having no use for Tindol, murdered him, his wife and children and a great darkness fell upon Kirana.

"Ginter, Tindol's youngest son, had been overlooked by Sosna and survived this attack. Saved by one of the servants, Ginter was taken to live with his cousins in the forest, but the fairies rejected this plan fearing that Sosna would find both Ginter and the trinity of royal princesses and destroy them. They sent Ginter to live with the Dowager Duchess of Easton, Lady Bretton, who raised him as her own son at Swenwood Castle. As a young widow, Lady Bretton was delighted to have a child.

"When Riva's youngest sister, Zeilda turned sixteen and all three girls gained their mystical powers, The Order of the Heather who had been protecting Riva and her sisters in the forest, once again rose up to retake Kirana from King Sosna. Riva and her sisters, with the support of The Order retook the crown, defeating Sosna and the Kingdom of Mordith. Riva and her husband Philson were then the new leaders of Kirana and ruled for five years until trouble began again."

I was so intrigued, but I was also exceptionally hungry. The clock in the kitchen behind us explained why that was. It was dinnertime. Apparently, Adelio could tell that I was ready to eat my arm.

"Maybe we can get a bite to eat at the Boathouse just down the path on the loch and I can tell you more?" He suggested.

"Absolutely, but let me check on the twins and see if they want to come with us. We should probably all stick together." I left the living room and quietly crept up the stairs to the loft. The sun was still shining brightly outside, but the loft was shielded from the light by a partial wall. I opened the door slowly and whispered,

"Guys, hey guys…" No movement, "We're going to eat, want to come?" No answer. They were sound asleep.

"Avery, we can bring them back something and make sure Brother Thomas' men remain outside. We'll leave a note," Adelio told me through my thoughts.

"What if they wake up soon? I don't want them to be angry that we went without them." That was just the sort of thing my sisters would get aggravated about, especially Marena.

"Avery, concentrate and try to imagine what is going to happen when they wake." At first I was confused by this instruction, but I realized that Adelio was suggesting that I look into the future to see what my sisters' reactions to our absence would likely be. Without Adelio, it would not have dawned on me that I could do that.

I closed my eyes as I tried to focus my thoughts. I could see both of my sisters waking up, first Timber then Marena. They both come downstairs and it is dark, but we have left the hall and kitchen lights on. Timber reaches for a piece of paper on the kitchen counter. She tells Marena that there is food and drinks in the refrigerator, and that we will be right back with dinner. They both grab a bottle of water and some fruit and plop themselves on the couch. Marena turns on the television and they watch an episode of Dr. Who, laughing at how silly BBC shows are. They do not appear to miss Adelio or me. Soon, the living room door opens and Adelio and I enter with prawns and salmon we have brought back from the restaurant.

I was so excited that I could see this much that I ran down the stairs to Adelio who was already waiting for me at the door of the flat. He held it open and gestured for me to exit with him.

"I did it!' I exclaimed. "Guess what I saw…?" Adelio chuckled.

"I already know," he said.

"Oh," I replied somewhat deflated.

"Come on," he said as the door of our suite closed behind us, "I want to show you the loch."

20

A NEW FRIEND

The Boathouse Restaurant was the perfect spot for dinner. Located directly on the south bank of Loch Ness, it offered us great opportunity to continue my Kirana history lesson. The view up the loch was like nothing I had ever seen before in my life. As beautiful as Crystal Lake in spring and summer was back home, Loch Ness was breathtaking. Adelio told me that the loch was eight hundred feet deep - the perfect place to house a legendary creature like the Loch Ness Monster.

"She's not really a legend," Adelio told me over our appetizers of grilled prawns and fresh greens salad.

"Oh, ok," I replied sarcastically.

"Seriously, she lives in Loch Ness. In fact, one of the reasons we continue to return to Fort Augustus is to watch over Nessie."

"Who is we?"

Adelio leaned in to speak, but then he replied silently. "The fairies."

"The what?" I blurted aloud.

"You heard me," he replied aloud as well, "that's what I am. But let's avoid publicizing that to the entire restaurant." I looked around. Besides Adelio and me, there were only two other tables of people in the restaurant. They appeared to be local people, and they were sitting at the farthest corner of the room from us. I closed my eyes and concentrated on them, trying to hear them or hear their thoughts. No luck. I would have been more frustrated, but our dinner was served; salmon for me and venison for Adelio. Quite a big meal for a "fairy" I thought to myself.

"My people quite enjoy hearty meats, actually," he said as he cut into his meal. This comment only perpetuated my inappropriate joke, which I could tell Adelio neither understood nor cared for. It was not one of my best, for sure, and it was probably rather offensive. I decided not to bother explaining the joke to Adelio.

"Since you were wondering, they are staying at the Lovat Arms Hotel up the street. They're on holiday from Perth," Adelio pointed out nodding toward the younger couple across the room, "And those four came in on a sailboat through the Caledonian Canal and are headed up the loch toward Inverness tomorrow morning. Don't worry, you'll get better at it." He was practically devouring his venison.

"Thanks for the encouragement, but back to you for a minute. So you're a - well, I won't say it, but if you are that then where are you wings?" I asked. I was purposely being snarky. The princess business was hard to believe, but at least we had learned a little about the legend of Kirana when we were at St. Elizabeth. The fact that my sisters and I had developed these extra-sensory powers more or less confirmed the likelihood that it was true. What Adelio was telling me now was bordering upon the absurd.

"Only sprites have wings, Avery," Adelio answered me as if he were speaking to the most ignorant person on the planet. Admittedly, I was quite uninformed when it came to the enchanted forest creatures of the world. I took the last bite of my Scottish salmon. It was every bit as delicious as the server had promised.

Adelio finished the last of his pint of ale and motioned for me to get up to leave.

"Uh, don't we have to pay for this?"

"I have an account here through the abbey. It's already handled," he replied.

"Let me guess," I giggled, "you've put the bill on your 'Fairy Express Card!'" I was literally slapping his arm at my joke as we left the restaurant and headed over to the banks of the loch.

"My what?" Another bad joke, lost on my fairy friend.

"Never mind." I sighed. "So continue. Tell me more about your fairy-ness." We sat down on wooden Adirondack Chairs facing Loch Ness. The sun was setting and the sky was turning shades of purple. I tried to ignore the very annoying little bugs flying around us, which was a difficult thing to do, to enjoy the view. Ducks were swimming in the gentle waves of the loch that washed on shore. Adelio left his chair and walked closer to the water. He knelt down and began to sort through some stones.

"Here's a good one," he decided. He waved his right hand over the stones and magically, one of them levitated in the air. He then seemed to direct the stone toward me. It floated through the air and I put out my hand. The stone fell into my left hand. It was smooth and round, obviously a part of the geography of the loch for thousands, or maybe millions of years.

"How did you do that?"

"I told you before that I am a descendant of Jonwell. Jonwell was the leader of the fairies in Kirana. Fairies are mystical people. No wings, of course, but we do have a lot of the abilities you do, like ability to see into the future by reading minds and hear the unspoken thoughts of - um, well special people - ability to control the weather and elements - Avery, are you all right? You seem like I've said something to upset you."

I was slightly too shocked to respond. The floating rock trick was enough to render me temporarily speechless. He could tell I was having a hard time comprehending what he was saying.

"Here, come with me," he said walking over and reaching for my hand. I placed the stone he had floated to me, rather inexplicably, into my pocket. I stood from my seat upon command and met his left hand with my right. Our fingers intertwined and we walked hand in hand out onto a very long pier. The annoying bugs followed us, but with Adelio's hand in mine, I really did not care. I looked up at him and he was smiling at me, so I immediately put my head down and looked the other way. I took my right hand from him and thrust it into my pocket, feeling for the stone.

My crush was apparent, certainly. I tried to think other thoughts like how wrong Adelio was for me, how much older he was than me, and the fact that he clearly found himself attracted to my sister. The vision of Marena and Adelio cuddled up at the Drover's Inn provided me with the perspective I needed. There was no time to foster a romantic relationship with a boy who was more interested in my sister. I had to let this one go and focus on the important issues at hand: protecting my sisters and myself and getting to Aunt Bea before something terrible happened to her.

We stopped at the end of the pier. The sky was a beautiful magenta now with violet wisps of clouds painted through it with gentle brush strokes. Looking out over the loch, I began to remember some of my early childhood in Scotland. I remembered boat rides on the loch with Uncle Bob and playing on the grounds of the abbey behind the trees. I even remembered our cottage, which I could barely see through the pine trees over my right shoulder.

I stood facing as far north as I could see, avoiding eye contact with Adelio. I wanted him to understand that I was not interested in him in "that way," despite what my thoughts may have previously indicated. Really, he was here in Fort Augustus with us to do a job, to protect the Trinity, and I was not about to distract him from that task. Moreover, I did not want to face the disappointment I would encounter when I next saw Marena and Adelio together. Maybe we would all go to Kirana and he and Marena would get married some day and live happily ever after. Then Adelio would be my brother. I would definitely like that, which is why I was done with my crush. Just like that, I decided.

While I was declaring my intentions in my mind, Adelio seemed to be concentrating very intently on the water.

"What are you doing?" I asked. He did not respond. I came closer to him and sat beside him on the pier. I could see there was an animal there or something in the water swimming up to the dock.

"What is that?" I stood up. Whatever it was, it was enormous and headed right for the dock.

"Shh - don't scare her. Avery, this is Nessie! Come over and meet her. She won't hurt you." I knelt down next to Adelio. Sure enough, just peeking above the water was the head of what appeared to be the famed, and previously mythical creature. She peered at me, lifted her head out of the water and shot me in the face with water straight out of her snout.

"Ahh!" I exclaimed, slightly amused and at the same time grossed out. I thought Adelio was going to fall in the water with his laughter.

"You told her to do that!" I accused.

"Yes, but I didn't think she understood me! My ability to commune with nature is not as strong as some fairies' abilities." He put his hand back toward the water and waived it about. Nessie popped her head out of the water again, rubbed the top of it on Adelio's hand and dropped back into the dark, deep loch. This time, I got a better look at the creature. She looked exactly as I imagined she would – part seal, part dinosaur. At this point, I wondered if Adelio was also friendly with Big Foot.

Nessie swam about next to the dock and would periodically peer out from the water, as if to check on our whereabouts. Then she would spin around under the water and raise a flipper into the air as if performing at Sea World. We stood and watched her effortlessly glide through the deep, dark waters. After a few minutes, we saw Nessie dive down into the water, her back arching and tail splashing, and she was gone.

"Gee, is that all you got, Fairy Boy?" I gave him a punch on the right arm, "Floating rocks and sea monsters?" Adelio stood and faced me.

"In Kirana, these sea monsters are not quite so docile. We also have an occasional dragon sighting," he told me, excitedly. Adelio's eyes were glistening from the distant lights that had automatically turned on outside the Boathouse. He smiled a most alluring and charming smile and punched me back on my arm.

"Hey!" I protested and prepared to deliver him another playful knock, this time to his chest, but he blocked my right fist with his left hand. He held my wrist and gently rubbed it with his thumb. There was that electricity again. Why was he torturing me? He pulled me closer to him, and tenderly brushed my left cheek with his other hand. I felt a combination of nausea and lightheadedness as his eyes met mine.

Adelio leaned in and kissed me, ever so lightly on my lips. Was this really happening? I was not sure which was more unlikely, that Adelio was kissing me or that I had just had a visit with the Loch Ness Monster. I pulled away from his soft embrace and looked into his eyes. His expression answered my query so I gladly kissed him again. I closed my eyes and the world seemed to stop moving for a moment. This kiss was much more passionate than the first. My heart was fluttering and I knew I was not breathing. Adam Martin and any of the boys at Woodport High School were a distant memory. Then, suddenly I saw something.

"Oh my God!" I pulled away from Adelio and turned to face the loch. "They're coming! They're coming for us!" I saw a boat cloaked by mist with five large men in it coming toward the very pier upon which we were standing. It was very dark, but I could see the men readying the boat to tie it off on the cleats attached to the dock. "We have to get to my sisters!" I grabbed Adelio's hand and pulled him so that we could run up the pier to our residence.

"No, you're having a vision…I see them too. They are not here yet, but we probably do not have a lot of time. A day, maybe two. Let's get back to Timber and Marena. We're going to have to leave Fort Augustus soon."

21

HARNESSING POWER

The next morning arrived rather quickly, I thought. When Adelio and I returned from our time at the loch, my sisters and I had spent the evening learning more about Kiranian history and the people of Kirana, including the fairies. We also learned about the Kingdom of Mordith in the north. It seemed that Mordith was always causing some sort of trouble for the Kiranians, but especially now that King Anyon maintained control of Kirana. Since defeating our mother, Anyon had turned Kirana from a united, peaceful land to a land of paranoia, hatred and turmoil. The treasury was all but empty and many of the members of the Order of the Heather had been captured and jailed. Some of them, including our father, King Philson were presumed lost forever. This sobering information was almost too much for us to hear, despite the fact that until this week, we assumed both of our parents were nonexistent.

The most important conversation of the night was our plan. Adelio explained just how we were to leave Fort Augustus. It seemed simple enough and this morning, we were packing up whatever we had unpacked upon arrival. After breakfast, we were to head to the dock where Brother Thomas would be waiting to send us off to Kirana.

I lay in bed staring at the ceiling. Sunlight was streaming through the windows in my room. I could not help smiling at the memory of the last time I was on the dock. It was only last night, but already the memory had become legend to me although I could still feel his lips upon mine. I could smell his sweet scent and my heart fluttered imagining the most wonderful moment in my life. I did not want to leave my bed knowing last night's events would be just a memory if I moved. But suddenly, I had little choice.

The door swung open so violently that it sounded as if the knob had smashed through the wall.

"Knock much?" Was all I could stammer out of my mouth before she was practically on top of me.

"I tried to stop her, Avery. I tried to explain…" Timber was right behind Marena whose face was purple, her eyes glassy and watery.

"That's what you were doing last night? You left us here, alone so you could steal my boyfriend?"

"Your boyfriend? Rena, what are you…?" I realized that plausible deniability, my usual strategy was not going to be successful here.

"Don't try and deny it! I heard you just now!" As much as I thought that I could keep my thoughts to myself, clearly it was a near impossibility to keep a secret from either sister for very long. I hadn't done anything wrong. I knew that, but I could not escape the feeling of irrepressible guilt. I got out of bed and pushed past both Marena and Timber to avoid making eye contact. I made my way into the bathroom.

"You can't run away from this Avery!" She shrieked as I closed the bathroom door. "Open up - open up - now!" Marena was pushing on the door with her hip, trying to muscle her way inside.

"Ok, ok - move." I opened the door and faced her. Her blond hair was pulled back into a bun at the nape of her neck, but random tendrils were now stuck to her cheek from the tears I caused. Her eyes were no longer just glassy. They were bloodshot and tired looking. The sight of her sorrow broke me and forced me to look to the wood flooring beneath my feet. Marena began to poke me in the chest.

"You knew I loved him - you knew and…" I needed to end this drama quickly. I hoped Adelio was not in the suite to witness this ridiculous display of sibling rivalry.

"Love, Rena? It's been two days," Timber interjected.

She had been hovering close behind Marena, as if to prevent a physical altercation. My sisters and I had not had a sisterly slap fight since we were about eight and ten years old and we were fighting for the attention of our neighbor, Logan Mitchell and the use of his toy. Logan had this battery powered ride-on Jeep that we loved, but only two people could ride in it at once and Logan always had to be one of the two people. This one time in particular, it was getting dark and both Logan's mom and Aunt Bea had called us in for dinner, but we wanted to ride in the Jeep. Logan said the winner of a race from our mailbox to his, which had been two doors down, could take the last ride with him in the Jeep. Kids never think there will be another opportunity for fun. It's all about the immediate thrill and I suppose we weren't thinking that we could just ride in the Jeep the next day.

So the three of us took off down the road. Timber was clearly the frontrunner with Marena and me just behind her. Intent on winning, Marena caught up to Timber and shoved her out of the way to win the race. Needless to say, we never did ride in the Jeep that night. We ended up in a heap on the Mitchell's lawn, pushing, slapping and hollering. Actually, I don't believe we ever did ride in that Jeep again or play with Logan for that matter. A few weeks later, Uncle Bob caught Logan and Marena playing "mommy and daddy" in our bedroom and that was the end of our play dates with Logan.

"Rena, please…I'm sorry," I wasn't sorry, really, but I didn't know what else to say. I wasn't sorry about kissing Adelio, but I was sorry that I did not have the ability to block my thoughts from Marena.

"Sorry? Sorry?" I had never seen Marena this angry before this moment. Timber and I caught each other's gaze and she looked as frightened at Marena's rage as I did. Before either of us could say anything, Marena let out this piercing scream and threw her hands into the air. With that motion, we heard a great crash behind me in the bathroom. I turned around to see the shelving in the bathroom collapse along with my toiletries. This distracted all of us briefly, but Marena, seemingly frustrated that Timber and I had turned our attention to the destruction over the bathtub, screeched once more. She threw her hands into the air again and waved them over her head as if she were throwing a soccer ball. Now the framed picture in the bathroom came crashing to the floor.

"Marena, stop it!" Timber yelled and grabbed her twin's arms, pinning them to her side. Marena was breathing heavily and sobbing. I was stunned. Could Marena be causing this destruction? It did not make any sense.

"Are you girls all right?" Adelio emerged from his room down the hall and rushed toward us. It was hard to believe he did not respond when this chaos first began, although I was aware that he probably had heard every word through me. "Was that glass breaking?"

"Oh, perfect!" Marena turned her back to Adelio and headed up the stairs to the loft, leaving the scene of the crime.

"I'll go," Timber followed her sister, but before she made it upstairs, she said to me silently, "She's jealous, Avery and she isn't used to not getting what she wants. I will speak to her. Don't worry, she'll be all right." I was grateful to Timber for playing mediator, but at the same time incredibly irritated with Marena. Her penchant for the dramatic was bad enough, but I was accustomed to that. This violent display of irrational anger was just unbelievable.

"She's coming into her power, Avery," Adelio explained as we surveyed the damage.

"Being a complete jerk is a power?" I said as I collected what was left of my makeup and necessities. My powder had broken apart and gotten all over the rest of my brushes.

"We're going to have to help her cultivate it. It's a strong ability as mystical powers go. Controlling her emotions and keeping an even temper are going to be important to avoid - well, this sort of catastrophe," he clarified.

"You mean she can move objects, just by being mad at me? Great!"

"No, she can move objects by concentrating on them. The emotions, as you have just witnessed, can cause unintended destruction if she isn't careful." We picked up the pieces of the glass frame and moved them into the trashcan. Luckily, the frame did not shatter completely. Adelio took my hand, forcing me to look at him.

"Are you all right, Avery? I was worried that she hurt you," Adelio spoke to me silently. He touched my left cheek with his left hand. I smiled when I felt the touch of his fingers on my skin. His touch gave me the tingles inside.

"I am. We should talk - uh - about last night…" Nervousness even caused my thoughts to stutter.

"Not now," he replied gesturing toward the upstairs loft, "I do want to speak with you regarding last night, Avery. It was wrong of me to try and kiss you and cause a problem with your sister. You are both such wonderful girls, Timber too. I let the ale go to my head, I guess. It will not happen again, I assure you. I have a job to do, and I am going to do it. We have a big day ahead of us today, so perhaps we should put this all behind us and focus upon our trip to Kirana." I was confused.

"Wait, but last night - I thought…" I could not complete the sentence. Adelio squeezed my hand really hard, almost as if to tell me to "shut up." This conversation was for my sisters' benefit and I played along. "I see. Well, Adelio I respect your feelings. Let's just be friends, ok?"

"Sure," he replied smiling. We shook hands and continued to clean up the mess in the bathroom in silence. I filled my head with thoughts of the task at hand, and within what seemed to be only seconds, Marena appeared at the bathroom door, still whimpering.

"I'm sorry, Avery. I don't know why I got so mad at you. I guess I must have misinterpreted something. I heard your thoughts just now and - I don't know. I feel like such a mean jerk."

"You are a mean jerk - I'm just kidding. It's fine," my sister was truly ashamed of her behavior. She stood at the bathroom door with her head down and eyes on her bare toes. Marena was rarely apologetic about anything she did, which typically required that Timber or I would have to break down and apologize to her when we fought. *This* Marena was frightened by her capabilities.

"Adelio, I'm sorry you had to see us like this. I don't know what came over me," she continued.

"It's your power, Rena. And please don't worry about before. It's happened to the best of us."

"Really?" She inquired hopefully.

"Well, no. That was just bizarre!" Adelio laughed which caused Marena to laugh. "Come now, I'll make us all some tea and we'll have some breakfast, right?" We nodded. Adelio winked at me as he put his arm around my sister and walked down the hall to the living area and kitchen. I was not sure what it meant, since he somehow was blocking his thoughts from me. Timber appeared at the bathroom door fully dressed. She did not say a word to me; just shook her head as if to say "can you believe what just happened?" After last night and everything we now knew, I could.

22

REUNION

Adelio made us tea and we ate toast and fruit. We talked about our powers with him. It was amazing how much he knew about us already. He told us that once we got to Kirana, our powers would intensify and become stronger. The closer we got to Kirana, the more powerful our abilities would become. In fact, since coming to Scotland, he said our powers had been growing stronger every day, theoretically anyway. Our mind reading talents were certainly developing.

Marena listened intently as Adelio described what he envisioned to be our full powers. Apparently if properly developed, Marena had the power of telekinesis as we had already witnessed, Timber had the ability to communicate with and control nature, and I was going to be able to read the thoughts of people other than just my sisters and foresee future events.

Adelio explained that Marena and Timber's abilities to share thoughts with each other and with me could be described as a silent conversation. If any of us was thinking about the other, then that sister could hear our thoughts. This is how Marena apparently heard my thoughts about Adelio and the dock from the night before. Even though I didn't realize it at the time, I must have been thinking of her in some way.

"How come Avery gets two powers?" Timber questioned.

"She's the oldest and the mystical powers were conferred upon her first by birthright," Adelio answered, "Avery will also become Queen of Kirana and - uh, her husband will become King. But it is the Queen and her sisters, the Crown Princesses who rule the kingdom. The King sits at the head of the Royal Council and is the liaison to the Order of the Heather. Timber and Marena's husbands will become Crown Princes. One will lead the Royal Guard and Seafarers and the other will be the Minister of Justice. Both will also serve the Order of the Heather."

"Oh, we know what the Order of the Heather is. It's the ancient group of mystical leaders from all over the land. We learned that when we went to Aunt Bea's college library," Timber acknowledged. "Although it isn't clear what they do."

"Well, the Order of the Heather is the protectorate of the Trinity. They see that you are the balance of power between benevolence and malevolence, between good and evil. They believe that as long as descendants of Hazaro are in power in Kirana, peace will prosper throughout the entire land so they dedicate their existence to protecting that peace for every man, fairy, and creature in our world. And to do this, they employ their mystical powers." Adelio explained as he spread strawberry preserves on his toast.

"Wait just a tick - we're going to be expected to stay in Kirana? We can't do that. We have school and tennis and we already committed to working at Camp Sacagawea this summer!" Timber exclaimed. "We can't just leave Woodport and never come back! What about our friends? What about Tulip and our house and Uncle Bob?" Timber was becoming slightly frantic as reality began to strike her. We all knew that coming to Scotland against Aunt Bea's wishes would probably change our lives forever, we just never imagined it would be this severe.

"Your uncle is on his way to Fort Augustus and is coming with us. He called Bea and Brother Thomas as soon as he realized where you girls had gone. He just needed to make some last minute arrangements with Father Dan. His flight landed three hours ago and he is on his way to Inverness by train. One of the brothers will retrieve him from the train station. Don't worry, he brought your cat," Adelio told us.

"Oh thank goodness!" Timber sighed with relief. She no longer seemed concerned about friends or leaving Woodport since she now knew the cat was coming with us. Marena was not so easily appeased.

"Well, wait a minute. So it's true? We aren't coming back? We can't just get Bea and come home?"

"I'm afraid not, Marena. It has always been your destiny to return to Kirana to claim the throne and the Order of the Heather has worked very hard to protect you," Adelio sounded like he was making a sales pitch for the Order.

"Actually, Aunt Bea and Uncle Bob have worked very hard to protect us," Marena corrected him, "in fact, it's not until we ran into you that we suddenly have all these problems."

"Rena, Timber, we were born for this task. You have to think of going to Kirana as something we would be doing no matter what, whether it's today or next week," I tried to reason.

"Easy for you to say 'Your Majesty,' you're going to be a Queen over there," Marena mocked. I knew this would be the sticking point with Marena. Adelio came to my rescue.

"You can't look at it like that, Marena. While Avery might eventually be the figure head in Kirana, you and Timber are as important as she is. In fact, she cannot rule as Queen and maintain her powers without both of you. And for that matter, her right to the crown is not conferred upon her until the birth of her first child is foreseen by the Order. But right now, your mother Queen Riva is completely powerless against the forces of the Kingdom of Mordith and Anyon because her sisters are gone," Adelio explained.

"Gone? You mean…?" Timber interjected.

"Yes. Murdered by Anyon's soldiers prior to his last invasion of Kirana. Your mother is only alive because Anyon knows that you are still alive and the only way to get to you is through her. They took Bea because they knew you'd follow her."

"How does he know we even exist at this point?" Marena asked.

"You'll learn more about the inner workings of your heredity when we get to Kirana, but basically they have spies who not only knew you were all three alive and of age, but that you were coming to Scotland. We think they were able to read Bea's thoughts. I don't know how, after all this time, they were able to get this information from Bea, especially since Bea has been coming to Fort Augustus for years. I suspect that one of the fairies who came to meet with her was compromised." Adelio and I began to clean up the dishes from our quick breakfast

"You mean, one of your fairy friends sold her out?" Marena asked.

"It would appear that way, Marena." Marena rolled her eyes. She was not exactly sharing her thoughts with me, but I knew what was going through her head. We were expected to just trust Adelio and head to Kirana when he could not even trust his own people. Marena pushed her chair back from the dining table and stood.

"Ok, well I'm going to get myself and my stuff together. I'd really appreciate it if you don't suddenly betray us and give away our position, while I'm upstairs, Adelio," she said. "I'll be right back." She winked at Adelio and pranced out of the room. He smiled at her. I could feel my blood pressure rising, not out of anger at Marena, but loss of Adelio's attention and affection so soon after I had had it. In fact, I felt the same way I did the day in the CVS parking lot when I realized Adam Martin had chosen Kerri Jeffers over me. I ended those thoughts abruptly to focus on what lie ahead of us. My heart would have to wait.

⌒◯

We waited in the abbey's common room for Uncle Bob to arrive. Marena listened to her iPod while Timber and I played cards. Rummy 500 was our game of choice because it was a long game that we could adjourn and reconvene at any time. By the time the heavy gilded doors creaked open and Bob walked into the room, I had 235 points. Marena was the first to greet him.

"Bob!" Our uncle was not quite as enthusiastic to see us as we were to see him. He appeared uneasy and even older than just a few days ago. Tulip was meow-ing in her carrier.

"Tulip!" Timber was clearly more excited to see the cat and ran over to take her from Bob. "Of course we wouldn't forget you, Tulip. How could you ever think such a thing? Poor Tulip says 'she was afraid she would never see us again.'" Timber translated, headed back to our spot on the couch, and removed Tulip from her carrier.

I had walked over to Bob to hug him. I was so relieved to see him that I started to cry. My crying caused Marena to cry as well.

"Bob, we're just so happy to see you," I reported, "and we're scared. Why didn't you tell us about Kirana and our powers and well, any of it?"

"We were waiting for the right time and we hoped that it was not a conversation that needed to be had for at least another year. But don't you lasses worry. We have been planning for our return to Kirana since we left sixteen years ago. Why do you think Bea spends so much time in Scotland each year?"

"What do you mean?" Timber picked her head up from Tulip, "She had to come here for her research for the college, for that annual conference."

"Well yes, that was part of it, but she also visited with Brother Thomas, here and some people from our home land would meet with her as well," Bob replied.

"You mean fairies, not people?" Marena stated. We were aware of a lot more information than Bob assumed. He laughed and rubbed the top of Marena's head.

"I see your friend here must have provided you with quite an education!" Bob exclaimed as he walked over to Adelio and enthusiastically shook his hand. Actually, it was more of an "arm shake" like in the movie Ben-Hur. "Look at you," he said to Adelio, "how are you, old friend. You've hardly changed at all and look at me, practically an old man!" Old friend? Apparently Bob and Adelio were well acquainted during some prior life of which my sisters and I were completely unaware.

"How do you two know each other?" Marena asked as she grabbed Adelio's arm and began to caress it with her other hand in an overly intimate manner. I wanted to scream when I saw her doing this, but I just focused my attention on Tulip so as not to show my frustration. When I looked up again, I noticed Bob's eyes widening at this sight of his sixteen year old niece stroking an older man's arm and I saw him make direct eye contact with Adelio. This caused Adelio to shake his head and shrug at Bob, as if to ask "I know, but what am I supposed to do about it?"

"Your Uncle served in your father's Navy, what we called the Seafarers in Kirana, and we met on an expedition to recover a fishing boat in distress," Adelio told us as he wiggled his left arm out of Marena's grip. He walked over to his backpack, picked it up and needlessly adjusted the straps, only to set it back on the floor. It was an obvious tactic to avoid contact with my sister, I thought.

"Actually girls, your father, King Philson was on that fishing boat when it sprung a leak, so it was official state business that we were conducting. That is why Adelio was there. His position in the royal court was very - is very important," Bob added. I was interested in what Bob meant by that last statement about Adelio. I looked at Adelio and asked him myself and he responded, "I'll tell you soon." I hated waiting. One of my great pet peeves is when someone tells you that they have something important to share, but they can't tell you right now. Not that the answer to my question was overly important, it was just that I really wanted to know more about Adelio.

"So what happened?" Timber inquired, seemingly more interested in the part of the story about our father.

"We came upon the boat and King Philson himself was bailing out water in a bucket and he said 'ahoy, good timing boys! My boots are not soaked through quite yet. Forget me and save the boat!' The boat, which he had named RMS Petal was a wedding gift from the Queen's parents," Adelio continued and laughed aloud at this memory. "Your father had quite a sense of humor."

My sisters' thoughts began to race as mine did at mention of the word "petal." In our mutual dream, the old-fashioned woman, who we all now assumed was our mother, referred to us as "petals." We all agreed that it was an interesting connection.

Brother Thomas entered the room and seemed excited and anxious.

"Friends, it is time for your departure. Please let's get to the shore. The brothers have packed some food and water for your trip." Just then, I saw a boat coming through fog on the loch. In the boat, there were five men in black cloaks. As they floated into shore, they unsheathed long swords and traveled with swift determination toward the abbey coming into contact with one of the abbey's security guards. With one immediate strike with a sword, the security guard crumpled onto the ground outside the door to the corridor of the building we were presently inside.

I gasped and looked with horror to Adelio, who had clearly witnessed this atrocity as well.

"We have to go, now. They are already on their way!" Adelio shouted to us as he grabbed his backpack as well as mine.

"Get your things and follow me." Neither my sisters nor Uncle Bob said a word, they just acted according to Adelio's command.

23

JOURNEY TO KIRANA

What I considered an oversized boat for our group of five was tied at the end of the long dock. It was probably about thirty eight feet long but only about fourteen feet wide with a cabin below the deck. The name painted across the stern was "Three Petals." We continued our quick pace, which was just short of a jog, to the end of the dock. My heart rate quickened, not from the brisk walking but from the site of so much fog and mist that was creeping up to the water's edge. It reminded me of my visions. I took a deep breath and noticed that the air smelled sweet, like Adelio. I reconciled that it must be "fairy dust" that created the cologne on Adelio and the odor in the air.

"Ok, girls," Uncle Bob instructed as he boarded the boat, "you know what to do." After many years of boating, both on sailboats and powerboats with Uncle Bob and our Crystal Lake friends, we knew how to conduct ourselves on a boat. We piled in and piled our bags in the cabin. Timber took Tulip out of her carrier and connected her leash to a latch in the aft cabin, located at the back of the boat in the cabin. I could hear Timber soothing the cat, telling her to rest and not to worry.

"Whose boat is this?" Marena asked. I was wondering the same thing.

"It belongs to you girls," Bob replied. "A gift from the Order of the Heather to assist in your safe passage back to Kirana."

"Wow! This is a nice gift. Looks brand new! I like these Heather people," Timber said as she emerged from the cabin. "Did you see the flat screen TV down there?"

"Let me start the engines before we untie the lines, Brother Thomas," Bob said. That was a cardinal rule he taught us about boating; always make sure the engines start before you detach from your mooring or the dock. Both of the inboard motors started right up and Adelio began to untie the fenders protecting the boat from the dock as Brother Thomas untied the lines from the cleats on the end of the pier. Uncle Bob pulled away from the pier very slowly.

"Good bye, children!" Brother Thomas called after us, "May God bless and keep you safe!" We waved at Thomas as our boat pulled further into the thick fog. The engine was incredibly loud, but I could hear my sister's thoughts loud and clear. They were frightened. They huddled together on the seat near the captain's chair, close to Uncle Bob, in the cockpit. I sat on the stern next to Adelio and could hardly see him through the fog. The breeze began to pick up and gust.

"How do we know where we are going?" I asked Adelio, trying to ensure that I was heard over the engines.

"You'll see, just hang on," he replied. Bob turned around and pointed to something in the fog toward the bow, but on the starboard side. Adelio stood up and grabbed a set of binoculars.

"Girls, into the cabin. Hurry!" He commanded us. My sisters stepped down into the kitchen area of the cabin. I stood to follow them.

"No, Avery stay up here with Bob and listen," Adelio dropped down into the cabin, "Timber, I need you to do something." I still was unclear as to what was going on, but then I saw the other boat coming through the fog toward us. It was the same sailing boat from my vision, barely visible through the dense mist. I could make out five figures.

"Remember, we're not being paid to be gentle, boys. We are paid to spill their blood. Ready your swords, we are close to the shore," said their leader.

"Sir, another boat," one of them reported. Just then, a huge wave came up out of the water and swamped the sailboat. I could hear the men yelling and scrambling for cover. I watched as the infamous Nessie lifted her head out of the water and head butted the boat until it capsized.

"Oh my goodness!" I exclaimed. "Did you see that?" Timber poked her head out of the aft cabin window.

"Did it work?" She asked.

"Did you do that? Did you talk to Nessie and tell her to do that, Timber?"

"Uh-huh. She's so sweet, but I did tell her she could eat the men if she caught them. Was that wrong?"

Adelio came back up to the deck and laughed a hearty laugh.

"Those men want to kill you, Timber, so I think it's quite all right for Nessie to have a little snack," Adelio was still laughing. Bob laughed too.

We continued on, apparently headed to the sea via the River Ness. We passed through the city of Inverness, where Bea had said she was performing research at one time or another. That probably was never true. I wondered what other secrets Bea and Bob had kept from us. The most obvious, of course, was that my sisters and I were to be the leaders of a magical fairyland. Despite all that had happened up to this point and all that was to come, I still could not help feeling a bit resentful toward my loving aunt and uncle. Had we known about our true background and identities sooner, the better prepared we would have been for what we were about to go through.

The sea began to get a bit choppy and the air was cold. I went below deck to retrieve a hooded sweatshirt from my backpack. I realized I needed my jacket too, so I dipped back into the cabin to grab it.

"North Sea?" I asked Uncle Bob as I came back into the cockpit.

"You bet. This ride is about to get interesting. Lasses, come back up here on deck so you don't get seasick in the cabin. We're about to hit a storm. Bring your slickers," Bob charged. Ahead of us, the fog seemed to become thinner, but the sea was churning violently. What seemed like at least twelve foot swells were breaking ahead of us as currents from three different directions were converging around us. The "storm" as Bob called it, was not exactly a rainstorm or a thunderstorm. It was probably worse, causing our small powerboat to twist and turn among the whitecaps. Seawater began to splash over the bow and onto the windshield. Even with the windshield wipers on, I could not imagine how Bob could see anything.

"Hang on gang. This is going to be a bumpy ride."

⌒っ

After what seemed like an agonizingly long time, our boat made it through the rough sea. We were all worse for the wear and wet. Marena got sick overboard twice and I could feel myself turning a bit green as well, while Timber seemed to enjoy the harrowing ride. We were very lucky to have Uncle Bob at the helm.

We still could not see land for the fog and mist, but the air was now still and the current calm. I noticed the air warming as well. We had slowed our pace temporarily and were traveling at trawler speed, about eight knots from what Uncle Bob said, so that we could eat and discuss our game plan.

"By now, Anyon already knows that his murderous plot failed, but what is bothering me is that he was able to send men to Fort Augustus at all," Adelio said as he bit into a sandwich of ham and cheese. "A member of the Order has clearly betrayed us."

"How do you know for sure? What if Anyon just found a map to Loch Ness and Fort Augustus?" I asked. Perhaps it was a naïve question, but I thought it was worth asking.

"For one thing, only the Order of the Heather is capable of travel to or from Kirana. I know this sounds strange, but a great degree of magic is involved even with our trip currently. Someone has shared this ability with Anyon, maybe by force or maybe through betrayal. Beyond the actual travel issue is the fact that Anyon knew you were in Scotland. Bea would not have told anyone, nor did she know you had followed her to the abbey until Bob called the Abbey and alerted her. Once I recognized that Bea was in danger of being taken from the abbey and you girls had already landed in Scotland, she had already been taken to Kirana."

"Seems like you just screwed up," Marena stated rather bluntly, "bad timing." Adelio seemed to become defensive at Marena's callous statement.

"Rena, you don't understand. Everything involving you and your family is carefully orchestrated and has been that way since you left Kirana. Something went wrong and I do not know what or how. That's a great problem when my task is supposed to be to protect you," Adelio argued. I suddenly understood the issue.

"So, we could be walking into a trap if we go directly to Kirana? That's what you are thinking?" I asked.

"Precisely, Avery. And I don't know whether the Order of the Heather has been compromised. I have not been able to see anything in Kirana since we initially saw those men coming through the fog for us last night. It is almost as if something is blocking my ability," Adelio told us. "We may be on our own for a while."

Uncle Bob, who had been silent and listening added, "Well, we should recover Bea first. We do not know whether she is in danger or not."

"Yes we should," Timber agreed, "but won't the bad people expect us to do that?"

"Listen, I had a dream about Bea leaving the abbey in a boat with one man. It was more like my other visions and…" Bob was immediately interested in what I was saying.

"Avery, what did the man look like? Was he old? How tall was he?" Bob inquired.

"He was not old, exactly, maybe a few years younger than you, Bob. He was much taller than Aunt Bea, but he seemed like he knew her very well. He had sort of sandy colored hair and, oh yeah, I almost forgot, he had these violet eyes," I reported.

"Like color contact lenses?" Marena asked.

"Yes, but he was wearing old fashioned clothes and…"

"A cloak," Both Timber and Marena finished my sentence.

"Yes, a cloak," I concluded.

Adelio looked at Bob with an inquisitive expression.

"Do you think it was Ginter?" Adelio asked Uncle Bob. Bob shrugged his shoulders and replied with an expression that seemed to say "couldn't be."

"Ginter? That's who Ginger, the cat in Luss, told me took Bea from the abbey," Timber blurted.

"Who is Ginter?" Marena asked.

Adelio answered, "Ginter is your mother's cousin and Kirana's Regent. Essentially, he heads the Royal Council in place of your father, but since Anyon conquered Kirana, Ginter has been presiding over the Council on behalf of Anyon. Yet, he has been loyal to your family, especially the Queen, so why would he try to lure you girls back to Kirana by taking Bea?" Adelio was problem solving aloud. This was all for Bob and my sisters' benefit, since I already knew what he was thinking.

"He wouldn't. There must be another reason Bea went with Ginter," Bob answered.

"In my vision, Bea appeared to be very conflicted, but I could tell she didn't seem to have a choice in leaving," I added.

"And that makes sense, because the vision I had showed Bea not leaving of her own accord, but Avery I saw five cloaked men in the boat with Bea, not just one," Adelio said.

"Well, there were other men in the big boat that took her, but just one man, this Ginter I guess, who spoke with her on the shore and then helped her into a row boat. The part of my dream in the big boat was not clear. There was a lot of that fog and mist you people seem to like so much so I couldn't see faces, just figures," I clarified.

"I suppose we won't be able to make sense of any of this until we get to Kirana," Bob stated and headed back to the captain's chair. He increased our speed and the engines roared once again.

❧

"Are we there yet?" Timber whined.

"No Timber, as I told you twenty minutes ago when you asked. When you see the sun beginning to break through the cloud cover, you will know we are close," Bob replied.

"So are we close?"

"Oh yes, we are close, Timber. Why don't you go down into the cabin with your sister and Tulip and sleep? The seas are calm now," Bob suggested.

"Rena will probably puke on me! Fine, I'll go, but I'm sleeping in the aft cabin, and not with the barf bag!" She headed down into the cabin. Timber always seemed to revert to childhood when she needed sleep and became a whiny, crank pot.

I was happy to see her agree to sleep. I, on the other hand, was too keyed up to rest. I felt as though I needed to be doing more to plan our trip to our homeland. Adelio could hear and sense my anxiety and came to my side. He took a seat next to me and reached for my right hand, forcing me to make eye contact with him. Silently, he spoke to me:

"Avery, I know a lot of what has happened has been confusing and I know that I have not made it easy for you with my evasiveness. I need to have a long conversation with you, but I need to do it without Marena knowing because I fear what I am going to say to you will affect her as well, and not in a positive way. It might hurt her feelings a bit."

"What is it? What do you mean?" I asked directly into his crystal, ocean eyes.

"You are not trained to block your thoughts from your sisters yet or me. That skill takes some time to develop and I will help you, but for now I need you to just listen without a reaction and then you must focus on another thought. We need to clear your mind so that Marena does not hear your thoughts."

"What is it that I am trying to hide from her? You know I can't keep secrets from my sisters," I replied. This new round of evasiveness elevated my anxiety level. It did not seem that Adelio could ever just say what he wanted to say to me.

"Avery, you and I are meant…"

"Oh my God! Oh my God! Ewwww!! Gross!" Timber was screeching from the aft cabin. She popped the hatch window open, which happened to be directly across from where Adelio and I were seated. I threw my head back in frustration. Timber's timing was flawless, as usual.

"Tulip just threw up on my leg," she whined and then she shook her head at Adelio and me and mouthed the words, "Rena is waking up." This was Timber's attempt to run interception, but it was also evidence that I was not able to block my thoughts at all.

"Oh, calm yourself lass, and grab a towel from under the sink," Uncle Bob yelled down to her.

"I will," she replied rolling her eyes. "Tulip didn't do anything," she whispered to us," I made that up to - you know - interrupt." Timber popped her head back down into the aft cabin. I could hear her offer to bring Rena some water from the cooler and some crackers. Rena was still not feeling well, apparently.

"We'll continue this another time," Adelio told me aloud with a sigh. I just smiled and nodded. Obviously whatever he needed to tell me was not life and death, but I truly could not piece together this secret without more information. I decided to join my sisters in the cabin for a snack. They were spreading peanut butter and jelly on crackers. Marena offered me an "hors d'oevres," as I sat down on the bench seat with Timber. Marena seemed in very good spirits considering how sick she had been only a few hours earlier. Timber pulled out a deck of cards and we decided to play a few hands of Rummy while Bob and Adelio spoke above us. I concentrated to try to hear Adelio. I don't know how, but Adelio recognized my attempt to read his thoughts and addressed me:

"Sorry Princess Avery, this is between your Uncle and me for the present time, but I promise I will speak to you again before we reach Kirana."

"Uhhh!" I groaned out loud. "I hate secrets!" Before my sisters could ask, I told them, "Never mind."

24

A MISUNDERSTANDING

Our boat drifted through a canopy of green. If not for the melodies and calls of the resident birdlife, the silence would have been deafening. The only other sound was the muffled whimpers of Marena from inside the boat's cabin. Sunlight streamed through the intertwined branches, which hung across the slow moving, but deep river leading us deeper into the forest.

The warmth of the sun on my face dried the damp tears that had made their way from my eyes to my cheeks. I could feel that my throat was scratchy and dry, a common side effect of teenage misery. I rubbed my eyes with the back of my right hand.

My body began to shudder once again with the silent words from Marena that floated into my mind:

"I will never forgive you for this," she whispered through her thoughts, "never."

"Avery, get up!" I could feel the weight of both Timber and Marena on my back and my legs. This was a common method of waking one of us up at our house.

"Get off, fatties! Oww! You're breaking my back!" I teased them.

"We can see it! We can see Kirana, come look!" Timber exclaimed as she rolled off my left leg and proceeded back up to the deck. This was the same tone of voice and excitement I remembered when she first saw Cinderella's castle at Disney World when she was nine years old. Bea and Bob took us on the obligatory trip to Disney when I was in fifth grade. I remember that Marena told us that when she grew up, she was going to be a princess and live in a castle.

Timber was going to be her maid, but Marena would let her wear pretty dresses and live in the castle. Bea suggested that they both could be princesses together and Marena reluctantly agreed. I chuckled in my head at the irony of that memory as I flipped my body over beneath Marena, who had been straddling my back.

"Ok, you need to get up, Rena."

Marena grabbed my wrists and held them over my head on the pillow. This move usually preceded a "tickle attack," but instead Marena leaned in and whispered into my left ear, singing: "I know something you don't know." She giggled with glee and jumped off of the V-berth mattress onto the floor.

I sat up quickly, probably a little too rapidly as I felt a bit dizzy.

"What do you know? Come on Rena, tell me," I whispered trying to coax the secret out of her. I had a butterfly feeling in my stomach because I was fully aware that my sister could never keep a secret and would tell me. I was not confident I wanted to know. The raw memory of the dream I had just had was causing my trepidation.

"Ok, but don't tell Timber yet because I want to tell her. Swear?"

"Yeah, fine. What is it?" The suspense was beginning to hurt. Marena took my hands in hers and squeezed them. It was a an uncharacteristically affectionate action for Marena and it caught me very off guard, so much so that I pulled my hands away from her and folded them at my chest.

"Well?" I prodded.

"Adelio and I are getting married," she whispered, "isn't that wonderful?" She grabbed me and gave me an enormous squeeze. Although I recognized the words she used, I was unsure of what I actually heard.

"He asked you…?" I could not complete the sentence. I could feel my chest tighten, my stomach churn and my ears beginning to get hot. Marena's declaration was completely irrational and made no sense to me whatsoever. It could not possibly be true.

"Oh no, he didn't come right out and ask or anything. I mean, I'm too young to get married now anyway and I'm sure Bea would say 'no' until I'm at least eighteen," Marena was starting to babble in an overly joyful manner, which ordinarily would not have bothered me in the least, so I had to interrupt.

"If he didn't ask you - I don't understand…"

"Ok, so get this," she began, "because you, me and Timber are the chosen Trinity thingy, our future husbands are chosen for us by the Order of the Heather and there is a special ceremony where we are sealed to one another. He said that this is the way it's been done since the beginning of the Hazaro line of succession." She took a breath and continued. I could tell by her recount of the conversation she had had while I was sleeping that she didn't quite understand all of what she was told, Marena heard what she wanted to hear.

"So Adelio said that before we all left Kirana, we were sealed to our future mates. Usually the ceremony takes place when we are fifteen years old, but because our parents were sending us away from Kirana, the ceremony was held secretly after Timber and I were born. The three of us were sealed the night before we were taken from Kirana and sent to Scotland. Isn't that amazing?" I didn't respond because, despite asking the question, Marena had no intention of allowing me to answer.

"Adelio is my soul mate! Of course, I knew that as soon as we met, I mean we are so perfect for each other, but isn't that so amazing?" Now I could sense that Marena was fishing for a response from me.

"He told you that you were his soul mate? That you were sealed to one another in Kirana?" That was the obvious question, a detail Marena left out of her account.

"Adelio didn't have to because I just knew it when he explained the whole thing to me," she replied. "Oh, and get this - your soul mate can hear all your thoughts so you can talk to each other like we do and you can train your thoughts so that no one else can hear your conversation. Isn't that wild? I'm sure after I learn more about our powers and practice, I will be able to hear Adelio's thoughts."

"So you don't hear them now?" I asked.

"Not yet, but I can already tell what he is thinking. We have that kind of a special bond already," she replied. My uneasy feeling began to wash away as I realized the import of our conversation. Just as I was about to ask another question, Adelio made an appearance in my head and in the cabin.

"Avery, please end the conversation," he instructed abruptly. "I really made a mess of things with your sister, I tried to explain it all to her, but let's not worry about it right now. Once she meets her soul mate in Kirana, all will make sense to her. The truth can wait for now," Adelio promised. I rolled my eyes and smiled.

"Girls," he said aloud, "we're home. Come on up and take a look. It's a bonnie day outside and we can see the coastline and the city already." Marena smiled at me, took my hand and guided me toward Adelio at the steps.

"Remember what I told you," she silently said to me, "this is a secret that I want to tell Timber." I nodded in agreement. I once again recalled my most recent dream and connected the dots. I knew I had to at least try to prevent what might have been the inevitable.

"Your secret is safe with me," I told her silently.

❦

The scenery before us was simply breathtaking. We did not speak aloud, but my sisters and I shared our thoughts. Timber was too excited to even finish a complete sentence in her own head and Marena was distracted by Adelio. Kirana was obviously a land of rainbows and butter-flies. Golden sunlight streamed across green rolling hills in the distance while the same sunlight glistened off of the buildings and structures that we could see in the forefront. One particular building stood out from the rest, and without really knowing what it was, I knew it was our home, the palace.

Pilton Palace looked as if it was torn from the pages of an English history book. It reminded me of the artistic renderings of Hampton Court from Elizabethan Times. It was a grand estate, and I was sure, even more amazing inside. Marena took a moment away from staring at Adelio to admire our home.

"Is that Pilton where our mother lives? Is that where we're going?" She asked.

"It is, but no we aren't going there," Bob replied.

"We need to get you girls to the Order of the Heather. Undoubtedly, Anyon knows we have arrived in Kirana, but he won't be able to get to us if we have the protection of the Order," Adelio stated. This was a logical and well-reasoned decision that seemed to have been made on our behalf, but my sisters were not happy about it.

"Yes, but we haven't seen our mother in sixteen years. Can't we meet her and then go hide with the fairies?" Timber inquired. We already knew the answer.

"No we can't do that, sorry girls. You'll see her soon, don't worry yourselves," Bob replied. Timber pouted anyway.

As we approached the coastline, Uncle Bobril asked us to go down into the cabin and remain there until he decided it was safe. Neither he nor Adelio wanted to take any chances that we would be seen by any inquiring minds, which was completely understandable. However, the last place I wanted to be was in close quarters with Marena who was clearly obsessed with her perceived betrothal to Adelio.

To avoid the painfully unavoidable conversation, I told my sisters I was going to take a nap in the aft cabin. I grabbed my iPod, which I had been able to charge through the power on the boat, and connected to my favorite playlist. Unfortunately, I could not completely block out Marena's dialogue with Timber, planning her bridesmaids' dresses. Nor could I avoid hearing that I was apparently "jealous" of Marena's good fortune, having found her soul mate. Ordinarily, these types of Marena comments would cause an argument, and I summoned every ounce of restraint I had in my body to avoid sharing a negative thought with either sister. The music helped me through that challenge, and I made a mental note to honor the singer, Taylor Swift, in some way when I became Queen of Kirana.

25

THE GROOM OF THE WOOL

After what seemed to have been hours, Adelio lifted our banishment to the cabin and invited us back up to the deck.

"Whoa! Where are we?" Timber asked as she emerged from the cabin holding Tulip.

"We, Princess, are on the Throagtone River headed to Prenmar Forest," Adelio answered.

"This is so cool! It looks like a ride at Disney or something! Doesn't it, Rena?"

"Don't be so juvenile, Timber," Marena criticized.

"Marena, be nice. I agree with Timber, this looks like one of those pirate rides we took at that Walter Disney's World," Bob added.

"Walt Disney, Uncle Bob," Timber corrected him.

"Right, well I'm sure his mother calls him Walter," Bob laughed.

"You're unusually quiet," Adelio commented to me silently. He touched my shoulder and I turned to look into his dazzling eyes. Every time I looked at Adelio or thought about Adelio, I felt as though my heart grew in size. Right now, I was exceptionally nervous and my thoughts explained why that was.

"We have to try to prevent that from happening," Adelio replied.

"I know, but look around you. This is the exact scene from my dream. It's only a matter of time before she knows. Maybe if I avoid her?"

"Maybe," Adelio shrugged, "I think you also should avoid me at this point if you want to prevent hurting Marena." My heart sank but I knew he was right. I nodded and he squeezed my shoulder as if to say goodbye for now. I could feel the tears welling up inside of me, but luckily, Timber interrupted my sad thoughts. She sat right on my lap.

"What are you doing? You're going to crush me!"

"No I won't!" She giggled and then whispered to me, "I'll help you. I'll be right here." Then she added silently, "Adelio tried to tell her. But you know Marena. Avery, you're not responsible for Marena's irrational emotional responses, although we should avoid them or she might sink our boat." I smiled at my little sister and she winked back just as Marena also decided to add herself to my lap. She obviously had not heard our conversation. I was glad that Marena's mind reading abilities were for some reason developing more slowly than mine or Timber's.

"Ok! Get off me!" I yelled at them as I felt my knees practically crushing under their weight.

"Ha! Fine, I'm sure Adelio won't mind if I sit on his lap," she teased.

"No, but I would Rena. That is not appropriate, lass. Not at home and especially not in Kirana. You are a princess and must act accordingly. Princesses do not sit on strange boys laps," Bob admonished her.

"He's not a strange boy, Uncle Bob. Adelio is my…"

"Friend!" Timber completed the sentence for her and Marena quickly understood the message, at least she thought she did.

"Right and I was just kidding Bob. Lighten up, old man!" She teased our Uncle.

"Adelio, you hear that? Old man? Can you believe it? I'm an old man!" Bob laughed.

"You wouldn't think your Uncle an old man if you heard some of the stories I have…" Adelio told us.

"Really? Like what?" Timber probed. I could tell Bob was starting to get uncomfortable as I could see his cheeks flush, but I was very curious to hear Adelio's stories of our uncle.

"Ha, ha ha…" he laughed, "Well, my favorite one involves Bobril, a herd of sheep and a certain young lady…"

"Oh brother! That one?" Bob interrupted.

"Tell us, tell us, tell us," Timber chanted while Marena joined her.

"All right, twist my arm - remember the story about how your Uncle Bob and I met, helping King Philson and his boating debacle? Well, this story occurred a few months later. Since Philson was so grateful that Bob was able to save his boat, he gave him a special position at the royal court - Groom of the Wool," Adelio began.

"What's the Groom of the Wool?" Timber asked the obvious question.

"Let me guess," I said, "You're the guy in charge of sheep?" I said to Bob.

"Good guess, Avery," he replied. "Yes, the sheep. Wool really. One of our major exports is Kiranian Wool. It is some of the finest wool in the whole world and in great demand. Over the last two-hundred or so years, we learned how to export it to the mainland of Scotland without any question as to its origin. One of our chief defenses against Scottish or British invaders has been our wool trade. We send the wool to a select number of Scottish clans throughout the nation, and they work to ensure our secret existence is safe. To be sure, I would guess that most of the wool products made in Scotland come from Kiranian Wool, although people think it is from places like the Hebrides or Shetland. But that's another story. Sorry Adelio, continue…"

"Right, so Bob's job was to oversee the production and export of wool from the royal herds, which produced the finest quality wool in all the land. Really, the system ran itself since the men and women who raised the sheep and sheared them had complete control of the production. Within a few days of assuming this position, Bob realized that other than reporting on numbers, you know - profits or losses - there was not much he needed to do. But, this was a very prestigious position in the Court so in an effort to impress a certain lady…"

"Awww, Aunt Bea?" Marena interrupted.

"No lass, this was some time before I met Bea. I was courting another young woman - I mean, dating as you girls would say. Her name was…"

"Celista," Adelio declared with Bob in chorus, "Lady Celista of Langford was the youngest daughter of the Duke of Langford, Lord Alby Jons. Lord Jons was a high ranking official within the Royal Council and let's just say was not pleased at the attention your Uncle Bob paid his daughter, or the attention she paid Bob."

"I was not good enough for Celista, for sure, as far as her father was concerned. I was a working man with nothing of my own, other than what the gracious King, your father gave me. As far as Lord Jons was concerned, his daughter would be married to a Duke or a Viscount, someone of noble blood. Of course, after raising three girls myself, I totally understand that now. Anyway, go on Adelio…"

"Celista was quite a beauty and sort of a wild girl, ready to have fun. One night after a rather raucous evening celebration, your uncle and Celista along with some other young members of the royal court wandered out to the barns where the sheep were kept to continue the party. Keep in mind, I was not present, I just heard about this story as it spread like wild fire through the court. Somehow, Celista and Bobril were alone in one of the barns. Celista wanted to pet the sheep so Bob opened a pen, not realizing it was the only pen in the barn. The entire herd escaped and made its way into the Palace courtyard."

"Uncle Bob!" Marena laughed. "What were you thinking?"

"I was thinking I would do anything for this Celista Langford, is what! Well, needless to say, I was collecting sheep until the wee hours of the morning. Celista fell asleep on a hay bale in the barn waiting for me. Her father's men came after me and roughed me up pretty good. Lord Jons wanted to charge me with indecency with his daughter, but the King was more concerned about the sheep. I was relieved of my position as Groom of the Wool, but I remained on the Royal Council as Privy Liaison to the Seafarers, a much more appropriate position for me."

"What about Celista? What happened to her?" Timber asked.

"Well, Lady Celista was sent to the country to her mother and did not return to court, except for special events like your birth announcements and sealing ceremonies," Adelio replied.

"So you never saw her again?" I could tell Marena was concerned that Bob had some unrequited love connection with this girl.

"Oh no, I did see her on occasion and for a while we would secretly meet and talk, but as the months passed, and she stopped answering my letters I knew it was over," he told us.

"Aww, Bob. That's so sad!" Marena commented.

Bob laughed, "I suppose, things work the way they do in the world for a reason. Bea and you girls are the best things that ever happened to me, so I have no regrets about Lady Celista Langford."

"Hey, is that a guy waving at us over there?" Timber was pointing ahead of us to the river-bank. Adelio grabbed the binoculars and suddenly became very excited. He was waving back to the man exuberantly.

"Is it…?" Bob asked him.

"'Tis. We are closer than I thought," Adelio answered. Bob headed closer to the shore and activated the windlass to drop anchor.

"'Tis whom? What's going on?" I asked them.

"Barlow!" Adelio exclaimed. Just then a rather swarthy young man swinging from a vine like Tarzan, landed on the bow of our boat. He was dressed in what appeared to me to be a pirate- meets-Robin Hood costume. He looked about Adelio's age and was very handsome in a rugged, outdoorsy, "hasn't bathed in weeks" sort of way. He had longer dark brown hair pulled back with a leather strap at the nape of his neck and dark blue eyes.

"Barlow, meet the Princesses de Hazaro; Avery, Marena and Timber," we each waved, reluctantly, as Adelio introduced us. Barlow bowed his head to us, which gave me a little shiver since it was really the first time anyone recognized our position in Kirana. "And I think you already know this gentleman…"

"Good God, when did you get so old? Ha ha! How are you my friend?" Barlow had a deep, but laid back voice with a strong accent. I recognized it as more English than Scottish. He jumped down from the bow as Bobril stood for a long awaited, friendly embrace.

"Old? We're practically the same age, you rascal! I am well, and you? How is life treating you now?"

"It's a challenge day to day. I am surviving, though," Barlow stated as he wandered down to the stern where we were seated. "Well, well well! I daresay there is no fairer Lady, fairy or otherwise in all of Kirana than these three here. Bobril, you have done well. Luckily, they look nothing like you!" This comment made Timber snicker. Barlow winked at my sister and gave her a charming smile. I could tell that she was blushing as she put her head down and stared at her feet. Timber was never overly comfortable with attention, especially from boys.

"And you, Princess Avery?" Barlow took both of my hands and kissed them. Now I was blushing. "You will be the most beautiful Queen ever to rule Kirana. I can see it already." He knelt down on one knee and kissed my hands again, slowly and deliberately. In all honestly, I was quite taken with Barlow's attention and unsolicited adoration until I heard Adelio in my thoughts complain:

"Avery!" My conscience reminded me I was spoken for, sort of. I recovered my hands from my newest fan and smiled.

"Thank you for the warm welcome, Mr. Barlow, but may I ask what you are doing here?"

"It's just Barlow, Princess and yes, I am here to offer you safe passage to and through Prenmar Forest and I offer you my services as protectorate of the blessed Trinity," he answered.

"We should get moving while we still have the light of day," Adelio answered, joining us on the stern. He unlatched the dinghy attached to the back of the boat and lowered it to the water. Only one line now connected the inflatable boat to Three Petals.

"Girls, go get Tulip and only bring your backpacks with whatever you absolutely need for the next few days. Hear me? One bag each!" Bobril instructed us. "And Timber, we can't take Tulip's hard carrier, it will be too difficult to carry. We can put her in my backpack with the mesh bits on it, like we did when we went camping that one time in Stokes Forest." I could see the dismay on Timber's face. That camping trip with Tulip was a bad idea, but Timber insisted that the cat be part of our weekend adventure. Timber remembered, as I did that Tulip was less than a good sport about riding in Bob's backpack, mesh or not. Bob had the scars on his arm to prove it.

"Fine, but I will carry her, Uncle Bob and you can carry my backpack. I guess I don't need my laptop here," Timber compromised.

We all grabbed our necessities from the cabin, which for me included a few pudding packs, just in case, as well as what was left of my clean clothes and my asthma inhalers. Adelio had already thrown his bag into the dinghy. We made an assembly line from the cabin stairs to the swim platform at the extreme rear of the boat, and passed our belongings to him to place in the little boat. The last bag passed along contained Tulip, and Timber warned Adelio to "be careful" with her little friend.

Barlow was already in the dinghy and Bob joined him. Bob started the engine and gave Adelio the "ok" to start the boarding process for my sisters and me. Marena carefully stepped into the little boat, lingering unnecessarily while Adelio offered her his hand. Next, I reached for Adelio's hand for assistance, but before I could make contact with his fingers, there was a splash to my left, followed by "I'm ok!"

"Princess overboard! I'll save you, Your Grace!" Barlow reached his right hand out to my sister.

"Don't bother getting in the water or anything, geez!" Marena noticed. Barlow smiled and offered Timber his left hand as well.

"You'd better get out of the water before anything decides to take a nibble. We've got plesiosaurs - you know, Nessies in here, lots of them, and they don't always limit their diet to shell fish, if you catch my drift," Barlow told her.

"I'm ok. They won't hurt me," Timber said, "besides, it's really nice in here. How can this place and this water be so warm when Scotland is so chilly most of the year?" She was floating alongside the dinghy, holding on to the ropes attached to the sides as Barlow lifted her back into the boat.

"Well, Your Grace, we have a lot more sun than the mainland. In fact, in summer, we have sun just about all of the time. The rest of the year, we only have about three hours of dark and we get up to seven hours in winter," Barlow explained as he pulled my drenched sister into the Zodiac tender.

"How do you sleep?" Marena asked.

"What do you mean? When we are tired, we sleep. We do have drapery and shutters." Now the Kiranian sense of time was starting to make a little sense to me. Adelio and Bob had mentioned to us that time occurred differently in Kirana and to a degree it explained how Uncle Bob aged sixteen years since leaving Kirana, but Adelio only aged about two years since we left. Adelio had used the phrase "Kiranian years" in describing how long it had been since we were sent from Kirana.

My sisters began thinking about what it meant to have perpetual sunlight as Adelio and I climbed into the boat.

"Your Highness, you should sit by me so I can protect you," Barlow bragged. There was something about his boldness that I really enjoyed so I slid next to him on the edge of the boat. He put his arm around my waist.

"Can't have another of you fall in, can we?" He joked squeezing my middle into his body. I shook my head. I liked the way his arm felt around my sides and I leaned into his body. I could tell Adelio was not pleased with the way I had become so comfortable with Barlow. He sat with his arms folded, just staring at Barlow. Barlow noticed too.

"Sorry my friend, do I have something you want?" Barlow asked Adelio.

"No, no - it's nothing. I'm just thinking..." While I knew Adelio could not say what he probably wanted to say to Barlow with Marena sitting next to us, I was somewhat disappointed that he did not at least protest the attention Barlow was paying to me. Of course, we had more important issues at hand.

Uncle Bob maneuvered the small watercraft toward the eastern bank of the river. Apparently, the plan was to leave the big powerboat on its anchor so that it could be recovered by the fairies who would tow it downriver toward the castle at Swenwood. Adelio thought that this plan would keep Anyon in the dark a little longer regarding our exact whereabouts, giving us time to come under the full protection of the Order of the Heather. Barlow agreed with Adelio, in any case, and we just went along with this plan. I felt even safer that we had Barlow in addition to Uncle Bob and Adelio protecting us on our journey.

As we approached the riverbank, Barlow squeezed me closer to himself and he whispered into my right ear:

"Majesty, can I just say that I am truly humbled to be of service to you and your sisters?"

"Thank you, Barlow," I replied not really knowing what this unsolicited compliment meant.

"Your husband will be a very lucky man and I envy the fool already knowing he will have the privilege of basking in the glow of your exquisite beauty each day." I knew I was blushing and with this over the top compliment, I looked to Adelio who had obviously heard Barlow's comments to me. He was looking at me, smiling.

"I shall be a lucky woman too," I told Barlow. He removed his hand from my waist and rather swiftly, jumped out of the boat into the shallow water. Adelio followed Barlow and the two of them pulled the boat onto the shore.

"Everybody out! Girls and cats, everybody out," Uncle Bob sang. We all grabbed our backpacks and walked to the front of the boat to exit. Adelio and Barlow were at the bow to assist us. I looked ahead of us. Despite the sunlight, the forest in front of us was quite dark.

"Now what?" I asked, "Are we going in?" I answered my own question.

"Yes, lass. Welcome to Prenmar Forest," Barlow answered.

26

TIME KEEPS ON SLIPPING

The path through the trees had clearly been well traveled and as the light of this very long day waned, the sounds of birds calling changed to insects chirping.

"What time is it?" Timber asked Adelio.

"It's twilight-time," he replied.

"Yeah, but what *time* is it? 7 o'clock? 9 o'clock?" She asked again, this time yawning. Her yawn was contagious and Marena and I joined her and yawned too.

"Kirana time is different from what you are used to in the rest of the world. We deal more in periods of time relative to where the sun is in the sky," Adelio explained. "Our day starts at dawn, then comes morning, which lasts until the sun is high in the sky at high noon, then it is the afternoon followed by dusk when the sun goes down, and finally, nighttime.

"It is the springtime so there is much less darkness than during the winter. The darkness will last about two, maybe three hours until dawn begins to break and the sun rises again. In the summer time, there is no darkness at all," Adelio continued.

"Well then how do you measure a day of life?" I inquired.

"Well, a day is from dawn to dusk. So in the summer when there is no darkness at all, no night, the day lasts until the darkness returns again. You'll understand it more as the days pass," he assured us.

"Holy moley! So one day could last comparatively for months? No wonder you people don't age normally!" Marena exclaimed.

"Well, now I get your tans. No one in Scotland has a tan unless they went on vacation somewhere else," Timber added.

"So, if I'm tired now can I sleep now?" Marena asked.

"No, lass. We need to get to the encampment. Don't worry, it's not far and there'll be plenty of food and merriment once we arrive," Barlow promised. Suddenly, Marena was not quite so sleepy.

"Really? Like a party? Well, who will be there?" She asked.

"Some folks from the Order of the Heather, I suppose," he replied. Marena was very excited at the prospect of a party. She grabbed Adelio's right arm.

"Will there be music and dancing?" She asked.

"Of course, your Grace!"

"You'll dance with me, right?" She asked Adelio, whispering. He unhinged her fingers from his forearm and nodded. Marena squealed with excitement and ran ahead to where Timber was walking with Uncle Bob, right behind Barlow. I could hear her explaining her connection with Adelio to Timber. Timber turned around to look at me, knowing that I could hear their conversation. I just shrugged back at her. At this point, what was I supposed to do? Marena always heard what Marena wanted to hear and given her developing powers and her last reaction to my thoughts of Adelio and me, telling her the truth now was not a good idea. Timber shook her head, as if to say "you're making a big mistake here." I just shrugged again. This decision was not mine to make. When Adelio was ready to reveal our betrothal, it would be revealed.

We had both agreed to wait until we reached the palace, once everything is sorted. Of course, I still had the lingering memory of my vision of a very sad and angry Marena. I could only assume that this issue would cause her that pain. Part of me just wanted to get it over with already so that Adelio and I could be together as was intended. The other part of me, who loved my sister more than anything in the world, wanted to protect her from pain. This sacrifice, however small, would likely make all the difference in the world to her in the end. It seemed that we just had to get her to meet her own sealed partner, and then she would forget all about Adelio. I hoped that would happen soon.

We continued along the path deeper into Prenmar Forest and as afternoon slowly turned to dusk, we saw the light of a large fire ahead of us as we traversed a rather steep hillside and reached its summit.

"Oh, thank goodness!" I exclaimed aloud, completely out of breath. "We're here, right Barlow?" I felt like I needed my asthma inhaler, but tried to cough which caused me to have a bit of a coughing fit. I was so embarrassed, and I knew I would be fine in a moment if I could just reach my inhaler in my backpack. I began to rummage through the front pocket. It was never where it was supposed to be located when I needed it.

"Indeed. Highness? Do you need help, Princess?" Barlow rushed over to me. I shook my head, still coughing. I realized my wheezing was probably frightening to Barlow and

Adelio. Uncle Bobril and my sisters were very accustomed to my asthmatic episodes, which had improved quite a bit as I grew older.

I triumphantly raised my Albuterol inhaler into the air, still coughing.

"She'll be fine. This happens all the time if she over exerts herself, physically," Timber assured Barlow and Adelio, who appeared rather alarmed. She was a bit out of breath as well. The hill we just climbed was deceptively steep.

I sucked in two puffs of the medicine, coughed a few more deep coughs and immediately regained my composure. My eyes had watered and teared and I knew my face was completely red at this point, so terribly embarrassing.

"Princess, you need medical assistance. I will carry you to the encampment where you can be properly treated," Barlow instructed me and without any additional warning, flung me over his shoulder in a firefighter's carry position.

"Not necessary! Please, put me down," I yelled, startling my would-be hero. He returned me to my feet and bowed his head in obedience and respect.

"Sorry, your Majesty. I only wanted - sorry," he mumbled.

"It's fine, Barlow. Thank you for your concern, but I'm just fine," I assured him gratefully. He bowed his head again and began walking toward the fire. As we got closer to the encampment, I counted six to eight people gathered around the fire. I concentrated to try to hear them, but for some reason could not.

"Fairy minds are most difficult to read," Adelio told me silently, "but you'll learn." There was a lot I had to learn, clearly.

⁓

"May I present to you, Her Royal Highness, Princess Avery de Hazaro…" All of the men and women at the encampment stopped what they were doing and faced us in deep curtsies and bows and acknowledged me in chorus.

"Your Grace," they all replied to Barlow's announcement. He similarly introduced Timber and Marena. Timber physically shuddered at the announcement of her full name, which made me giggle. She really did get the short end of the name stick and I know Timber had a lot of questions for our mother about it. Hearing her own name to Timber was like hearing fingernails scraping along on a chalk board.

Barlow introduced Bobril too as "His Grace, Duke of Easton," which caught him by surprise.

"Since when?" He asked Adelio. Adelio slapped Bob on his back.

"Since you left Kirana. His Majesty, the King granted you all of the lands and titles associated with Easton including a seat on the Royal Council. This, for your service and bravery to the Royal Family. He granted you this position without consideration of his sister, Beata's titles so he has given you Easton in your own right," Adelio informed him. I could tell Bob was floored by this information. He was speechless but obviously excited.

"Of course, I'm sure Anyon has probably altered the property maps by now," Adelio snickered, "but your place on the council remains for you, under Ginter of course since he serves as Regent of Kirana."

"I - I just can't believe it," Bobril stammered, "Me - a Duke?"

"Wow, Uncle Bob," said Marena, "That job probably beats your old one with Port Authority, huh?" Bob laughed and hugged his niece.

"Yes, I would imagine this is a bit of a promotion."

"Come everyone, I want to introduce you to some wonderful people," Barlow urged.

"Can we put our things somewhere and clean up a bit? I feel like I have a week's worth of dust and dirt on me," I asked. I recognized that personal hygiene was not a major priority in the woods, but I was feeling quite ripe and at the very least needed to change my clothes.

Barlow agreed and led us to a rather well decorated and billowy white tent at the south side of the campsite. Inside the tent, layered tapestries created the outer walls and curtains partitioned the living space. A number of young women in gold colored gowns scurried about and then came to attention as we all entered. They curtsied before us.

"These women will care for you while we are here in Prenmar. Whatever you need or desire, they will help," Barlow told us. The women curtsied again, acknowledging their role.

"Oh my gosh, we have servants!" Marena exclaimed through her thoughts. "This is going to be totally awesome!" I laughed and decided to introduce myself to the one older woman who seemed to be in charge of the others.

"Hello, I'm Avery and these are my sisters Marena and Timber," I told her. "What's your name?"

"I am Honora, your Chief Chambermaid and here are Donnelle, Mergard and Pentil," she said referring to the three other women behind her. They all curtsied to us again. "Let us help you dress, you must have had quite a journey, your Graces." Honora directed us toward what seemed to be a more private area in the tent, separated by long and beautiful drapes. Already this tent seemed to be more nicely appointed than our house in Woodport. Now I sort of understood from where Bea's expensive tastes in home decorations came. She had obviously been accustomed to a luxurious lifestyle when she was home in Kirana. I wondered if there was a Pottery Barn in Kirana.

"Come gentlemen, we can leave the ladies for a moment and I will show you where you can dress and leave your bags," Barlow led Adelio and Bobril out of our large tent, bowing to us as he exited.

"I'll be right next to you, Avery," Adelio told me in my thoughts.

"Thank you, we'll be fine," I replied although I appreciated knowing Adelio was so close. It was getting to a point where he would leave my sight, even for a few moments and my heart would ache. I was working very hard at not letting my growing adoration of Adelio be apparent to others, but I wondered how long I could keep this charade going. The fact of the matter was that some natural force was driving my heart, my mind and maybe even my soul to fall madly and deeply in love. The inability to demonstrate how I was feeling was becoming cumbersome in itself. I just wanted to be with him, now and always.

Honora lead us over to three ornately carved chests and gestured for the other three maids to open them.

"What's this?" Marena asked.

"Just a few gowns that were made for you in anticipation of your blessed and glorious return to Kirana," Honora told us with a triumphant tone to her voice. She reached into the trunk in front of me and pulled out what looked like a costume from a movie. It was beautiful; purple with gold trim and it looked like it would fit me.

"I'm to wear this? Now?" I asked.

"Of course, Highness. You can't stay in these - these - whatever these are," she remarked pointing to my jeans and gray "Legally Blonde: The Musical" t-shirt. We had gone to see the show at the New Jersey Performing Arts Center with our neighbor, Amanda for her birthday a few months ago. Marena especially loved it, more for the reason that she thought she could sing all of the songs and actually be in the show in the not too distant future. The show, based on a movie about a girl who follows her boyfriend to Harvard Law School, made me think that I might want to be a lawyer someday.

"Well, it's just that I don't want to mess up this nice dress sitting around a fire, you know in the dirt and stuff," I told her. I was amazed that gowns had already been made for us and wondered how a dress maker who had never met or seen us could know our measurements. Then I remembered that Bea had us measured for dance costumes for the North Jersey Scottish Cultural Society's Robert Burns Supper this past January. We had never had to be measured for that event before so Marena, Timber and I thought it strange that all of our measurements - from bust to hips to inseam - were measured when we ended up wearing the same tartan skirts we wore the prior year. Bea obviously was up to something at the time, and apparently it had to do with these gowns.

In thinking about all of that, I began to think about Aunt Bea, hoping that she was all right. Since arriving in Kirana, we had not heard anything about where she was or what was happening to her, although it was useless to worry about something completely out of our control. No one seemed to believe she was in any danger. In any case, I still did not feel like climbing into a stuffy gown to sit around a campfire.

"Come, ladies. Let us get you presentable and beautiful," Honora announced ignoring my concerns. Honora motioned to the other ladies to start whatever process they had planned. Marena was very excited at the prospect of this quasi-royal makeover. Timber and I, however, were skeptical and not overly interested in putting on a dress at this point. I was hoping Honora, who seemed completely in charge and kind of bossy, would reconsider when suddenly she said: "On second thought, why don't you just wear what you prefer and we can save the gowns for more of an official coming out."

"Oh, thank you Honora. You read my mind!" I laughed.

"No dearest Highness, I do not have such powers, nor should I ever profess to," Honora replied.

"Oh, that's just an expression we say back home in - well, in the rest of the world. I know you can't read my mind," I said. Really, I did not know very much about anyone or anything in Kirana. Why was I supposed to wear a costume that an actor at a Renaissance Faire might wear? Why was this place stuck in the Middle Ages?

Frankly, I kind of liked the historical aspect and the formality of it all. It was if we had traveled back in time. I was pretty sure we hadn't undergone any actual time travel, although even that would not have surprised me given all we had experienced already in getting to Kirana.

Honora helped us wash up and change into clean clothes. As a compromise, we agreed to wear flowers in our hair that the ladies plaited, or braided for us in complicated styles and we agreed to put on these extremely comfortable satin robes over our clothes. I caught my reflection in the full-length mirror as we walked out of the tent. Even with my jeans and sneakers sticking out from the bottom of my flowing purple robe, I looked somewhat regal already. I certainly smelled a whole lot better.

We joined Adelio, Uncle Bob and Barlow by the fire and sat down in folding cloth chairs. There were musicians playing what sounded like Celtic folk music and everyone seemed to be enjoying him or herself. We were presented with full plates of fruits and vegetables to eat and wine. Before we each took a sip, we looked to Uncle Bob.

"Yes girls, you may drink the wine. The rules are a bit different here than back home, I mean in Woodport. Help yourselves to whatever you want, whether it is the ale or wine. Just take it easy and do not overdo it." Marena was particularly excited about the prospect of having permission to underage drink, although it was not underage drinking in Kirana. She always liked the idea of doing something she probably should not be doing.

As we dined, the women and men at the encampment came to us one by one and introduced themselves to us. Everyone was very kind and genuinely excited to make our acquaintances. They all wanted to touch us and kiss our hands, which was weird. Marena did not find it strange at all and basked in the glow of her admirers. She looked like a natural royal in her posture and demeanor. Even Timber seemed to be getting the hang of smiling and nodding appropriately and she could be extremely awkward in social situations. Where I might stutter or slur my words, Timber could say the weirdest things. On many occasions, Timber would end up offending someone involved in the conversation, not because she was trying to be funny or mean, just because she did not know the more appropriate thing to say. More often than not, Timber would listen to a conversation rather than participate.

Once it had appeared that everyone at the campsite had met us, two taller and very distinguished older men approached us. Adelio introduced them as members of the Order of the Heather, Lankin and Remble. Apparently, these men were to become our tutors over the next few days. They seemed very kind and soft-spoken. They reminded me of the school psychologist I was forced to meet in middle school after I wrote an essay for the D.A.R.E., anti-drug program at school. It was this mandatory class New Jersey implemented in all of the schools in the 1990s. In sixth grade, I wrote my essay about my parents and the consequences of their drug use. Since no one had any idea about our background, my teacher believed I was reaching out for help. The school decided I should visit with the school psychologist, Dr. Brad, every day for a week until Dr. Brad agreed that I was completely well adjusted and not negatively affected by any of the elements I wrote of in my essay. Dr. Brad agreed that I was just fine, and he even gave helpful advice on being the oldest sibling. Remble definitely reminded me of Dr. Brad, who probably wasn't a real doctor, come to think of it.

The night wore on and I became extremely sleepy. Marena and Timber caught a second wind and were dancing with Adelio and Bobril. I excused myself and made my way back to the tent. With the assistance of Honora and the other chambermaids, I undressed and went right to sleep in one of the surprisingly comfortable cots.

27

THE GREEN MONSTER

Daybreak came much more quickly than I had expected and I awoke as the sunbeams began streaming through the white fabric of the tent. As I lay awake, I figured that the intention of all of the darkly colored tapestries hanging in the tent was to block out the sunlight. They seemed to do a good job, but the top of the tent and its opening were without the tapestries, allowing the light to flow through the ceiling. Poor design, I thought. It appeared that I was the only person awake in the tent, and I did not hear anyone stirring outside at all.

I lay on my back staring up at the blue sky that was sneaking a peek at me through the branches and leaves of the forest. I had a strange feeling in the pit of my stomach - kind of a cross between what happens when I eat too much fruit and when I am nervous about a test in school.

The last dream I remembered was surprisingly about Barlow, but I could not recall what the dream was actually about other than Barlow seemed upset about something. I wondered if this dream was a premonition or simply a dream. I figured it was nothing for which to be concerned or I would have remembered more of it. My mind began to wander and just as I caught myself thinking about Adelio, I heard one of my sisters stirring. Someone's cot creaked and I heard a loud sigh. Then I heard Timber's voice tell Tulip she was taking up too much room. I was relieved it was not Marena awake, but I took this as a sign to clear my mind.

I rose, threw my satin robe over the flowing white nightgown Honora had forced me to sleep in, and wandered over to the opening of the tent. As soon as I placed one foot outside, a hand grabbed my left arm, startling me.

"No, dear. You must not venture out alone. I will come with you," Honora stated absolutely. She was quite a stern woman, like how you would imagine a librarian or old-fashioned school marm, which was surprising because she did not appear much older than Aunt Bea.

"I have to use the um…" I really had to pee, like I always did when I woke up in the morning, but somehow telling Honora that "Her Royal Highness had to pee" did not seem appropriate. Moreover, I realized yesterday that "bathroom" was not in Kiranians' vocabularies.

"Necessary?"

"Yes, the necessary room - er, house," I repeated. I had forgotten what they called it. It was an outhouse at this campsite, not unlike the "Port'o Potties" at the softball fields in Woodport. My sisters and I had our own "necessary" room here, which we appreciated.

"Very well, let's go to it," Honora directed. "We have a busy day today, Princess."

"What are we doing?" I asked as Honora lead me to the outhouse around the back of our tent.

"Lessons," she replied. I did miss school so in a weird, nerdy way I was looking forward to learning from our tutors, Lankin and Remble. I had many questions I hoped they could answer for me. I finished my necessary business and washed my hands and face in the warm rose water outside the outhouse. Honora offered me a cloth to dry my hands and face and she led me back to the tent.

"Come, the ladies will dress you appropriately this morning and we can break our fast together while your tutors prepare your lessons," she told me.

"Oh, we don't really have to put on the fancy clothes yet, do we?" I was hoping to avoid the freak fashion show. No such luck.

"Yes, you do," Honora replied and I left the subject alone.

⁓෮

The ladies dressed me in an extremely comfortable dress, which surprised me. It was a linen dress in pale mauve. I expected to be a wrinkled mess by midday.

By this time, my sisters were also awake and dressing. It was explained that these were essentially our "play clothes" and that before supper we would have to change into gowns that were more formal.

"Oh, I love this one," Marena said about her blue, flowing dress. "Look how big my boobs look!" Timber cracked up at that comment and so did I. "I hope Adelio likes it," she remarked as she skipped out of the tent with Mergard.

"Try not to let her bother you," Timber told me silently. I nodded in agreement. Really, this misunderstanding was not Marena's fault. Still, she was getting incredibly annoying.

"Listen to your sister, Avery and do not get upset," Adelio also told me through my thoughts. I loved hearing his voice like that. It gave me the chills.

My sisters and I dined in our absurdly large tent along with Bob and Adelio. Barlow was apparently off arranging for our boat to be delivered to a place called Swenwood later in the day. I was mildly disappointed that he was missing, especially as I watched Marena attempt a game of "footsie" under the table with my alleged betrothed. Adelio sat between Marena and me on one side of the table with Timber and Bob across from us. It was difficult for me to focus upon the conversation with Marena acting in this overly flirtatious manner.

"Do you want to cool it, Rena? Jeez, you're making everyone uncomfortable," Timber chastised her silently. My little sister to the rescue again, I thought.

"What?" Marena said aloud. "Stop acting all jealous. Avery understands. She doesn't mind, right?" I did not answer her because I was afraid of what might come out of my mouth at that point. Clearly, my sister did not know me very well, or worse, did not care about me. Timber stood and spoke aloud.

"Rena, of course she minds and frankly, I'm sure Adelio minds that you can't keep your paws off of him or leave him alone for one stinking second! God! You can be so clueless sometimes!" I rarely heard Timber instigate an argument with Marena, but when she did it would typically end in tears for both of them. I needed to intervene.

"Ok, ok - enough, I don't mind, ok?" I lied. Marena was now standing, facing Timber across the table.

"Girls…" Bobril warned. The twins ignored our uncle's admonition.

"What is your problem all of a sudden?" Marena was now raising her voice. Given her last show of anger, I was nervous about where this argument was headed. Seemingly, Adelio was concerned as well.

"All right, ladies. Why don't we just sit down and finish our meals. Your tutors are likely ready to begin your first lessons this morning," Adelio calmly suggested. I could tell that his tone was meant to help lower the blood pressures at the table.

"No, Adelio. I want to know what my sister's problem with me is. Out with it, Timber!" Marena was not giving up this argument. This was usually where Aunt Bea would order one or all of us to neutral corners to collect our wits, but I could tell this sort of issue was well above Uncle Bob's head.

"Fine, Rena. I'm sick of you spitting in Avery's face, that's my problem," Timber replied. This was not going to be an easy battle and my stomach was already turning.

"What are you talking about? Oh wait, are you talking about Adelio? Come on, Timber. Give me a break. It's not my fault that he chose me. I mean, I am sorry to say this Avery, because I know you have a little crush on him and everything, but did you really think he would pick you? Can't you just be happy for me?" I could not believe what I was hearing. Marena was always a little selfish and self-centered, but she had never insulted me in such a bold manner. I stood up now and turned to the right to face Marena. She was combing through the ends of her hair, coyly with her left hand.

"What?" I shrieked. I could feel the back of my neck starting to burn as the tears were collecting in my eyes. Adelio reached for my right hand, perhaps to comfort me or perhaps to prevent what he believed I might do. Marena glared at Adelio and then at me when she saw this.

"Adelio, don't patronize her. You know, you might be the future queen and everything, but you can't have everything, Avery. Adelio and I were chosen for one another, like I told you and there's nothing you can do about it," Marena gloated.

"Rena, that's enough! And what are you talking about, you and Adelio - I don't think you understand… " Uncle Bob was now trying to salvage the situation.

"Yes, your uncle is correct, Rena. Please drop this, all right? We have more pressing issues to address now, anyway," Adelio interrupted Uncle Bob before he could reveal any semblance of the truth to Marena, but Marena could not stop.

"You just can't take it, can you?" she hissed as she placed her hands on Adelio's shoulders. I just glared at her. Adelio's expression was sheer terror and helplessness.

"Avery, you've never been able to get a boyfriend, so why are you both so surprised that Adelio is with me? Of course, he is with me. Get over yourself! You too, Timberose." With that last comment, Marena sat back in her chair. Timber and I looked at each other, too stunned to reply.

I never imagined my own sister could be so cruel. I was not only mortified that she embarrassed me in this way in front of Adelio, but also that she was embarrassing herself. She was the only one in the room who did not know that Adelio was my betrothed, that he had apparently been sealed to me in some sacred and mystical ceremony, that he was my soul mate - my one and only true love. At least, that was according to the second hand information I had received from Marena.

What was worse than her not knowing the truth was the fact that because we were all so afraid of what the truth could do to her, we were keeping her in the dark. I could no longer be responsible for her emotional reaction and I could no longer take her abuse.

Speechless, I pushed my chair back from the table.

"I…you…" I stuttered. I wanted to just throw the truth right in her face, but I could not even organize my thoughts let alone my sentences. Instead, I just stormed out of the tent, brushing past one of our tutors. He greeted me with a genial, "Your Grace," but I did not acknowledge him. I marched across the campsite and caught Barlow in my sights. He smiled as I approached, but his expression soon changed when he saw the tears streaming down my face.

"Princess? Is everything all right?" He asked as he bowed to me.

"The boat," was all I could manage to mutter.

"What about the boat?"

"Is it still there?"

"Yes, but you can't go, Princess. You can't leave the camp, it's too dangerous," I had already started running toward the path we had taken when we arrived at the encampment just last night. He began running with me.

"Don't follow me," I mumbled at him but I realized that once again my wishes were not going to be obeyed. I stopped running. "Please," I pleaded, "Just let me go! I have to get out of here," I moaned. I pushed him so hard that he stumbled. Barlow looked at me, in utter surprise.

"Your Grace, my job is to provide you safe passage. I cannot let you leave."

"You can and you will," I ordered, "And don't tell the others where I've gone. I just need…" I started to cry again and attempted to suck the tears back into my heart broken body. "I have to get away - I'll be back before it gets dark. I know the way," I promised and started jogging into the woods. There were no footsteps behind me and as I got to where I believed no one could hear me, I let out the deep cry of pure anguish that had been trying to escape from my body since I ran out of the tent. I leaned against an old tree trunk to steady myself and just sobbed.

28

A BAD IDEA

My mind was clear and all I could hear were my own wounded thoughts for once. Since my powers began to develop, I never felt like I had any peace and quiet anymore. Adelio told me that once I began my training with the tutors, I would learn to control what I hear and whom I hear.

The silence now was almost deafening since the only reflections running through my head were my own. While I was perhaps a tad bit dramatic in my escape from the campsite, I desperately needed time away from Marena as well as time to consider everything that I had learned over the past week and what the future potentially held for me.

As I walked along the path through the woods, I remembered that when we were dressing this morning, Timber had mentioned that she forgot Tulip's back medicine in the boat. According to Timber who could now fully communicate with Tulip, the cat was complaining that her back was sore. A month or so before we left Woodport and the lives we knew, Tulip had had a bit of an accident on the basement stairs.

Frightened by some innocuous noise, the cat ran down the stairs and lost her footing on the last five steps. She bounced, on her back, to the floor. Although she seemed all right at the time, Timber insisted that she be taken to the Twenty-Four Hour Emergency Animal Hospital in Newton. $1250.00 and three hours later, the Vet "on call" told us Tulip was going to be just fine, but he prescribed a medication for her just in case. He also prescribed a supplement for her to take every day as well. Allegedly, Tulip was requesting her supplement. At this point, I figured at least I could help the poor cat and Timber, and get the vitamins.

The well-traveled pathway through the forest was well lit by the morning sun. While I did not want to rush my trip to the boat, I did not want to dilly-dally either. Admittedly, walking alone, while somewhat refreshing was also somewhat disconcerting. I did not remember this part of our hike yesterday and every subtle noise caused my heart to skip a beat. I decided to quicken my pace.

As I continued on my mission, I thought about breakfast. With space came some perspective and I concluded that Marena was not like Timber and me. She was not considerate of anyone's feelings but her own and while I knew she loved me as her sister, I wondered just what that meant to her. To me, the love and lives of my sisters were my paramount concerns. I had always felt protective of them, but now given this incredible responsibility recently posed to me, I felt even more of an obligation to guard their safety and well-being.

Marena was clearly not herself, or not in control of herself. I had never fought with her in such a mean-spirited way.

Despite what had just transpired, my sister was not a mean girl. She could be insensitive, at times, but not cruel. I wondered if her powers had something to do with her terrible attitude.

Perhaps, Marena just needed to hear the truth about Adelio from me to understand just how I felt when she cut me in half with her thoughtless words. She would need me to comfort her and maybe in time she would understand how much I love her and that she loved me too. Maybe then, she would see that we are on this road together and that working together is the only way to prosper and be successful as the next rulers of Kirana. This disastrous situation at breakfast ultimately forced me to consider that Marena and my differences in personality needed to be dealt with if we were to stand side by side as the leaders of Kirana.

Proud of my realization and adult perspective, I recognized that I was close to the river. I could hear the water and gentle current flowing just feet from where I was on the path. Despite its cover among the brush on the shore, I easily found the rubber dinghy and dragged it to the river's edge. I decided to paddle it rather than use the motor. While I did know how to drive the tender, without any premonition, I could foresee a problem if I attempted to use the engine on my own. It seemed that the big boat was closer to the shore than it had been yesterday when we abandoned it.

I paddled over to the boat and tied off to the swim platform, since it was the only reasonable place I could reach. I carefully boarded the boat and went into the cabin. I found Tulip's medicine right away on the counter by the stovetop and placed it in the satchel tied at my waist. It was then that I realized I did not mind wearing a dress as much as I thought I would. In fact, I had not even noticed that I was practically formally dressed while I walked through the forest.

I sat down on the V-berth and took a deep breath, then another and then another. I felt as though this issue with my sister Marena was resolved on my end. I had to literally be the bigger sister and talk it over with her. Despite Adelio's consternation, the truth had to come out and the best way for that to happen was for me to unveil it to her.

Just then, I caught a glimpse of the inverter we had been using to work the appliances on the boat and charge our electronics. I reached into my satchel, took out my cell phone and plugged it into its charger. I recognized that I needed to not only turn on the inverter, but also to turn on the boat to charge my phone, which was useless in this foreign land in any case. I decided that I should go ahead and charge it anyway. At the very least, I could keep track of time, I figured.

I went up to the helm of the boat, but of course, the key was not there. Then I remembered that Uncle Bob often left an extra boat key in the head, attached to the mirror. Why would this boat be any different? Sure enough, the keys were taped to the side of the vanity-sized mirror above the marine bathroom sink. I grabbed one, went back to the cockpit and put the key into the port engine ignition. It started right up and I was able to drop back into the cabin and turn on the inverter.

The little battery icon on my phone lit up indicating that the phone was charging. I looked at the time and date on my phone. It was clearly still on Scotland time. According to my phone, it was July 15th at 3:34 pm. In just what I thought was a maybe a week from the time we landed in Glasgow and ended up in Kirana, two months had passed in the rest of the world. That was just remarkable and a bit sad to me.

In just a week, I had missed the junior prom, the AP exams, the chorus and band concerts, and the first weeks of the summer program at Rutgers University in public policy and government into which I had been accepted. I had really been looking forward to this particular program since I was one of two students from my entire county accepted into this prestigious summer program. At this point, the directors were probably wondering what had happened to me, as was the faculty and administration at Woodport High School.

We were likely quite a story in Woodport. "The MacLeod family disappeared without a trace - did you hear?" would be the sentence most heard and uttered around our town. Inhabitants of Woodport loved good gossip.

As I considered what else I had probably missed back home, I began to also consider what my new life was going to be like here in Kirana. There was so much here that I did not know or understand and I was quite eager to learn. Abandoning my first lesson with the tutors was not a good start, of course. I figured I should probably swallow my pride and get back to the camp before anyone realized I had gone missing.

I turned off the boat and replaced the key. I also grabbed the last of the pudding packs, but changed my mind about bringing them back to camp without a bag to put them in. Apparently, we were going to have access to the boat when needed as it was headed up river to Swenwood, wherever that was.

Just as I had come to the boat, I returned the dinghy to the shore where it had previously been hidden. I felt as though I was no longer alone.

First, it was a hand over my mouth and then a forearm around my midsection lifting me into the air. Another figure came from the brush and drew a dagger-like knife that looked like the *squian dugh* Uncle Bob kept in his sock when he would wear a kilt on special Scottish holidays. The figure was dressed in the same black cloak as the men who were after us in Fort Augustus.

"Finish her!" He commanded the man holding me. With all of my might, I threw my right elbow into the nose of my attacker, something I had learned in a self-defense class at the local

YMCA. The attacker dropped me and I fell into the dirt. As quickly as I could, I scurried to my feet and tried to run back toward the path in the woods when the other cloaked man caught my arms. He held the blade to my throat.

"Squirming is only going to make this worse, Highness," he said facetiously.

"No, please, no," I pleaded. I was too shocked to freak out, cry, or even move.

"Just do it," said the other man. Blood was dripping down his face. He walked up to face me and slapped me so hard with the back of his hand I thought my left cheek was going to fall off my face. Then I heard an abrupt thud. The man who slapped me grabbed at an arrow that had been driven into his left shoulder, gasped and fell back. The man holding me suddenly became nervous.

"Who's there?" He called out into the forest. Just then, we were both knocked to the ground. I hit my head hard on a rock or log or something. My attacker had fallen away from me and was now pleading with someone.

"Let me go, you don't want to do this," he begged and those were his last words. Barlow ran him through with a sword and then turned to finish off the other cloaked man.

"Are you all right, your Highness?" He rushed over to my side on the ground. I was stunned. "How did you...?"

"Followed you. I told you not to be out here by yourself. I couldn't let you." Barlow tried to help me to my feet, but for some reason my legs would not cooperate. My right ankle was throbbing like crazy. I leaned on his arms.

"Thank you," I told him. He just smiled at me then without a word, he lifted me in his arms and carried me through the forest. My head started swimming and the world was spinning. I closed my eyes.

29

ENOUGH TRUTH FOR ONE NIGHT

"Here Princess, please take this elixir," Honora was holding up my head and trying to force-feed me some medicine.

"What is that?" Marena asked.

"It is called 'aspirin' and it will take away her pain," Honora replied. Her tone was somewhere between offended that my sister would second-guess her nursing skills and her usually bossy attitude.

"Oh no you don't!" Marena grabbed the small cup of liquid from Honora. "Aspirin gives her a stomach ache. Hold on, I brought Tylenol, you know just in case." Marena wandered away from my cot for a moment and returned shaking a bottle of CVS brand acetaminophen. We never bought name brand.

"Ahh, loud…" I complained. Marena stopped shaking the bottle.

"Sorry, here. It says you should take two, but I think you can take four." I put out my hand and accepted the blue and red capsules.

"Highness, are you certain you should take these?" Honora asked. I recognized the concern. Obviously, there were people in Kirana who wanted me dead and who is to say that someone had not tampered with our over the counter pain medications? I resolved that the likelihood of anyone getting into Marena's backpack and poisoning them was remote and swallowed each of the pills.

"Honora, would you please give us a moment?" Marena asked. Honora bowed her head and backed out of my private sleeping area.

"Avery, I'm so sorry about that fight this morning at breakfast. I mean, I don't even know what came over me. Timber is still mad at me and not talking to me and I just couldn't take it if

139

everyone was angry with me, you know?" That was a constant theme in Marena's life. She could not stand the idea of people not liking her or harboring ill feelings toward her.

"I'm sorry too. Rena, there's something I have to tell you - and you're not going to like it," I said attempting to sit up. "Oww..." I moaned. "Feels like I got hit in the head with a softball bat." I took a deep breath to overcome the throbbing I felt on the back of my head and cheek.

"Look, if it has to do with Adelio, don't bother. He broke up with me," she replied, "and I totally deserve it for being such a jerk to everyone," Marena started to cry. "He said that he needed space to think about things," she whined.

"Oh," I was surprised to say the least, "he didn't tell you anything else?"

"No, well except that we would talk again about it when we got to the palace. That might be days," she moaned.

"Well, maybe this gives you time too - to pull yourself together, you know?" I tried to comfort her. "And who knows, maybe Adelio and you are not meant for each other after all. Maybe you will meet someone else when we get to the palace. Someone even more handsome and charming and who won't put you into time out," I tried to joke with her but I could see that my humor was a bit premature.

"Thanks, sis. I think Adelio is the one for me, though. I love him. I just need him to figure out that he loves me. Maybe when we start learning our powers and I can read his mind, he will be in love with me again," she stated hopefully. Her blue eyes glistened with tears, which she tried to wipe away without leaving those red streaky marks that were often inevitable when you cry. Marena was quite good at looking lovely even during moments of emotional distress.

"Maybe," I replied.

"So, are we all right now?" She asked me.

"Yeah, we're cool. Just stop being so mean to me, ok? I can get a boyfriend, Rena. I just need to find the right one," I reported.

"I know," she said as she smoothed some of my hair behind my ear. "I'm going to see what's going on out there. I'll be back. Now that you're awake, I'm sure Timber and Uncle Bob want to see you too." Marena opened the curtain and permitted Honora to re-enter my private pseudo-room. Adelio was right behind her. Once again, Honora excused herself from our presence.

"Hi," I said to him with a smile. I was so glad to see him. Adelio took my hands and kissed them.

"Try to clear your mind," he said to me silently. I nodded that I had. I realized that I had been getting a little better at my selective thinking recently. He kissed my hands again and continued: "We need to get out of here."

"What? Why? I thought we were safe here!" Adelio's tone frightened me. He seemed frightened as well, which made it much worse for me.

"After today, I know we are not - you are not safe. For now, we have armed guards stationed around the camp. I lost you today, Avery," Adelio seemed hurt when he said this. I didn't quite know what he meant.

"No, Barlow…" Adelio interrupted me.

"Barlow followed you, Avery and that was a stroke of luck, perhaps. But I lost you. Could you hear me when you left the camp because I couldn't hear you - at all," Adelio was somewhat panicked as he tried to explain this to me. I did notice that I was alone for the first time in a really long time, but I thought I had accomplished that feat on my own. My eyes widened as I came to this realization.

"Yes," Adelio said, "someone or something was able to infiltrate and block our thoughts from one another. We can't take any chances. We're leaving at day break for the boat."

"Where are we going?" I recognized that my question was naïve as Adelio shook his head at me.

"You'll know in the morning. We know where Bea is and we're going to get her," this plan sounded great to my ears. I missed Aunt Bea so much and although everyone said she was just fine, I was worried for her.

"Rest now and I will send Barlow in for your safety. You know Avery, we owe him your life," Adelio told me as if I didn't already know that. I nodded humbly. He kissed my wounded cheek, a little too hard and long.

"Ouch," I said aloud. "That hurts!" I wanted to add "dummy" to the last part of that complaint but then suddenly, my cheek was no longer throbbing. I reached up to touch it. It was no longer swollen and the gash that resulted from the cloaked man's ring striking my face was healed.

"Hey! How did you - fairy medicine?" I asked.

"Precisely. I need you in proper form, dearest Princess," Adelio bowed his head and exited through the tent. I sighed one of those long, content sighs of someone in absolute love and then I laughed at myself for doing so. I lowered my head to my pillow and fell asleep.

The campsite was abuzz with activity while my tent was completely quiet. I looked up through my tent "sky-light" and could see a zillion twinkling stars. The moonlight danced along the walls. Apparently, it was now "nighttime." I sat up in my cot and stretched. Despite my tumultuous morning, I felt just fine. My head did not ache and my face was no longer swollen and throbbing. I placed my bare feet on the tent floor and stood and stretched again, yawning. A shadowy figure rushed toward me causing my heart to race out of my chest. I screamed.

"No, no, no! Oh my God, no!" I was trapped and alone. I threw a snap kick into my attacker's mid-section and he crumpled to the floor.

"Princess, it's me…," Barlow moaned from the floor.

"Barlow! Why didn't you say it was you, dummy!" It wasn't nice, but I felt "dummy" was an appropriate name for Barlow at that moment. "You scared me to death!" I helped him up off the floor. "Did I hurt you?"

"No, just surprised me is all. Didn't Adelio tell you I was going to be watching you?" Clearly, I had forgotten this important bit of information.

"Sorry, Barlow and thank you for saving my life today. I still can't believe what happened." Barlow and I walked out into the common area of the tent.

"I told you, that is my job and my pleasure. Your protection is all that matters to me," he replied.

"Well, I certainly appreciate your dedication to your work, but you could have been hurt or even killed."

"No matter what happens to me," he said humbly.

"Matters to me, Barlow," I told him and I meant that comment. There was something genuine about Barlow that I really liked. I trusted him. Barlow bowed to me.

"Come lass, let's join the others, eh?" I nodded and we came out of the tent together. I put my arm in his and my head on his shoulder. I felt safe with Barlow at my side. He excused himself from me and headed over toward the rest of the group.

I found a nice spot on a large rock in front of the fire. I was just thinking and relaxing when Barlow plopped himself, practically on top of me, on my rock.

"Can I sit with you, Princess? He asked, handing me a mug of what I assumed was ale. I accepted the mug gladly. Having little experience drinking alcohol, I had nothing to compare the taste of Kiranian ale to other than Natural Light, the first and only beer I had ever tasted. This ale was much, much better.

"Sure," I replied. I took a sip from the mug and licked the resulting foam from my top lip.

"Why aren't you dancing with your sisters and the others?"

I shrugged, "Don't really feel like it, I guess. Why aren't you dancing?"

Barlow shrugged back at me, "Same," he replied, "Adelio and Princess Marena seem to be getting along quite well. They seem to fancy each other quite a bit, I think," Barlow told me. I wanted to inform him that any fancying between them was a one-way street, but I didn't have the energy even though it was beginning to hurt my heart that people here seemed to think that Adelio and Marena were a couple. I wondered what had happened to Marena's "time out."

"Oh, yeah - I suppose," I mumbled to Barlow without lifting my gaze from the dancing flames.

"Your Highness, may I speak with you plainly? I have something - something important that I need to tell you. Something only a few people in the world know, but I want to tell you. I feel I owe you the truth about me."

"Why on earth would you want to tell me?" I tried to read Barlow without him having to say anything because I could not imagine what this secret was, but his thoughts were moving too slowly for some reason. I figured I might as well let him tell me what he wanted to say.

"What is it, Barlow?" He inched closer to me on the rock. Whatever he needed to tell me was clearly serious.

"I committed a horrible atrocity and I fear I shall never be forgiven," he whispered. He had my attention. I didn't know what this horrible thing he did was, but I could tell by the tone of his voice he was broken hearted over it.

"I'm sure it cannot be as bad as you describe, Barlow," I said.

Barlow took a deep breath, "It was, Princess. It was the worst thing I could do," he whimpered.

I was shocked, partly because Barlow was confiding in me his terrible secret and partly because his secret really was that terrible. Barlow told me the story of why he had committed his life to ensuring my safety and the safety of my sisters:

"Soon after you girls were smuggled out of Pilton Palace and disappeared from Kirana, Anyon and his legions from the Kingdom of Mordith invaded Kirana. Once we were overtaken and conquered by Anyon, anyone with a connection to you girls, to the Trinity, were killed or imprisoned. My brother and I were members of the Royal Guard, charged with the task of protecting the Royal Family. Since the Royal Family had been broken, for lack of a better word to describe what had taken place, the Royal Guard disbanded and all eight of us were sent from court.

"Systematically, one by one, they came for us. Anyon had us captured for questioning about the whereabouts of you girls. We of course had been instrumental in your safe passage. They came for my brother and me, but we had no idea they were after any of us. Anyon's new guard came into the inn in Braventon-shire where our family was from. We had traveled home after our release from service and we were out carousing with our cousin Markel and some local boys when they came into the tavern. They asked for the name 'Corwin,' our family name. My brother and Markel responded. I was at a table at the other end of the tavern talking with a farrier about the shoddy work he had done on my horse's shoes, but I saw what was happening. I did nothing. I said nothing.

"Anyon's guards took my brother and my cousin, arrested them for treason and brought them to the Tower. Still I did nothing. Well, that is not entirely accurate. I ran. I first ran back to court to find out what was happening and I found the wife and young son of my friend in the Royal Guard, Jaxson who told me what had happened. Lady Jaxson told me that Ginter, under orders from Anyon arrested and imprisoned all eight of the former Royal Guardsmen, and questioned them about the Trinity. Anyon ordered them tortured and then killed. Lady Jaxson was fearful for her own life and was leaving court that very day.

"Then she asked me the question I was dreading…"

"How did you escape capture?" I filled in the blank. I still could not believe that Barlow was sharing this story with me.

"Yes. I did not have an answer so again, I ran. This time I ran to the Prenmar Forest, found an encampment of the Order of the Heather and pledged my allegiance and service to them and to you girls.

"But you see," Barlow's voice was cracking, "I will never forgive myself for what I have done, nor should anyone else. My cousin, Markel was like a brother to me, and because of my cowardice, there are two little girls and a lovely woman without their father and husband. I did that and they know it. I can never go back to Braventon."

"Surely they understand that this was a situation of mistaken identity. You're family. They will forgive you," I tried to reassure him. I did not know his family, of course so my words were likely hollow. Barlow had his head in his hands. I put my arms around him and held him to my chest. I held him and rubbed his back while he attempted to contain his emotions. Finally, he picked up his head and let out a moan.

"Ahhh! Your Grace, I am so sorry to put this on you. It has not been that long since this terrible thing and I - no one knows. Not Adelio, not the members of the Order, only you, my family and Lady Jaxson. The rest of the world assumed I died too," Barlow was attempting to apologize for his behavior.

"I'm glad you told me - it's important that you not keep these sorts of secrets completely to yourself. It is too difficult to bear. And Barlow, you are not responsible for your brother or your cousin's deaths. You must know that. Anyon ordered their deaths." While I tried to comfort Barlow, I only half-heartedly believed what I was saying. Of course, Anyon was the obvious responsible party here, but I could not help thinking about what I would do in Barlow's situation. I could never run. I would do everything I could to save my sisters. In that sense, I understood completely the torture Barlow must have been enduring and the tremendous regret he carried with him.

"Well," he said, changing the subject, "This must be an exciting time for you, Princess. Until your eighteenth birthday, you will be groomed to rule this kingdom. You must have been dreaming of this day for quite some time."

"Actually, Barlow we didn't know anything about Kirana or our role here until a few days ago. Yes, I am excited. But I'm more fearful than anything else. I couldn't even run my school's student council effectively, let alone an entire kingdom. I don't know how I'm going to do this," I replied candidly. This year in student council, the president was out of school with mono for two months. Our constitution allowed nominations from the floor for an interim president. No one wanted to do it so I volunteered, thinking it would be a good opportunity to do some good at our school. It was a bad experience, to say the least. Even our adviser, Mrs. Grost, lost confidence in my ability to lead our student government by the time my short term had concluded.

"You'll have plenty of help, your Grace, and you will be surrounded by people who truly believe in your cause," now Barlow was reassuring me.

"There's just so much I don't know or understand and I can't imagine that I'm going to be able to do what everyone expects me to do - I just..." I stopped mid-sentence feeling the tears surfacing and pooling around my eyes. I dropped my head to stare at my hands.

"Princess Avery?" Barlow asked tenderly and lifted my chin to look at my face. "Princess Avery, you are going to be a powerful leader, whether you know it now or not, and all of Kirana will sing your name in praise. We believe in you and your sisters," he told me. His words were incredibly sweet and reassuring if I was nervous about a USTA tennis tournament back home, but this situation was quite different. The fact was, he didn't know me. None of these people, magical or otherwise, knew me. My biggest fear in life next to poisonous snakes was disappointment, and I could not see a way of avoiding disappointing these people.

I slid off the face of the rock where we had been seated this whole time in front of the fire. I was starting to sweat, partly out of anxiety and partly because the fire was really roaring. I walked back toward our fancy tent, into the shadows. Barlow followed me. I could hear his footsteps behind me. He was thinking of ways to make me feel better, which was very sweet. I turned to him.

"It's all right, Barlow. Thank you for listening and for trying to make me feel better," I said.

"No, thank you, Princess." Barlow was standing close to me now and looking at my face intently. Even if I had not been able to read his thoughts at that moment, I knew what was coming next and for some reason, I chose not to prevent it. In fact, I practically encouraged Barlow and I hoped neither my sisters nor Adelio were listening to my thoughts at that moment.

Barlow lifted my chin, this time to meet his lips. I could feel his cool breath on my face. Barlow parted his lips ever so slightly to meet mine. I could smell the sweet ale on his lips, but I pulled away from him before they touched mine.

"No, Barlow. We can't do this," I told him. Barlow immediately dropped into a deep respectful bow and lowered his head to me.

"Your Grace - I - I'm sorry, so sorry - I just - wanted to…"

"It's my fault, Barlow. Believe me, I wanted you to do it, but that was so wrong of me. My heart belongs to someone else," I tried to explain. Barlow looked up at me and appeared crushed.

"I meant no disrespect, Princess. You are the most beautiful and wonderful girl - woman in Kirana. I just…"

"Please, Barlow. Don't apologize. I think you are pretty special too, but we could never be together…" I was trying to speak in nebulous terms to avoid having to explain myself. The truth was that by nearly kissing Barlow I could feel my heart burning for Adelio. The force of what I already felt for him was so strong, I really couldn't explain it. But then, I didn't have to say anything. Adelio was standing right there. I caught a glimpse of him out of the corner of my left eye. He was standing at the front of his tent, staring.

"Adelio!" I called out to him. "I'm so sorry - I…" I stuttered. I didn't know what to say. Adelio walked over to my side and faced Barlow.

"Avery, please step aside so I can talk to Barlow," he asked. I didn't want any fighting over me or for anyone to get needlessly hurt, emotionally or physically, but I followed Adelio's instructions.

"Avery and I are sealed, Barlow. She is my soul mate and I hers," he told Barlow rather bluntly.

"Adelio, I didn't know - I'm so sorry," Barlow responded.

"Now you do and I expect you will respect me and Avery accordingly," Adelio was so forceful in his tone.

"Of course," Barlow bowed and just walked away from us.

"Well, that was awkward," I tried to joke, but the joke was lost as usual on Adelio.

"Yes it was, and that's my fault," Adelio said. "I should have made our situation known to everyone, including Marena. You know, she's naming our children already?" Adelio grabbed me and gave me a hug. With my head resting on his chest, I could feel his strong heart beating. I closed my eyes, never wanting to leave this spot, but my moment of pure contentment was abruptly interrupted by an emotional shriek. I gasped.

"Marena!" Adelio left me standing behind the tent.

"Stay here," he directed as he walked toward the fire.

30

PITY THE FOOL

All I could hear from where I had been standing behind the big tent was Marena shrieking so I decided I should make my way over to her. The closer I came to the fire and Marena, the more volatile I realized the situation had become. My presence would probably make the situation as bad, maybe worse, but I couldn't leave Adelio alone.

"Please, Marena," Adelio pleaded, "You must try to understand. Avery and I were sealed to one another a long time ago."

"Why did you lie? Why didn't you tell me? You let me walk around thinking you were in love with me," she cried. "And you," Marena saw that I had joined the fray, "How could you? You've made me look like a fool - like a desperate idiot! You think this is funny? Are my feelings a joke to you?" She directed at me. Timber had also joined the commotion. Through her thoughts, she told me not to say anything, not to respond because that would only make matters worse.

Marena raised her hands into the air in exasperation and as she threw them down at her sides, we heard what sounded like creaking or crackling. Tree branches came crashing down in front of us.

"Rena, you must calm down!" Adelio begged her. "You are not in control of yourself."

"Calm down? After what you put me through - both of you? You have to be kidding me! And you?" Now Marena directed her anger at Timber who stood by her twin's side, sheepishly. "Did you know about this?"

"Rena, I…"

"Oh great! So everyone knew this secret except me?" Marena flailed her arms around as she often did when she got angry or upset, and almost as if she commanded it, fire jumped out of the pit to her left and landed between Adelio and me and the bonfire. The branches she carelessly forced from the trees above us caught fire around us, essentially trapping Adelio and me.

"You have to be kidding me!" I shouted. "Rena, what are you doing?" It was getting hot in this fiery cell she created and no one seemed to be jumping into action.

"I - I - I don't know," Marena replied. "Oh my God, what am I doing? Timber help me get somebody - water…" The camp inhabitants were already throwing water on the fire surrounding us, but it wasn't going out for some reason.

An ember danced its way over to the bottom of my robe and began to burn. This situation was more serious than I initially thought. Adelio ripped the robe from my arms and fed it to the fire.

"Come on!" I protested, "I love that robe!"

"Avery, be serious for a moment, we're in a bit of trouble here," Adelio said to me. He seemed genuinely concerned with our situation as the deadfall continued to burn around us. I saw his point. I was becoming accustomed to being the damsel in distress and almost expected that either a giant sea monster would intervene and help me or either Adelio or Barlow or both would save me. I was beginning to see that Adelio and I needed to think fast. The flames were getting closer to us.

"This is not good," was all I could say. I could see Timber closing her eyes on the other side of the fire ring.

"Hey, a little help? Napping is not helpful, Timber."

"Shhh - I'm trying something…" She replied without opening her eyes. A few raindrops fell on my bare shoulders and then a cloud above us opened up and dropped a deluge upon us and the entrapping fire around us.

"I did it! I did it!" Timber was jumping up and down as if she had just won the third grade spelling bee.

"You did this? But how…?" I couldn't believe it. The fire in the pit and the fire that Marena had caused smoked and smoldered around us as the rain tapered off. I was now soaked, my nightgown literally sticking to my body. Apparently, the entire look was a little too revealing for both Adelio and Honora. Adelio wrapped me in his shirt and Honora came running to my side with a blanket and covered me, holding her arms around me in a protective bear hug.

"Ok, Honora. Thanks. I'm just fine - not even cold, just wet," I told her and further wrapped the blanket around myself, grabbing the ends from her hands. She bowed and backed away from me.

"If you must know, I spent my day in lessons with Lankin and Remble. Something you and Marena should have been doing. Anyway, I am learning how to use my powers. Now in addition to understanding cats, I can summon birds and I guess make it rain. Pretty cool, huh?" Timber seemed very pleased with herself. I was very pleased that she was a diligent student and a fast learner or Adelio and I would have been in some serious trouble.

"Well done, Timber," Remble congratulated his new pupil.

"Thank you, sir. Where is Lankin?"

"He is making preparations for our swift departure come day break, Princess Timber," Remble replied. Apparently, one day was quite a productive, bonding experience for my youngest sister and her tutors. Timber nodded and Remble bowed to her, then to me and then excused himself.

⌒◦

Marena was sobbing in Uncle Bobril's arms and as I approached her, Bob shook his head at me and Timber as if to say "not now, Avery." I nodded back in understanding and headed into our tent to pack my things with Timber.

"You know," she said, "it's bad enough that some weird caped guys are trying to kill you and now you have Marena trying to kill you."

"She wasn't trying to kill us, Timber," I replied, "she just doesn't know how to channel her emotions and her powers in the right manner yet. Of course, I hope she figures it out soon or who knows what sort of problems she will cause."

"We probably should have told her about you and Adelio before we left Fort Augustus. Then at least she would have had time to deal with it and maybe turn her attention to someone else for while, like Barlow," Timber stated. Her hindsight was appreciated to a degree but the fact of the matter was that "I told you so," Timber's favorite expression, was not helpful here.

"Well, it wasn't my decision. Adelio didn't think…"

"Adelio doesn't know Marena like we do. Are you going to let him make all of your decisions for the rest of your life?" That was a blunt and harsh question coming from my sister, but she had a point.

"No, of course not," I replied, "I just thought, in this case, he might be correct, but the reality is that keeping anything from you two is difficult without magical mind reading skills, let alone with them. Besides, I don't want to keep anything from you. If we are going to rule this place together, we need to work together and that means no secrets."

"I totally agree. Lankin and Remble were telling me some pretty cool things about our ancestors. Get this! Our whole family tree started out of a love affair between this Hazaro guy and a fairy woman. 'Mixed' marriages were not condoned in Kirana, but they were so in love that the fairies and the men saw their union as the key to peace in Kirana so they blessed it. Isn't that sort of neat and romantic?"

"Yeah, it is," I replied as I folded my jeans into my backpack. One of our ladies had washed our clothes for us and my jeans had a "been out in the sun without fabric softener feeling" to them. I probably wouldn't have a chance to wear them again anyway with the expansive gown wardrobe that Pentil and Donnelle had described to us.

I awoke just before dawn to Barlow breathing very heavily on my floor. The sky was still dark but I could see that the sun was struggling to make its appearance, as the colors outside became a kaleidoscope of blues, pinks and oranges. I rolled onto my side to watch him sleep. He seemed so perfectly content. I wondered what he was dreaming. My sleep was restless and filled with visions of Marena turning her back on me metaphorically and literally. In one vision, she even told me "now you know how I feel" and walked out of this cavernous, 16th Century-looking hall with the train of her dress flowing like water behind her, dramatically choreographed to her statement.

I had another dream that was bothering me even more than the ones about Marena. It was about Barlow and it was not so much what happened in that dream that concerned me as much as how I felt about it. In this particular dream, he kissed me with all of the passion of someone desperately in love. Not only did I let him kiss me, I kissed him back, meeting his passion with my own. Although it had only been a silly dream, and probably understandable given what almost occurred last night, it felt so real and worse than that, I liked the way it felt.

Just then as if on cue, Barlow opened his eyes and caught me staring at him. I tried to pretend I had not been watching him.

"Everything all right, your Highness?"

"Um, yes. Fine, thanks," I replied nervously and flopped onto my back. Barlow slid over to the side of my cot and sat up looking at me.

"Are you unable to sleep? Is something frightening you?" If only he knew.

"No, no. I'm ok, Barlow, really. I just had a strange bunch of dreams that I was thinking about is all. It's almost dawn."

"Almost," he replied. He seemed as if he had more to say.

"What is it Barlow?" I asked. Barlow sighed, hesitated and then whispered:

"Princess, I know you are sealed to Adelio, but I…"

"I know," I told him and I did. I knew what he wanted to say to me, but I couldn't allow him to keep going. In a strange way, although my body and soul were so tightly connected to Adelio, part of my heart was coming under the powerful control of "what if?" What if Adelio and I were not sealed by some mystical force; would we still feel the way we do about one another? What if I had met Barlow before I met Adelio? Would I be forced to put aside my feelings for Barlow? And just what were these alleged feelings I had for Barlow all of a sudden?

"Barlow, sometimes what is left unsaid is more intimately understood than what is declared," I advised him sounding like a Jane Austin novel. "Matters of the heart are - difficult to endure if impossible to reconcile. But maybe what we both know, but do not say is more - is more…" I couldn't think of what would appropriately finish the sentence.

"Precious?" A voice in my head suggested.

"Nah, not precious," I disagreed silently. Then I realized with whom I was disagreeing. Adelio had been listening to my thoughts. I hoped he hadn't heard every bit of what I was thinking about with reference to Barlow, but I realized it didn't matter. He had probably heard enough.

"More what, Princess?" Barlow was eager for me to complete the sentence.

"Uh - valuable?" I was both mortified and irritated that I could clearly never have a private moment. Now I really regretted missing my lesson with the tutors yesterday, and not just for the whole almost getting killed by bad guys thing.

"I understand. You are an amazing woman, Avery," Barlow complimented.

"Thank you. You're all right yourself," I said giving Barlow a playful punch on the arm.

"You know, I think we're going to be famous friends," he said with sudden enthusiasm. His energy was contagious and I recognized that we were going to be the best of friends now that all of the awkwardness was past us. I hoped, anyway.

"Yes, we are! The best of friends, I think," I sat up in my cot and faced Barlow, "Now excuse me, while I get dressed. We probably should get moving."

"Oh, I think I should stay in here and…"

"Out!" I commanded.

He bowed and backed out of the curtain.

"Be quick, friend," he called back to me in a loud whisper, "And we can be the first to the strawberries and cream this morning!"

"Shh!" I replied. Strawberries and cream did sound delicious. I slipped my nightgown off my shoulders and it floated to the floor. The light from the rising sun allowed me to see that my dress for our journey today was already hanging on a hook at the side of the tent. I assumed one of the ladies was supposed to be helping me, but I had dressed myself with little assistance since I was probably three years old so I went ahead with my plan.

My bare back was to the curtains leading into my private tent chambers so I did not realize at first that Adelio had snuck in to see me until I reached for the dress on the hook. He handed it to me and I suddenly choked on the air.

"What the? - Hey, get out!" I hissed trying to cover myself with a blanket. "What do you think you're doing?"

"I need to speak with you, urgently," he replied.

"Why? Are you going to chastise me for my thoughts? You know, I don't appreciate you listening to every private conversation I have. The first thing I'm asking the tutors is how to block my thoughts!"

"That's a good idea, but it's tutor and that's what I need to tell you. Lankin is gone."

"Gone? What do you mean by gone?"

"Not present, not at the camp, and nowhere in the vicinity. We think it was he who put you in danger. He's working for Anyon."

"What? Why would he do that?"

"It may not have been intentional, but we don't know and we don't have a lot of time to guess. Our suspicions are that he is headed to where he believes we are going. The Order of the Heather is aware of the situation and they have sent guards to find him, so there is nothing to worry you. I just wanted you to be aware of the situation. I'll wake and alert the others.

We should probably get to the boat. Hopefully, it's still there." Adelio did an "about face" and headed for the curtain.

"Wait!" Adelio stopped walking. "Are you angry with me?" I asked him.

"I am, but we can speak about that later. Or perhaps what is left unspoken is more - valuable," he mocked. I did not reply and he continued through the curtain.

31

PULLING STRINGS

Between the time that Adelio spoke to me to the time it took to walk to the boat, the sun had completely risen, awakening all of the birds and forest creatures. While I was never one to ignore nature, unfortunately I did not have time to truly take in just how lovely Prenmar Forest was. During our swift hike back to the boat, we passed by a number of grazing deer and even a red fox. Tulip must have also noticed the fox since she ducked into her backpack and did not pop her head up again until we reached the safety of the boat.

We were a larger crowd this time. In addition to Bob, my sisters, Barlow and Adelio, on this trip Remble, Honora and our ladies had joined our group. The rest of the encampment was traveling the opposite direction, apparently to Thistelton on the Eastern border of Premnar Forest.

We carefully boarded the boat in three shifts using the inflatable, hard bottomed tender.

"You know," I started to Barlow, "if Kirana is this antiquated place with few modern conveniences, if any, how are we going to be operating this boat for much longer?"

"Aren't you clever, lass? Nothing to fear, the Order has stores of fuel used to operate some modern machinery, although, we do not have a lot of modern machinery to speak of here. A few power boats, like this one, a few tractors in some of the northern counties and towns where the earth is more difficult to plow, but that is about all we have." That answer satisfied my curiosity and my concern that we would run out of gas somewhere on the river and get eaten by a sea creature. I quite liked the idea that my next car in Kirana would probably be a horse.

Soon, we were underway and headed up river. We still did not know where we were going, but Bob knew and seemed quite delighted at the course he had set. Marena had not spoken to any of us since last night and was still sulking. Donnelle sat very close to her. I could tell that she was comforting my sister. I could also tell through her thoughts that Marena was not going to move on from the events of last night so easily. Marena caught my glance and I smiled back at her as if to say, "We're ok." Tears began to run down her cheeks and Donnelle pulled my sister close to her chest. Then she silently uttered the words I wanted to avoid hearing:

"Avery, I will never forgive you for this - never." I looked away toward Adelio and my eyes began to fill with water. This was the moment we had been attempting to prevent. We were told that the Trinity was only as strong as its parts - the three of us - and if one of us was not going to cooperate, our powers would be useless.

"It will be all right in time, love. I promise," Adelio offered into my thoughts. I had no response for him and turned away. His promise provided me with no comfort at all since my sister was suffering now and we would all be forced to suffer along with her. I concentrated on the scenery surrounding us. This part of the river reminded me very much of our rafting trips down the Delaware River during the summers with not only the deep green foliage but also the steep rock faces and waterfalls that cascaded into the river.

⌒〇

Suddenly, I was in a dark hallway in my nightgown holding a candle in order to light my way. I came to a partially opened door and peered inside where I could see Marena and the man with the violet eyes embroiled in what appeared to be a heated discussion. He was holding both of her arms tightly and speaking to her in hushed tones, but I could hear him:

"Do you mock me, Marena?" He asked her.

"Of course not, I love you!" She protested.

"Then why do you insist on disobeying me?"

"I didn't - I - I couldn't get what you wanted. There were too many people in the room, but I will get it. I promise!"

"That's my good girl," he said in a calmer, sweeter voice. The man embraced Marena and kissed her passionately. "You will be the most beautiful Queen of Kirana to ever rule this Kingdom," he told her as he released her arms.

"And you will be my King," she promised him.

⌒〇

The river became narrower as we continued our travels. Barlow had taken a seat needlessly close to me near Uncle Bob at the helm. As he spoke to Bob about the doings of the kingdom over the past sixteen years, which for him was only about two years, he nonchalantly placed his arm on the seat behind my head forcing me to lean on it. Every so often his hand would leave the cushion and touch my shoulder. I would shoot him a look and he would just smile at me, like a child who was caught snatching an extra cookie at snack time. Adelio walked out to the bow of the boat. I could tell by the sparse thoughts that he was allowing me to hear that he was concentrating heavily on something, but I could not tell what.

I knew Adelio was busy, but I felt like I needed to share my vision with him.

"I need to tell you something which I think is important or maybe nothing. I don't know," I spoke to Adelio silently. He did not respond.

"Really, so Ginter is running the Royal Council without the Order of the Heather?" Bobril asked Barlow.

"Ginter is just a puppet from what I have heard, but he has been able to keep Queen Riva safe all this time, which is remarkable," Barlow replied.

"And what of her husband, the King?" Barlow did not respond to Uncle Bob so I knew the answer was unpleasant and probably horrible. We had all been under the impression that he was "presumed dead" which still allowed us hope that he could be alive.

"Is he dead? Is my father dead?" I interrupted. I stood up in between the captain's seat and Barlow. Still no one responded. Marena looked up from Donnelle's lap and Timber emerged from the cabin holding Tulip.

"Well, answer!" Marena demanded.

"Yes," Barlow replied bowing his head out of respect to us.

"But how do you know for sure?" Timber inquired.

"Your father, the blessed King was captured and imprisoned in the Tower soon after our defeat against Anyon. He tried to escape one night and almost succeeded but was caught in the very act and murdered by Anyon's guards in the Tower. He was to be put to death the next day along with other men whom Anyon deemed to be traitors to his cause," Barlow looked at me. I realized that our father was in the Tower with his brother and cousin.

"I'm so sorry, girls. Your father was a wonderful man. He would be so proud that you have grown to be such bright and lovely young ladies," Uncle Bob tried to comfort us. The truth was that we were not overly surprised by Barlow's information. We never knew our father and knowing he was killed for trying to protect us was a sad fact in the fantastic tale or our lives. Certainly, we were disappointed that we would never meet him, but our emotional responses ended there. We could not mourn someone we never knew.

The billowy tree limbs above the narrow river dipped lower over the boat causing Adelio to have to move off the bow or risk being swept off by what appeared to be weeping willow branches. We turned slightly to the right around the river bend and before us, rising out of the river itself, was a white stone castle. Uncle Bob quieted the engine as we drifted closer to what appeared to be a gate of some sort with two men in official looking costumes standing before it.

Adelio walked out onto the bow of the boat once again in order to speak to these guards. I could hear him tell them that we had come for the Duchess of Easton and Preck and please open the Watergate. I assumed he was referring to Aunt Bea. Surprisingly, these men obliged and the metal bars lifted out of the water. Uncle Bob slowly steered our boat into the water passageway, which was lit by torches along the wall. He brought the boat to a dock and Adelio tied us off to one of the cleats.

"All right everyone, we're here."

32

SWENWOOD

We left Honora and the other ladies in the boat to watch after Tulip while we recovered our aunt. There was no one to greet us as we made our way up the winding stairwells to the main floor of Swenwood Castle. The walls of the stairway were stone; what you would expect in a medieval castle. Small windows allowed the sunlight to guide our way and unlit candles lined the stairwell. I wondered whose unfortunate job it was to have to light all of those candles at night.

We came into what appeared to be the Great Hall and the beauty of the castle equally awed my sisters and me. Timber's mouth was agape as we walked through the room with its remarkably high ceilings and ornate furniture. Gilded doors adorned with fantastic mythical creatures were closed on the other end of the room.

"Where is everyone?" I whispered to Barlow, who was walking next to me. He shrugged and shook his head. I could tell he was not comfortable and was on high alert. Barlow's eyes darted nervously around the room.

"Probably at Pilton Palace. This castle is your summer residence," Remble replied quietly. Despite the fact that it appeared no one was present in this castle, it was clearly lived in as I noticed fresh flowers in large vases on the right hand wall.

As if on cue, the gilded doors opened and in walked a tall man in one of those popular cloaks with five costumed guardsmen trailing behind him. He took extremely long strides and walked with determination. Barlow's right hand reached across his body and he gripped his sword in its sheath. As the distance between the man and our group decreased, I noticed that this man had glowing violet eyes. This acknowledgement caused me to gasp and I hid behind Barlow.

The man addressed Uncle Bob, who was at the head of our group with Adelio.

"My Lord," he said as he bowed slightly to Bob and gripped his left arm. "At last, you have returned to your home." He then pushed through Bob and Adelio and addressed my sisters and me, "Your glorious Majesties," he said as he entered into a much deeper bow now, "this is a most wonderful day. Come, give your good cousin an embrace!" Neither Timber nor Marena nor I moved; we were too surprised, but Timber spoke first.

"Where is Aunt Bea? We want to see her."

"She will be with us shortly. Once I heard that she had been taken here to Swenwood Castle, I immediately organized my men to ensure her safety and comfort."

"But you took her from Fort Augustus. You brought her on a boat to Kirana," I piped in from behind Barlow. I walked around and stood with my sisters facing this stranger from my visions.

"Your mother the Queen has not been well for some months now, and had asked for your Aunt quite regularly. In an effort to comfort Her Majesty, I traveled to Fort Augustus to retrieve her, just so Queen Riva could see her for a few hours, but as we crossed into Kiranian waters, Anyon's men overtook my vessel. They took your Aunt Bea into custody against my word and my wishes. I only learned of her captivity here yesterday, but I can assure you, she has not been harmed at all. In fact, she has been kept as a Duchess should be kept."

"And who are you?" Marena asked.

"I am Ginter de Hazaro, Princess, cousin to your mother and acting Regent of Kirana. Come, let us reunite with your Aunt," Ginter swept over to Marena and Timber and put his arms around their shoulders. Timber's expression spoke volumes and Remble intervened.

"It's all right girls. Ginter is a loyal friend and ally. You must forgive their trepidation, your Grace. They have traveled a long way and have been in grave danger for most of their journey," Remble's voice was soothing and calm.

"You are safe now. You can trust in me," he said humbly.

"Caution, Avery. I am not certain of Ginter's motives. He remains under the command of Anyon," Adelio advised me silently. I nodded in understanding.

"Surely, you are aware that I have considered my duty of protecting the Queen as the most important obligation I have. Of course, now that the Princesses have been safely returned to the realm, they are my most important obligation," Ginter spoke directly to Adelio, which I found rather strange. Perhaps he could tell that Adelio was skeptical.

"Why don't you lead us to Bea? We are all eager to see her," Uncle Bob asked Ginter.

"Of course. This way!"

Ginter lead us through the gilded doors into another grand hallway, which was brightly lit by the sunlight streaming through the floor to ceiling windows. Surrounding the windows were opulently designed velvet drapes in deep maroon. Colorful stained glass panels took the place of clear glass on the upper portion of the windows. Lining the walls of the hall were enormous portraits of what appeared to be Kings, Queens, Princes, Princesses and other regal looking people all dressed in a similar medieval manner.

"Doesn't look like the fashion trends have evolved very much since the Dark Ages!" I remarked silently to my sisters. Timber giggled and agreed. Marena was still ignoring us.

"Are these our relatives?" Marena asked aloud.

"Your ancestors, Princess Marena," Remble replied. "Here for instance is King Hazaro himself, the savior of Kirana, with his wife Queen Amara and their daughters," he said stopping in front of what appeared to be a very ancient oil painting. Marena walked ahead examining the portraits and reading the inscriptions.

"Is there a special girl gene in Kirana or something? There are very few boys in any of these pictures," Marena remarked.

"Here's one!" Timber replied pointing to a painting of four young children.

"Yes, that is my father, Tindol, and your grandmother is right there," Ginter instructed, pointing to a blonde little girl wearing a long green gown. I recalled the history lesson Adelio had given me while we were still at the abbey.

"Ginter's father betrayed our grandmother and her sisters. Isn't that right Ginter?" I asked in a less than kind manner. I believed it was necessary that my sisters were aware of Ginter's family history.

"Avery! That will do." Uncle Bob exclaimed, apparently surprised by my bluntness.

"That is true, your Highness. My father made a very grave mistake. He did not accept his place, serving his sisters, and he desired power. However, he was blinded by his own ambition, and he trusted the wrong people. I have paid the price time and again for his error. Orphaned, I was raised in the nursery of this very castle. It was through the grace and acceptance of your mother and father that I have any sort of purpose to my life now. They have allowed me to serve my duty to Kirana and I am most grateful. Your Lady Mother, the Queen has restored my titles and land, which I can someday pass on to my heirs."

Despite Ginter's candor, I felt uneasy. Something in the way he spoke to us seemed less than authentic. Adelio had warned me to be on guard with Ginter and maybe I knew too much about him to remain open minded. Perhaps I was harboring a bias against him based upon the stories I had heard of his father.

Conceivably, my feelings we based upon the visions of Ginter that I began to have prior to leaving Woodport. Whatever it was that was causing my anxiety, it did not taste right and I was going to remain on high alert around Ginter. At the same time, I felt obligated to remain open minded. I did not want to punish the son for the sins of his father. The fact was, Ginter was loyal to our mother and had protected her since we left Kirana.

We continued to follow Ginter through the hall and at the end, we made a left turn down another long hallway. Marena was now walking beside Ginter asking questions about castle life.

As she spoke, she smiled and touched his right arm. Timber elbowed me and raised her eyebrows. Perhaps Marena would be over Adelio and past our conflict more quickly than we had originally hoped.

We walked about two-thirds of the way down the hallway to a door that was guarded by two men. Ginter had said that Bea was in no danger while at Swenwood, so I found the guards' presence to be rather peculiar.

"I asked that the guards monitor visitors to your aunt, to keep her safe of course," Ginter replied to my silent notion. He must have been reading the pensive expression on my face. The guards opened the doors and we entered what looked to be a rather spacious apartment. Bea was reading a book in a chair by the window.

"Aunt Bea!" Timber exclaimed and ran to her side. Marena and I followed.

"Girls! Thank goodness you are all right. I have been so worried about you! Look at you-you look like princesses already. You know, you're grounded!" With this last statement, Bea laughed and stood up to receive an embrace from each of us. She kissed us on the tops of our heads.

"All right, lassies, my turn," Bob directed and we stepped aside so that Bob could reunite with his wife.

"Oh, Bobril. I am so happy to see you. Ginter told me you were coming here today and I just could not wait to see you all! Adelio, thank you for helping our girls and for keeping them safe. I cannot tell you how anxious I have been!" Bea told us.

"We should get moving if we're going to get to - where we need to be when we need to be there," Adelio said mysteriously.

"Are we going to the Palace to see our mother? Oh please say 'yes!'" Marena begged.

"Uh-huh," Uncle Bob replied.

"Bea, what do you need to take with you? We should go!" Marena responded.

"Nothing. Everything I need is at the - palace," she replied.

⌒○

"Are we actually going to the palace?" I asked Adelio in my thoughts once the boat was underway. Adelio shook his head.

"Why the secrecy? Where are we going?" Again, Adelio shook his head.

"You'll see and there I can guarantee your safety," he replied. Adelio and I sat in silence next to one another on the bench close to Uncle Bob. Bea sat at the end of the bench and spoke to her husband about her treatment at Swenwood Castle over the course of the past few days. She corroborated Ginter's assessment and told him that, although she was taken against her will by Anyon's men, she was treated rather well at the castle once Ginter found out she was there. In fact, she was informed specifically by Anyon's guardsmen that they were given strict orders to obey her every command, but she was not permitted to leave the castle. Bea had heard through

Ginter that Anyon had sent a group of henchmen into Fort Augustus to murder us, but that they were intercepted by a great sea creature.

"You know what was weird?" I asked aloud, rhetorically, to Bea. "That Ginter told you we were coming to get you today. How did he know that?"

"That's a brilliant question, lass. I do not know. I thought to ask him before he left Swenwood for Pilton Palace, but I changed my mind hoping we would come up with a plausible answer ourselves," Adelio said.

"I did not think anything of it, to be honest," Bea said, "But it is rather peculiar unless perhaps Ginter spoke with one of the members of the Order, although my understanding is that the Order does not communicate for the most part with Ginter."

"We didn't tell anyone where we were going. In fact, Adelio and Bob didn't even tell us where we were going just in case someone could hear our thoughts. How could Ginter know we were coming if we didn't even know? That's what I found so strange," I reported, "Do you think it's Lankin?"

"Perhaps," Adelio answered, "although that means he is still able to read my thoughts despite the fact that I had blocked them, or believed I had. There really is no alternate explanation, but I highly doubt he is in communication with Ginter or Ginter with him. Bea is correct. Due to his family history, the Order does not communicate or work with Ginter especially since he helped facilitate their expulsion from Pilton Palace and the Royal Council."

"Well, that's not fair!" I replied. "He's not his father. Why should the Order hold such a grudge?"

"I don't know, lass, but I'm sure they have good reason to mistrust Ginter. He has been more than loyal to your mother and your family since the invasion, but the Order still finds something untrustworthy about Ginter," Adelio stated.

"Coincidence, perhaps," Uncle Bob muttered.

"That's some coincidence, Bobril," Adelio countered.

33

LESSONS IN HISTORY

We continued our journey down river. Marena and Timber sat with Remble on the stern of the boat. I could hear him further explaining the mystical Kiranian method of measuring time and age.

"But how is it that we were able to age sixteen years when we lived in the normal world, but now our aging slows down? I mean the rest of the world and time moves on, right? We're all on Earth and the Earth revolves around the sun in the same way. They have a lot of sunlight in Alaska, but they don't measure time your weird way so how do you account for the difference?" Marena inquired.

"There is a mysterious and mystical power that governs time here, dearest Princess. Without it, of course, you would age like the rest of the world. However, here, over the centuries the mystics and fairies have developed a powerful spell that protects youth. And although our enemies have tried, the spell cannot be broken even through dark magic."

"What about the whole 'olden day's' theme we have going on here with all the medieval costumes? Don't get me wrong, I like the dresses, but you can't be that far behind the rest of the world. I mean, where's your computers or cars or phones?" Marena added.

"Hahaha! We rather enjoy our way of life and our 'costumes,' as you call them. We are of course capable of living like the rest of the world, but we choose not to do so. Over the centuries, we have seen the horrors that exist in the modern world. The Order of the Heather, following the Spanish Inquisition of the late 15th Century and Hazaro's rise to power here in Kirana, made a determination that we would live our lives without association with any formal religion. Instead, we have weekly community meetings in town halls where we celebrate national festivals and fellowship with one another. Kiranians are free to worship in their own ways as well, if they choose, and many do continue the religious traditions of the outside world. But these are private matters.

"As time went on here and in the rest of the world, the Order saw very plainly that modernization and industrialization were not necessarily positive changes - we lead such simple lives here, what would we need of motor vehicles or telephones? Certainly, we know they exist in the world and we teach about many aspects of the modern world, but as a cautionary tale to avoid the excesses of modern living. Certainly, we have many of our people trained to use tools of the modern world when they are called upon to travel to Scotland, but we do not require those things here. We are a self-sustaining Kingdom and what we need of finances, we find plenty in our export of fine wool and linens.

"There are many rich people in Kirana, but they are rich in a way perhaps foreign to you in the modern world. Surely there are people here of the ruling class who have over time won the favor of the royal family. But even such appointments and titles bestowed on people here tend to be based upon the merit of a person and not necessarily based on wealth."

"Wow! Timber exclaimed. "That still sounds so old fashioned and you are completely ignoring or discounting all of the good things that come from a modern world. What about communication and shared information? You are missing out on the internet. How do you Google?"

"Our scholars have compiled thousands of volumes on ancient world history through modern world history. Anything you need to learn, you can learn from them. As for your telephones and computers, well, we just find them to be a distraction from everyday life - what is important in life; family and recreation, true relationships and interaction. The modern world breeds greed and jealousy. We live in perfect harmony here in Kirana." Remble remarked.

"Perfect harmony? Isn't my mother being held hostage?" I added.

"Well, I meant among us in Kirana. Forgive my thoughtless comment, Highness. Mordith broke from Kirana many, many years ago as did Vilarr and Bolckar, the two islands to the east of Mordith. They became three independent Kingdoms, but it was not until more recent times that those in power in Mordith sought to seize power in Kirana."

"Why?" Timber asked innocently.

"Greed, I suppose. Kirana is an enchanted oasis and we are happy here. Mordith is dark and damp and it has been that way since the fairies and magical creatures that once resided there were banished or destroyed. The only mystical beings there now, as far as we know are the banshees and the brownies that employ dark magic. Vilarr and Bolckar are very, very small islands. The people there, having found their soil to be terrible for most crops, rely primarily upon fishing to sustain themselves and they have become expert ship builders. Often, the Kiranian Royal Seafarers would call upon the ship builders of Vilarr to design and build boats for them.

"But not long ago, the Kings of Vilarr, Bolckar and Mordith aligned themselves against Kirana, citing unfair trade restrictions with the outside world as their chief complaint, which at the time was unfounded since only those living within the borders of Kirana itself were restricted in their travel. This threat caused the Order of the Heather to close all borders and disallow travel completely. Imagine if these aggressors could travel to the modern world and bring back sophisticated weaponry or soldiers. We would all be doomed. Accordingly, the Order cast a spell upon Kirana and the islands of Mordith, Vilarr and Bolckar as well as the surrounding seas which keep people from traveling more than twenty miles from our shores."

"But Anyon's men were able to come to Scotland, to Fort Augustus and Ginter came to get Aunt Bea from Kirana," Timber pointed out to her tutor.

"Well - I can only surmise that Ginter had permission to travel out of Kirana from Queen Riva and had the assistance of the Order to do it. I cannot speak to how Anyon's men were able to achieve such a feat. It has been quite some time since this restriction has been in place," Remble stammered.

"Well, when we rule Kirana I think everything should change," Marena opined. I think people should be able to travel wherever they want and wear whatever they want," she stated. Remble sighed.

"Princess, when you rule Kirana I imagine some monumental changes to our way of life," and then Remble chuckled sort of a patronizing laugh.

∽○

"Whoa! Are we where I think we are?" I asked Adelio silently as we approached grand castle walls. Various flags adorned the front of the castle and waved proudly from the rooftops. Each of them was sort of a deep purple, gold and cream with various Celtic looking symbols on them. One flag had a unicorn, birds and a sword.

"We have arrived in Thistelton, Princess. The stronghold of the Order of the Heather. We are completely protected here, thank goodness. Those flags you are admiring are the standards of the Trinity - your colors. I'm sure your tutors will explain the meaning of the symbols and colors," Adelio replied.

We docked the boat rather easily with the assistance of what appeared to be winged small boys. They were little creatures, no taller than my waist and absolutely adorable.

"Sprites," Barlow whispered to me as he assisted me onto the dock, "mischievous little guys, but they know how to tie a good knot."

At the end of the dock stood a very tall and distinguished looking older gentleman in a white cloak. He had a gray-cropped beard and slightly resembled Sean Connery, I thought. He certainly sounded like him, with a strong Celtic brogue. The man bowed his head to us as my sisters and I approached.

"Your majesties, I am Ealdred, Chancellor of the Order of the Heather. Welcome to Thistleton. Please, follow me through the gates. We have much to do," he bellowed to us.

"Does this guy sound like Indiana Jones' dad from the third movie or what?" Timber asked silently and Marena giggled in response. I smiled and caught Marena's glance. Once we made eye contact, as if she had forgotten for a moment that she was angry with me, she abruptly stopped smiling and looked away.

"Seriously, Rena?" I quipped through my thoughts, "this is how you're going to be? We need to get passed all this Adelio stuff already. The man of your dreams is probably waiting for you on the other side of this wall. I can't keep apologizing to you forever," I told her.

The entryway of the castle had to be at least three stories high. Two doors opened into the castle, or what we had initially thought was a castle, and we entered. The structure was more of a fortified gate than an actual castle. A long passageway lead us directly into a courtyard filled with what appeared to be thousands of people gathered as if waiting for a rock concert.

Before we reached the courtyard, Ealdred led us up a flight of stairs that twisted up what seemed to be a tower. At the top of the stairs was a platform or balcony decorated with the purple standards and flags I saw when we first came upon Thistleton's walls. Something that sounded like a horn blew as we approached the edge of the balcony, then drums sounded and then bagpipes played. The crowd cheered and Ealdred allowed them their excitement for a few moments. Then he raised his arms and as the crowd quieted, he spoke:

"Brave men and women of Kirana. Today is the day for which we have waited. Our Trinity has returned to us!" The crowd roared with enthusiasm and then one by one, the men and women knelt down and bowed to us. Ealdred continued:

"We have come to the hour; the moment for which we have prepared these last years. Peace, prosperity and freedom shall be returned to you…" The crowd roared once again and I could feel a ball of anxiety building in the depths of my stomach.

"I suppose we're expected to bring this peace, prosperity and freedom, huh?" Timber commented silently to us.

"Apparently," I responded. Adelio was standing behind me and put his hands on my shoulders and gave them a reassuring squeeze. I looked up at his sapphire blue eyes and smiled.

"Don't you worry, lass. You were born for this, you'll be fine," he said as he patted my shoulders. I rolled my eyes as if to say, "Says you," and he laughed.

"Come now, you have your sisters and you have me to help you," he replied to my sarcasm. Ealdred continued speaking as the crowd quieted again:

"Our young Trinity has arrived to lead us to victory. Let us make them proud and serve them with honor, loyalty and bravery and even in moments of imminent danger, let us not forget our purpose! We have devoted these years to the preservation of our way of living and today the battle to restore that life begins!" The crowd reacted again to Ealdred's words and cheered loudly.

Marena elbowed me, "We should have had this guy at our football games and pep rallies," she joked. I laughed and nodded in agreement, as Ealdred pushed me forward on the platform toward the edge.

"They want to hear from you, dear Avery," he whispered.

"From me? What the - no, I - I don't know what to say," I stammered as the crowd began to come under control.

"Yes you do," Timber stated, "acceptance speech!" She declared. When we were in middle school and obsessed with the idea of becoming an all-girl rock band based on our playing abilities on the Xbox video game, Rock Band, we had practiced what we would say when we received our first Grammy Award. Since my speech was decidedly the best of the three of us, Timber and Marena decided that I should be the spokesperson when we won our awards. Having no time to prepare here, I figured I would use what I knew.

"Uhh…" already I was not off to a rousing start, and I could feel my nerves in every part of my body, "thank you - thank you loyal Kiranians. We are so blessed and excited to be here with you - we have dreamed of this day for a long time and with your support and the support of so many people - Aunt Bea, Uncle Bob - this day has become a reality…" I was speaking much slower than usual so that I could have a moment to consider the words about to fall out of my mouth. I had arrived at the part of my speech where we thank the rest of the band and our agent so I had to skip ahead a bit.

"We only hope that we can exceed your expectations time and time again. Thank you for supporting us - peace out," I probably could have left the last part out, but I was not sure how to end. I backed up into the crowd on the balcony as the crowd below us cheered for me.

"Wonderful job Avery, I'm so proud of you!" Aunt Bea exclaimed giving me a hug and kissing the top of my head.

"You forgot to say "rock on" at the end," Marena joked.

"Ha! I know. That was nerve wracking. I hate not being prepared, I'm such a bad public speaker on my feet," I complained. My hands had turned clammy and tingly from my nerves, so I shook them out as if that would help revive the feeling in them.

"Nonsense," Ealdred assured me," those were exactly the words your people needed to hear. Rest assured, you will have many opportunities to address your people with preparation and without. Certainly, you will be practiced in this art, Avery. In fact, all three of you will be bonnie speakers in no time," he said.

"Well, I have no problem speaking to crowds so I'm sure I'll be really good at giving speeches," Marena added. No one acknowledged her statement. It was true, Marena was a natural on the stage and enjoyed the limelight much more than I.

We were brought to our lodgings, a beautiful apartment within the castle where we each had our own bedroom as well as our own trunks. One trunk contained gowns and I could hear Marena cooing over hers in her room. The other trunk contained armor and a long sword in a beautiful leather sheath. I removed the sword from my trunk and unsheathed it. It was a stunning piece of hardware that had an ornate Celtic carving on the handle and engraved down the shaft was the phrase "Je Suis Prest." I remembered hearing those words in one of my dreams. The sword was heavy, but it felt as though it was made exclusively for me. I turned it over to examine it and the other side of the sword had an engraving as well, "A. de Hazaro."

"Well that answers that question," I said aloud to myself, "it *was* made for me." I swung the sword over my head with two hands and then thrust it into an invisible enemy just as Adelio poked his head into my room.

"Be careful there, lass. You don't know how to wield that thing yet," he warned.

"Sure I do, I had a Light Saber when I was little," I joked knowing that Adelio did not know about Star Wars or Light Sabers.

"I'm sure you did, but this sword has some magical abilities when in the proper hands."

"Really? Like a magic wand or something?"

"Well, or something, yes. So you might do everyone here a favor and put it back until you have been properly trained in its usage." I obeyed Adelio and placed my sword back into its sheath.

"Can I help you with something? What are you doing in here? You're always trying to sneak into my bedroom," I teased.

"Actually, I would like to introduce you and your sisters to some friends of mine who I am sure in short order will become very close friends of theirs."

"You mean…?" I did not even need to finish the sentence and Adelio was nodding his head. "Oh, hallelujah! Maybe Marena will be less of a pill now!"

I followed Adelio through the apartment to a common sitting room where two young, handsome men sat obviously waiting for us. The young man on the left was very tall and thin with dark blonde hair and crystal blue eyes. He wore what appeared to be a military dress uniform - a white tunic with burgundy trim. He looked tremendously heroic in his uniform, even seated. The other boy appeared to be a bit younger. He had dark brown, almost black hair closely cropped to his head. His eyes were a blue green color, a lot like Timber's eyes. He wore riding boots and a fur lined vest over a linen shirt. Marena and Timber were right behind Adelio and me.

"Ladies, I would like to introduce you to Egan and Verner," the boys both stood and bowed. Marena's eyes sparkled and her cheeks flushed as she and the boy on the left, Verner, made eye contact. Timber, on the other hand, stared at her feet.

"I trust you four will get to know each other very well over the course of the next few days while we are in Thistleton," Adelio stated, "we are expected at dinner in the grand hall at dusk. You might want to rest before then."

"I'd like to walk. Verner would you come with me?" Marena asked.

"Of course, your Grace. I would be honored," he replied.

34

TRAINING CAMP

The next three days were very long. As the Kiranian summer approached, there was already significantly less darkness at night and the days were warmer. We spent our days studying the proper use of our powers with Remble and learning to use our swords. Of the three of us, Marena appeared to be the most powerful now that she could channel her emotions properly. She was able to not only move objects through the air, but also people. That was impressive, although Remble was becoming obviously aggravated with her new desire to play musical chairs with us.

Timber's powers were extremely dependent upon her ability to concentrate so Marena's joking around was not overly helpful in Timber's practice sessions. Despite Marena's obstacles, Timber had become able to change the direction of the wind, cause a rainstorm and summon all sorts of forest creatures to her command. She was able to train Tulip to speak to the creatures as well, and the cat appreciated the opportunity to be useful. At least, that is what Timber gathered.

As for me, I was becoming increasingly frustrated with my abilities. My mind reading skills were developing well, but I had become unable to read future events through my visions. My visions were increasingly less clear. It was almost as if that mysterious fog that had been such a large part of our initial dreams had invaded my visions too. I could easily hear my sisters' thoughts and we spoke freely with each other. As I understood it, we would be able to understand each other's thoughts as if in conversation as well as the thoughts of our sealed partners. We might even continue to share certain dreams.

My ability, however was supposed to be enhanced. I did not necessarily have to be in direct contact or conversation with my sisters to hear their thoughts. To hear mine, I would have to be addressing them or thinking about them in some way. I could essentially enter other people's thoughts to read their minds, and I had started to develop that ability the more time we spent in Kirana, however now, it was almost as if I had developed a mental block of some sort.

Remble hinted that all of the stress of the last few days was affecting my powers and he assured me that once I was able to truly relax, my powers would progress. Marena suggested that I was not being assertive enough or persevering enough. What I found strange was that I had been able to perform these feats on a modified scale prior to actually studying how to do them properly. I resolved to speak to Adelio about my frustration and ask for his advice.

"There is something strange afoot. I have noticed some difficulties in hearing you and definitely a decrease in visions, which is really disturbing me," Adelio told me after supper that evening as we danced. Marena and Verner were also dancing, staring adoringly into each other eyes, while Timber and Egan were working on throwing grapes in the air and catching them in their mouths over at the head table. Both of my sisters were obviously in love. I wondered if they felt the way I did when I was close to Adelio - that electrical current that caused my entire body to tingle.

I rested my head on Adelio's chest as the music slowed. I had to adjust myself so that the conical headdress Honora set upon my head did not poke Adelio in the throat. These stupid hats were on my list of items to ban in Kirana when I became Queen.

"So what do you think is happening?" I asked him silently.

"I don't know, but I mean to find out."

༄

The next day was warmer than usual and I missed my regular clothes more than ever as we practiced our archery skills with Uncle Bob and a man named Robert MacGregor. Robert was the first person we had met in Kirana or from Kirana who had a "normal" name. We learned that he was orphaned as a child and left by his parents at the abbey in Fort Augustus. The nuns who had taken residence in the east wing of the Abbey raised Robert. While there, he was educated by the nuns, and he assisted the Brothers in maintaining the grounds.

During their travels, some of the fairies met Robert when he was a teenager and immediately admired his quick wit and work ethic. Robert told them how much he desired to see Kirana, which he had read about through some of the essays at the abbey and how he wanted to join the Royal Guard. The fairies decided to take the young Robert to Thistleton as they believed he could be a great help to the Order of the Heather and he has been serving them ever since. Robert had become one of Kirana's foremost experts on Kiranian history and politics.

Through Robert, we learned that there were thousands and thousands of people in Kirana who were transplants from Scotland and even Spain. Many of them were victims of shipwrecks and some of them were descendants of historically oppressed people. He described that the government of Kirana was set up much like Britain in the Middle Ages. The Queen was the ultimate ruler, but the Royal Council was headed by the King and made up of the fourteen representatives from each town, which included two members of the Order of the Heather, the Crown Princesses and their betrothed, and four additional appointed members from each geographic region. The representatives from each town were typically the highest ranking noblemen in the town.

According to Robert, while the aristocracy did historically govern Kirana, every citizen was allotted a piece of land that they could pass on to their heirs. The land could be used in the best interests of both the citizens and the town. For example, in areas of more fertile soil, it would be expected that land would be used for farming. Thus, many of the artisans and craftsmen tended to live in towns like Glenridge and Pivko, where the soil was less conducive to growing crops. Every town traded freely with one another and markets were opened in each town center. Under the reign of Queen Huldi, a monetary system was established to simplify trade, but it was soon abandoned in favor of the traditional barter system. Any trade disputes over values of particular items or trades owed were addressed and resolved by the member of the Royal Council appointed as the Commerce Secretary.

As we were finishing up with archery and preparing for horseback riding, Timber's absolute favorite activity of the day, we saw Barlow approaching with another man. It was Lankin.

"What is this traitor doing here?" Uncle Bob asked in a menacing voice I did not recognize.

"It's all right Bobril, and I think we all need to listen to what he has to say," Barlow replied.

We all sat down at the dining table in the apartment my sisters and I shared. Donnelle brought us tea and biscuits. Adelio joined us with Aunt Bea a few minutes into our impromptu meeting.

"So you'd like us to believe that Remble is and has been working for Anyon and he is to blame for the attack on Avery?" Adelio challenged.

"I would very much like you to believe that, because it is the truth," replied our former tutor, sheepishly, "I fled the encampment for Thistleton to warn the Order of this treachery. Remble has been able to manipulate your thoughts and conversations so although you believed that your silent, private conversations were actually private, Remble was able to hear you. He did this through a Transparency Spell found in the Book of Shadows. I was shocked when I saw this book among his belongings when we were at the encampment."

"What is the Book of Shadows?" Marena asked.

"Dark magic, lass," Uncle Bob responded.

"Oh, this is very Harry Potter!" Timber exclaimed.

"You're an idiot!" Marena barked. "Those are books, this is our life!"

"Marena, watch your tongue. This is no time to be nasty," Aunt Bea scolded.

"Yeah, jerk. I was just joking anyway," Timber sulked. Egan took her hand to comfort her and she smiled at him sweetly.

"Well, what should we do? I mean, does Ealdred know what Remble has been up to?" I asked.

"I spoke to the council members when I arrived here and they suggested that I stay out of sight for a few days so that they can try to confirm my accusations, but so far they have been unable to do so, which is why I have decided to speak to you on my own. Remble has always been a good and loyal member of the Order. I cannot fathom why he would suddenly turn against us or against you. If the Order confirms Remble's misdeeds, I shudder to imagine the unfortunate end to which he will come."

"You mean, they will kill him?" Timber asked. The silence in the room answered my sister's question.

"If I am correct in my findings, and I am certain that I am, you are all in grave danger. But the only way to guarantee that I am right is to create a situation…a trap, if you will," Lankin said.

"What do you suggest, old man?" Adelio asked. Lankin proceeded to explain his plan to us and we all agreed to execute it this afternoon at our magic lesson.

35

SUBTERFUGE

I was sure that our awkward silence was a dead giveaway that we were up to something, but Remble passed off our stillness as simply fatigue.

"You will become better accustomed to our seasons and measure of time, your Graces," he assured us. I decided to break the quiet with some questions for our tutor, who I was still not convinced was a traitor. He was so kind to us and appeared genuinely concerned about our education and our progress.

"Remble, geographically speaking, where is Kirana. I mean we were told that we are off the northeast coast of Scotland, but then how can it be so mild and sunny here all the time?" I inquired.

"Excellent query, Avery. We are indeed about 200 kilometers east of Inverness in Scotland, right in the North Sea. We are south of the Shetland Islands and the Orkney Islands, which are also off Scotland's east coast. You would imagine that our climate would be rather unpleasant, wouldn't you?" Remble unrolled a map of Great Britain, which included Scotland and bits of Northern Ireland.

"Well," he continued, "it was a bit colder out here for many centuries, but with the near constant sunshine we receive and a bit of magic, we were able to stabilize our climate and create an almost tropical paradise."

"Magic - I see," Marena said.

"Yes, it is magic, just like the way we control time and aging. The fairies bless the Island and Kingdom of Kirana. You see, the fairies do not age like humans and many, many centuries ago, this island was inhabited exclusively by the fairies and we were able to keep our existence unknown to the rest of the world. However, sea travel and world discovery became an important part of human life and existence and soon, we were not alone on this island. Viking, Celtic and even Spanish explorers found our shores and created some of the first settlements here and we needed to come to an understanding with these people so that we could co-exist in peace. Our new neighbors immediately agreed to maintain our secret existence and in exchange, the fairies gifted the humans with youth and beauty and together we created a utopian society.

"Time and human history lead us to close our borders for fear of Crusaders, which was when we created the magical portals to our world," he continued.

"You mean the fog and storms?" Marena asked.

"Precisely. When Kirana was still united with Mordith to the north and the islands of Bolckar and Vilarr, coming and going to Kirana required the use of fairy magic. When the treaty was signed granting severance to Mordith and the small islands, we agreed that the storms would only preclude travel to and from Kirana. Once our neighbors to the north became adversarial, we closed all borders once again. Of course, every now and again, a ship would be caught in our mist or storms and the survivors would find their way to Kirana. Most stay; very few ever leave."

"We read about these guys who were shipwrecked here in like 1500 or something and they went back to Britain and told some Bishop about Kirana and…" Remble interrupted Timber's rather ineloquent recitation of the article we had read prior to leaving for Scotland.

"Yes, of course. Those poor men! They were with us for about one year, which is about eight years in your time. The great Hazaro came to us with these men, but Hazaro was the only one who wished to stay. The others, devout Catholics I believe and servants of Katherine of Aragon's household at the time, were rather frightened by the mystical qualities of our world. We allowed them to leave, but we never anticipated that they would share such detailed reports about Kirana with the Catholic Church, for no one ever had. If not for the quick thinking of our Order, establishing such a strong relationship with the Abbey in Fort Augustus, we might have been under siege by England, Scotland or both." This information was mesmerizing to me and I had already forgotten that we were supposed to be setting a trap for Remble, when Adelio walked into the room as we had planned.

Adelio bowed respectfully as he entered the room only coming in as far as the thick door frame.

"Sir," he addressed Remble, "I must speak to the Princess Avery at once." Remble nodded and I walked to the doorway.

"Avery, you and your sisters are to travel to Marshton this day," Adelio said silently.

"Marshton? What is in Marshton?"

"All I can tell you now is that there is a very powerful weapon which is stored there. Something that only you and your sisters can utilize but the Order has been keeping at bay awaiting your return," he told me. Honestly, my imagination began to wander to dragons and mystical beasts until Adelio tapped my shoulder.

"Yes, of course," I answered. "I will gather Marena and Timber. What shall I tell Remble? I assume this weapon is a secret."

"Very much so," Adelio replied, "In fact no one can know what you are doing and only one guide will be attending to this task with you. Tell the old man that you are being called out on urgent state business," he said with a chuckle. I laughed too. Although at some point, "state business" would be a valid reason to do something, it sounded very silly right then. I turned back to the group to speak aloud. They were clearly anxious to find out what was so important, but I remembered another important detail:

"You mean we will have only one other person to protect us?"

"Yes, this is why it is so important that no one know of your plans. With the exception of me, no one else is aware of where you are going except Ealdred."

I turned back to my sisters and told Remble we had important state business to attend to and had to cut our lesson short. He agreed to dismiss us and we hurried out of the room. No one spoke a word until we reached the confines of our bedchamber.

"Well, let's get moving," Timber said. "I want to be back by dinner time. I spoke to the Master Chef and he is going to make us a pizza, sort of."

Lankin's plan seemed to be a good one, although I thought Remble would have to be overly naïve to believe we would be left practically defenseless and unarmed. Lankin believed Remble to be just that gullible and desperate to provide Anyon with information. Our job was to leave Thistleton on foot in the direction of Marshton, crossing the river, with one guide. Our chosen guide for this task was a man named Tereblyn who was probably 6'5" and 300 pounds of muscle with wavy red hair and a Scottish brogue that was barely understandable behind his beard. We figured if something were to go wrong, we would have a chance to run for it while Tereblyn handled whatever bad thing tried to hurt us. Waiting for us along the trail about fifteen minutes from Thistleton were three young looking female fairies dressed in our clothes and wearing hoods. These girls were supposed to be our decoys.

Because Lankin believed that Remble was able to see our plans and intentions through Adelio's thoughts, he only told Adelio exactly what he reported to me in front of Remble. Adelio was to wait back in Thistelton and attend to his ordinary course of business, which this morning was archery target practice with some of the clans.

After we crossed the narrow bridge that connected Thistelton to Marshton, over the Throagtone River, we walked silently along the river path. We were afraid that any word might alert Remble to our plan. Within what seemed more like an hour than fifteen minutes we reached the decoys and their entourage. We traded Tereblyn for three substantially smaller fairies who were armed with daggers, swords and crossbows. Tereblyn nodded and directed the three decoy princesses to continue along the trail.

"Now what?" Marena asked aloud. While I was not sure we were permitted to speak quite yet, it was refreshing to hear her voice.

"This way," directed one of the fairies pointing to a branch in the trail that seemed to lead into the woods. We began to walk and Marena stopped,

"Are we sure this is what we are supposed to be doing?" She asked Timber and me silently. Her trepidation was warranted as Lankin had not revealed any part of his plan after trading places with the decoys. I shrugged at Marena but as a measure of reassurance, revealed that I was wearing my sword under my cloak.

"Oh great," Marena groaned through her thoughts, "You've brought a tripping hazard." Timber laughed and so did I, but we agreed to follow our fairy protectors into the forest.

36

SEAWEED PIZZA

"I think I want a winter-wonderland wedding," Marena stated dreamily as we sat in the grass in a clearing."

"Duh. It's always summer here, so how are you going to pull that off?" Timber teased.

"I'm not, you are," she replied.

"Oh, yeah. I probably could throw something together for you," Timber realized. "What kind of wedding do you want Avery?" To be honest, I was not really paying attention to my sisters' conversation. I had matters that were more urgent on my mind like retaking Pilton Palace, rescuing our mother - minor issues in their world, apparently. I did not want to weigh down their dreamy exuberance.

"I don't know. Maybe something small, under the stars?" I added.

"No, no, no. If you're going to be Queen of this place, it has to be grander than that!" Marena protested.

"Well, I haven't really given it much thought, but when I do you'll be the first to know," I said.

"We should continue back to Thistleton," one of the fairies escorting us directed. Timber, Marena and I stood and followed him. As I stood, a vivid vision came to me. Three cloaked women were being attacked in the woods. I gasped and then realized the vision was not of my sisters and me, but rather of our decoys. Lankin's plan had worked, or at least would be successful sometime in the near future. I just hoped the decoys would survive the attack since I was sure Anyon did not intend for my sisters or me to survive.

Without providing any detail to us directly, Lankin had essentially framed Remble knowing that he would be interested in separating the Trinity from Thistleton and interested in a weapon in Marshton. When we returned to Thistleton, we found that Remble had been taken into custody for questioning and that the Book of Shadows had already been found among his personal affects. I felt a mixture of sadness for what was likely to become of Remble and apprehension because I really thought we could trust Remble. Who else was waiting to betray us?

My sisters and I went to our chambers to prepare for dinner. Timber confirmed we were going to partake in Kiranian pizza.

⸎

The hallways intersected and intertwined almost haphazardly, but some force drew me closer to my destination as I guided my sisters through the long corridors of Pilton Palace. We came upon a heavy looking door, not unlike the other doors that we had passed, but this one had a doorknocker in the shape of what appeared to be a rose or a flower of some sort. I did not want to alarm her or cause an alarm for that matter, so I carefully turned the glass doorknob so as not to make any noise and I slid into the room with my sisters gliding in after me.

⸎

"Hey dreamy!" Marena was attempting to catch my attention. She was passing a small wooden bowl with freshly grated cheese as she sprinkled a spoonful onto her pizza. "You just zoned out again. Did you see something important?"

"Yes, I think so," I replied as I took the cheese from her. I made the mistake of sniffing it, which caused me to pass it across the table to Adelio, who chuckled at my reaction.

"Probably aged goat cheese," he told me. "It's quite good, if you do not mind the strong odor." Adelio dumped a heaping spoonful onto his pizza. I shuddered imagining how strong the taste of the cheese must be as well.

"Don't be so provincial, Avery. When in Kirana…" Marena stated in her most sophisticated voice. Verner smiled at his lovely bride to be.

"Well, what was it? What did you see?" Timber asked impatiently.

"I think it was Pilton Palace and I think it should be the next stop on our hit parade."

"You mean to see our mother?" Timber asked.

"Uh - huh," I nodded as I stuffed a piece of pizza into my mouth. It was not as good as Frank's or TJ's pizza back home, but it was a valiant effort by the chef, especially since he only had Timber's description to go by. The cheese had a funny aftertaste and the sauce was more sour than sweet, but the toppings of fresh herbs, mushrooms and green stuff that I thought was spinach at first - it was actually seaweed - made the pizza pretty delicious. Timber was clearly satisfied as she had already inhaled two pieces and was reaching for her third.

"Avery, the last place you should be is Pilton Palace. It is overtaken by Anyon's men who will be happy to imprison you or much worse…likely much worse. The only safe place for you is here, with me and your soldiers," Adelio advised.

"You're right; he's right," I said to my sisters, "we'll just have to wait." I smiled and squeezed Adelio's knee, giving him my best "yes dear."

Nevertheless, I did not intend to wait to see my mother. I had already waited sixteen years. I needed her to know that we were in Kirana and she was going to be safe.

Dinner this evening was a briefer affair than usual with the whole Remble debacle looming over Thistleton. Adelio was meeting with some of the elders and Ealdred to question Remble about his treachery, which provided me just enough time to get to Pilton without detection. As I fetched my sword from my trunk, my chamber door flew open.

"No way are you going by yourself to see her, Avery. We are going with you."

37

SORRY DEAR

"You know, when we're trying to be sneaky, it would be nice if we had the cover of darkness or something to help us along," Marena said in the loudest whisper I have probably ever heard. I glared at her. It was probably 9 pm, but the sun was still dancing in the sky as if it was late afternoon.

"Shhh - you seriously do not know how to whisper. Silent talking, please," I said to her through my thoughts.

"Ok, ok!"

We crossed the courtyard casually, giggling to one another about a phony conversation we were having and we caught the attention of the two guards at the gate.

"Good evening your Graces. Going somewhere?" The tall one on the right tower asked us as we came to the enormous door.

"A walk along the river, and maybe a boat ride," I yelled up to him.

"You know you cannot go out all three unaccompanied," the guard on the left piped in with a very thick Scottish brogue.

"Of course not, which is why our protector, Barlow is meeting us at a specific spot by the river to walk with us. He's only a few yards out to the left. Can you see him?" I had to admit this was not our best-laid scheme, having Verner pose as Barlow by the river with Egan hiding in the bushes, but we knew that the guards' scopes or "look-sees," as they were called here, were not powerful enough to distinguish exactly who was waiting for us. The guards were not fairies or any other mystical being so they were not blessed with any power that would allow them to clearly see that it was actually Verner.

"Oh I see him," the taller guard said and began to turn the lever to open his side of the gate. It creaked as the pulley system strained to open the door and my sisters and I shimmied out when the crack was wide enough for us.

"Thanks!" I yelled as we sprinted up the riverbank toward my sisters' boyfriends. I listened for the guards thoughts - they seemed confused, wondering why we were running if we were planning on a walk. Both guards concluded that we must be excited to be out of the fortress, "the poor wee dears."

"Hey!" Marena yelled to Verner and jumped into his arms nearly knocking him over as she did. Verner cradled Marena for a moment then set her down ever so heroically.

"Careful my love," he laughed and helped her into the wooden boat that was tied to a rock on the shore. As Verner took my hand to help me into the boat, which seemed to be a cross between a canoe and a raft with its somewhat flat shape, Egan emerged from his hiding spot behind a bush to greet his love. Even without my ability to gaze into the future, I saw this coming: in her excitement to see Egan, Timber thought she would duplicate Marena's move and jump into his arms, but Egan was not ready for her.

"I'm ok," she whimpered following the loud "thud" sound her bottom made as it hit the damp ground. Marena immediately began cackling,

"You clutz! Oh my gosh, that was hilarious!" Timber tried to get off the ground, but crumpled back down again.

"Your Grace, are you hurt?" Egan picked Timber up in his arms in one move. I was impressed! He must work out or something, I thought.

"I think I twisted my ankle when I fell. It hurts - owww, it <u>really</u> hurts," she said as she tried to put weight onto her right foot.

"You have to be kidding me, Tim! Well, now we can't go…"

"Rena, be a little sympathetic, will you? Timber really hurt herself," I said. "Can you walk?"

"I don't think so. Look," Timber lifted her skirt to show us her swelling right ankle.

"Oh for God's sake!" Marena muttered in her thoughts as she rolled her eyes. Egan slowly carried Timber down to the boat and sat her on a bench seat. He got in the boat and signaled for me to get in as well, so I did.

"Ok, we can't pull off our plan with a gimp, so what are we doing?" Marena asked. No one answered her. Egan hovered his hands over Timber's swollen ankle and then without warning, he grabbed her ankle with both of his hands and seemingly squeezed it. Timber let out what sounded like a small dog's yelp, the noise a dog makes when you accidentally step on its little foot.

I turned toward the gate to listen for the guards' thoughts, hoping they had not heard Timber or noticed what was actually happening. Luckily, a conversation about weaponry - whether a dirk or a claymore was a better weapon in close combat - currently occupied them.

"Oh my gosh! Look! The swelling is gone!" Timber said as she rotated her ankle, "It feels fine now. Thank you! How did you do that?"

"I can be pretty handy, my Lady," Egan replied smiling.

"Can you do that?" Marena asked Verner.

"No I cannot do that. Egan comes from a long line of healers."

"So, what is your talent then? Being gorgeous?" Marena teased as Verner untied the boat and pushed us away from shore. Egan, Verner and I grabbed three of the four paddles and Timber grabbed the fourth, while Marena lounged on the bench seat next to Verner.

"You want to see what I can do?" Verner asked. Marena nodded.

"All right, my bonnie Lass, hold this paddle." Verner rubbed his hands together very quickly and then opened them revealing a fireball in his palms.

"Oh no wonder your hands are always so warm," Marena said, "Ok, so now what?"

"Timber, when I say 'go' you're going to have to put this thing out for me," Verner said.

"I have to do what now?" Verner took his fireball into his right hand, stood up and threw it like a baseball about fifty yards. It landed along the shore and engulfed every piece of grass.

"Holy moley!" Timber yelled. She lifted her right arm and then made a wave motion, which apparently directed the river water to cover over the flames. The fire was out and luckily, the grass was only slightly singed.

"That could come in handy when we take down Anyon and his forces," I said.

"Seriously!" Marena agreed.

We continued down the river toward Pilton Palace. Finally, the sun was beginning to set. Egan lit one of the four oil lanterns in the boat to help guide us up the river.

"Is that light a good idea?" I asked. Egan blew out the wick as quickly as he lit it.

"Probably not," Egan replied.

"Avery, don't be so bossy," Timber said.

"It's all right, my love. Avery is right. We need as much camouflage to get up to the Palace undetected as possible. But thank you for being protective of my feelings," Egan said. Timber smiled at Egan in a way that made me think she had known him all her life.

"Here's something I am dying to ask - sealing. Is everyone in Kirana sealed to somebody? Is everyone matched to their soul mate?"

"Not exactly," Verner responded, "Sealing became a very important part of the Hazaro line of succession because once King Hazaro and his Queen had a trinity of daughters, and power succeeded to them, the Order was concerned that the competitive nature of men would interfere with the ability of Hazaro women to rule."

"You mean men might be jealous that their wives have all the power?" Timber asked.

"More or less, yes. It was recommended that mystical sealing be employed to create the undying bond between a man and a Hazaro woman to protect the line of succession. Sealing establishes a union of souls that only death can break. A sealed man and woman live to protect one another and are so uniquely connected that they can hear each other's thoughts and can sense when the other is in danger. Their love is so strong that they feel electrified by the presence of one another. Every fairy in Kirana is sealed to his or her mate when they are very young, so it was decided that the children of the Queen would also be sealed to their mates. Many children of noble birth are betrothed to their spouse at a young age. Sealing is a mystical betrothal."

"Well, that explains some things," I commented, "but how is a mate chosen? I mean who chose you for Marena, for example?"

"Your parents and Ealdred chose us for you from a pool of eligible young men. Keep in mind, most of Hazaro's line is sealed in a special ceremony when they reach the age of fifteen, before coming into their powers. You three were sealed to us as babies - infants, really - so that you would have our undying love, devotion and protection from day one. We didn't know at what age you would be able to return to us or even if you could return to us so the Order found it prudent to seal us before you left Kirana," Verner answered.

"Ok, but what was it about Adelio that made our parents choose him for Avery, specifically?" Marena asked. That was my question too.

"Well, I suppose they wanted someone with extraordinary powers to love and protect Avery. Egan and I are only part fairy - we have mixed blood - but Adelio is full-fledged fairy. It is rare for a full blooded fairy to be considered for sealing with one of Hazaro's line, but the Order believed this union to be the strongest possible given the needs of the Kingdom."

"What powers does Adelio have that you guys don't?" Timber asked.

"What can't he do?" Egan laughed.

"Can he fly or something?" Marena asked.

"No, dummy. That's sprites," I corrected her.

"Adelio has a great harness on the power of the mind, the body and nature," Egan said.

"So basically he can do all the things that we can do individually?" I asked.

"And then some," replied Verner.

"My boyfriend is awesome!"

"Too bad he has to marry a dork!" Marena added sarcastically.

"What is a 'dork'?" Is that a reference to Avery's ability to read into the future?" Egan asked innocently.

"No honey, not even close," Timber answered, laughing.

We came around the river bend and the waterway widened dramatically. Pilton Palace was directly ahead of us, illuminated by what looked like a million twinkling white lights. As we drew closer, we saw that candles were lit in seemingly every crevice in the castle walls. Music and voices became louder and louder the closer we approached.

"A party! Oh we're definitely getting in there!" Marena said.

"I doubt we're on the guest list, Rena and what if someone recognizes us?"

"I don't believe anyone could recognize you, but you can wear our hoods. Perhaps that would obscure your faces," Egan suggested.

"I have a better idea," Marena reported, "Is there a back entrance or side entrance?"

"Sure but the whole palace is crawling with Anyon's guards. If we paddle that way, we can tie off to the loading dock and try to come in through the servants' gate," Verner said pointing toward the palace.

"Perfect. Just follow my lead everyone." I was concerned about Marena's plan. She laid it out through her thoughts and it seemed a bit ill-conceived. Of course, if it worked it might go down as the best idea ever.

38

THAT'S ENTERTAINMENT

"**N**o entrance here," a very scary man who must have been a guard told us at the gate. "Oh no," Marena whined, "This is entirely my fault. You see, we are the entertainment for tonight and we are late because I could not find a proper shoe to wear to perform before the great Lord Anyon. We are a surprise from Sir Ginter to Anyon and I've just ruined it," she cried. I was mesmerized by Marena's performance, especially since she was able to conjure what looked like real tears.

"She's good," commented Timber silently.

"Uh, please sir, can we enter here? If we enter through the other gates, the surprise might be revealed."

"I don't know..." the guard seemed sufficiently confused but not convinced.

"Please oh please, sir? We promise we won't tell anyone that you let us through here!" Now Marena was batting her eyelashes and running her hand up the guard's left arm. I could tell Verner was becoming uncomfortable.

"Well, all right, but don't tell nobody." The guard opened the heavy wooden door and we all ran inside.

"We won't!" Marena yelled out to him, "Thank you!"

"Which way?" Timber asked as we faced a hallway with four possible directions.

"Follow me," I said. I felt as if I had been in Pilton Palace before - maybe through all my visions and dreams over the course of the last year. Somehow I knew where to go. We ran to what seemed to be a back staircase and began our ascent.

"How high does this go?" Timber asked causing all five of us to look up. The stairway seemed to climb toward forever.

"I think this is the staircase that leads to all levels of the Palace. Only the servants would use it or maybe guards so we should get moving," Egan said.

"We need to be on the third level, I think. That's where her room is," I told everyone.

We continued to climb up and up the winding staircase. Considering how dank and dingy it felt, the stairs were remarkably well lit with torches on the walls. There were no decorations and no windows except random slits cut into the stone. I could feel the breeze blowing through the openings and could smell what I perceived to be a barbeque. Timber smelled it too.

"Mmmm…smells like summer," she commented, "I wonder what they're making down there."

"I hate to be the bearer of terrible news, but I don't think it's anything you'd want to consume, Princess Timber. They've likely caught one of the fairies and…" Marena stopped Verner before he could complete his sentence.

"Ok, ok, let's just keep going," she said.

We made it to the third door on the way up the stairs, which I assumed led to the third level. I listened to hear the thoughts of anyone who might be passing by who would not be thrilled with our intrusion. I heard nothing so we opened the hall door and made our way down the hall in silence.

"How will we know which room is hers?" Marena asked me silently. A valid question, for sure.

"There will be a rose or some sort of flower shaped door knocker and a glass door knob. I think it's purple or reddish in color," I told them.

Verner ran ahead of us with Marena toward the end of what looked like a never-ending corridor to check those doors. As Egan, Timber and I ran along the hall, I remembered that our mother's room was down another corridor. I stopped for a moment and I could see myself turning right into a much shorter hall.

"No, guys. This way," I whispered to Marena and Verner and motioned for them to follow me. I ran ahead of Egan and Timber and found the hall in my vision. There was only one entrance to one chamber down this hall and it had a large flower shaped doorknocker and a glass doorknob. I knew our mother was behind the hand carved wooden door.

We all stood outside her room, and the common thought between my sisters and I was, "now what?"

"Should we knock?" Timber whispered. I did not answer and turned the knob shaking my head.

"She already knows we are here," I said. I pushed the door open only as wide as necessary to slink into the chamber. It was dark, lit only by candles and the fireplace and smelled like the spices of my dreams. I breathed in the scent that seemed so familiar and comforting. Egan entered the room last and closed the door behind us. A woman immediately greeted us by the door.

"Your Highnesses," she said and curtsied.

"That's not her is it?" Marena asked in her thoughts. The woman was much older than we imagined our mother to be and probably "old" by Kiranian standards. She reminded me of my piano teacher, Ms. Shripp who would always start each lesson with the tale of the amazing thing her grandson, who was also my age, did that week. The older woman motioned for us to follow her into an open area that looked like a living room. Carved wooden chairs with deep purple cushions and matching benches were set out in the space near the fireplace. We walked around the furniture toward a large window. There was another deep purple, upholstered bench under the window, and seated on the bench was a young woman dressed in a cascading burgundy dress.

As we approached, she stood and her long, auburn hair shifted from her right shoulder to her back. It was kept off her face by a gold crown and her neck sparkled with a gold necklace with a purple jewel at the end.

Marena broke down first, and rushed at the young woman with her arms outstretched. Marena fell to the floor and clutched the woman's legs. She buried her head in her dress and whimpered,

"Mama, oh mama…" Her emotions were contagious and as much as I tried to fight them, warm tears filled my eyes and began to run down my face. Timber began to cry as well. At that moment, I realized I had not called anyone "mother", "mom" or "mama" in my life. Perhaps I had referred to this woman as my mother before being swept out of Kirana so many years ago, but if I had, I had forgotten.

"My girls," the woman whispered, "My sweet petals." Timber and I, almost simultaneously reached out for our mother's arms. She embraced the three of us and held us close to her. After a while, she loosened her hold around us and took a step back. She examined our faces intently. Our tears of joy faded to permanent grins.

"Look at my baby girls. You are women now. Beautiful women. I have thought of you every day. For many months, Beata was able to send me life like paintings of you girls. Look, I have kept them here," our young Queen mother gracefully glided over to a trunk next to the fireplace. She opened the trunk, moved some items around, and soon she emerged with a wooden box, which she opened to reveal a collection of photos. Timber practically lunged for them.

"These are all pictures of us at the abbey," Timber remarked. Our mother nodded.

"I have so much I need to tell you. Soon the guards will be alerted to your presence," our mother said.

"We will stand guard by the door, Your Majesty," Verner told our mother and he and Egan bowed to her and backed toward the doorway.

I thought I knew what she wanted to say, that she was sorry for sending us away so I figured I would save her some more emotion:

"It's all right, Mother. We know everything. We know about Anyon and Hazaro and every-thing - we're here to restore you to your rightful throne," I announced.

"Oh sweet Avery, that is not why you are here in Kirana. You must understand…"

"But we do, mother and we're going to get you out of here," Timber said, interrupting.

"Girls, listen to me. I do not believe you understand what Anyon can accomplish. He has powers and weaponry beyond our capabilities and he will stop at nothing to destroy you and everything Kirana has built over these past centuries. He has spies everywhere - trust no one except the Order of the Heather."

"I don't even know about that. Anyon had a spy hiding in our camp and acting as our tutor who it turns out was trying to have us killed," I told her.

"I know. Ealdred told me. He's been able to communicate with me now and again thanks to my cousin Ginter."

"What about Ginter? Is he trustworthy?" I asked. Our mother laughed.

"Well, our cousin is trying a great deal to gain my trust, but I cannot confide in him and I do not believe he always has my best intentions in mind. However, he has kept me safe these past few years."

"I get a weird feeling about him," I told her. She nodded and then told me silently:

"Trust your instincts, Avery, but keep your feelings to yourself. You and your sisters will need Ginter," I acknowledged my mother's words with a nod.

"We are gathering our forces, mother and we are going to retake this Palace and get you out of here," Timber reported.

"I know you will, but please do not concern yourself with my condition or captivity. When you attack Anyon's forces, I will be with you, guiding you. You must direct your focus to Kirana and freeing our people, can you do that, girls? Do you understand?" We all nodded and answered in the affirmative, although I was not quite sure what she was driving at exactly. Before I could ask, loud footsteps down the hall alarmed us all.

"We have to go," Verner instructed.

"This way," our mother instructed, "this is a secret staircase. No one, not even Ginter knows it is here. It will lead you below the main level of the Palace. When you reach the lowest level, take the corridor to the right and it will lead you to the outer perimeter. Once outside you will be safe to return to your boat. I will be sure Anyon's men are preoccupied. Come," our mother lead us into her bedroom. I recognized the wardrobe and mirror from my dreams and visions. She pulled the tapestry hanging on the wall directly across from her bed to the side and then pushed on the wall behind it. The wall pushed open - the secret door to the secret staircase, apparently.

"In here, my petals." Starting with Verner, we all began to file into the stairway. The older woman came rushing into the room with a lantern.

"You will need this," she told us. Egan, who was closest to the woman and the last of us to through the doorway, took the lantern and handed it down the stairs to Verner.

"Will we see you again soon?" I asked our mother practically into Egan's chest.

"I will wish every day for our true reunion. Now go, be safe. I love you all," and with that, our mother closed the door to the stairway and almost complete darkness overtook us.

39

PART OF ME

"**Y**ou know," Marena began in her non - whispering, whisper, "she didn't answer your question."

"Shhh - you seriously have to learn to whisper, Rena," Timber said.

"Sorry, but do you agree that she totally evaded the question? I mean jeez, it has been sixteen years already! Couldn't she just lie? Tell us 'soon - I'll see you again soon?'" I saw Marena's point, but I did not think our mother could guess when we would see her again, or even if we would see her again. Future altering events were about to occur in Kirana and we were at the center of it all.

Just then, I was able to see into our mother's room. The man with the violet eyes was addressing her:

"Please Your Majesty, to whom were you speaking? Who was in your room? I need to protect you and in order to do that you must be candid with me. Were they here? Were the princesses here?" Our mother, Queen Riva laughed.

"Do not be silly, dear Cousin Ginter. If anyone was present in this chamber, you would have seen them come and go. I was speaking to my ladies and perhaps we were speaking more loudly than usual to hear each other over the celebration, is all."

"Anyon has ordered these men to search your chambers, Riva."

"Fine, fine. Let them search if they are interested in young women and needlepoint. That is all they will find. Come now, dear Ginter. Escort me to the party. This is still my home, as you have said, and I would like to join the merriment." Riva took Ginter's arm and began to lead him to her doorway.

"You are aware that the festivities are to commemorate Anyon's rule over Kirana and your captivity, Highness?" Riva laughed.

"So I should be the Guest of Honor!" Ginter chuckled aloud.

"I appreciate that you have maintained your quick wit, Majesty. All right, come with me." Ginter and our mother left her room and I realized we were on the lowest level of the Palace.

"This way," Verner said as we followed him into the right corridor, like our mother instructed.

⤳⟲

The guardsmen outside the palace did not detect our presence as we quietly made our way back to our little boat. This was probably due more to the fact that an amazing fireworks display was underway and everyone's attention was directed to the sky above the palace and had less to do with our group's ability to be stealth-like. In any case, we were grateful to be back to the boat. We each took our places and our oars and silently paddled away from Pilton Palace. The multi-colored fireworks reflected in the river and they lit up our faces upon explosion. Marena finally spoke:

"I am glad we did this," she said.

"Me too," Timber added, "Now I feel like we have a good reason to fight Anyon."

"Dearest, we already have a good reason to fight Anyon," Egan told her, "He is the oppressor of Kirana."

"Yes, but it's more personal now. He's got our mom and…well, I just want my mom," tears were rolling down Timber's face, illuminated by the fireworks that were quite a distance away already. Egan placed his oar on the floor of the boat and embraced his bride-to-be. I knew exactly how Timber felt because I felt the same way. We may have just met this woman, but there was no denying the connection we sensed when in her presence. This was our mother and we needed her.

"Timber, we're going to fight that much harder to be with her, that's all," I reassured her.

"Yeah, and we're going to send Anyon and those jerks back to whatever stupid place they came from," Marena added and Timber began to laugh.

"I hope that's your motivational speech to the soldiers, Rena. Very powerful stuff…"

"Very funny!" Marena pouted and grabbed Timber's oar from her. "Come on, paddle! Let's get back to Thistleton before anything bad happens. Maybe there is more pizza!"

⤳⟲

Before we reached the main gate to Thistleton, I knew we were in trouble. Not grounded for a week without TV in trouble, but definitely in for some scolding and added restrictions on our ability to leave the presence of our protectors. I did not have a vision about this and I did not hear anyone's thoughts about this. My gut was telling me, we were in for it, or at least I was.

As we approached Thistleton and the shoreline, we could see lanterns and a number of people clearly awaiting our arrival. Adelio was the first to greet us.

"Hi!" I said enthusiastically. I was excited to see him. He did not look directly at me or speak to me at all. He just shook his head as if to say, "You are in for it!" Adelio assisted Verner and Egan by helping to pull the boat onshore. Once on the sand, I jumped out and began to justify our trip.

"You know I had to go...we had to go...to see her...and..." I stuttered. I was not even convincing myself that we did the right thing by traveling to Pilton Palace.

"I know you did, and that is why neither Barlow nor I decided to follow you. But you still defied my instruction, Avery and you must not do that anymore," Adelio replied through my thoughts.

"Wait," I said aloud, "Since when are you my boss? It is my understanding that I am to be Queen so who are you to tell me what to do? I made a decision, we had a plan, and we are all back in one piece. No harm, no foul." I was steamed. How dare Adelio treat me like a child? I turned from him and marched up the riverbank toward the gate.

"Well, you're not Queen yet, Princess, and the job I have been entrusted with is to make sure you are alive to become Queen," Adelio announced to my back, "Avery, I want to protect you. Let me protect you," he pleaded with me, silently.

"I don't need your protection. I need my mom!" I yelled. At that moment, I recognized that the group assembled outside Thistleton's main gate included Aunt Bea, who for the last sixteen years had been our mom. I immediately regretted my last statement. How could I be so immature and insensitive?

"Aunt Bea, I didn't mean..."

"I know, lass," she took my arm. "Come inside and we can talk about the next step to getting you your mother." Aunt Bea began to lead me inside. I turned back to see my sisters, Egan and Verner following us. Adelio was standing on the edge of the riverbank throwing pebbles into the ink black water. I looked at Aunt Bea and she nodded, understanding that I needed a moment. The rest of the group walked back inside the gate.

"I am sorry, Adelio," I said silently, "I know you are doing your very best here to keep us from harm, but we have waited our lifetimes to see our mother. I do not know if you can understand what it meant to us or how difficult it has been for us knowing she was only miles down this river. We had to go. And I am sorry I yelled at you. I do need you. We all do." Adelio stopped throwing stones and turned toward where I stood. The others had already passed through the gate, giving Adelio and me the moment we obviously required to resolve this quarrel.

"Avery, my heart hurts when you are away from me. I do not know how else to describe the feeling. I have had this sensation, this ache since you were taken from Kirana so many years ago. It was only when I saw you at the airport in Glasgow, that first day that this empty feeling began to subside. You are a part of me - a part of my soul. You are the fiber of my being. But I feel that perhaps you do not share this connection with me. Perhaps our sealing was not meant to be." Adelio was now standing directly in front of me with his hands gently laid upon my shoulders. His eyes filled with water. I could not bear to see this specimen of a man so obviously hurting.

"Oh Adelio," I said to him. I was speaking aloud, but my voice shook with the uncertainty of what I was going to say. What could I say? I loved him so much and I barely knew him.

"Adelio, I love you. I love you so much I cannot even put words to the quantity and quality of love I feel for you. The funny part is, I cannot even explain why I love you. I barely know anything about you. I don't know where you live. I have never met your family or parents. I don't know your favorite food or color. Heck, I don't think you even told me your last name. Despite all these small mysteries, I can feel my heart growing in size when I see your face. Even thinking about you makes me happy, and I feel safe. When I am near you, I feel as though I can do anything - even lead an army to victory. Before I met you, I could hardly decide on what shoes to wear in the morning without some consternation. Now, I feel powerful, confident. Mostly, I feel adored. I think I am going to be who Kirana needs me to be because you are a part of me. I do not know or understand much about the sealing process, but I can tell you that our bond makes perfect sense. I am supposed to love you and I do...I..."

Adelio responded with a kiss upon my parted lips. This kiss rivaled the passion on the dock at Loch Ness. I was not quite finished with what I had to say to Adelio, but I decided he must have gotten the point.

Images began to stream into my mind - visions of Adelio and me in all white and on horseback waving to crowds gathered along a street. Timber and Egan followed behind on horses with Marena was behind them by herself. Marena did not look to be enjoying the festivities like the rest of us, as she reluctantly waved to the people on the street.

Then I saw Adelio, still in all white, kneeling before me as he kissed my hands. We stood in what appeared to be an open, grassy courtyard. Flowering bushes created an archway directly behind us, which led to a garden that was blooming with the most amazing roses I ever saw. The air smelled of their fragrance.

Adelio pulled his lips from mine, and my visions dissipated.

"Those things are the least of what is to come, your Highness," Adelio whispered into my right ear and then gently kissed it. I felt my whole body shiver as he brushed his lips passed my cheek. I reached up with my right hand and pulled the back of his head toward me so that his lips met mine again. I never wanted to stop kissing Adelio.

"Ahem..." Timber was giggling and pretending to cough as she poked her head out of the open doorway at the gate.

"Can we help you, Princess Timber?" Adelio asked.

"Sorry to interrupt - sort of - but Ealdred has gathered all of the leaders in the main hall. Anyon knows we are here in Thistleton and that we are organizing our army. Ealdred wants to attack before Anyon can muster his own troops. First thing in the morning, in fact."

"Oh my gosh! This is really happening!" My stomach began to gurgle with a combination of fear and anticipation.

"Come on, Chef made more pizza!" We followed Timber through the gate. I reached for Adelio's hand, we interlocked our fingers and he squeezed my left hand in his.

"Ready?" He asked me silently.

"Do I have a choice?"

40

THE WAR ROOM

"Aunt Bea," I whispered, "Why is he here?" The cloaked man with the violet eyes, the man who haunted my dreams and visions for so long stood at the head of the long, hand-carved wooden table. Before him, large hand drawn maps on old looking parchment paper lay with different colored stones on them representing our various regiments.

"Ginter will be important in helping to defeat Anyon's forces. Anyon trusts Ginter and has shared his plans to defend Pilton Palace."

"I'm glad the bad guy trusts Ginter, but since when does the Order trust him? I thought they wanted nothing to do with him," I was very concerned. After our experience with Remble, I wondered how much we should trust a man who had essentially been acting as our mother's jail guard. Even our mother was not convinced of his loyalty to our cause.

"Sometimes we must do what is expedient. Right now, Ginter is able to tell us what Anyon's plans include. He knows how Anyon will defend his position in Pilton. He knows how many men Anyon has on hand to meet us on the battlefield and he knows where weapons are stock-piled. In fact, we have a team headed toward Pilton this very moment to inhibit the guards' ability to use their long bows," Aunt Bea continued, speaking very low to me so that the other participants of this important meeting could not hear.

"Really? Are they going to steal all their weapons?"

"No, but their arrows might be temporarily relocated for a while," she said. I nodded, impressed that there were members of our group courageous enough to execute this job.

"Ealdred, the only way to overtake Anyon's forces is to send in waves of cavalry following the ground troops that will surround the palace. Anyon will have no place to go. We will trap him and take him captive until we hear surrender," Ginter instructed causing many of the leaders in the room to cheer. Others seemed to disagree with this strategy and grumbled with dissatisfaction. Ealdred shook his head in a kind manner, but it was clear he too disagreed with Ginter.

"Ah, no lad. We must not surround our enemy for he will have nothing to lose and may cause great casualties for his men and ours. No. We must keep to the original plan. Meet Anyon straight away on the battlefield and push forward. Attack at the North, East and West points. Leading our troops from the South will only mire them in a swampy nightmare. They will be perfect sitting targets for the long bow," Ealdred explained.

"I have men who will follow me. Men loyal to the Queen. I can lead them from the South." I could not understand why Ginter was being so obtuse on this issue. Why did he feel that attacking from the South, through a marsh was such a good idea? Maybe he knew something the Order of the Heather did not. I could sense Ealdred was becoming aggravated with Ginter, so I wanted to break the tension and ask,

"Ginter, why on Earth do you want to lead your men through the swamp? What is so important about attacking from the South?"

"Your Grace, I know that I can infiltrate the palace walls from the South. Look here," Ginter held up one of the maps that appeared to be of the palace grounds, "There is a way around most of the marsh." Sure enough, Ginter showed us what appeared to be an old trail or road that came through a wooded area to the east of the swamp. It only crossed into the swamp for the last fifty or seventy-five yards at which point the topography appeared to become hilly leading up to the palace.

"You can make it through here, without horses or men being caught in the swamp?" Adelio asked.

"Absolutely. I know it can be done. Anyon took this path when he invaded the palace initially. I watched helplessly as an entire column of his men overtook the few members of King Philson's guard on the South end. I tried to organize our long bows, but it was too late. Yes, it can be done," Ginter declared.

"Yet, it will not. We cannot risk losing an entire platoon of men on the South side. If he was able to infiltrate the palace from this point, he will expect us to do the same. Ginter, we respect your willingness to assist and your bravery, but we are best to remain with the original plan, yes?" It did not seem as though Ealdred was truly asking Ginter to agree. He was speaking in an almost patronizing manner, as if to say, "Nice try, young man, but the adults will work this out." I did feel a little badly for Ginter. He seemed sincere and eager to fight with us.

"Very well," Ginter sighed, "I will join Lessig and Glenridge on the East side.

"Good. Now that we have settled this matter, who would like to try more of that delectable pits-ah?" Apparently, Ealdred was also a fan of Timber's Kiranian pizza.

Looking around the room at all of the people gathered to plan our attack on Anyon was humbling. Present were members of the Order of the Heather - fairies and men alike. Then there were members of various Scottish Clans whose relatives had settled in Kirana in the mid-1700's during the Jacobite rebellion. There were groups of Jewish settlers whose ancestors had initially come to Kirana at the time of the Spanish Inquisition, during the Russian Pogroms and the Holocaust. There were even some African Kiranians who had escaped the bonds of slavery in Europe and Africa in the early centuries. All of these people sought freedom from oppression when their ancestors found their way to Kirana so many years ago, and now they were willing to support my sisters and me in our fight to free them once again. Despite the diversity of their ancestries, they were all Kiranians, dedicated to freedom from tyranny. This realization elevated my sense of duty and I felt more than ever that here, with these people, was where I belonged.

Once the twenty-five or so people gathered in the Hall had their fill of Kiranian Pizza, they reassembled and took their places at the table. During the break, I noticed that Adelio spent a great deal of time speaking with Ginter. I was curious about that conversation.

"What was that all about?" I asked him silently.

"A bit of reconnaissance. I was attempting to determine Ginter's motives," he replied.

"And? Did you just come out and ask him?"

"No, I did ask some probing questions about how he knew we were coming to Swenwood to get Bea, for example. His explanations are completely plausible, but I did notice something interesting when he spoke to me."

"What?"

"He rarely looked me in the eye and when he did, it was only for a few seconds."

"So?"

"So, I have a feeling that perhaps your Cousin Ginter is not exactly who he says he is," Adelio told me.

"Adelio, I think we need more evidence than shifty eyes to accuse him of treachery or treason," I said.

"I know, I know," Adelio replied in haste. "It's just this feeling I have."

"Well what should we do?"

"What can we do, Avery? We have no direct proof of wrongdoing, just gut instincts telling us something is a bit off," Adelio said.

"Let's keep our eyes open, then. As if we don't have enough to worry about," I sighed. Our plates were all quite full so to add, "Ginter monitoring" to the list was a lot to ask. Still, perhaps this was the best time to determine Ginter's true loyalty, to us or to himself.

Adelio and I turned our attention to the meeting. A rather strapping young man with a red beard, wearing a red-plaid kilt was speaking to the other group leaders. His name was Alexander from Fort Reamer in the North, and he seemed to know quite a bit about hand-to-hand combat. I found that somewhat surprising considering Kirana had a relatively peaceful existence, generally speaking.

"Aye, the Clans will be here 'a here," Alexander pointed to spots on the map and moved two blue stones to those areas. "We will take 'em 'a the bridge. They canna come 'er go." Alexander's thick brogue was difficult to understand.

"What the heck did he just say?" Marena asked me silently from across the table. I had almost forgotten my sisters were in the room. Both of them had been so quiet. Like me, they were sensing the gravity of the situation and were taking in all the conversations, debates and ideas strewn about the room. It was a lot to digest.

"Alexander is going to lead the Clans to the bridge that crosses Throagtone River and connects to the road toward Braventon. We don't want to allow additional troops from Mordith to come into Pilton or any of the troops already at Pilton Palace to leave," I explained.

"Is that what this guy just said?"

"Not in so many words, but I'm following. Shush, Rena, and pay attention," I directed.

"Fine, fine…"

Following Alexander, some of the noblemen of the various Kiranian towns all stood at the head of the table to tell us where their men would be during the battle. They all seemed excited that they were going into battle at sunrise. Although my sisters and I had been training for a few weeks, which was likely the time equivalent of a few months back home, I still felt we needed more time. My powers were not as strong as I had hoped they would be at this point. I was finding great difficulty in seeing impending events despite the visions and dreams I would have. Those visions did not always have obvious meaning and I could not anticipate when in the future they were to occur. I found this fact to be troubling because by the time I figured out that one of my dreamy predictions was actually transpiring, it might be too late to stop or prevent a bad thing from happening.

However, over the last week I had become a passable equestrian, considering I had only been on ponies at the Sussex County Farm and Horse Show, the local county fair, as a little kid. I called my horse, Pearl, due to her shimmering white coat. After throwing me in the mud two days in a row, Timber had a "conversation" with Pearl, and she and I seemed to come to an understanding. If Pearl did not throw me, I was more than happy to reward her with extra carrots and apples at the end of the day.

In addition to learning to ride Pearl and communicate with her, I also became adept at using my sword. I was hoping I would not find myself in a hand-to-hand combat situation, but if I did, I was ready. My sword was special - like no other sword and made only for my use. As long as I was threatened and had the sword on me, it would literally fight for me. I just had to keep my hand tight around the grip. I was astounded during the first training session.

Barlow was responsible for my sword training and he instructed one of the men to come toward me baring a large, Claymore sword. As soon as I touched the handle of my sword, it released itself from the sheath on my left hip. A blue-ish glow emanated from the metal blade and the sword thrust itself at my presumed attacker. The sword literally engaged my sparring partner in a duel with very little input from me. Barlow instructed that I needed to keep my right arm relaxed, my legs shoulder length apart and my body turned to the side and let the sword do the work.

"This sword makes me feel patronized and discounted," I jokingly complained to Barlow.

"Well, Princess I am sure the fairies can turn it back into an ordinary sword if you would prefer. I am sure you are well versed in the art and science of combat," he teased.

"Oh, that won't be necessary. I'll just get used to this thing," I replied.

I was also told that this sword had another power as well. It was not another magical power, but rather a more symbolic strength. The sword was created by the Order of the Heather from a special metal found on the sunken ship Hazaro had traveled upon when he came to Kirana. The oldest child of the Queen was always presented with this special sword upon her coronation, but in my case due to the circumstances of having to lead an army against foreign invaders, I was provided the sword without traditional pomp and circumstance. It was a symbol of tradition and leadership that was said to inspire Kiranians to acts of bravery. I hoped that was true.

Barlow was now at the head of the table describing where my sisters and I would be during the battle. We would hold the high ground on the West side of the field. That seemed like a logical spot for us to be, along the ridge, where we could keep an eye on the action. Part of me wanted to be in the fray on the battlefield with the rest of these warriors supporting our cause, but realistically I knew I did not belong there.

"Would it not be more strategically advantageous for the Trinity to lead a battalion from each direction of attack?" Marena asked. This caused a great uproar from the assembled group. Apparently, no one else agreed with this idea.

"Separating the Trinity is madness!" One of the leaders exclaimed.

"Hear me!" Marena called out over the fray. She stood to address the room: "I only suggest this to demonstrate a sign of strength. I am not suggesting that each of us stay on the battlefield once the battle gets underway. I merely mean to offer that if Anyon is watching our attack unfold, we can make him feel immediately surrounded by the power of the Trinity. This is more of a symbol of strength than anything else. And once the horns have sounded and my sisters and I have called for the charge, we retreat to the high ground and hold a position there." The resounding opposition of a few seconds ago faded to contemplative murmuring. This did not sound like a terrible idea.

"The symbol of strength, my dear Lady Marena, will be evident by the thousands of well-trained men on our side fighting Anyon's forces. We need not endanger our Trinity for symbolism. We need not risk your lives at all," Ealdred responded.

"Yes, we'll do it," the words spilled from my lips and the eyes of the room were upon me. I was standing and looking to Adelio and Timber for support. Timber stood first.

"Yes," she said, "we will lead the charge from each side." Timber and I both looked to Marena. Her thoughts raced, which seemed a bit odd since this was her idea. After a slight pregnant pause, she smiled and stood with Timber and me.

"We can do this." She looked to Verner who smiled proudly at his bride to be. He stood, which prompt Egan to stand and soon the entire room was standing and cheering for us. A wave of pride and perhaps foolish bravery came over me and again, I had the feeling that my sisters and I were in the right place doing the thing we were born to do.

41

THE EVE OF WAR

Adelio lead me by the right elbow into the hallway once we were excused from the Great Hall. I was making attempts to silently speak with him but he was ignoring me. Moreover, he was annoying me. Before he could drag me anywhere else, elbow first, I pulled away from him and stopped in the hall near the entryway to the courtyard.

"What is your problem?" I hissed at him. Adelio sighed.

"I am sorry you did not realize the problem."

"What are you talking about?"

"He wants you separated. Don't you see? If you and your sisters are apart, Anyon can pick you off one by one and destroy the Trinity." Adelio began to pace and had his hands to his face. I had never seen him anything but calm and confident. His anxiety was frightening me, especially since I knew he might be correct in his theory.

"Ok, ok. So then we don't go through with it. I mean, what does Marena know about this stuff anyway? I'd be lying if I said I had to hold myself in my chair from falling on the floor when she suggested *we* lead the charge. I was as surprised that she was paying attention long enough to say anything valuable." I could tell Adelio was not listening to me. I was attempting to calm him, perhaps help him identify a solution, but his mind was clearly elsewhere. We were completely silent.

"Come," he said aloud, breaking our silence. "We must rest for a few hours."

"If this is such a bad idea, why didn't Ealdred overrule us? Surely Ginter knows of Anyon's intentions. Why wouldn't he speak up?"

"I do not pretend to know what sorts of things go through Ginter's mind when it comes to you, but I can imagine that Ealdred did not want to dampen the spirits of the people by calling

Marena's plan 'the worst plan ever concocted' right there in front of everyone. I am sure I will hear from him shortly and we will devise a more suitable plan for you and your sisters."

"I hope so. What if we lead the charge, but rather than come from three sides, we charge together. The effect Marena spoke of would still be achieved, wouldn't it? But we would be together and ready for whatever we had to face." Adelio thought about my proposal.

"Still too dangerous. Princesses, especially those smuggled away from the Kingdom and raised in a foreign land, just don't lead charges."

"Isn't there a first time for everything?" Adelio laughed but I was serious.

"Still does not make it a good idea," he replied.

"Fine. Maybe I just need to get over the shock that Marena came up with this plan in the first place."

"True," Adelio agreed, "perhaps a small ale will help us to figure it all out."

"That's so funny," I replied, "that is exactly what my Uncle Bob would say to Aunt Bea."

"Well, Bobril is a charming fellow. Smart too."

Adelio lead me from the hall toward our chambers.

"I've been meaning to ask you, Avery, have you had many visions lately?"

"A few dreams, but I can't tell whether they are visions or just dreams. It seemed that before I actually started to try to conjure visions or hear thoughts, I could do it."

"I only ask, because I too have continued to experience a weakening of sorts of my own powers. And do you ever have that strange feeling that someone is watching, listening to you even when you are alone?" He asked.

"You know, I do. Even after Remble was - uh - removed from camp, it seemed that our actions were still being monitored. Ginter knew we had been to our mother's chambers and come to think of it, I did not see him coming. Verner and Egan literally heard him and we just happened to be about one step ahead of him that we managed to escape undetected. Maybe he can read minds like we can," I surmised.

"In Kirana, only those of fairy blood have that ability. But the attribute is diluted in Ginter because his father, Tindol possessed this talent. His mother did not," Adelio explained.

"So then, maybe Ginter has cultivated this ability so he can read minds too?"

"Maybe, but he knows full well he is not entitled to possess this skill. In fact, everyone is aware of that. Only fairies and the Trinity are permitted to mind read."

"That sounds like a completely unenforceable rule, Adelio. I mean, how can the Order of the Heather control minds in that way?"

"There is an understanding here, and if someone has learned to read thoughts who should not read thoughts, the punishment is banishment from Kirana. This rule is in place to protect the Trinity."

"Wow! That is a harsh punishment. Surely, every person who has even a fraction of the ability who tries to develop it cannot be tracked and punished, right?" I asked. I felt that this particular rule was quite hypocritical and perhaps a bit ironic in a land that cherished freedom.

Adelio was basically telling me that the Order of the Heather was acting as the "thought police" I read about in George Orwell's *1984*, one of my favorite summer reading assignments for Honors English Sophomore year.

"Actually Highness, they can. Certain fairies have been specifically trained and designated in this capacity. And this is just another reason why it is so unbelievable that Anyon was able to learn of Aunt Bea's presence at the abbey in Fort Augustus and subsequently your arrival there as well," Adelio lamented. Adelio clearly did not watch as much Law and Order or CSI type shows as I did. He was missing the obvious answer:

"Ginter bought the thought police to help Anyon!" I announced proudly, probably louder than necessary.

"The who?"

"Your fairy mind reading protector people. Come on, think about it. He needed Remble to learn to read minds and Remble just happened to be our tutor, always close to us. That was easy. Remble just had to report to Ginter what our next move would be - Thistelton, Swenwood Castle - and Remble was obviously compromised since he was fooling around with the Dark Magic stuff, right? He was able to block our abilities to see into the future and hear each other for a short amount of time, long enough for Anyon or Ginter to try to take me and my sisters out of the picture," Adelio was listening intently as we walked into the courtyard and toward the archery range. I was on a roll:

"So, we figure out what Remble was all about thanks to Lankin, but not before Remble was able to instruct Ginter on the methods of intercepting thoughts and hiding the evidence. He was probably training in that long before we even heard of Kirana. In fact, maybe that is how he knew Aunt Bea was coming to Fort Augustus."

"But you cannot 'hide the evidence' as you say. They will know he is reading thoughts," Adelio said attempting to deflate my hypothesis.

"Not if he bought those fairies off - you know, bribed them in some way - same as he did Remble. And he would only need to control one of them. That fairy would probably cover up his illegal activity. It all makes sense, doesn't it?"

"And you say I live in a fairy world. My darling, I appreciate your theory. I do. But it is all quite impossible. Ealdred surely would know of Ginter's alleged plot and if he did, he would never have invited him to Thistelton."

"Oh, yeah. So much for that theory," I stated. I was disappointed, to be honest. Certainly, I did not hope that our cousin, and the person closest to our mother, was a traitor to us or to our cause. There was just something about him that gave me pause. My instincts were telling me that something was not as it seemed with Ginter.

Adelio said and grabbed me into an affectionate embrace, "Well, if what you say is true, I just might have the smartest woman in the entire world," he said, "A mastermind at seeking the truth."

"Well, smarter than you," I teased.

"Come, let's get to our chambers. And put your complicated scheme to rest as well as yourself. I assure you, it cannot be. I am not sure what to do about Ginter. I do not trust him any farther than I can throw him, but we have a bigger task at hand once the sun rises. He is your kin and he has pledged his allegiance to your mother, the Queen, and to the Trinity. Really, we should accept his word and his sword."

"You're right. But how is it I am supposed to sleep?"

Of course, I could not sleep. None of us could. Timber, Marena and their boyfriends sat in our common living room area playing Rummy 500 while I lay in my bed trying desperately to see what events would transpire during the coming day. Visions swirled around and I tried to make sense of them. As I expected, they were blurry and confusing. Most of them were frightening and I thought perhaps this lack of clarity was due to my anxiety. I wondered how many seventeen-year-old high school seniors lead battle charges. My knowledge of history told me probably quite a few. Still, I did not know anyone personally who faced the prospect of a bloody medieval battle, other than in video games.

Some of the visions I did have were more troubling and specific than others. I saw my sisters, Verner and Egan fighting off an approaching group of what must have been Anyon's men. Marena seemed to be able to use her talent of telekinesis as I saw the men fly into the air and crash into the side of a rock wall. I envisioned running through the Palace calling out for my mother, but when I arrived at her room, I saw nothing but a trail of blood.

This premonition in particular gave me great pause. I knew I had to protect my mother and prevent what I saw. I also knew that this would be a deviation in our battle plan, so I had to keep my intention secret, especially from Adelio. I lay in my bed, tossing about. My nervousness surpassed any feeling I had ever experienced. No math test in school ever caused me this much anxiety. I decided to get dressed and join my sisters. Through their thoughts I could tell that they were much more relaxed than I was.

I spun my body to the left side of the large, four-poster bed and dangled my feet to the wooden floor. I shimmied down the side of the bed to stand up, but my legs felt weak so I braced myself on the side of the bed. I took a deep breath as I let go of the bed, then another yoga style deep breath. I walked to the trunk at the end of my bed and began to take out pieces of battle-garb. I found a helmet, chest plate, leg guards - the equipment reminded me a lot of Timber's catcher's gear. Then it dawned on me that I did not know what was supposed to be worn underneath this surprisingly lightweight metal protective gear. I poked my head out into the common area where my sisters, Egan and Verner were still playing cards.

"Do you guys know what we are supposed to wear with this armor?" All four of them looked up at me as if they had previously forgotten I was in my room.

"Huh? Are we supposed to get in that stuff now?" Timber asked nervously.

"No, uh I don't know. I'm just bored and - well - trying to get organized. I don't want to wake up Honora or the others to bother them about it. I thought maybe you knew," I said.

"Nope," Marena replied and turned back to her hand of cards.

"Sorry," Timber added. I could not figure out why they were not more concerned about the impending day, but decided to avoid picking a fight with them. Verner, however, seemed to be a bit more focused on our upcoming task and he rose from the velvet sofa.

"Come with me, lass. I'll show you what to wear," he said. I smiled and followed him back into my room. As I crossed the doorway I heard Marena yell, "Rummy!"

Verner helped me lay out my battle wardrobe on my bed, which consisted of the armor, a linen blouse and my jeans. Apparently, it was customary for women in battle to don a battle gown.

"No way!" I told Verner. It was one thing to wear a skirt in a tennis match but quite another to be dragging a heavy gown around while bad people were trying to kill me. I told my sisters through our thoughts that they too should track down the jeans we wore when we came to Scotland so many weeks ago.

I thought back to our arrival in Glasgow and the first time we met Adelio. The truth was, I had no idea exactly how long ago that occurred. It felt as if we had been in Kirana for maybe three weeks, but I knew from the time I checked my cell phone on the boat that time had been racing forward in the rest of the world. While I prepared for battle, my friends were probably preparing for SATs or maybe beginning their first year of college.

I stared at myself in the mirror. My thin, sleeveless nightgown barely touched my body, but as I gazed closer at my reflection, I noticed a change. I appeared more mature and physically stronger. I stretched my arms over my head and then flexed my biceps like a body builder.

"Err! You're no match for me, Anyon!" I told my newly sculpted, muscular arms. Then, as if on cue, laughter.

"Ha! What are you doing?" Adelio asked.

"Nothing. Getting psyched up to kick some butt is all. Where have you been?"

"Making some plans with Barlow for your protection, but I can see you will not be needing any of our protection, Highness," he chuckled.

"Laugh it up, fairy boy! What kind of protection?"

"We are going to designate some additional men to join your ranks whose job will literally be to watch your backs," Adelio said.

"That's it?"

"Yes."

I sighed, "All right. That is probably all we need," Adelio could sense my trepidation.

"What is it?" He asked.

"My sisters and their boys - they seem overly relaxed, as if they don't even know what is about to happen in only a few short hours. It is strange. They have been playing cards and giggling for hours while I have been thinking and worrying - I just don't get it," I reported.

"I saw Ginter speaking to Marena after you lasses were excused from the strategy meeting," Adelio told me.

"Well, why didn't you say anything?"

"I did not think much of it, but now I am wondering about that conversation," Adelio walked out of my bedroom and right into the common area and spoke to the group:

"Marena, what did Ginter tell you earlier?"

"Umm - nothing really. He just said that he would personally make sure we were safe. He says he will have three-thousand men surround our position to make sure nothing happens to us," Marena said.

"I see. Just remember, you must follow the detailed instructions Ealdred provided you this evening. Understand?" Adelio spoke very plainly.

"We know, but we're not worried," Timber said.

"What do you mean? I'm freaking out like crazy," I admitted. Marena shrugged.

"I have faith in our cousin and everyone else. No one is going to let anyone hurt us. Besides, we outnumber Anyon by a three to one margin. We're going to crush him and chase him out of the Palace and Kirana. Even Ginter says that," she said as she tossed a grape into her mouth. I wanted to argue, but her misguided confidence was refreshing. Surely nothing is pre-determined in war or battle, but Marena and Timber were accustomed to being winners. Before a big tennis match, they would be completely relaxed. Their quiet confidence seemed off putting to many of their rivals. They imagined they would win every match, and for the most part, they did win. Why should I mess with their pre-game ritual now?

"Why don't you four put your battle garb together. Avery and I have to head to the blacksmith to sharpen her sword. We will meet at sunrise in the courtyard. Be sure to eat something and pack up your bags with plenty of food and water," Adelio told them. I went into my room and collected my armor and sword and Adelio helped me carry it out of our chambers.

"Maybe we should let Ginter know we are on to him," I suggested as we picked out fruit from the kitchen. I did not know exactly what I was taking. I had never seen some of the fruit that the cooks had set out for us. I took in the sweet odor of a yellowish-pink piece and then added it to my bag.

"We cannot complicate our task, Avery. No, we need to keep a cautious eye out for Ginter, but we need to defeat Anyon first and foremost. Ginter shares this goal. In these last years, Anyon's control of the Kingdom has not brought Ginter any additional power. Yes, he is Regent and he would not normally be in this position if your mother and her sisters were still in power, but if Ginter hungers for full control of Kirana, he needs Anyon out and you girls gone. So first things first. Let's have him help us rid Kirana of Anyon and then we can focus on controlling

Ginter's ambitions, if they are truly adverse to your interests. Perhaps we have allowed our imaginations and suspicions get the better of us. Based on all the evidence, we seem to be dead wrong about Ginter." Adelio was right of course, but I did not see the harm in multi-tasking. I'd keep my eye on Ginter.

"Do you think we can talk about something else for a while?" I asked Adelio as we entered into the courtyard.

"Of course," he replied, leading me to a wooden bench. We put all of our equipment down in a heap behind the bench and sat. There was a lot of activity around us as the soldiers - my soldiers - readied themselves for battle. Adelio sat close to me and put his arm around my shoulders.

"Want to play a game?" I asked sheepishly. Adelio chuckled.

"A game? Now?"

"Sure, why not? A questions game. I ask you questions and you have to answer them and then you can ask me questions."

"Sounds more like an interrogation," he replied. "All right, ask away."

"Ok," I began, "where are you from, originally?"

"I come from Southington, which as you can imagine is in southern Kirana. Nice town, along the coast. My turn?" I nod to him and he asks: "What do you fear most?"

"Gee, that's a deep question compared to mine! What do I fear?" I giggled. "Just about everything - no, that's not entirely true. I guess I am afraid of failing and letting everybody down," I sighed. "Oh and I am also afraid of poisonous snakes."

"Well, my love, there is no need to fear failure or snakes. Preparation, desire and your strength will lead to your success here. And, we don't have poisonous snakes in Kirana," Adelio assured me.

"That's right, you just have giant man-eating sea monsters!" I laughed. "Ok, my turn again. What are your parents like?"

"My blessed mother is a lot like you actually. Beautiful and witty. Strong and vulnerable at the same time. She is the kindest person I know. Although she is of fairy blood and my father too is of fairy blood, when you and I were sealed by the Order of the Heather, they gained the titles of Lady and Baron Southway. Usually fairy families are not honored with titles. With those titles came a gift from the Royal Treasury to build a beautiful castle home, but my mother chose to build a primary school for Southington, a library and a community flower garden and park. She said she had no need of a castle, but the children of Southington had need of books and natural beauty," Adelio told me.

"She sounds like a wonderful lady," I remarked. "What shall I call her when I meet her?"

"I am sure she will call you daughter and you will call her mother," I smiled at that notion. I had lived most of my life with a surrogate mother, and now, in only a matter of weeks, I had three living mothers.

"What about your father? Is he as lovely as Lady Southington?"

"Indeed! My father is a ship builder by trade and a retired Royal Seafarer. He is a very brave man and fought during the uprising when Tinol betrayed his family. Father is very proud of our lineage. You remember I told you we are descendents of Jonwell, one of the early leaders of the Order of the Heather? My father takes great satisfaction in that fact and it has always been his justification for working that much harder. 'We are kin of the Great Jonwell. Much is expected of us, my son,' he would tell me."

"I wish I knew my true parents," I lamented. "That's my next question: what were my parents like, before Anyon took the kingdom?"

"Wait a moment, Princess. Are you changing the rules of our game? Am I not permitted to ask a question of you, first?"

"Sorry. I just have so many questions. I want to know everything about you and me, for that matter," I told him.

"In time, you will. First, I must ask you a serious question: do you feel love for Barlow?" My eyes must have bulged out of my head at that question. I did not foresee such a personal and serious question. Adelio must have sensed my surprise or read my mind. "I only ask you because of that time in the encampment..." I stopped him mid-sentence because even without the ability to read his thoughts, I understood his concern.

"If I am being completely honest, yes. But it is the love of a sister for a brother and nothing more. At first, and especially after he saved me from the attackers at the river side in Prenmar Forest, I felt somewhat enamored by him. He is very charming. I even felt a bit of desire, perhaps. No more than a short-lived crush. Not true love though. Not the pure incomprehensible and full-bodied love I feel for you. I am glad for Barlow. I am glad we are friends and he is my protector and counselor. But it is your heart that speaks to me, Sir Adelio Southway!" Adelio smiled at me and kissed my cheek.

"My last name is actually Gallo," he whispered.

"Huh?" Was my not very eloquent response.

"You wanted to know my last name? Gallo. Lord Gallo or Sir Adelio, if you prefer. My father is Baron Southway. I stand to inherit his title, property and wealth upon his death. Of course, we are fairies and tend to live exceptionally long lives," he laughed. "Oh, and green. My favorite color is green."

"Mine too!" I exclaimed. "We should get married. We have so much in common," I joked. "Won't you receive another title? Won't you become King of Kirana?"

"We have to win a battle first, Majesty. We should meet the others. Come." Adelio stood and reached for our gear at the side of the bench. I reached over and grabbed his hand to stop or at least delay the end of this truly wonderful moment together.

"Oh, but I have more questions, and you never answered the one about my parents. Come on - please? Just one more," I pleaded. Adelio sighed and returned to his seat on the bench next to me. He took both of my hands in his and kissed them delicately, as if they were made of fragile glass.

"How can I resist you? King Philson was both generous and commanding. He was quick with a smile and a joke, like you. He never took himself too seriously. I daresay he was handsome too. If not for your parents sealing, Philson would have been the lady killer of the court. He was both charming and fair. I admired him so very much as a friend and my father-in-law. You are like him, Avery, although you are the spitting image of your mother. But I must say, I see many more similarities between Queen Riva and Marena.

"Riva is kind of course, but also strong willed and determined to get what she wants when she wants it. Her husband's leadership style, one of consideration and compromise, differed with hers. She was decisive and pointed. Not in an overly despotic or dictatorial manner; she just knew how to accomplish her goals. But the death of her sisters, your aunts, and the invasion of Kirana by Anyon changed her from a strong willed woman to a woman questioning every decision she made. Time and again, she asked the seers of the Order of the Heather to read her future and yours. She would plead with them to tell her she made the right decision in sending you away for your safety. She became sad and untrusting." Hearing this about my mother made me concerned for her well-being.

"She seemed gracious and relaxed when we saw her at Pilton Palace. She appeared as a Queen should, I suppose," I told Adelio.

"No question, Queen Riva is a most noble and poised ruler. I believe your safe return to Kirana has lifted her spirits and reaffirmed her faith in the Order of the Heather."

"Now we just have to win back her throne."

"Yes, there is the matter of that," Adelio said.

"That reminds me, why didn't the Order and all the Kiranian people just rise up and take back the Kingdom in her name when Anyon first invaded? Why did they have to wait sixteen years for my sisters and me to wander back into Kirana?"

"Kirana, under the rule of Riva and Philson, had neither a standing army nor an organized force large enough to withstand the invasion from the Kingdom of Mordith. As it was, they mustered as many trained soldiers as were in Kirana at the time, and most of the Lords volunteered their fellow townspeople to fight. It still was not enough. We stood a chance if the ruling Trinity had their full powers, but as you know, Anyon sent in spies and mercenaries who killed Riva's sisters, destroying the Trinity before the invasion. This prompted your parents to devise a plan to remove you from Kirana and hide you from Anyon and his murderous plot to destroy the Kingdom of Kirana. Preserving the Trinity was the only way to preserve Kirana," Adelio said.

"Well I get that, but why not just send us away from Pilton for a while?"

"With Riva virtually powerless, it would be sixteen long, Kiranian years before you or your sisters would come into your powers. A long time to hide you, safely in Kirana. The Order thought it best to send you to the other world, the outside world, for safety. This is where the time difference between our worlds comes into play. The Order recognized that you would return to us of age and coming into your powers fairly quickly if you were sent out of Kirana. For us, it has been only about two years since you first took safe passage from the Kingdom.

"I remember that day well. Along with some of the other seafarers, I helped lead your boat out of the harbor. There was a fog created to conceal your boat, and the fairies of the Order created a storm much closer to our shores to afford you a safe way toward Scotland. But after only a short time in Scotland, somehow Anyon became aware that you were alive and living at the abbey on Loch Ness. The Order decided that the only way to keep you safe was to send you to the United States, far away where no one could find you."

"Wow!" I exclaimed. "This preservation of the Trinity stuff sure gets complicated in a hurry, doesn't it? Well, I am glad that we all made it this far. I mean everyone worked so hard to keep us safe, we probably owe it to Kirana to stay alive at this point," I was half joking, but then I realized something, perhaps a piece to the puzzle that was missing.

"Ginter," I blurted out and stood in front of the bench. "Ginter knew we were at the abbey in Fort Augustus from the beginning, didn't he? He told Anyon where to find us in Scotland. Think about it - it was Ginter who came to the abbey to fetch Aunt Bea, under possible false pretenses, I might add. He knew where we were going all along. He helped Anyon destroy my mother's Trinity and invade the Kingdom. How else could they get in so easily without detection? And he has been ruling the Kingdom ever since, if you think about it. Ginter would not be so arrogant as to declare himself King of Kirana knowing my sisters and I were still alive. But that is what he wants. Destroy us, become King of Kirana, just like his father Tindol wanted. It's just too easy. And now, we will be separated on the battlefield, woefully under-skilled in our powers and as you said we can be picked off one at a time. Oh, Adelio. This is bad. Very bad."

"That is a sound theory, but I hope that Ealdred or any of the Order would have considered the idea of Ginter as traitor from the beginning. They obviously do not fully trust him. Until now, he has never been in close contact with the Order about anything. But your mother told Ealdred that she asked Ginter to fetch Aunt Bea from the abbey in Fort Augustus. Queen Riva confirmed Ginter's account. That doesn't explain why both you and I had visions that appeared to show Bea being kidnapped from the abbey, but sometimes our visions can be deceiving," Adelio explained.

"I think maybe I should give up on accusing Ginter of treachery," I told Adelio with a sigh.

"So do I. In any case, we cannot worry about it now, dearest. We have a Kingdom to free and you have a speech to make soon." Adelio and I both reached for our battle garb and silently made our way to the meeting point where our very long day was about to begin.

42

THE FIGHT FOR FREEDOM

The heavens glowed with the anticipation of morning. The stars were still brightly shining in the jet-black sky and the moon appeared to be dancing over the trees to the west. A banner of purple and blue clouds dissipated into what remained of the night sky. I stood on the stage where I had delivered my first speech to the people in Thistleton and faced out at the crowd. Torches and gas lanterns lighted much of the courtyard. Once again, my sisters, Aunt Bea, Bob, and Ealdred stood with me. Ealdred quieted the people assembled in the courtyard and as if I had addressed them a million times before, I spoke:

"People of Kirana, thank you. Thank you for standing with us for what is right. We are fighting for our freedom, for justice. Together we are strong and mighty. We are skilled. The passion for liberty and justice runs through our veins and is what will guide us on the battlefield this day. There is no cause more dignified or justified than that for which we fight today, for ours is the cause of all men. It was the cause of our ancestors who led their families to Kirana to escape the tyrannical forces in their native lands.

"So today, when we drive Anyon and the forces of Mordith out of our lands we will prove our strength. We will demonstrate the power of our people. And you will tell your children and they will tell their children of the courage with which you have fought for the freedom of all Kiranians!"

The crowd cheered and I took a deep breath. I had been thinking about my speech for some time. I tried to recall the St. Crispen's Day speech delivered by Henry V before the Battle of Agincourt in the Shakespeare play. I had read it over and over again for my Honors English class and found it incredibly motivating. Nothing I had said rivaled the eloquence of William

Shakespeare, of course, but I hoped the people staring up at me from the courtyard felt even remotely inspired.

The reality was that personally, I had little idea what we were fighting for. Certainly I understood that Anyon was the "bad guy," that he invaded Kirana, killed my father, imprisoned my mother, emptied the treasury and took away the rights of the Kiranian people to own land or speak freely, among other things. His soldiers pillaged our towns and attacked men and women alike, terrorizing the countryside. But I had not experienced the alleged horrors of this tyranny. I learned of them second-hand. I just knew that it had become my responsibility to bring Kirana back to its people and I was going to do it.

The assembly began to organize into columns at the end of my speech. An obvious challenge to our planned invasion was getting to Pilton Palace. Some groups would march on foot, some would be on horseback, and some would be transported by barge. My sisters, our sealed partners, our horses and I would be transported to the rallying point, on the Western edge of the proposed battlefield, by one of these barges. Once there, and hopefully still under the cover of some darkness, we would go to our "attack posts," as Ealdred called them.

My sisters, Egan, Verner, Adelio and I boarded our barge with our horses. The other barges were lined up along the dock where we first came into Thistleton. I could not help but recall first seeing the gates of Thistleton upon our initial arrival and seeing the flags of our ancestry waving over the tower. The reality of our mission had not struck me at that point. Now of course, it was a stark reality. We were going into battle, facing danger we had never contemplated.

I took a deep breath as the ferry pulled away from the dock.

"You ok?" Marena asked me silently. I shrugged.

"You?" I asked her in return. She shrugged.

"I think I might barf," she told me.

"Please don't!" Timber ordered aloud and moved away from her twin on the bench located beneath the railing on the boat. The armor on her right leg scratched along the seat, leaving a mark.

"This stuff is worse than my catcher's gear," Timber complained.

"Maybe, but I doubt your catcher's gear can stop an arrow from penetrating and reaching your skin," Egan replied.

"I don't know. You'd be surprised by how good my softball equipment is. Woodport's booster clubs raise a lot of money so we always have top of the line stuff. I bet my chest plate could stop a bullet," Timber bragged.

"You're such a dope, Timber. Of course it can't," Marena told her.

"Oh yeah, well Beth Ikeman's pitches are like bullets, and - ok, probably not," Timber shrugged. Based on the silly conversation, I could tell Timber was now nervous, despite her earlier calm demeanor.

"Hey gang, can we focus for a moment?" Adelio asked. We all looked in his direction. It was dusk already and the hint of sunlight rising over the tree line became daunting. Daylight meant attack.

"Right, I know you are all a bit on edge. But remember, you have been training for this these past weeks. If we stay together and follow the instructions provided by Ealdred, we will all be just fine at the end of this. More than fine, we will be victors and peace will fall upon Kirana once more. We must listen to one another and know where each of us is among the fray. Neither Egan, Verner nor I will leave your respective sides and if for some reason we should become separated, look for your sisters, listen for them," Adelio told us. He seemed so confident and I was immensely proud of him. I could envision him as King of Kirana and that thought calmed me in a way.

"Ok," I said, "Remember, the plan is lead the charge toward the battlefield, then at the half way point, hold up, let the cavalry pass you, turn around and we all meet at the top of the hill on the West side. Got it?" Everyone nodded.

"If you accidentally get caught up in the fight, just alert one of your sisters so we can decide what to do," Adelio added.

"What could possibly go wrong?" Marena asked sarcastically. No one answered her because the fact was, we all knew a lot could go wrong with this seemingly simple plan. Unfortunately, it was the only plan we had.

"We are coming to the rallying point. Get your gear together and get ready to disembark like we practiced," Adelio instructed. The shore closest to the rallying point was full of rocks and the water too shallow for the barges, so we had to jump out with the horses about twenty five yards off the beach with all of our stuff. Luckily, the water was only thigh deep, at most. Still, we decided to wear our jeans under the lightweight armor, and there was just about nothing worse than wet denim. I learned that the hard way at a water park when I was in middle school. I hoped the warm Kiranian breeze would dry my jeans, eventually.

We successfully made our way off the boats and to shore. Many of the groups that had left Thistleton by horse and by foot were already in the encampment field. Most of them left prior to my speech, which meant I would be expected to deliver another rousing address to the soldiers. As we reached the tent that had been set aside for the leaders of the clans and battalions, I could already hear dissention.

"Ah, no laddie! Ye canne go the swamp wey," Alexander was telling Ginter. "It's sure death and these are my boys."

"I appreciate your concern, sir. But it has already been decided. They have given me their word. Your Graces," Ginter said as we entered the tent. Alexander bowed to us and then left in a huff.

"What was that all about," I asked our cousin.

"Nothing more than a strategic disagreement. Some of Alexander's clansmen have decided to join me in our attack from the South and he would rather them not," Ginter explained. "It is the easiest way to infiltrate the Palace. Ealdred and the others have agreed to it."

"Hmm," was all I could say. Was I expected to say something important? I did not know.

"I am sure you can understand why Alexander would be disturbed. You are gutting his regiment and placing them at the pointy end of an arrow," Adelio muttered casually.

"Yes, but I'm sure you'll keep them safe, Ginter," Marena said, glaring at Adelio.

"Indeed. Come, I believe the ferries are all in from Thistleton and the lines are assembling. The Noblemen from north of the Throagtone River marched down during the night. Stearns, Preck and Pivko are waiting for instructions from the battle leaders," Ginter directed us toward the center of the field where a platform was set up. "I must go and speak with Sir Duffy, the Duke of Stearns. Together, we will lead the Southern charge. Excuse me," Ginter bowed and left us.

"Are you ready? This is the speech that counts!" Adelio joked.

"Great. What was the other one?"

"Practice."

～◦

"No one will forget this day. For it was on this day that we declared to our neighbors, the oppressors of Kirana, that freedom, justice and the strong will of the Kiranian people are no match for intimidation. They are no match for fear and tyranny. No! It is on this day that we declared we do not accept the leadership of those who would destroy our core values as a people. Today, let us be victors and declare our freedom and our strength so that none shall dare try to take our will from us ever again! This is our day and our time! I will see you again, dear people of Kirana, on the field of victory where we..." I did not get a chance to finish my speech. The field erupted in cheers and then the thousands assembled began to break into their respective battle groups, still cheering.

"Well that went over pretty well," Timber said as she nudged me with her elbow.

"I didn't even finish," I said, mildly disappointed, "I didn't even get to the good part yet about 'our children and their children...'"

"I think they got the point, listen," Adelio said directing my attention to the field. Thousands of men were all chanting "Trinity, Trinity, long live the Trinity!"

"Yeah, yeah, yeah!" Marena started shouting with the group, which only made them break from their chant to cheer again.

"Holy cow! I feel like I'm at a concert or something!" Marena shouted to us over the noise.

"Come on rock star, we have to get into position if we are leading a charge in a few minutes," I said taking Marena by the arm and leading her back down to the ground.

43

CHARGE!

"Why is this taking so long?" Marena asked me through our thoughts.

"Relax," I told her. "This is the way they do things around here." I took a deep breath.

"Everything all right?" Adelio asked.

"Just Marena. She's anxious to get going, I suppose. Is this 'parlay' supposed to take this long? What could our side and Anyon's possibly be talking about?" It was not as though I could hear the representatives from our respective sides negotiating on the battlefield. We sent Verner, two young members of the Order of the Heather and one of the noblemen out to meet some of Anyon's men.

When Adelio first explained parlay to me, I could not help imagining that these men were going to participate in a coin toss or something to start the "game." Really, we were sending Verner and the others to meet with Anyon's leaders to inform them of our demands. Basically, it was a last, peaceful effort to allow Anyon to remove himself and his troops from our land. I could see Verner and the other two men riding at a full gallop toward our position to the East. Based on the fact that Verner did not ride to speak with me, it was evident that final negotiations were not successful. We were going forward with our attack.

As I sat upon Pearl with Adelio to my left and four armed guards around me, I closed my eyes to try to see what was about to happen. No visions would come to me.

"I know," Adelio said to me silently, "I couldn't see anything either. I could not hear the conversation at parlay, either."

"What's with that?"

"I think it is the interference we spoke about. I also think that as the battle begins, we may be able to regain some of our ability since conceivably everyone will be a bit preoccupied, but who knows? Don't worry, we'll go through this together," Adelio assured me. I nodded and then took a deep breath.

"Do you have your breathing medications?" He asked.

"My breathing - oh, my inhaler? Yes I do," I replied.

"Good. Can't have you losing your breath mid-charge," Adelio teased.

"Thanks, I'll be fine." A horn blew in the distance *"Doot doooo. Doot doooo."*

"Right, that's the call," Adelio said. To my right, a horn replied *"Doot doooo. Doot doooo."*

"Ready men?" I yelled.

"Ready!" Was the shouted reply. This was it. This was the moment that would determine the future of Kirana, and it was surreal. I raised my sword into the air and it glowed with a blue tint. At this very moment, my sisters were yelling the same thing:

"Charge!" I yelled as Pearl and I and about 3500 men raced toward the battlefield and Pilton Palace. From my position, I could see my sisters leading their charges to the right and to the left of my group. The thundering sound of hoof and heel on the ground was nearly deafening. If Adelio or anyone else was attempting to speak to me, silently or otherwise, I wasn't going to hear it. The earth trembled with our charge as the field of battle got closer and closer.

As we reached the even ground of the battlefield, at about three hundred yards from the Palace walls, arrows began to fly at us and like a choreographed dance, we all lifted our shields in defense. I looked behind me and saw that some of my men had fallen, that some of their horses were struck. I could not allow that sight to distract me, however. We needed to reach the walls of Pilton. Once there our men could easily infiltrate the Palace and take control. From what our scouts told us, Anyon was only able to muster an armed force of perhaps 5,000 men. Despite the obvious advantage of our numbers, what I did not anticipate was being met with so much opposition outside of the walls.

"Turn back Avery, you must turn back," Adelio ordered. I couldn't stop though. I raised my sword and aimed it at the soldier headed straight for me, thrusting it forward. I struck him and he fell.

"Onward men!" I yelled amid the chaos and the sound of metal striking metal. We pressed forward, fighting our way through the line of soldiers Anyon sent out to slow us down. There were not many of them, comparatively speaking, but they were standing between us and our goal. I hoped my sisters' were able to turn back to safety without any conflict, but I doubted it.

More arrows were flung at us and large stones were catapulted in our direction as well, but we kept going. More men had fallen behind me - I heard the sounds of agony and mortality - but I knew I could not worry about those brave souls, lost to our cause, at least not yet.

From where I was, I could easily see the entrance of the Palace and I knew I had to get inside without alerting Adelio to my plan, or lack thereof. I had had a vision of my mother in deep trouble, injured inside her room and I knew I had to get to her before she could be hurt.

As we pressed ahead through Anyon's soldiers and the Western entrance to the Palace became visible, I began to see three or four men with swords heading down the hallway toward my mother's chambers.

"Ya!" I commanded Pearl.

"Avery, don't! Stay with us. This is exactly what he wants you to do!" Adelio practically shouted in my thoughts.

"They're going to kill her, Adelio. I have to get there!" I cried. I was resolved to get to my mother in time.

Pearl and I zigged and zagged our way through the rushing forces until we had the steps of the Palace within our reach. The Earl of Westport's men were engaged in hand-to-hand combat with some of Anyon's men along the steep stairway into the Palace. Anyon's men were clearly trying to prevent our forces from entering the castle. Bodies had fallen all over the stairway. I could not make out from that distance whether they were our men or Anyon's who littered the entrance.

I jumped from Pearl's saddle and ordered her to return to Timber. I slapped her on the behind and she galloped in the direction of the high ground. I turned and faced the battlefield. There were men everywhere. I listened carefully for my sisters' thoughts, but heard nothing more than the beating of my own heart, jumping out of my chest.

"Damn it!" I screamed. How could I know if they were all right? I just had to hope that they were following instructions, unlike me, and headed back up to the high ground. Just then, I turned to face an aggressor. Before I had time to grip my sword, I was on my back bleeding from my mouth. I could not see this person's face through his mask, but I saw him raise his sword over his head. Before I realized what I had done, my sword was drawn and now stuck through my attacker. I pulled the sword from his chest and the man fell to the ground.

No sooner had I defeated this enemy than I heard someone cry out:

"There she is! Get her!" I turned toward the West and saw about a handful of Anyon's men running toward me. About one hundred and fifty yards to my right, I saw another ten or so men on horseback racing in my direction. I froze even though my sword glowed with anticipation. Surely, I could not outrun a horse, let alone a dozen. I was still too far from the Palace doors to make a run for it and get there safely. I looked around me and saw I was surrounded by men fighting for both sides. I saw the standards for Westport and Preck in front of me.

Then someone yelled, "battle square," and before I understood what was happening, I was completely surrounded by forty men with pikes. One row of them knelt down with their pikes facing upward with the butts of the long staffs in the ground. The next row stood with their pikes facing forward and still another row stood behind the second row, with their pikes in ready position. I realized they had formed a protective square around me.

As the men chasing after me on horseback approached the square, they were cut down in their tracks by the pikes.

"Oh no!" I cried out from inside as I realized the horses were probably getting hurt too.

The line of men on foot, similarly went down as they faced the battle square. Many men standing with the first row were injured or worse, but as they fell, they prevented anyone else from breaking formation. I recognized this as a brilliant strategy, even though it caused a lot of injury.

Once the attack on me seemed to die down, the square opened. A man on horseback offered me his hand.

"Your Grace, I am your cousin Murris of Colvin. Please let me take you to safety." I recognized his name from the family tree Adelio had showed me when we were still at the abbey.

"Thank you, cousin," I gave him my hand and he hauled me up onto his saddle. "Can you get me to the entrance to the Palace?"

Murris pushed through the fighting and stopped at the foot of the steep stairs.

"How is this, Lady Avery?"

"Perfect. Thank you, Murris. Thank your men for saving me back there. You will all be rewarded when this is over and we have won. Be safe, cousin," I told him. Murris nodded humbly.

With my blade drawn and glowing, I rushed up the Palace steps. Westport's men must have seen me running because I heard one of them call out the others:

"Men, push 'em from the door. Let the wee one pass!" His men created a passage for me and I pushed through the heavy wooden door into the ornately decorated foyer of the West wing of Pilton Palace.

I breathed heavily and began to wheeze. Of course, my asthma had to start kicking in like it always did at the least opportune moment possible. I placed my sword back in its sheath, and I reached into my leather pouch, designed specifically for my inhaler and took two puffs of my medication. I took a deep breath and then another, replaced the inhaler, re-drew my sword and began to run.

There was blood on my right hand that began to turn from bright red to dark brown. I rubbed my hand on the part of my jeans sticking out from under my leg guards. I could tolerate the sight of blood, ordinarily, but this was not my blood. I continued through the maze like corridors until I came to her door. It was already open and my heart jumped into my throat.

"Mother? Mama?" I whispered. I heard the sound of footsteps in one of the corridors nearby, but I ignored it as I came upon a pool of blood by the window. Just as in my vision, I was too late. She was no where in sight.

"Please, please..." I pleaded with no one in particular as my bottom lip began to quiver. I saw this event coming so how could I be too late? I followed the trail of blood with my eyes from the window. Drops of blood seemed to have been left in two different directions. One path led to her bed-chamber and the other out the door. I walked toward the chamber, but I didn't see her. I did not see any more blood either. The tapestry hiding the door to the secret stairway seemed eskew. I breathed a deep sigh of relief.

I heard footsteps in the hall, now closer to our mother's room. I ran back into the sitting area by the window and glanced out of the window. The scene outside was serious. Our mother's chambers looked out onto the forest and swamp to the South. I looked for Ginter and Alexander's men, but I could not see them. There were a number of men and horses stuck in the swamp, as Ealdred had feared, but they appeared unopposed.

I also wished that my sisters made it to the high ground to the West without much difficulty. It was about time I joined them, I thought to myself when someone grabbed me from behind. I screamed.

"It's only me, Highness. We must get you out of here. Anyon's men were here and - your mother - she is gone," my violet eyed cousin reported.

"Gone? Gone where?"

"Do you see this blood? It is her blood. I - I tried to get here in time, but I was too late. They stabbed her and she lay here bleeding and lifeless when I came upon her. When Anyon's men saw me, they chased me. I outran them and hid in a corridor, and I am only returning now," he reported.

"Well where is my mother now? I need to see her one last time," I ordered.

"I do not know, but we must leave the Palace. Our forces have penetrated the walls and Anyon's men cannot withstand the invasion. They are retreating, but they are fighting for their lives. Another fifteen hundred men from Mordith were spotted marching south through Colvin. They will be at the battlefield to reinforce Anyon's lines in less than one hour. We have to get you to safety before anyone knows you are here. Come," Ginter told me as he took my arm. Like mine, his right hand was covered in blood. I noticed that his shirt was blood soaked on his left side, below his ribs.

"Ginter, you are bleeding! Are you all right?"

"A flesh wound is all, Highness. Hurry!" I followed him out of the room and raced down the stairs to the main hall. Men were pouring into the Palace from outside, their swords clashing. I would have to force my way out, I realized and held my sword in the air.

"I am Avery de Hazaro and this is *my* house!" I announced at the top of my lungs and ran forward toward sunlight.

I had apparently lost Ginter as we pushed our way out of the Palace.

"Avery, do not fear for me. I am with you. I love you," a gentle and familiar voice told me.

"Where are you?" I asked.

"Do not concern yourself with me. Go to your sisters. Protect them. Fight for them. Fight for all of us, my brave petal, and I will be with you soon." I listened closely. I could hear Marena and Timber arguing over who reached the rallying point first. They were safe. I ran toward the western wall and followed it up toward the great hill. I could see my sisters sitting in the grass. I ran faster and faster. I just wanted to get there.

44

BATTLE ROYALE

"Where did you go?" Timber asked me as I reached the top of the hill. She was holding Pearl's reigns and petting her mane. "Pearl said that you were going into the Palace. Why?"

"I wanted to make sure our mother was all right," I replied, still slightly out of breath from my trek up the grassy hill.

"And?" Marena asked. "We couldn't hear your thoughts at all during the charge."

"I know. I couldn't hear you guys either, but I sensed you were ok. I think our mother was attacked in her room, but I also think she is ok. She escaped down her secret stairs and she spoke to me in my thoughts," I told them.

"Attacked? What do you mean?" Timber asked.

"I mean someone hurt her or tried to anyway. There was blood all over the place, but she's ok. Here's the weird part: Ginter told me she was killed and he saw her lying in blood in her room. He said that he tried to get there to stop the attack on her, but he was too late and the men who killed her chased him out of the room. He said that by the time he got back to her room, she was gone," I reported.

"Wait. I'm confused. Why is that weird? Is she alive?" Marena asked me.

"I'm almost positive she is, so I don't know why Ginter would tell me all of that, unless maybe he saw her before she was able to get out of her room and surmised that she was mortally wounded."

"Mortally wounded? What are you on CNN or something? How do you know she's ok?" Marena was getting annoyed with me.

"Because, I just know. I don't know, Rena. I just know. But I have to tell you something else. Ginter looked like he had been pretty badly injured too. I hope he is all right. He went back out into the battle," I added.

"I hope so," Marena said, "I like him and I think he's really brave for helping us." Timber gave me a look, rolling her eyes at Marena's comment. Marena caught this silent commentary as well.

"What, Timber? Why the eye rolling? Ginter is helping us and he's a leader. Maybe he's not perfect, but I think actions speak louder than words. He's working for us and for a free Kirana. That means a lot in my book," Marena said defending herself.

"Ok, ok. I just hope you keep an open mind. I don't know about Ginter, still. There is something fishy about him," Timber told her twin.

"Well, what do you think, Avery?"

"I think we should keep an open mind, but not forget that Ginter has an axe to grind against our family," I replied.

"He is our family! You are both so judgmental," Marena complained. I decided to let the disagreement go. There was no point in arguing with her, especially since she was right at this point. Ginter was one of our best allies in this fight.

"You're right, Rena. He is our family. Timber and I should try to keep an open mind." We all sat on the hill and watched the battle ensuing below. It was hard to believe that all these people, on both sides, were risking their lives because of us. We remained quiet and shared bits of fruit from our bags like preschool children enjoying an afternoon snack.

"This is crazy," Marena said pointing toward the Palace, "We're just sitting here, useless."

"Well, what would you like to do?" I asked.

"Fight!" Marena stood up and raised her arms in front of her. Then she mimed lifting something heavy. I watched as a large boulder lifted in the air from the ridge.

"Watch this!" Marena hurled the boulder toward a group of catapults Anyon's men had hauled into the field and aimed at our front line. The large stone rolled over all three of the catapults as if they were made of matchsticks.

"Strike!" Marena yelled triumphantly, "Your turn, Timber." Timber thought for a moment and then stood up next to Marena. Suddenly, flocks of large birds flew from the wooded area behind us and from the South of the Palace.

"Oh come on. That's it? Birds? Are they going to poop on everyone?" Marena laughed childishly.

"Nope. Look!" Timber's bird air force began to drop what looked to be stones in waves over Anyon's lines of fighters, stopping them from advancing toward our front lines.

"Ah, poop would have been better. Ok, your turn, Avery," Marena coaxed.

"Sorry, I don't know how to do anything cool," I replied taking the last bite of my yellow-pink fruit. The juice ran down my hand and I wiped the stickiness in the grass.

"Darn. Well, I've got another trick," Marena waved her hand toward Anyon's troops and then as if hitting a one-handed backhand, swatted the air. We watched about a hundred men fly into the air and crash into other men around them.

"That's 30-love, me!" Marena shouted down the hill and did what appeared to be a victory dance, as if she just won a point in a tennis match. Timber and I laughed at her, but even though Marena was being funny our giggling was misplaced given the seriousness of the day, and in any case it was interrupted by the announcement into my thoughts:

"Avery, you girls have to stop fooling around. Anyon's men know where you are now and they are going to come for you," Adelio scolded.

"Darn it!" I shouted. "Ok, we have to stop. We just put ourselves on Anyon's radar and he's sending men after us.

"What should we do? There are only like a hundred and fifty guys up here with us and all the men protecting the hill are down the hill now," Timber asked.

"Ladies, come with us," Egan and Verner rode up behind us on their horses. They were covered in mud as were their horses.

"Where did you come from? You guys stink!" Timber commented.

"South side - swamp. We had to pull some of our guys out of there and use some of our defenses to protect them from the onslaught of long bowmen," Egan replied.

"Ginter really got them stuck in the muck. He and about a dozen men made it into the castle before we got there, apparently. I do not know how they made it through so easily," Verner added.

"In any case, we've penetrated the Palace walls on all three sides. Adelio and Ginter have secured the North entrance so we are going to lead you down there where you will be safer," Egan explained.

"Yeah, but we have to ride through all of that to get there," Marena remarked, pointing at the battlefield chaos between us on the hill and the West entrance.

"We found a way around the Palace from the South side, which will avoid getting caught up in much of the fighting, but we have to get through the swamp. That is where Timber can be quite useful," Egan continued.

"Sure, I know just what to do," she said.

"Then let's get on your horses. We're winning this fight, your Highnesses. Anyon is almost totally defeated. We're winning back Kirana!" Verner announced and headed off to the right toward a trail at the edge of the woods.

45

SOUTH SIDE TROUBLES

We rode quite quickly toward the South side of the Palace, so quickly that I noticed the muscles between my legs began to ache from all this time in the saddle.

"Mine too," Timber told me silently.

I rode up closer to Egan and asked, "How is it really going out there? From the hill, it looks like we're rolling right over Anyon's troops. Are we really winning this?"

"Indeed, Majesty. We simply outnumber the troops from Mordith, but they are fighting hard against us. When Ginter's men moved in from the south, against everyone's wishes of course, Anyon's men acted liked trapped, rabid dogs. A longstanding rule in battle is to 'never surround your enemy' but that is what Ginter accomplished," Egan said.

"Of course. That is from Sun Tzu. I learned that in school when we studied Chinese history. Sun Tzu said to always allow your enemy an escape because if you don't, he will fight for his life. That is what Ealdred was trying to tell Ginter back in Thistleton when he told him not to take the southern side. What was Ginter trying to prove, anyway?"

"I'm not sure. But he and a few men were able to get into Pilton Palace quite easily. The rest were mired in the swamp, many cut down where they stood. Those who survived the onslaught of the longbowmen without injury were able to push their way through to reach the castle walls. Verner and I were pulling men and horses out of the muck for quite some time," Egan reported.

As we came to the swamp, Timber began to concentrate and stopped her horse a few yards behind us. We halted our galloping horses once we realized she had stopped.

"You guys might want to move back here," Timber warned and we all almost simultaneously trotted behind her. I felt a warm breeze blow past my back. A wind was picking up leaves and swirling around over the swamp, faster and faster.

"Ah, it's not working," Timber complained and the wind died down, causing the swirling leaves to drift into the swamp. She began to stare at the swamp again, focusing on her task. I could feel the air around me becoming rather chilly.

"Sorry guys, I'll try to make this quick," Timber said.

"Oh my gosh, Timber. Forget what I said about a winter wedding. I'm freezing! Hurry up," Marena said. With that, we could feel the ground beneath us beginning to harden, a regular occurrence in late October or November back home in Woodport.

"Ok, that should work if we get across the swamp quickly. It should stay frozen for a while," she told us. Verner lead the way over the formerly marshy land and we all followed him toward the Palace.

Suddenly, we heard the sounds of hooves behind us. Some of Anyon's men had tracked us and followed us, and they were beginning to surround us. There were at least fifty or sixty of them and they looked serious about what they wanted to do to us.

"This is not going to end well!" Marena muttered. Verner turned his horse around and galloped in front of Marena. He turned his hands, palms out to face our foes. A ring of fire began to form in front of us, separating Anyon's men from us. Their horses began to panic. A few closest to the fire jumped up on their hind legs and threw their riders.

"Oh no, the ground!" Timber yelled. The ice she created was melting under the warmth of Verner's fire.

"Go! Egan take them. I'll hold these men off!" Verner yelled.

"Come on your Highnesses, follow me!"

"No! Verner you have to come with us! Avery tell him!" Marena pleaded with both of us. Then she threw her hands into the air and quickly pushed them to the right, as if she was trying to push an object aside.

"What the?" Marena did it again and then again. "It's not working. My power isn't working! They won't move!" She yelled.

"They have harnessed dark magic. They are blocking your powers, Marena, with their own spell. But I can hold them here while you get to safety. My darling, I will be right behind you. Now go!" He told her. He pulled his horse next to hers, reached over, took her by the waist and kissed her strongly on her lips.

"Five minutes, my love," Verner assured Marena. She reluctantly turned and followed us as we raced toward the Palace.

We followed the Eastern wall of the Palace all the way around to the North side. Waiting for us was Ginter and about thirty battle-tired men, some on horseback and some on their feet, all of them filthy.

"Come, your Royal Highnesses. This way!" Ginter directed.

We dismounted and climbed the five broad stone steps to the long patio-like entrance to the Palace.

"Verner is coming, Ginter. From the swamp. He is holding off a group of Anyon's troops so we could get away. Will you stay and watch for him, make sure he makes it inside?" Marena asked our cousin.

"I will, your Majesty. You have my word! Now, you are to go inside and wait in the great hall. I have not been inside yet, but I do believe Ealdred and members of the Order have secured the entire main floor. You are safe here. Anyon and his men should all be out of the Palace and I dare say headed back to The Kingdom of Mordith as we speak. Alexander and his clansmen have headed to the bridge to stop their escape," Ginter reported.

"Good," I replied and the four of us ran into the Palace as instructed. Once inside, I slowed my pace. Adelio - I had not heard from him in quite sometime.

"I am coming from the bridge with Barlow. We've lined it with explosives and split Anyon's army. Alexander is already on the other side with his men ready to stop any who make it across. Oh, lass. It's just brilliant! We've got him right where we want him. Anyon is finished!" Adelio told my thoughts. His speech was quick and breathless, even in his thoughts.

"That is wonderful. Hurry back safely!" I told him. The feeling of victory was upon me - glorious victory! I continued toward the great hall slowly, admiring the furnishings in my new home.

⸙

The approaching cavalry turned rapidly in front of the entrance. The man on the lead horse was riding maybe thirty yards in front of the pack.

"Make way! Make way!" He announced.

"Ready men! Ready long bows. We're going to end this now! Fire!" A blanket of arrows flew into the air finding many of their targets. Men fell from horses and horses fell to the ground, tripping up other horses. Yet, the crowd of fifty soldiers pushed on past the fallen and injured.

"Make way!" The man on the lead horse yelled again to those protecting the North entrance. The men on the patio charged toward the attacking pack of horsemen with swords drawn. Men were pulled and dragged from their horses. More arrows were flung into the crowd and the chaos was overwhelming.

The lead horseman, caught in the fray tried desperately to break free from the fight, but as he turned to flee, a blood soaked hand pulled him from his saddle. He fell to the ground, stunned as metal struck through his chest plate. He breathed a shallow breath and closed his eyes.

"No!" I cried out and before I could make it to the great hall, I turned and ran toward the entrance from where we came. Marena came to the doorway of the hall and called after me.

"Avery, come back! Everyone said to stay here!"

"Adelio! Adelio!" I cried aloud.

"We're coming. Stay where you are. I saw it too," was his silent reply. "Don't worry and don't say anything about what you just saw to your sister. No reason to alarm Marena. I'm almost there! Alert them in the front."

I stopped near the front door and obeyed Adelio. I could see out of the window onto the patio. Ginter and his men were standing guard, but no one seemed overly excited about anything yet. I was relieved that we were not too late. I opened the heavy door.

"Ginter, Verner should be coming upon the north side here very soon," I announced.

"Yes, Princess Avery. I am aware and my men will be looking out for the chap," Ginter shouted to me over his shoulder.

"Yes, but he may be chased by a large number of..." Ginter interrupted me.

"We will do what we can to defend the Palace and ward off these men. Fear not, Majesty. All is won and all will be well soon. Please, go inside and relax," Ginter said as he walked toward me at the door. "Glory returns to Kirana once more."

"Yes - all right..." I replied and closed the door. I walked toward the great hall. On my way, I ducked into a small, round room to the right that appeared to be a chapel of some sort. Sunlight streamed into the room through elaborate stained glass panels that looked like they depicted a story. I examined them closely and realized they told the story of Hazaro and Amara from their initial meeting in Thistleton to a battle scene to a wedding and the birth of their three daughters. I wondered if anyone would think to make a stained glass rendering of the story of how my sisters and I, Varsity tennis players from Woodport, New Jersey, defeated the Kingdom of Mordith and its King, Anyon.

In the center of the room was a padded seat with what appeared to be a padded kneeler beneath it. I remembered the vision I had of our mother praying and begging for our return to Kirana and recognized that she must have been in this very room. I felt an immediate connection with her in that moment and I knelt down and looked up to the ceiling. Painted above me was the phrase "The Three are Strongest as One."

As I stood and prepared to head back to the great hall, where apparently I was supposed to be anyway, I heard a loud commotion outside. I went back to the window and saw Ginter's men charging against approaching soldiers on horseback. I gasped as I saw both Barlow and Adelio racing from behind, trying to get to Ginter.

"Stop him! Stop him! What is he doing?" I pleaded with Adelio in my mind.

"Ginter wait!" Adelio yelled to him and then an anguished shriek.

"Nooooooooooooo!" Marena came running at full force toward me at the door. I tried to grab her, to calm her down and assure her everything was fine, but I knew it wasn't. She knew it wasn't. Marena pushed past me and threw her body into the heavy door until it cracked open just enough for her to sneak through and just in time to see the bloodied, limp body of her true love carried up the stairs of the Palace.

Adelio and Barlow laid Verner on the ground in front of us. Marena collapsed at his side, hysterical, and gripped her chest.

"No, please, no..." she cried. Timber and Egan ran outside followed by Aunt Bea, Uncle Bob, some members of the Order and our mother. I turned and ran to her with tears streaming down my face.

"Gently love," she said as she raised her bandaged arm.

"You are alive! I knew it! Are you all right?" I asked examining her arm.

"I am. See to your sister!" She whispered.

"Please, help him! Egan, please, please!" Marena shouted. Egan knelt on the other side of Verner's body and placed his hands over Verner's chest wound. He closed his eyes, seeming to focus intently on the healing process.

"I can't - I - I - it is the heart..." Egan stammered. "He's gone, Marena. I am so sorry."

"Oh my God!" Timber cried, knelt down next to Marena and embraced her. Marena wailed uncontrollably. I left my mother's side and also knelt down. I hugged my sisters and sobbed with them.

46

WHEN YOU LOVE SOMEONE

Three long, Kiranian days had passed since our victory at Pilton Palace. As of last night, summer was upon Kirana and there was no longer darkness at night. This made the days much warmer. Adapting to the "time" change was actually easier than I expected. As Adelio told us when we first came to Kirana, we sleep when we are tired. Our rooms were all equipped with blackout shades and shutters.

Anyon was defeated and while he personally escaped Alexander's ambush at the bridge, Anyon lost a large number of his soldiers including his nephew, Honder. Honder was the heir apparent to the throne of the Kingdom of Mordith and reports from Mordith indicated that Anyon and his family were beside themselves over this loss. Anyon had no male children, only two daughters who were not entitled to rule Mordith. Honder, Anyon's sister's son, was therefore next in line to be King of Mordith. This blow to the ruling line in Mordith was perhaps more severe than if King Anyon himself had been killed. Talk of a civil war between the ruling families in Mordith had already reached the Order.

It had also been reported that it was Ginter who slayed Honder. Honder led the group chasing Verner from the swamp. Honder had hoped he would take down my sisters and me. Ginter struck him down at the north entrance to Pilton Palace. Of course, we had our own loss in Kirana.

In the Battle for Pilton Palace, approximately 3000 brave men and fairies sacrificed their lives for our cause. Despite our decisive victory, our losses were devastating. We lost Earls, Dukes and some of their sons, which destroyed lines of inheritance. Noblemen and common people fell together on the battlefield under the standards of their towns. There were many more tales of heroism than loss, which provided some comfort to me.

Our mother began to make arrangements for new appointments to the Royal Council. I made sure our mother knew that cousin Murris and his soldiers from Colvin saved my life with the battle square. I also described how the Duke of Westport and his men helped me safely get into the palace. I was saddened to learn that the young Duke lost his life soon after I made my way into Pilton Palace.

There was so much loss. I could not help but feel guilty. Women and children lost husbands and fathers all for my sisters and me.

"You cannot see it that way, Avery," Adelio told me over our breakfast.

"I can't help it. We were looking over the roster for the memorial service last night. It's just sad. As Rena, Timber and I watched the battle from the hill, we were removed from what was really happening down there. We were up there, laughing and joking around like spoiled idiots while all these brave men did our work," I said in a hushed tone so that the serving staff did not hear me over the sounds of hammering and sawing.

Pilton Palace was still being "renovated" to suit our needs. Luckily, it was spared any major damage from the battle. Surprisingly, Anyon did not modify very much of the palace's interior. The great hall needed some sprucing up and some of the apartments reserved for noble families when they visited court required some attention, but as our mother said many times, "it could be a lot worse."

"I know, love. I lost friends, kin and neighbors from Southington. This battle was bigger than just you and your sisters. We fought for our way of life and for our security. Do not take this the wrong way, but the Trinity is just the mascot for a very important cause," Adelio was right, but I could not help but think of the children forced to grow up without their fathers, like me.

After breakfast, Adelio and I met with our mother in her chambers to discuss plans for our wedding and coronation.

"We will plan for the winter time once Avery is of age," she told us.

"When is my birthday, anyway? We always celebrated back home - I mean in Woodport, on December 20th," I said.

"You were born on the first day of winter."

"How do you know when the first day of winter is here?"

"In the winter, we have seven hours of darkness. The first day of the winter season follows the first night of seven full hours of darkness. On that night, there is a full moon and a great celebration. You were born that first day after the celebration," Queen Riva told me.

"That makes sense," I surmised. "The first day of winter in the outside world is usually December 20th. But isn't a bit soon for a wedding and all that goes with it?"

"We need to secure your line, Avery, so that we can secure the future of Kirana. And to begin that process, we need to be married as soon as possible," Adelio added.

"You mean kids? We have to start having kids?" The idea of having children seemed so remote. Most kids my age were trying not to have kids at this point.

"Of course, petal," my mother replied. I took a deep breath. I was not ready for this conversation.

"It will all be fine, my love. You'll see," Adelio told me with a smile through his thoughts. I smiled back at Adelio. "Your Majesty, perhaps Avery and I should discuss some of the plans we have on our own and then we can present them to you for your guidance and approval?"

My mother sighed, "Very well. Just know that this has been my hope and dream since I sent you from Kirana. Please allow me some control over the planning." I stood from her dining table and kissed her on the cheek.

"Yes mama," I said and curtsied to her as I had been instructed to do by Lankin at my lesson on royal protocol yesterday.

"You may be excused, children. We must check on my darling Marena, the poor lamb."

⌒○

"Has she eaten today?" Riva asked Timber as Timber emerged from Marena's room.

"She still can't eat. She did try to eat soup, but it made her sick. I am making her drink water and that pink juice that Honora made for her, but unless I remind her to drink, she won't even do that," Timber reported to us.

"I will see her," our mother stated and opened the door.

"Me too," I said.

"Let mom go, Avery. Marena said something to me this morning that I wanted to talk to you about," Timber said.

"Shoot," I said as we both sat down on the wooden bench outside Marena's chambers.

"She thinks you knew that Verner was going to die and yet you did nothing to stop it," Timber told me solemnly, almost embarrassed to report this accusation. The truth was, I did have a vision, but I did what I could to stop the events I saw unfolding.

"What else does she think I could have done? I mean, I had a vision. So did Adelio and as soon as we saw what might happen, Adelio and Barlow raced to the Palace to stop Ginter from attacking in order to allow Verner a chance to get away. Both Marena and I warned Ginter to watch out for Verner. But in all the confusion, it didn't work. She does realize that there were like fifty or sixty of Anyon's armed troops on horseback, chasing Verner from the swamp, right?"

"I don't know what she knows or doesn't know. Avery, she is not herself at all. She just lost the only man she ever loved and when you love someone the way we love Adelio and Egan - well, you lose part of yourself when they go. But I know that Ginter has been to see her a number of times over the past few days. He seems to cheer her up. I tried to listen in on their conversations, you know, because I trust the guy as far as I can toss him, and for some reason I could not hear very much of anything. It all seemed innocent and superficial, but I can't help thinking he has been filling her with some unsavory ideas."

"What do you mean, 'unsavory'?"

"Well, I did hear him tell her that *he* did everything he could to save Verner. I also heard him mention that 'perhaps Adelio and Avery were more concerned with self preservation at the time Verner was killed'," Timber said.

"What is that supposed to mean?" I hissed.

"Meaning, you were worried about saving your own butts since you are to be Queen and King, essentially more important that the rest of us."

"That's ridiculous!"

"Maybe, but I can only imagine what other tidbits Ginter has shared with Marena," Timber said.

"I have to talk to her," I said. My voice was beginning to crack nervously, "I have to tell her exactly what happened." I stood up and went inside Marena's room and Timber followed me. Our mother, looking more radiant and regal than ever in a cream and gold gown, acknowledged us.

"There they are. Look, sweetness! Here are your sisters to see you and cheer you." Marena sat up in her bed. She looked as though someone had punched her in the face. Tulip was snuggled on a pillow next to where Marena had been laying. Marena's movement disturbed the cat who "meowed" quietly and found another comfortable spot on the end of the bed.

Marena's hair was matted to her face by her tears. I felt so badly for her, I wanted to cry as soon as I saw her red eyes.

"Hi guys," she said.

"I'm glad you are up," I said, "the last few times I came in here, you were sleeping and Honora basically kicked me out."

"They gave me some sleeping medicine to calm me down. I guess it worked. Look at me. I'm so calm," Marena told us. She spoke with a dull affect, slowly and without expression. She was certainly not herself, although I have never known a grieving Marena.

"How are you feeling?" I asked her and took her left hand in mine. She swallowed hard and her bottom lip began to quiver. Tears were forming in her eyes and racing down her cheeks, following the natural path they had taken for the last three days. Perhaps that was a stupid question for someone who just lost her true love.

"How do I feel? Like someone ripped my heart out and threw it down my throat. I can't breathe. I can't eat. I can't think. I just want to sleep. When I sleep, I can see him and I can feel him. He's right there and I don't want to wake up," she told us in the quietest voice we had ever heard Marena use. She pulled her hand from mine and continued:

"And you knew this was going to happen," she accused.

"Marena, we spoke about this already. You know that Avery only had a vision moments before Verner was taken from us and she acted as quickly as she could to stop it," our mother intervened. Riva spoke slowly and in a patronizing tone as if she was reminding a four-year old why she could not eat a cookie before dinner.

"Rena, it's true. I saw Verner caught up in the mess between Ginter's men at the Palace entrance and Anyon's horsemen from the swamp. Adelio did too, which is why he and Barlow rushed to stop Ginter's attack. It was total chaos and - and - we told Ginter and…" Marena interrupted.

"And you just watched the whole damn thing unfold, didn't you?"

"Marena, that is quite enough!" Our mother told her. I began to cry. I couldn't help it. Maybe she was right. If I had intervened myself and not waited for Adelio and Barlow, or counted on Ginter's men, Verner might still be alive.

"No," Riva said interrupting my intrusive thoughts, "Avery acted appropriately and it is a tragedy, certainly that Verner is gone, but we must remember that he bravely stood up to over fifty men on his own in the swamp in order to save and protect you girls. Marena, you must think about that. Verner is a hero. You are all the heroes of Kirana," she said.

"Doesn't bring him back to me, mother. Doesn't make it better," Marena said between her sobs.

"You forget, my darling. I too lost my love when your father, Philson was taken from me. It is a pain in my soul that has yet to subside. But I go on and you must go on as well, Marena. For Kirana, for your sisters, for yourself," our mother sat down on Marena's right side and took her into her arms. Marena could barely breathe she was crying so hard. My heart was breaking for her and I could not help feeling guilty, that I did not do enough to save Verner.

"Come, I will summon your ladies and you shall be dressed for the parade and memorial," our mother the Queen announced. She walked over to Marena's wardrobe, opened it and showed us a beautiful white and gold gown.

"Oh," Timber cooed, "She gets to wear that today?"

"You all get to wear a dress like this today. Today we celebrate Kirana's freedom and we celebrate the life of our dear Verner. Come my sweet girl," she said to Marena and offered her a hand out of bed. Marena slowly pulled herself out of her bed and our mother helped her to the wardrobe.

"We should get dressed," Timber said and we headed out of Marena's room.

"That didn't go well," I said as we closed Marena's chamber door.

"Nope, although it could have been worse," Timber remarked.

"How?"

"She could have thrown stuff at you like she did in Fort Augustus."

47

BEFORE THE PARADE PASSES BY

As we lined up to lead the processional down the main roadway through the small town of Pilton to the Palace's West entrance, I had a heavy feeling inside of me. I knew she could not help it, but Marena was like a black cloud following slowly behind the rest of us. But for the urging of our mother, I doubt Marena would have left her bed or her room. I could feel Marena's pain and I garnered every bit of thought-blocking ability to try to avoid her intrusive and sad thoughts.

"Please listen carefully," a small man below us instructed. He was apparently the Royal Groom of Revelry, Sir Jerod, out of work while Anyon controlled the Kingdom and clearly excited to be back in his position at court. Adelio had tried to explain that there were "people" to help us with every aspect of our daily lives from dressing to eating to cleaning to party planning. Many of them were of noble birth, trying to win the favor of the royal family so that they could advance themselves through appointments at the local government level or even through grants of property.

"The order of procession shall be as follows: guardsmen, who will be here shortly to lead us; Lord and Lady Easton; followed by her Royal Highness, Queen Riva; then Princess Avery and Sir Adelio; Princess Timber and Sir Egan; Princess Marena and Sir..." The Groom stopped his speech, recognizing his mistake.

"Go on!" Marena commanded.

"Please, I beg your forgiveness my Lady. Forgive my stupidity and insensitivity," Sir Jerod groveled at the hoof of Marena's horse. Marena just shook her head at him with disdain and glared. In only a few short hours, Marena transformed from a grieving "widow" to an angry person. She lifted her right hand and caused Jerod to fly into the air and land on his back at the front of our line.

"Marena!" Timber yelled at her.

"That will teach you to be so stupid!" She screamed at the Groom.

"Yes, yes your Highness," he groveled. Aunt Bea and Uncle Bob stood horrified at Marena's behavior. Aunt Bea left the line and trotted her horse back to Marena.

"Marena, please try to be civil. We know you are hurting, but…"

"You don't know a thing, Aunt Bea," Marena growled. Then she took a deep breath. "You're right. I need to reel it in. I'm sorry," she said. "And sorry to you, party guy," she yelled up to the Groom of Revelry who bowed to Marena.

"Forgive me for my tardiness," Ginter said as he trotted up to us on his black horse. He too was wearing an all white military uniform decorated with colorful medals.

"The farrier was shoeing Magic just when I needed to meet you. Hello Lady Marena, I hope this day finds you much better. You certainly look as radiant as the summer sun," Ginter told her. For the first time in days, Marena genuinely smiled.

"Thank you cousin," she replied.

"My Lord, we were just lining up for the processional," the Groom told him.

"Splendid! I will join Princess Marena so she can have solace in knowing her loving cousin is here for her during this time of sorrow." Adelio caught my eye and raised an eyebrow. I shrugged. Now was probably not the time to worry about Ginter's intentions, and Marena did seem to find comfort in having Ginter at her side. However, I remembered a vision I had not long ago, and that memory made me feel uneasy about this new relationship they seemed to have cultivated. But again, this was not the time to concern myself with such things.

The new Royal Guardsmen, twenty young and strong looking men in burgundy uniforms joined our group and the Groom of Revelry released us to begin our victory parade. Horns and drums announced our approach into the town of Pilton and then celebratory bagpipe music ushered us down the road.

"Hey Avery! Avery!" Timber shouted at me. I turned my head to look behind me, but Timber realized that I could not hear her so she spoke to me silently.

"Remember when the New York Yankees won the World Series the last time and Uncle Bob took us to the parade down the Canyon of Heroes in New York City?"

"Yeah," I replied.

"Well, this reminds me of that time except we're the Yankees!" She said excitedly. I laughed at her silly observation.

"What? You are such a goof. Ok, Derek Jeter, pay attention to your fans," I told her.

Thousands of people lined the street, craning to get a look at the Trinity and the Royal family. They threw flowers at our horses' feet, cheered and waved to us as we traveled the mile and a half to the palace gates. We smiled and waved back. I turned to look behind me as we approached the palace and saw that Marena was neither smiling nor waving, just as I had remembered from my vision. The gold brocade in her dress shimmered in the sunlight and she looked like a goddess with her long blonde waves pulled back away from her face. Marena stared ahead at the back of Timber's horse. Ginter seemed to be trying to speak with her, but Marena did not appear to respond with more than a few words. I tried to listen to their conversation, but could hear neither Marena's thoughts nor Ginter's.

"This is getting frustrating, Adelio. Somehow Ginter or somebody is preventing me from hearing their conversation," I told my betrothed silently.

"We'll have to get to the bottom of that soon, my love," he replied.

We made our way through the crowds to the West side of the palace. As planned, we all stopped in front of the gatehouse, turned to the crowds, waved and then proceeded up the pathway to the palace where about one-hundred fifty noblemen and women, members of the Order of the Heather, and leaders of our military action, greeted us. Everyone was dressed formally. Unlike our trip to the palace, no one cheered or threw flowers at us. They were present for a solemn memorial service lead by the Royal Family, de Hazaro.

We rode around the grounds and dismounted by a flowing white tent that was waving in the breeze. Under the tent were rows of chairs decorated with white material and separated by an aisle of white flower petals. It looked almost like a wedding ceremony was about to take place. Just outside of the tent was a large sculpture or monument of some sort, covered by a white sheet.

"That is the monument to the Battle for Pilton Palace," Adelio whispered to me.

"Oh," I replied, "And what's that one next to it, over there?" I asked pointing to another covered stone statue. That one was shorter than what Adelio called a monument, and much wider.

"That is to commemorate the dead. We call it an eternity fountain. The water will continue to flow through the fountain, forever. And we will remember the brave service of our brothers and sisters in arms forever," he told me.

"I love that idea," I replied. I walked over to the fountain and could hear water trickling beneath the cover. I lifted the end of the cover slightly to reveal a bronze plaque that read:

"To our Kiranian brothers and sisters who were lost to the noble endeavor of freedom - you live in our hearts and souls forever." Then it listed the names of all who were lost in battle. Verner was listed first, which I thought was fitting.

"Marena will unveil a separate plaque celebrating Verner's bravery that will be placed in the rose garden or wherever she wants it to be displayed," Adelio said.

"Good. That's a nice idea," I replied.

The Groom of Revelry ushered us to our seats at the front of the tent and the rest of our honored guests filed into the seats behind us. A musical ensemble consisting of a harp, bagpiper, and what looked like a xylophone played softly as everyone took their seats. Our mother stood and gracefully made her way to the front of the tent. Ginter joined her, although Riva seemed surprised by his appearance at her side, to me anyway.

"What's *he* doing up there?" Timber leaned over and whispered to me. She and Egan were sitting together, holding hands to our right. I shrugged, but found it interesting that Timber seemed to notice our mother's uneasiness with Ginter.

"Moral support?" I replied. "Keep in mind, he's been her surrogate husband, so to speak, over the past two years and I guess he is still Regent and head of the Royal Council since our father, the King was killed."

"Oh, I guess," Timber replied. Queen Riva motioned for Marena to join them at the front of the tent. Surprisingly, Marena stood and obeyed. She slowly ambled to the front of the tent with her white gown trailing behind her. She kept her eyes fixed on the ground ahead of her and stood next to our mother.

"Today we celebrate the lives of our brave men and women who sacrificed their lives for the greater good. While we grieve for our losses, we must not lose sight of what they and we have accomplished this past week. Our Trinity has returned to us and the de Hazaro line will continue, ensuring that peace, tranquility and our very way of life will persist here in Kirana. Those we have lost have guaranteed our rights to exist and our freedoms to live, love and prosper. And for this we are eternally grateful," Riva signaled the Guardsmen standing next to the tall statue and they pulled the cover from it. The crowd reacted with a chorus of "oohs and ahhs."

"How the heck did someone create that in three days?" Timber asked. The statue or monument as Adelio referred to it, was probably ten feet high and depicted my sisters and me standing together holding my sword. It was definitely an impressionistic rendering, but still an impressive piece of art. I was completely awed by the fact that my sisters and I were the subject of a statue. Nevertheless, I could not help asking:

"Is my butt really that big?" I asked Timber. She replied with an elbow to my right side.

"Marena, why don't you read us the plaque," Ginter suggested. Marena walked over to the statue.

"Three are strongest as one. Victory at the Battle for Pilton Palace - Avery, Timberose and Marena de Hazaro - Summer, in the 5th Year of Riva," Marena read aloud. Our guests applauded and slowly stood to recognize our accomplishment. Marena stood beaming by our statue.

"Wow! This is better than winning the State Tennis Tournament last year!" Marena told Timber and me silently. I was happy to see that she was happy, even if it was for only a fleeting moment.

"Way better," I replied. The crowd of our close supporters settled back into their seats. Riva then signaled for the Guardsmen to reveal the second memorial, the fountain.

"We commemorate the bravery and unselfish lives of our fallen brethren with this small token. May the waters flow eternally so that we shall always remember their sacrifice," Riva announced and indicated for Marena to read the next plaque. Marena studied it for a moment and her emotions began to overtake her.

"No, mama," she whispered, "I can't..." Ginter came to her side and held her. She buried her head in his chest and he proceeded to read the list of the dead.

"Verner Wallace, beloved by Marena de Hazaro; Harnish Tasker, beloved by Clara, Beau and Rossen Tasker..." Ginter announced the entire list and at the end, our guests rose in silence. The bagpiper began to play and our mother lead them in song:

"For them our hearts will burn and bleed, until we meet once more. Our love will never leave our hearts and the flame will burn forever more. Be not sad for one day soon, we will be together again. And on that day the joy of love will be with us once more."

Adelio squeezed my left hand causing me to look up at him. I noticed he had tears in his eyes as he smiled at me and mouthed the words, "I love you." My heart melted and despite the somberness of the occasion, I was filled with joy.

"I love you," I replied.

"Is it time to eat?" Timber asked as she stripped a tear from her cheek. "Sad, serious stuff makes me super hungry!"

"My darling, everything makes you hungry!" Egan stated.

"You know her so well," I told him. Egan kissed Timber on her right cheek.

"Yes, let's make our way to the hall. There is a banquet in there where you will receive all of your honored guests. Sorry, Timber, but that might interrupt the flow of food into your mouth," Adelio teased. She came up to him and punched him on his left arm and he laughed.

"Something funny about death?" Marena asked us with a scowl as she walked up behind Timber and Egan.

"No, of course not. We were just trying to make light of a very serious day," I replied.

"Hmm," she replied and walked away rejoining our mother and Ginter as they made their way into the Palace.

"Oh boy! This is going to be a really, really long day," Timber remarked.

White, fragrant flowers and white, flowing material decorated the great hall. The windows were all open, allowing the warm breeze to blow through and caused the material to shimmy as it hung from the ceiling. The whole room appeared ethereal. Tables were set up throughout the room and a buffet filled with colorful foods lined the right side. A head table was at the front of the room. Ginter and our mother were already there with Marena, greeting guests. Queen Riva motioned for us to join them. We took our places at the long table, on each side of my mother.

Although our food was served to us and we were not required to go to the buffet tables, due to the flow of dignitaries visiting with us, offering their condolences to Marena and congratulating us on our victory, our meal seemed to take forever. Apparently, the servers were not permitted to interrupt with dishes when people were visiting with us at our table. Timber left our table twice for the buffet and brought back plates of fruits, cheeses and shellfish for us to share.

While the four of us struggled to quell our hungry bellies, Marena seemed to bask in the attention she received from our guests. I watched her as she smiled politely, bowed her head and thanked everyone for "their kind words and thoughts."

"Thank you so much for being here," she told the Duke of Pivko and his young daughter, Sir Gallin Meller and Randa Meller, "I will remember your kindness, always."

"Bless you Princess Marena," Sir Gallin replied, "Perhaps there will be a place at court for my daughter who will be of age this winter? She has been well groomed and prepared for service to the Trinity."

"Yes, perhaps, Sir Gallin. I will see that Randa is properly considered for duty," Riva replied to him. He bowed and went back to his seat only to open a space for the next guests to greet us.

"Ugh! How much more of this is there? My Kingdom for a lamb shank!" Timber complained. Our whole table became silent. Ginter had been speaking with Uncle Bob about the status of the Royal Council and Aunt Bea was talking to Barlow about the needs of the people in Braventon. Suddenly, everyone directed their attention to Timber.

"Timberose!" Our mother the Queen scolded, "We do not offer the land of Kirana in exchange for dinner. Were you not present today at our memorial service? Have you forgotten the last few days?" Everyone stared at her and my sister turned completely red. Timber seemed mortified by her apparent *faux pas*.

"I - I - yes - I did not mean - it's an expression. I did not mean it literally. You guys know that," she said defensively.

"You're an idiot!" Marena told Timber.

"Rena, please. You know she didn't mean it. Riva it is just a common figure of speech when a person is hungry," Bea added. Aunt Bea was accustomed to Marena's name calling, but she had little tolerance for it.

"I'm sorry. Everyone, I am sorry. I didn't think before I spoke," Timber said.

"It's all right, petal. Now you know not to use that saying here in Kirana," our mother said.

"Anything else I should know? Maybe I should just sit quietly and think about the delicious lamb shank everyone else is enjoying," Timber pouted. Our mother raised an eyebrow at her and then smiled.

"May I have your attention? Ladies and gentlemen, as you can imagine this has been a long and tiring day for our family. At this time, we are going to join you in enjoying this feast and we will continue with presentations after supper!" Riva announced to the room.

"All right, dearest. Your lamb is on its way," she told Timber.

"And that my sisters, is how it is done!" I joked.

"It is good to be the Queen," Timber added smiling.

"Indeed," Egan said.

48

MEANT TO BE

The five of us walked together around the grounds of our new home. It looked quite different than it had during battle. The fairies had been in charge of "beautification" of the palace grounds, which meant the daunting task of burying the dead and magically "cleaning up." They apparently employed the same type of timely magic in sculpting our monument and the eternity fountain as they did in their cleaning efforts, because the palace and grounds were immaculate, and the little renovation that was needed was nearly completed.

The banquet was still carrying on inside the Palace and we could hear the music emanating from the great hall. Marena seemed to be getting tired and overwhelmed so we decided that it would be a good time to find a place for Verner's memorial plaque in the Rose Garden.

"Achoo!" Timber sneezed.

"Bless you, love," Egan said.

"I guess we're close - to the flower gar - achoo!" Timber tended to be allergic to flowers.

"Are you all right?" Egan was concerned with his betrothed's sudden sneezing fit.

"She'll be fine," Marena responded, "At least you know now not to bring her flowers on special occasions."

"I suppose not!" Egan laughed.

Multi-flora rose bushes lined the perimeter of the rose garden and the sweet nectar smell of flowers filled the air around us. Poor Timber began to sniffle.

"I'll be ok," she told us.

We followed the path into the garden. Rose bushes in all different colors bloomed proudly. Other colorful flowers were skillfully planted, and sculptures as well as benches were placed throughout the garden with care. Bees and butterflies made their way from blossom to bloom.

"This is one of your mother's favorite places here at Pilton Palace," Adelio told us.

"It's remarkable. I've never seen such beautiful roses," I said, "This one is so different," I remarked pointing to a broad, yellow bloom.

"That is the Timberose," he told us.

"Hey! Like me!" Timber declared before sneezing again.

"Eww, did you just wipe your nose on your dress?" Marena accused. Timber sneered at Marena and shook her head "no." Of course, I also caught her using her dress as a handkerchief, but I kept that to myself. Timber could still be so gross, but there was no need to call her out on it in front of Egan and Adelio.

"Here!" Marena announced, "Verner's plaque can go here so I can come visit him," she said pointing to a spot next to a patch of purple and pink flowers. "Everyday, I will sit right here in the grass and tell him how much I miss him and about what he missed." Marena sighed, kissed the plaque, which included a likeness of Verner etched in bronze, and placed it in the soil. Egan knelt down and helped her properly anchor it into the dirt and when they were both satisfied, they stood and admired the plaque.

"He was the best man I knew, Marena. My best friend, in fact. I will miss him too," Egan told her putting his right arm around her shoulder.

"Thank you Egan. I appreciate that."

"You guys want to check out whether dessert is served?" Timber asked.

"Seriously? Is that all you can think about?" Marena criticized.

"Pretty much," Timber replied sarcastically, which made Marena chuckle.

"Fine, let's go back," Marena acquiesced. I turned to follow my sisters out of the garden, but Adelio grabbed my arm.

"Wait, let's talk for a minute," he said. I nodded and let the three others pass out of earshot.

"We have a lot of work to do in the next few weeks, your Highness," he warned.

"I know, but I didn't want to think about that yet," I whined. Adelio put his hands on my shoulders.

"Oh, Avery! The work of a fair and just ruler is never quite done. We need to consider how we are to restore the Royal Council, we need to draft a feasible peace treaty with the Kingdoms of Mordith, Bolckar and Vilarr and we need find a time for a wedding," Adelio said.

"Ugh!" I said throwing up my hands and turning away from Adelio, "First of all, we need to determine what role the new Royal Council will serve and then we need to decide who should serve on it. Second, any peace treaty we draft has to consider lifting the travel restrictions on Mordith or at least provide them with easier means to trade with Scotland just like Kirana does and third..." I suddenly realized what Adelio's third point was and as I turned back to address him, I found my true love on his knee holding a yellow Timberose.

"What - what are you...?"

"Avery de Hazaro, my love for you began before you knew who you were and it will last eternally. I ask you for your hand…" I stared at Adelio and realized I was mouth breathing, with my jaw gaping open.

"This is the part where you give me your hand," Adelio whispered. Still stunned, I offered him my right hand. "Other hand," Adelio whispered.

"Oh, sorry," I replied. Adelio held my left hand in his right hand. Then he kissed the top of it gently.

"Avery, be my wife. My eternal partner," Adelio asked. I just began to nod profusely.

"Is that a yes?" Adelio whispered.

"Yes," I said, "But wait a minute. If we are sealed and meant to be together, do you even have to ask me to marry you?"

"Not at all. We've been betrothed since you were a toddler. But I have studied the traditions of the outside world and figured you might expect a good story to tell your sisters and our children. What do you think? Maybe we should start a new tradition," he said proudly.

"You are too much, Adelio," was all I could manage to say. He truly surprised me. Adelio reached into the pocket of his white jacket and took out a piece of jewelry.

"Oh, you don't have to give me anything," I told him.

"I want to. This bracelet once belonged to my mother and has been passed through my family. I want you to have this as a symbol of my fidelity and love," he told me. It was a gold bracelet with a charm in the shape of a star hanging from it. I immediately loved it.

"Thank you so much! I love it and I love you!" I hugged Adelio around his waist and squeezed. "I have to tell you, I don't really want to share this story with anyone but you. To be honest, I shudder at the idea of getting married in front of hundreds of people I don't know. I just want it to be us, but I know my mother has other plans for us."

"Do not worry, Avery. When the time is right, we will make plans for the ceremony we want to have," Adelio assured me. "Now, let's see about that dessert."

We spent the rest of the evening dancing. I could not stop grinning at Adelio. Our lives here in Kirana were about to get a lot more interesting and exciting. With such an exciting future to look forward to, I hardly missed Woodport or our old, normal lives.

Egan and Timber danced next to us and Marena and Barlow danced near us as well. Marena seemed very interested in Barlow, which could not make me happier. Although he was not of noble birth or fairy blood, an apparent pre-requisite to marrying a de Hazaro princess, Barlow was a hero of the Battle for Pilton Palace and was going to be awarded accordingly with a title, position on the Royal Council and land in Braventon. Of course, he didn't know it yet. But his rise in importance within the Kingdom was going to place him on the list of possible suitors for my sister. While the decision would ultimately be hers, I secretly hoped she would choose Barlow so he would become my true brother.

Adelio and I took a break from dancing and my mother called us back to the long table to meet our cousins, Iris, her husband Murris and their little girl, Petal. I had already met Murris on the battlefield, but he looked a lot different. He was not very tall or lean and he was balding. He appeared much older than our mother or even Iris. Our cousin Iris was also not very tall, but she was certainly pretty. Iris was the daughter of our mother's aunt, Jonna. Lady Jonna's first husband, Alby was killed in the conflict involving Tindol. She later remarried a nobleman, George, with the blessing of our great-grandmother, Huldi. George was the son of the Earl of Colvin. He and Jonna had Iris, who was a bit younger than Ginter.

In speaking with them, I learned that Iris was to be my mother's chief lady in waiting. Riva's former chief lady in waiting, Tartine, who was King Philson's aunt was looking to retire to the country-side of Preck and assist in the raising of her grandchildren. Iris had served my mother for many years, before her marriage to Murris and before Anyon invaded Kirana. During Anyon's occupation, Iris left court for Colvin where she married Murris and had Petal. Petal was only a baby, but if she had been sent to the outside world with us, she would be the same age as Timber and Marena.

"I look forward to knowing you and your sisters, your Grace," Iris said to me.

"I look forward to knowing you, Cousin Iris. Your husband is a hero, you know. He and his men saved my life," I looked to Murris who humbly nodded to me and smiled just as he had in front of Pilton Palace.

"Your Grace flatters me. I only did what any good Kiranian would do," he said.

"Perhaps, but that battle square? Where did you ever learn that?" I asked.

"My husband is a great scholar, Princess Avery. He studies great battles in history," Iris responded.

"But we are supposed to be a land of peace, not war. Why study warfare?" I asked Murris. His eyes brightened and he smiled.

"Oh, I just love the excitement of battle, your Grace," he responded cheerfully. I laughed.

"My AP European History teacher would just love you!"

⌒つ

The night wore on, although so did the sunlight. I began to feel my energy wane, despite the second and third wind the many glasses of wine and ale seemed to provide me. We continued to dance with my sisters. The traditional Celtic style music was something we were quite accustomed to when we were growing up in Woodport. We were even able to employ some of our Scottish dance knowledge to some of the tunes, which our adoring guests applauded greatly. Despite the fact that we were supposed to be mourning the losses of so many great Kiranians, we all had a lot of fun. My mother described the celebration as "mourning overtaken by revelry." All I knew was that they sure knew how to throw a good party in Kirana.

"What should we name our babies?" I slurred to my fiancé giggling.

"Oh, I don't know. I will let you choose the names. That is the tradition. The wife names the children after her family, typically," he told me.

"Well, not Kerri or Adam," I remarked.

"All right. I will try to remember that," Adelio laughed. I could tell he was just patronizing me. I had been drinking quite a bit and clearly the ale had gone right to my head. I started to laugh for no reason, which caused Adelio to laugh at me and that in turn caused me to develop the hiccups. Now Adelio was really laughing.

"What is so funny?" Marena asked as she and Barlow danced past us.

"He - I…" I couldn't even tell her. I could barely breathe, I was laughing so hard. Apparently, my affliction was contagious and Marena started laughing too.

"Why are we laughing?" She asked, barely able to get the words out. I shrugged, which made her laugh even harder. Barlow was just looking at the three of us as if we were absolutely crazy.

"Aren't you all a sight," he said. After a while, we all calmed down and ceased our laughing, only to start up again when my hiccups returned.

When our laughing fit finally subsided, my dear Adelio asked to dance with his soon to be sister, Marena. It was a very sweet gesture and I could tell she was happy to oblige his dance request. That left Barlow and me.

"I like her," he whispered to me, "quite a lot."

"I know. I can tell," Barlow smiled and shrugged.

"Do you think she likes me?"

"My sister likes attention but I think it is too early to know. She will be mourning Verner for a long time, maybe forever. Sealing is pretty serious business, Barlow. I want her to be happy. Our differences aside, I love her so much. Timber too. Marena deserves what I have with Adelio and what Timber has with Egan. Maybe you can provide that for her, maybe not. Just, please, don't lead her on with promises you can't keep. She's vulnerable and sensitive, and despite her public persona, I think she is quite - nevermind. Just be good to her," I advised.

"Of course, your Grace. I would never hurt her. I could never," Barlow smiled. We danced quietly, which gave me a chance to attempt to hear Adelio's conversation with Marena.

"Your mother already has a list of appropriate suitors for you from all over Kirana, but you need not worry about that now," Adelio told her.

"I cannot imagine loving anyone else. I thought I was in love with you, but I wasn't. That wasn't love. Maybe what Verner and I had was magically thrust upon us, but it was palpable. I would have given my life for him as he gave his for mine. Honestly, I just wanted to make out with you," she giggled. I remembered back to our time in Prenmar Forest and how infatuated Marena was with Adelio. I recalled how Adelio and I kept our sealing and love from her. What a disaster that was. But we had all come so far in only a short time. It was hard to believe that I would be married in the winter and probably Queen of Kirana by next summer.

"Cousin Marena, may I have this next dance?" Ginter asked her.

"Of course," she replied with a bright smile. Adelio bowed, gave Barlow and me a concerned look and the three of us returned to our seats at the large table. Ginter took Marena by the waist and spun her to the center of the room. The rest of the party made room for them on the dance floor.

"You did well today at the memorial service," I heard Ginter tell Marena, "I was very proud of you."

"Oh, that was nothing, but thanks," Marena replied.

"You conducted yourself like a Queen, Marena. A stunning, graceful Queen." Ginter caught my stare, smiled and gave me a nod. He whispered in my sister's ear. I could not hear any more of their conversation.

ABOUT THE AUTHOR

Lauren D. Fraser is a trial attorney in Sussex County, New Jersey where she lives with her husband Andrew, daughter Anna Elizabeth and cats, Henry Tudor and Chloe Marie. She is a partner with the law firm of Laddey, Clark & Ryan where she specializes in personal injury law. She is also the author of the blog, Full Court Mom, http://www.fullcourtmom.com, where she discusses life as a full time trial attorney, mom and author.

Connect with Lauren D. Fraser online:
Website: http://www.laurendfraser.com
Facebook: http://www.facebook.com/trinityldf

Coming Soon from Lauren D. Fraser:
Queen Makers, Book Two in The Trinity of Kirana series.

Made in the USA
Middletown, DE
30 November 2017